Reputation

Reputation

A NOVEL

Lex Croucher

ST. MARTIN'S GRIFFIN
NEW YORK

For Jane Austen. Sorry, Jane.

First published in the United States by St. Martin's Griffin, an imprint of St. Martin's Publishing Group

www.stmartins.com

Designed by Meryl Sussman Levavi

Library of Congress Cataloging-in-Publication Data

Names: Croucher, Lex, author.
Title: Reputation : a novel / Lex Croucher.
Description: First U.S. edition. | New York : St. Martin's Griffin, 2022.
Identifiers: LCCN 2021048558 | ISBN 9781250832832 (trade paperback) |
    ISBN 9781250832849 (ebook)
Subjects: LCSH: England—Social life and customs—19th century—Fiction. |
    LCGFT: Romance fiction. | Novels.
Classification: LCC PR6103.R673 R47 2022 | DDC 823/.92—dc23
LC record available at https://lccn.loc.gov/2021048558

Our books may be purchased in bulk for promotional, educational, or business use. Please contact your local bookseller or the Macmillan Corporate and Premium Sales Department at 1-800-221-7945, extension 5442, or by email at MacmillanSpecialMarkets@macmillan.com.

First published in 2021 in the United Kingdom by Zaffre, an imprint of Bonnier Books UK

First U.S. Edition: 2022

1 3 5 7 9 10 8 6 4 2

Chapter One

It all began at a party, as almost everything of interest does.

This particular party was by no means a grand affair. Dinner had been distinctly lacking. The man tasked with playing the viola seemed to be hurting it a little. A scarcity of candles—entirely due to poor planning on the host's part, rather than a lack of monetary means to produce light—meant that whole rooms were so dark as to be hazardous.

"It's romantic!" Mrs. Burton had said generously as they were given the grand tour a few hours earlier, narrowly avoiding a headlong collision with a serving girl carrying a tray of diluted punch, who stepped deftly out of the way and was immediately swallowed into the shadows.

It was not romantic. Her aunt had promised a night of skillful dancing, delicately blossoming friendships, and a wealth of eligible bachelors with shiny coat buttons and dashing mustaches. Instead, Georgiana was reclining in a gloomy alcove in the empty hallway, tying and untying little knots in her second-best ribbon and thinking wistfully of Viking funerals.

Norse warriors were often burned on pyres with their boats, along with a great many of their personal effects. She had read about the custom in one of her uncle's books, and had talked about it animatedly and at length earlier in the week at the Burtons' dinner table while eating her potatoes. She was just getting to the part about wives and thralls following their masters into death when her aunt had slammed her hand down onto the table in an out-of-character display of force and cried, "Are you *quite finished*, Georgiana?"

Georgiana had looked up from the potatoes to find her aunt's face the very picture of horror.

"I'm sorry, Mrs. Burton, but if you'd only let me finish, I don't think the wives and thralls *minded* following the Vikings into death. The Norse believed in a sort of heaven. If Mr. Burton were to fall on his morning walk tomorrow and dash his brains out on a rock, wouldn't you want to go with him? If heaven is as lovely as everyone says it is, it would be like a holiday. You're so looking forward to St. Ives in September—it would be like getting to go early. Wouldn't you throw yourself upon a flaming pyre if you could be in St. Ives tomorrow?"

Evidently, Mrs. Burton would not. The subject of Vikings had been banned from polite conversation.

In the thirteen days since Georgiana had come to stay with her aunt and uncle, she had come to know them far better than she ever had in the past twenty years of her life. It had become clear to her rather quickly that while the Burtons were very kind and accommodating people, they were also particularly skilled at filling whole days and weeks with the kinds of monotonous minutiae that Georgiana could take no pleasure in. Any suggestion of an outing or an activity that bore even the slightest resemblance to a thrill or a caper had been tutted down with the proclamation that they were still "getting her settled."

Georgiana already felt so settled that if she were forced to settle any further, she might lose sentience altogether and become an integral part of the structure of the house—the human equivalent of a load-bearing beam. She had recently spent an entire afternoon in her new and rather small bedroom being forced to try on every item of clothing she owned, while Mrs. Burton and her shy maid, Emmeline, checked for required fixes and alterations. By the time they were appraising her last gown, Georgiana had become itchy, quarrelsome, and alarmingly wild-eyed with irritation.

Clearly, in Mrs. Burton's eyes, the process of becoming properly "settled" required a period of boredom and loneliness so excruciating that it rendered its subject broken in spirit, and therefore far less likely to rebel against the usual rituals of the house. There were only so many times a person could read the local advertisements, or arrange hundreds of embroidery needles by size, or discuss upcoming meals for three people as if they were feeding the five thousand. The morning when a neighbor's horse had escaped and circled the garden, incoherent with freedom, was such a bright spot of excitement that she clung to the memory of it for days afterward.

This was not how fresh starts began in stories—and Georgiana had read a lot of them. A fortnight ago, she had dragged a trunk twice her weight to her aunt and uncle's house, full of the tomes she had been unable to part with from home. In all the books she'd read in which a heroine started over in a new town or village or castle, she had immediately stumbled upon a series of daring adventures, or got dramatically lost on the moors, or swooned into the arms of a passing (and very handsome) gentleman.

In absolutely none of them did the heroine spend two weeks staring at a patch of damp on a parlor ceiling, wondering if it looked more like a man falling over a stool or an owl playing billiards.

Georgiana had begged her aunt rather doggedly for some form of social outing, and she supposed this party was her penance. She had been hiding in her alcove for almost an hour, wishing she'd had the presence of mind to bring a book. From here, she was perfectly placed to observe the comings and goings of guests as they shuffled from dining room to drawing room, and to eavesdrop on them in passing. Unfortunately, their hosts, the Gadforths, seemed to only know men and women above the age of five-and-forty without a shred of personality between them. Georgiana had eavesdropped on the exact same conversation twice, between two entirely different groups of people, about whether the drapes in the dining room were red or purple, and which constituted the more garish choice. All involved on both occasions were in agreement that either would be unseemly, but that as it was too dark to settle the matter presently, they'd revisit the subject at a later and more convenient date.

"They're plum," Georgiana muttered to herself, reaching for her drink as the latest group of soft-furnishings experts ambled away out of earshot.

"Nonsense. They're sort of wine-colored."

The reply came from so close to her ear that Georgiana immediately knocked her glass over in shock. She felt Mrs. Gadforth's undrinkable punch soaking rapidly through her dress and petticoat as she twisted around to find the source of the voice.

The ledge Georgiana had situated herself on was tucked behind one of many mock-Grecian plaster pillars; clearly somebody else had been making similar use of one of the others for some time without her notice. She heard a rustle of skirts, saw a slender hand alight on the plaster, and then without conscious thought she was moving over so that the like-minded intruder could slide in next to her.

In the low light Georgiana made out a slight figure with a dark complexion and a lot of black, curly hair swept up intricately on top of her head. She was perfumed with something heady and floral, and as the stranger held out an elegant hand for her to clasp, Georgiana caught a glimpse of bright stones and flashing gold.

"Frances Campbell," the woman said in a polished voice, and then before Georgiana could reply, "This is without a doubt the worst party I've ever been to. If anything remotely stimulating happened I think they'd all keel over from the shock."

"I'm Georgiana," said Georgiana. "Ellers."

"Oh? I wouldn't be here at all, only my father sold a painting to these dreadful people, the Godforths. They were just beside themselves, carrying on about what a *triumph* it would be and what great *friends* they hoped we'd all become. It was a hideous painting—Father couldn't wait to be rid of it; he inherited it, for his sins. I suppose it'll fit in just fine here, though, with all of . . . *this*." She waved a hand at the offensive pillars.

"They're called Gadforth," said Georgiana, wondering why she was suddenly only capable of announcing names.

Frances Campbell didn't seem to notice; she had put a hand down on the ledge between them and then quickly removed it again.

"But what on *earth* has happened to your dress?" Georgiana had somehow entirely forgotten about the spillage, but Frances must have put her fingers directly into it. "I hope it wasn't a favorite. Another tragic casualty of this vile punch. Here, don't fret—have some of this."

She passed Georgiana a small flask, which Georgiana accepted and brought to her lips without question in a sort of daze, spluttering as something much stronger than punch burned in her throat.

"It's cognac. Dreadful, isn't it?" Frances said delightedly as Georgiana coughed. "Have some more."

Georgiana did.

She had never before met somebody capable of making such a bold impression in such a short period of time. She had known Frances Campbell for perhaps fifty or sixty seconds and was already dreading the moment she'd slip off the ledge and abandon

Georgiana to the rest of her solitary evening. She was certainly no swashbuckling adventurer or windswept nobleman, but Georgiana knew at once that she was in the presence of a Main Character.

"I can't believe they have the audacity to call *this* a party," Frances was saying, gesticulating violently with her free hand as she took the cognac back with the other. "It has all the joy and charm of a dog's funeral. And why is it so *dark*? I almost tripped on my hem and fell through a window earlier, and then I thought, actually, on the whole, that might be preferable. We are on the ground floor, after all."

Georgiana snorted with laughter, and then felt immediately embarrassed to have made such a repulsive noise.

"Who dragged you here, anyway?"

"Oh." Georgiana cleared her throat, her voice croaky and disused from an evening where she had mostly communicated via the humble nod. "I'm staying with my aunt and uncle, the Burtons. I believe they've been friends with the Gadforths for quite some time. They're lovely, the Burtons," she said hurriedly, seeing Frances's dark eyebrow twitch, "but I cannot account for their taste in parties. Believe me, if I had thought of the window I would be but a distant dot to you now, gathering speed as I rolled down the hill."

Frances laughed. She took Georgiana's empty glass and filled it with cognac, handing it back to her and then raising the flask as if to make a toast.

"Cheers—to our monstrous families, and to the infinite number of far better parties we're missing this very instant! May our friends wreak sensational havoc in our stead."

Georgiana did not think the Burtons particularly monstrous, and due to her current and miserable lack of connections she had absolutely nowhere better to be, but it seemed rude to bring that up at the minute, so she clinked her glass against the flask and drank deeply. Frances sighed wearily, wilting against the pillar as if there were truly no agony in this world greater than enduring a below-par social occasion.

"The only consolation in all of this is that the lady of the house is truly a *character*. Have you seen her dress? It's all pink satin and questionable corseting. She looks like a strawberry blancmange that somebody's grabbed hold of and squeezed. I imagine Mr. Gadforth will have to rub her down with goose fat to slide her out of it later."

Georgiana giggled, flushed and giddy from the attention and the cognac, which seemed to spur Frances on. She was just describing Mr. Gadforth's mustache—"Have you ever seen a squirrel that's been trampled by a horse?"—when they heard the tapping of metal on glass, followed by a lapse in the hubbub from the drawing room that indicated somebody was about to make a speech. Rolling her eyes, Frances got to her feet and smoothed the folds of her dress, tucking the flask neatly away in her reticule.

"Come on. Mr. Gadforth is about to cry with joy and offer his earthly body and immortal soul to my father in thanks for that damned painting, and I should be there to smile and curtsy—or at least to restrain him when he goes in for an openmouthed kiss."

She offered an arm to Georgiana, and they walked back into the party looking to all the world like dear old friends and closest confidantes.

Mr. and Mrs. Gadforth were, in fact, standing directly in front of what must have been That Damned Painting, beaming at their guests and clutching overfilled glasses in their somewhat sweaty hands. She now couldn't help but see poor Mrs. Gadforth exactly as Frances had described her, and bit down on a snort of laughter as their hostess clumsily adjusted her bodice, heaving her bosoms optimistically skyward. Frances laughed, too, making absolutely no effort to conceal her mirth, and then unlinked her arm from Georgiana's and gave a brief, sarcastic bow of farewell before crossing the room to stand with two people Georgiana assumed must be Mr. and Mrs. Campbell.

Suddenly feeling exposed without a new friend or relative to hide behind, Georgiana stepped to the back of the room as Mr. Gadforth cleared his throat and began to speak. She didn't hear a word of what she was sure was an excruciating monologue; instead, she was looking at the Campbells.

Frances's father was a handsome man: tall, pale, and broad-shouldered, dark hair and mustache neatly combed. He looked imposing and almost military in his bearing, and had fixed a small smile upon his lips that, though it may have wavered a little as Mr. Gadforth got louder and more enthusiastic, never faltered. His wife was also tall and striking, but she was slender where he was well-built, and her skin was very dark; Georgiana thought she must have originated from Africa, or perhaps the West Indies—undoubtedly somewhere far less gray than England. Upon first glance nobody seemed to be paying her any mind, but when Georgiana looked again, she noticed that the gentleman standing a few feet away couldn't stop his eyes from returning to Mrs. Campbell every few seconds; a servant, passing by with a tray of drinks, stared openly. She was dressed in sumptuous navy silk, with thick, tight black curls expertly shaped and pinned in place; the necklace at her throat was unmistakably frosted with real diamonds.

Impressive as her parents were, neither compared to Frances.

Georgiana could see her clearly now, for Mrs. Gadforth had obviously concentrated her candle budget in this room and this room alone. Frances's dress was cut simply but meticulously bejeweled, so that she seemed to shimmer whenever she caught the light. Her cheeks had a certain luster, which probably gave the impression of a lively, youthful glow to all those unaware that the effect had been achieved through copious quantities of French brandy. There was something about her eyes—gold-brown, startlingly bright against the dark amber of her skin—that implied she had just thought of something extraordinarily funny. Everything from the ribbons in her hair to the way she held herself spoke of unimaginable wealth, and the unpracticed elegance that went with it. Georgiana felt instantly unworthy of such company, coupled with a much more urgent and desperate desire to somehow woo Frances and win her as a friend.

Mr. Gadforth, meanwhile, was clearly reaching the climax of his speech.

"This fine painting—this *exquisite* work of art—has completed our home, and I shall think fondly of my extraordinarily kind friend, the most highly esteemed Lord Campbell, whenever I look upon it."

Georgiana startled, almost spilling her drink for the second time that night, then stole another awed glance at Frances's parents—not Mr. and Mrs. Campbell after all, but *Lord and Lady* Campbell. She looked back at Frances, who was positively smirking at Mr. Gadforth now; he was smiling back benignly as he raised his glass, as if he were in on the jest rather than the unfortunate subject of it.

The speech concluded to polite applause, and Georgiana's stomach clenched uncomfortably. If Frances and her parents were to escape now, it would put an abrupt end to this brief and sparkling recess from the monotony of her life with the Burtons. If she had to endure another week consisting solely of conversations about the thread counts of shawls or the right conditions to grow turnips, she knew she'd lose control of her rational mind. Frances held the promise of future witty conversations, esteemed company, and parties one did not dream of escaping by rolling down a steep hill and landing in a stagnant ditch. Frances felt like the beginning of something—a story Georgiana desperately wanted to follow through to the end.

As voices rose all around the room and general socializing resumed, she didn't dare look up to see whether the Campbells had made a graceful exit; she felt light-headed with relief when a cool hand touched her arm.

"You look terribly lonely back here," said Frances. "Like you've just suffered a jilting. Come and meet my parents instead." She steered Georgiana across the room to make introductions.

"Are you summering here, Miss Ellers?" Lady Campbell asked, once formalities had been exchanged.

"In a sense I am, Lady Campbell, although I may outlast the summer," Georgiana said, affecting what she hoped was a light and jocular tone, as if her circumstances only faintly amused her. "My mother has been unwell, so she and my father have moved to the coast, for the air. They thought it best that I remain closer to civilization. My aunt and uncle—the Burtons—have been most kind as to take me in. They live just over the west bridge."

The location of the Burtons' house—too close to town to constitute a grand domain, yet too far away to be fashionable—revealed enough about their means (or lack thereof) that Georgiana thought she might be received a little less warmly. She needn't have worried; the Campbells seemed like the sort her aunt would describe as "fine, upstanding people"—this meaning "people who do not openly mock others for the state of their financial affairs"—and they simply asked politely after the Burtons' health.

Standing a little way across the room behind the Campbells, unaware that she was the precise subject currently being discussed, Mrs. Burton looked up and saw who Georgiana was conversing with. She gave her niece a small, stiff smile and then urgently muttered something in her husband's ear, looking concerned. Georgiana rather suspected she was recalling Viking funerals.

"Frances, my love—could you speak to Mrs. Gadforth and

help Miss Ellers find something to complement her dress?" Lady Campbell was saying quietly, with a hand on Frances's arm and a quick glance down at the large, blotchy punch stain that Georgiana had quite forgotten in all the excitement.

"Of course!" said Frances. "Goodness, and I was just standing here with you all sad and sodden. Come with me."

Georgiana curtseyed and then allowed herself to be whisked from the room, pointing out to Frances as they began to climb the darkened stairs that they were traveling in the exact opposite direction from Mrs. Gadforth's heaving bosom.

"Oh, you are a sweet little thing—nobody will notice," said Frances consolingly. "And besides, I'm just *dying* to see the rest of her wardrobe. My money's on endless gold brocade and some sort of festive hat topped with fruit."

The cognac seemed to be working its magic; Georgiana really felt she ought to protest but somehow ended up willingly following Frances instead, their arms linked once again, as they searched for the dressing room. It was easier said than done in the near-dark, but eventually Frances wrenched open the right door and clapped her hands together in gleeful celebration.

Georgiana took a seat on Mrs. Gadforth's pink velvet footstool, watching as Frances pulled out more and more outrageous items of clothing from the wardrobe—a shawl of peacock feathers, a mask that seemed to be made of leather, a gray dress so low-cut it could never be expected to contain the human nipple—until they were both beside themselves with helpless laughter. Frances gestured for help unbuttoning the back of her dress, and Georgiana paused uncertainly for a second before assisting her with fumbling fingers, and then watched as Frances explored the wardrobe with renewed purpose.

"Here," she said eventually, swiping the flask from Georgiana, who didn't remember taking it in the first place. "Try this on."

She threw an unidentifiable mass of fabric at Georgiana and

then disappeared from the room. Georgiana considered it for a moment—it looked both too large and tastelessly frilly—before pulling it over her head. Left alone, the entire thing suddenly felt beyond ridiculous, but she found herself grinning foolishly into the vanity mirror anyway. Her hair was coming unpinned, and there was a general drunken *messiness* about her that she had never seen in her reflection before. It didn't seem to matter very much; it all paled in comparison to how wonderful it felt to have a silly, easy moment of friendship after weeks of loneliness—even if so far that short-lived friendship did seem to entirely revolve around bullying a portly, middle-aged couple.

"Mrs. Gadforth, you look simply ravishing," Frances said in a comically deep voice as she reentered the room.

A fresh shout of laughter burst out of Georgiana when she saw that Frances was doing her best impression of their hostess's unfortunate husband; she had somehow procured a morning suit and top hat that were far too large for her, and she had to hold them up as she walked or risk becoming suddenly unclothed.

"Oh, Mr. Gadforth, you *rogue*," Georgiana replied in a ridiculous falsetto. "Eat me like one of your French puddings!"

Frances cackled with glee as she shuffled toward Georgiana and then collapsed onto the footstool next to her. They kept laughing, somewhat hysterically, as Georgiana helped Frances decorate herself with a wonky mustache drawn in Mrs. Gadforth's kohl liner; once properly mustachioed, Frances took off one of her own rings and pushed it onto Georgiana's finger in place of a wedding band.

It was in this state—both sitting astride the footstool professing their deep, matrimonial feelings for each other ("Mr. Gadforth, next to this painting you're a veritable work of art!" "Oh, *thank you*, Mrs. Gadforth, and might I say I did admire the vaguely pornographic topiaries you've commissioned on the back lawn")—that Lady Campbell discovered them.

Georgiana froze in place as soon as the door opened, suddenly so ashamed and horrified that she felt she might combust on the spot. To her surprise, Lady Campbell didn't look angry; she just looked tired.

"Wash your face and fetch your cloak, Frances," she said quietly. "Your father says we're leaving." She turned on her heel and exited without another word.

Georgiana was overcome with mortification and turned to Frances, expecting to see the same emotion reflected in her expression; on the contrary, Frances simply looked exasperated.

"Right on cue. The slightest hope for some fun, and there she is to throttle the life out of it. She's a *dreadful* bore."

She stripped down to her slip and began to dress as Georgiana, red in the face, pulled Mrs. Gadforth's frilly gown off over her head and placed it carefully back in the wardrobe. Frances left Mr. Gadforth's suit pooled on the floor, stepping away from it as if it were absolutely nothing to do with her, and then reclaimed her ring.

"Hopefully I'll see you at the next one, at any rate." She saluted Georgiana with a flick of her wrist before turning to leave the room. "It's been a pleasure, Miss Ellers."

Suddenly alone again, Georgiana picked up the pile of discarded clothing and started hurriedly putting everything back in its rightful place. She returned Mr. Gadforth's suit and was just rushing downstairs, wondering what exactly Frances had meant by "the next one," when she bumped into the Burtons.

"What on earth have you been doing, Georgiana?" exclaimed Mrs. Burton. "Why are you so red? Have you fallen? Are you ill?"

"Not at all, I'm fine," said Georgiana, feeling her face with the back of her hand and finding it hot to the touch.

"Well, come along then," said Mrs. Burton, eyeing her with utmost suspicion. "Your uncle ate a funny grape and isn't feeling at all himself. We're going home."

Chapter Two

THERE WEREN'T A GREAT MANY ROOMS IN THE BURTONS' house, and they weren't very finely decorated, but they made up for this deficit—in Georgiana's opinion—by having a well-stocked and cozy library, which faced west and enjoyed the benefits of the last of the evening sun. There was a general shabbiness about the place that Mrs. Burton seemed constantly at war with, bubbles in the wallpaper and knocks in the furniture that could not be polished away, and although this extended into the library, Georgiana did not think the room suffered because of it. She made a habit of retiring there after dinner each night, settling into her uncle's cracked leather armchair for hours of reading, and although Mrs. Burton frequently entreated her to join her in the drawing room to do ghastly things like embroider fat little kittens onto cushions, generally she was left alone.

When she had first arrived at the house she had tried to ask her uncle about his collection of the written word, which he now seemed to have eschewed completely in favor of the endless newspapers he resided behind, and had received the rather unsatisfactory reply, "Ah, yes. Books." Mr. Burton had been a lawyer before his early retirement, and Georgiana often wondered if he had used up an entire lifetime's worth of words during his career, leaving him with very few left for his twilight years.

She therefore endeavored to explore the contents of the library alone.

At home she had kept her own carefully curated collection,

which paled in comparison to the shelves and shelves inhabiting almost every wall in the rest of the house, and to the study, which housed her father's personal library. Her father was the master of a rather self-important boarding school, and their small house was situated in its grounds, so if Georgiana ever found her own bookshelves wanting, she had only to provide him with a list and he would return from the school library with a fresh stack for her to peruse. Her parents were great readers themselves and could often be found of an evening still sitting at the dinner table long after their plates had been emptied, engaged in rousing debates about literary styles or a particular author's overfondness for hyphenation or run-on sentences. Georgiana was not authorized to borrow books without express permission; there had been a particular incident with ink-stained fingerprints on a priceless first edition that had never been quite forgiven, even though she had been four years old at the time.

It pained Georgiana to think about any of this now: the house, the study, the books. Their home was gone, and her parents were likely arguing about punctuation without her, while enjoying a brisk, coastal, child-free breeze.

She had decided not long after conversations about moving had begun in earnest that she would certainly not feel sorry for herself, or entertain thoughts of being abandoned, mislaid, or left behind. Her parents had always been enormously practical people, and her mother had been experiencing regular headaches for so long without improvement that a drastic change was the next logical step. Any rational person could understand their reasons for not wanting to take their adult daughter with them as they entered a new phase of their lives. Her father was to take up a new post, and the lodgings provided by this new school could hardly be expected to house both Georgiana *and* her father's books.

Georgiana had cried just once, when they signed the documents that handed the house and her entire life so far over to the new schoolmaster—a man with a smiling wife and three happy, chubby children in tow—and then resolved to never cry again. In the dark recesses of her mind, she imagined prostrating herself at their feet, begging them to take her on and make her their fourth child; she would offer to confine herself to her father's study and have meals delivered through the door, haunting them like a sorrowful literary ghost. In reality, she knew she was a child no more, and that she was very lucky indeed that her aunt and uncle had agreed to take her on when her lack of marital prospects so far indicated that she was a very poor investment. She had pulled herself together, her cheeks dry when her parents shook her hand in farewell, experiencing the ever-so-slightly discomforting feeling that something inside her was dying a painful, permanent death.

Her father had promised to write once they were settled, but they were far away with many affairs to get in order, and Georgiana had heard no news as of yet. Mrs. Burton had raised the subject a few times but had displayed an unusual amount of tact in dropping it when it had not been well received. Georgiana knew that her aunt would be entirely baffled by her sister's rather hands-off approach to parenting; she had always been treated as an equal at home, an adult in miniature even during childhood, whereas Mrs. Burton—new to the office of guardian and having had no children of her own—constantly wanted to bake Georgiana pies, fuss over her hair, and rebuke her soundly for the crimes of "staying up too late" and "walking too briskly."

Unfortunately the absence of correspondence from her parents was often at the forefront of Georgiana's mind, as there wasn't much else *to* dwell on. Her few friends from home had not written either, likely caught up in summer excursions of their own, or perhaps already forgetting Georgiana now that she was not sitting right in front of them at every dinner party and card game. Her parents had often had fellow academics over for evenings of lively scholastic debate, and their children had been Georgiana's constant companions; they had been quiet literary types, all cut from similarly somber cloth. Some of them were blessed with a little conversational wit, but it was mostly wasted on extensive, vicious debates about particular subsections of Roman history, or trying to distract each other into making unforgivable mistakes during long, terse games of chess. On one particularly memorable occasion, a boy had crudely split an infinitive during conversation and they had all talked of nothing else for a week.

Nevertheless, she had known these people since childhood, and their silence hurt. When Georgiana was not conjuring up elaborate and biblical punishments for them for ignoring her, all she could do for entertainment was to eat an excess of bread, walk the nearby lanes and woods in fair weather, and then upon her return sequester herself in the library with a well-worn copy of *Robinson Crusoe* or a volume of Mrs. Radcliffe's.

While her books did provide some comfort and distraction, Georgiana soon found herself reaching a hitherto untouched limit to her joy of the written word; she would cast a book aside after long hours of reading, look around for some other source of entertainment, then sigh and pick it back up again when no livelier company was to be found. The Burtons would not countenance letting her go out on real excursions alone in search of stimulation; their house sat far enough into the outskirts that it was twenty minutes by carriage into the town proper, and they rarely felt the need to go themselves.

They were content for the most part to sit about the house and garden, watching Georgiana go quite mad.

A few days after the Gadforths' party, Georgiana joined her aunt in receiving a visitor in the cluttered, wheat-yellow parlor at the front of the house. Their near neighbor Mrs. Clenaghan, who lived in an almost identical house just a few hundred feet down the lane, was elderly, bad-tempered, and prone to extended outbursts about not much in particular. She was far from Georgiana's ideal company, but her blunt demeanor and never-ending mental compendium of local gossip compounded to make her company just about tolerable—even slightly amusing, at times. Most of the unfortunate victims of her stories were friends and acquaintances of the Burtons who did not interest Georgiana, so she entertained herself for a while by running her fingers along the frayed upholstery of the armchair she was sitting in and counting Mrs. Clenaghan's mustache hairs—but they were just taking tea when she heard the name "Campbell" and immediately snapped to attention.

"Their youngest daughter is giving them a world of trouble, I hear. Flighty, unsettled thing. Prone to hysterics. A good boxing about the ears ought to cure her of that, but alas—I'm told the box is going quite out of fashion. Last summer, Mr. Grange—you know Mr. Grange, he has that goiter and only two pairs of boots— well, he claimed he saw her down at his old mill with some of the dreadful types she hangs around with, and they were"—here she leaned in, as if afraid of being overheard in the otherwise empty room—"*half-naked.*"

Mrs. Burton looked appalled. Georgiana instantly pictured Frances in a state of disrobe and blushed to the tips of her ears.

"Yes, well—you may well blush, my dear," said Mrs. Clenaghan with an air of great satisfaction. "The Campbells are a particularly old, exceedingly important family. Lord Campbell is a military man of excellent stock. He had frequent business in the West Indies, I believe, and on one such trip he returned with *Lady* Campbell. Well, I don't mind telling you, it caused quite a stir at the time. People have grown used to her in his circles by now, but his own family would have cut him off, had he not already inherited. It was too much money for one family—I would personally be embarrassed to hold so much wealth. Their house, Longview, is magnificent. In my opinion there are none in the county that better it—and it has been said on occasion that my good opinion is rather hard-won. I never thought much of *Lady* Campbell, never quite got over the shock of her as others have, but apparently they always hosted the most extravagant parties and dinners. I think parties are rather vulgar, and luckily have never been invited, but in any case—they seem to have stopped throwing quite so many of late. Their elder daughter, Eleanor, was married around five years ago, reported to be a perfectly agreeable girl by all accounts. Frances Campbell must be of an age with you, Miss Ellers, perhaps a year or two your senior—it *is* a shame that she seems so likely to ruin them."

"A livelier spirit than yours, Mrs. Clenaghan, does not necessarily amount to ruination," said Georgiana, rather more sharply than she had intended to. Mrs. Burton gave her a reproachful look.

"Oh?" Mrs. Clenaghan narrowed her eyes at Georgiana and leaned forward in Mrs. Burton's best armchair, clearly enjoying herself. "A friend of yours, is she, Miss Ellers?"

"Georgiana and Miss Campbell were acquainted at a party only last week," interjected Mrs. Burton, flustered. "They're hardly friends—and besides, I'm sure if Georgiana were privy to any manner of impropriety from Miss Campbell, she would have the good sense to cut her off—with good manners, of course, but with great haste."

Georgiana thought guiltily of cognac, and frilly dresses, and Frances's jaunty eyeliner mustache.

"You'd do best to stay away, Miss Ellers. There are plenty of well-connected ladies about town whose company I'm sure you'd enjoy. Why, I know of a group who meet every Saturday for tea and cards. And they do it," Mrs. Clenaghan said, raising her populous eyebrows, "with their clothes *on*."

Georgiana thought a little nudity might lighten up the sort of card party held by any friends of Mrs. Clenaghan but merely smiled tightly in response.

The truth of the matter was that she would have swapped all the tea in England for another moment in Frances's company. Georgiana had already replayed the events of their meeting over and over again in quiet moments, had even started inventing further conversations they might have, future meetings in which Georgiana impressed Frances with her wit and charm, confirming a lifelong friendship and setting in motion the many adventures they would undertake together. Frances would likely open the door to all manner of glamorous parties and enchanting outings, but more importantly, she would be Georgiana's partner in crime. Her confidante. Her captain.

Georgiana had even gone so far in her daydreams as to imagine a handsome brother, a future Lord Campbell of good humor and pleasant features, whom she might marry to ensure a permanent sisterhood with Frances. They would all go out riding together across the nearby windswept moors; he'd help her out of carriages, his hand lingering on hers just a moment longer than necessary; they would not be showy with their wealth, once wed, and would prioritize taking long holidays in far-off lands, restricting themselves to just two or perhaps three houses out of town.

Her newly acquired knowledge that Frances only had an elder sister, already married, put a damper on this dream but could not extinguish it entirely. Perhaps there might be a dashing cousin? A childhood friend, returned from some dastardly war? She'd even settle for a young uncle, at a stretch, as long as he had shapely arms and most of his hair.

Conversation in the parlor had turned to repairs on a nearby bridge, so Georgiana felt it safe to stop listening again, being neither a bridge engineer nor an utter bore. The real challenge now was the likelihood of bumping into Frances again, when the Burtons were so chiefly concerned with activities like sitting down in a quiet corner and being in bed by half past nine. Mrs. Burton had reassured Georgiana that summer would bring outings aplenty, but what she had seen so far of the Burtons' social calendar had not given her much reason to hope. Short of writing Frances a letter, Georgiana did not know how to rekindle their connection, and she could hardly imagine what she'd say if she attempted to put pen to paper.

Dear Miss Campbell—I did so enjoy our drunken cross-dressing the other night, and hope to make it a regular occurrence.

Yours faithfully,
Georgiana Ellers

Perhaps not.

Once all the tea had been drunk—Georgiana thought Mrs. Clenaghan must have had some sort of enchanted refilling teacup, it took her so long to reach the bottom of it—and their visitor had left, Mrs. Burton turned an accusatory eye on her niece.

"Don't think I didn't see you with Miss Campbell at the party, Georgiana. What on earth were you doing, squirrelled away upstairs?"

"Oh—having deep discussions, Aunt. Discussions of a . . . cultural nature."

"*Discussions of a cultural nature?* Which culture, may I ask, were you discussing?"

"Oh, the drinking culture," Georgiana answered, straight-faced and wide-eyed. "It is a scourge, you know, upon our society. People are falling down in the streets—engagements broken, lives ruined.

I have heard that the Thames is running at almost seventy percent gin."

"Oh, *Georgiana,* of course it's not," Mrs. Burton scoffed, and then hesitated. "Is it?"

"They're looking into it," said Georgiana vaguely.

Mrs. Burton sighed. "I know you must find it a little dreary here at times, but I'm sure there shall be more parties, more dinners. You must be patient. There will be plenty of appropriate company—ladies *and* gentlemen—who don't incite rumor and gossip the way Miss Campbell does. Be wary of her, Georgiana. She is of immeasurably high station, it is true, but that only means she has all the farther to fall."

"Oh, don't worry," said Georgiana tersely. "I'll be on the lookout for wanton behavior and sudden nudity when the Gadforths throw their next party to celebrate the acquisition of new tablecloths."

"Georgiana, there is no need to be rude. I have said my piece. Now," she said, smiling tightly in an attempt to return them to friendship, "I'll get my embroidery and you can finally make a start on yours. I've got a lovely pattern with some terribly winsome cherubs on it that I think you'll find to your liking."

They passed the rest of the afternoon in a silence that Mrs. Burton probably imagined was peaceful and amiable, unaware that Georgiana had considered driving the embroidery needle through her eye and into her brain once she had seen the horrifying, leering little angels she was to be immortalizing in thread. She was rather jealous of Mr. Burton, who was often successful in avoiding Mrs. Burton's whims by taking many walks "for his health"; he had a standing appointment with the fresh air each morning and evening, but his excursions became far more frequent when his wife was in a particularly talkative or trying mood, with new and exciting routes sometimes occurring to him spontaneously when she was midsentence. He returned from his latest outing—one that Georgiana could only imagine had become extremely pressing when he heard of Mrs. Clenaghan's impending arrival—just in time for them to sit down to supper.

"It's such a shame that you missed her, Mr. Burton."

"The Middletons have planted sunflowers," he replied, somewhat ignoring her. She did not notice.

"Sunflowers! Well, I hope they keep them in check. *Garish* things—when they get too tall they put me in mind of peeping Toms, ogling over the wall at you as you pass."

Georgiana tried to put this comment aside and get on with the business of eating quietly but found she could not. She put down her knife and fork.

"Is the sunflower the lewdest flower, do you think, Mr. Burton?"

Mr. Burton choked on his ale and took quite a long time to recover. Georgiana kept looking at him expectantly.

"Ah . . . I expect so," he eventually replied.

"I find many flowers quite aggressive in that way," said Mrs. Burton with a shudder. "There is something very vulgar about them."

"I quite agree," said Georgiana nonchalantly, reclaiming her cutlery and tucking into her chicken. "They should be banned."

"Banned?" said Mr. Burton in quiet horror. "*Ban* flowers? Ban the natural world's crowning glory?"

Georgiana pretended to think very hard upon the matter.

"Well, if not *banned*—trimmed. Trimmed into more appropriate shapes."

"Yes, I think that would do," said Mrs. Burton approvingly, while her husband looked at her, aghast.

"I saw a flower once, you know, in the exact shape of a gentleman's—"

"Georgiana!" her aunt exclaimed.

"—top hat, Mrs. Burton. Honestly! Sometimes I don't know where your mind goes."

They resumed eating in stony silence.

*L*uckily for the Burtons, Georgiana was soon distracted from her attempts to torture them at the dinner table. Just a few days later, she was sitting alone with a book in the dining room, breathing in the smell of wood polish and watching dust motes dance through shafts of sunlight, when Mrs. Burton entered triumphantly, clutching a letter above her head.

"Is it Mother? Or Father?" Georgiana asked, brightening at once and making to get up.

"Oh no, dear, I'm so sorry, it's not—although I'm sure they'll write with as much haste as the situation allows."

Georgiana sat back down, her heart feeling leaden in her chest. She knew she was hardly some sort of impoverished orphan—was not begging in the streets for coins or squaring up to fight a malnourished bear on London Bridge to earn a paltry meal—but she would have liked some indication that her parents remembered they had a daughter. And besides, she had been left behind in the dullest county in England; it might have been quite an interesting change of pace to take on a bear in hand-to-hand combat.

Mrs. Burton came to the table and placed the object that had inspired such hope in front of her niece. Georgiana took it, finding the paper of surprisingly high quality.

"It's an invitation," she said, trying to read as fast as she could. "To a party—who are the Woodleys?"

"A great family indeed! They have a daughter about your age. I haven't had the pleasure of their direct acquaintance, but I put it about that we had a fine young lady to stay who was in need of company, and it must have reached them!" A thought seemed to occur to Mrs. Burton, and she wrung her hands in sudden despair. "Oh, but we must have new dresses—and I'll need to see about Mr. Burton's shoes—we'll have never attended such a party! Their house is ever so large, and they keep *such* an extensive rose garden."

Georgiana felt a jolt of nerves, but it could not compete with the more pleasant emotions of hope, delight, and exhilaration; a large house and *extensive* rose garden sounded like exactly the sort of place where one might be lucky enough to bump into one flighty, ruinous Miss Frances Campbell.

Chapter Three

Mrs. Burton, infamous for her ability to fuss over almost anything, was a sight to behold when she genuinely had reason to do so. New fabric was ordered for dresses—plain ivory muslin, although Mrs. Burton took great pains to point out that it could be improved with a little lace—fresh ribbon was cut for their hair, and come the evening of the party, Georgiana even saw Mr. Burton standing very still, newspaper in hand, allowing his wife to trim his mustache with sewing scissors.

Her aunt kept up a constant rattle of conversation during the rickety carriage ride there, and Georgiana was gripped by a sudden urge to fling open the carriage door and fall gracefully out into the hedgerows just to get away from her. Luckily, by the time they arrived, Mrs. Burton had talked herself to the point of exhaustion, and they sat in awed silence as they traveled up a grand driveway to the biggest house Georgiana had ever seen up close. Mr. Burton, half-asleep, seemed unmoved.

A thrill of nervous excitement coursed through her as she entered the busy front hall, trying to turn her head in small increments to make it less obvious that she was struggling to take it all in. This room alone was so large it was a wonder that they'd managed to fill it with guests, but fill it they had; at least fifty people were laughing politely, fanning themselves, clinking their glasses, and calling delightedly to their friends across the crowd. An enormous tapestry depicting a biblical-looking battle presided over the curved staircase, emblazoned at the top with what seemed to be the family crest, and a chandelier that looked positively weary with crystal hung above their heads.

Georgiana wondered if the owners of the house might be some poorer relations of God.

Mr. and Mrs. Burton were fussing over something behind her in the entryway—probably occupied counting the rosebushes—and Georgiana took the opportunity to step away from them and disappear into the gilded crowd, accepting a drink as she did so. This was truly no painting unveiling at the Gadforths'; the dresses were all rustling silk and dazzling trim, the champagne flowed freely, and the gentlemen were well combed and upright in their neatly starched linens.

It had taken Georgiana three hours to dress and prepare for the evening. The maid, Emmeline, had taken the utmost care that every curl was pinned precisely in place, every ribbon tied and tucked neatly away, smiling shyly at Georgiana in the mirror when she had finished. Georgiana did not find her own reflection particularly inspiring—she knew her hair to be too dull a brown, her pale face grossly marred by a light sprinkling of freckles—but she had made an effort and thought the result possibly as comely as she had ever looked.

Even with so much time set aside for preparation, the Woodleys' house was so intimidating that Georgiana now felt she may as well have fashioned an outfit out of dishcloths. She kept tugging at her dress and smoothing her hair as she made her way through the throng, most likely achieving the opposite effect to that intended and disheveling herself further. In reality nobody was sparing her a second—or even a first—glance, but she still felt as if every eye appraised her and found her wanting; at any moment someone might spot her and cry "Oh, good God—a poor little match girl!" and throw sympathetic coins at her feet.

Georgiana navigated a long hallway lined with imposing oil paintings and constipated-looking marble busts until she found the main ballroom, carefully avoiding dancers and revelers as she walked the perimeter. There were more beautiful young men and women in this one room than she had ever seen in her life, and they seemed incandescent in the candlelight; it was hard to take them in individually, as they blurred into a mass of elegant hands touching gloved wrists, polished heels clicking against the marble floor, and well-bred mouths lowering to whisper in flushed, dainty ears.

Everybody here seemed in some way Of Consequence. Not one of them looked as if they had ever experienced more than ten seconds of boredom in their entire lives. Georgiana felt like a starving person who had stumbled upon a feast.

A few people nodded politely to her as she passed, and she returned the gesture shyly, thinking that soon she might be forced to loop back and rejoin the Burtons—but suddenly there was Frances, standing near the open French windows in the glow of a candelabra, and looking even more magnificent than the last time Georgiana had seen her. Then, she had been withering away in the dark, drab hallway of the Gadforths'; now she was absolutely in her element, radiant in shades of palest green and gold, with a wineglass dangling from her hand.

She was engaged in lively conversation with a group of young men and women who looked so glossy and well put together that Georgiana felt far too afraid to approach, let alone *speak* to them, lest they take offense and spit on her.

Gripped with the sudden anguish of indecision, Georgiana made to turn away, intending to take another lap around the room to fortify herself before making an approach—but then she heard Frances call her name. She had barely raised her voice, but somehow those four syllables cut through the clamor of the crowd and the music to reach her ears instantly, like a whistle to a dog.

Flushed with nerves, Georgiana made her way over to the group.

"Well, look who it is," said Frances, looking genuinely thrilled. "My erstwhile wife!"

Georgiana was introduced to each of those present in turn. Miss Cecily Dugray was tall, pale, and exceedingly handsome, with hyacinth-blue eyes and a delicate pillow of a mouth; she put one in mind of a golden palomino. Miss Jane Woodley, whose family's party they were attending, was short, darker, and plainer; she was a little stockily built, drawn in much bolder strokes than Miss Dugray, and her expression was guarded as she took Georgiana's hand in a perfunctory sort of way.

Of the two gentlemen present, one—a Mr. Jonathan Smith—was effusive in his greeting, sweeping back the strawberry-blond hair that had fallen into his smiling eyes as he bent to kiss Georgiana's hand. The last, Mr. Christopher Crawley, who sported a well-waxed mustache and was quite shockingly dressed in scarlet, gave her a roguish wink that startled her so much she almost forgot to curtsy. She was instantly reminded of a description of a pirate she'd read, and felt a little uneasy, as if he might be about to hold her at sword point and plunder her for her hairpins that very instant.

So far, not one of them seemed the least bit inclined to spit on her.

They returned at once to the conversation they had been having, and Georgiana was content to listen, delighted by the first-rate company and her inclusion in it—plus more than a little concerned that if she opened her mouth to speak she might say something extraordinarily foolish about the weather, or the life cycle of a frog.

"No, I'm telling you—if Mr. Weatherby looks at me askance again on Sunday I shall publicly name him a pervert, and tell the congregation that when I adjusted my position during the service he tried to get a good look at my ankles," Frances was saying, to much general amusement. "Honestly, it is no wonder I hardly attend—it's enough to drive a woman into the loving arms of the devil. When he gazes at me while preaching of family and duty, I can see what he's imagining—me his wife, fat around the middle with a litter of children, opening my legs once a year for the sole purpose of procreation and thinking keenly of God all the while."

Georgiana choked on her drink, and accepted with many quiet thanks when Mr. Crawley smoothly offered her his monogrammed kerchief.

"Well, if not the venerable vicar, who will be gazing freely upon those ankles, Franny?" asked Mr. Smith with a familiarity that instantly gave Georgiana the impression that he himself would quite like to see the limbs in question. "I've heard plenty a rumor, but I do like to go directly to the source."

"I couldn't possibly comment," said Frances, sipping her drink and flashing the other ladies a smirk. Georgiana wished she knew what it was that Frances was being coy about, so that she could join Miss Dugray, who was giving her a knowing smile in return. Miss Woodley's only response was a barely audible sniff.

"Who is the lucky man?" asked Mr. Crawley. "Oh, Frances, don't tell me it's that puffed-up, arrogant dandy—the *inimitable* Mr. Russell?"

"You're quite as puffed up as he is, Christopher, and you know it," returned Frances. "And you're wearing velvet in June, for Christ's sake. A little self-awareness might do you some good."

"Well, yes—but I have the dignity and good grace to know and accept all of my many advantages and scant flaws," said Mr. Crawley, not seeming the least bit offended. "*He* pretends to have no inkling of his few, inexplicable charms—all twenty thousand a year of them—and affects a positively baffled expression every time another mother approaches with a brood of daughters practically swooning in her wake. He's been like that ever since Eton. And besides," he added smugly, with the air of someone in possession of portentous intel, "he took Kitty Fathering to bed."

The ladies gasped in unison. Georgiana felt her eyes widen and took pains to return them to a more appropriate size.

"He did not, and you know it," said Frances sharply. "Kitty Fathering probably fell down drunk in her father's stable and slept in an amorous embrace with a particularly handsome pony, convinced it was Jeremiah by the color of its forelock."

"And the smell," said Mr. Crawley over his drink.

"Miss Ellers, we must be frightfully dull, speaking of people you're not yet acquainted with," said Mr. Smith. "Mr. Russell lives half the time up in some dreary city in the Midlands, but he comes here for the shooting and for most summers with his cohorts and his family. I'm surprised he isn't here, actually."

Georgiana was a little flustered to be addressed so directly and simply smiled.

"He *is* here," said Mr. Crawley reluctantly. "I saw him in the gardens with a few of his hangers-on when I went to smoke."

"Well! Kept that to yourself, didn't you?" said Frances, scowling prettily at him.

Miss Woodley laughed humorlessly. "Afraid you'd be outdone, Christopher?"

"All right, all right, let's pay him a friendly visit and give poor Franny something to think of other than God the next time she opens her legs for a passing farmhand," said Mr. Smith, steering Frances toward the French windows as she attempted to hit him playfully with her fan. Miss Woodley continued to look as if she'd rather be anywhere else—which was unfortunate, Georgiana thought, as this was *her* party.

She had never in her life heard so many outright references to fornication—her mother and father had skirted awkwardly around the subject, referring to it once, after Georgiana had seen

two pigs getting amorous, as "the special embrace." She was trying to affect an air of nonchalance about the fact that Frances and
her friends were as foul-mouthed and salty as a crew of peculiarly well-shod sailors. Sex was something that happened behind
closed doors, in broken-in marital beds or the dark recesses of
bawdy-houses; it was what happened *after the end* of romance
books, or sometimes, in the more risqué of her novels, what was
briefly alluded to and then quickly skipped past for decency; it
was *not* something you discussed openly at a party, as if com-
menting on the weather or the price of butter.

Georgiana trailed behind Frances and the others, clutching
her drink and trying not to draw too much attention to herself
as they walked out onto the expansive patio. She thought there
was every chance that they might turn and ask her why she was
still following them like a demented duckling. A group of young
men—perhaps Georgiana's age, or a few years her senior—were
lounging around an ornate fountain, cravats loosened at their
necks, laughing loudly and unrestrainedly. As they approached,
one of them leaned backward over the fountain's lip and opened
his mouth so that water cascaded into it; he spluttered, coming
up coughing and grinning, and the others cheered. Given that
the woman depicted in the fountain's design seemed to have forsaken clothing and sprung a leak from somewhere *most* unfortunate, it wasn't difficult to imagine what they found so amusing.

One of the men wasn't laughing; in fact, he was exhibiting
the kind of polite smile one might employ when meeting one's
dentist or hearing a detailed account of a banking transaction.
He was dressed simply in crisp whites and navy blues, with his
hands clasped behind his back, as if he were standing at attention; upon closer inspection his whole body was rigid, tension
radiating from him palpably, entirely at odds with the others,
who were so laid-back they were almost horizontal. He was tall,
with a brown complexion—perhaps some Indian heritage, Geor-

giana thought, although she had a limited frame of reference to place him—and with unfashionably long, loose curls that were half-heartedly pulled back from his face. His brown eyes were large but downcast, giving him a quiet and melancholy air, and the line of his jaw was so sharply defined that Georgiana thought it would probably be painful to the touch.

She immediately wondered why she was thinking of touching it at all.

While the other men met the approaching party with jovial cries of greeting, he gave a polite bow and turned to look out over the gardens.

The best-looking of the bunch, and their natural leader, was clearly Mr. Jeremiah Russell. He was tall, well-built, and classically beautiful, with pale, neat features and expertly coiffed blond hair. Georgiana wondered how many manservants it had taken to get one single lock of hair to fall so attractively over his left eye. Frances was obviously very taken with him; as hands were shaken and kissed, she couldn't keep her eyes off him, giggling with surprising girlishness when he lingered with his lips pressed to the backs of her fingers.

"And who is this?" he cried, turning his charming smile on Georgiana, who immediately blushed crimson.

Despite a certain excess of coiffing, he *was* very good-looking.

"The enchanting Miss Georgiana Ellers," said Frances. "I discovered her hiding in a wall at a dreadful party, and she made an intolerable evening bearable. She's *new,* Jeremiah—staying with her aunt and uncle nearby."

Georgiana curtsied self-consciously.

"In a wall?" Mr. Russell replied, raising an eyebrow as he appraised Georgiana, a faint smile playing about his lips. "How droll."

He turned his attention back to Frances. "Would you like something a little *special* to smoke, Miss Campbell? We were just entertaining the thought of taking a turn about the garden."

"Oh, you are terrible—but I suppose I would," replied Frances, beaming at him.

Georgiana tried to parse this exchange and failed; "taking a turn about the garden" clearly meant something quite different in this particular circle.

"We *all* would," said Mr. Crawley pointedly, and without further discussion the procession moved down into the dark grounds, leaving behind only the hostess, Miss Woodley—who rolled her eyes and waved them away with a shrug—and a few of Mr. Russell's friends. Georgiana noticed that the curly-haired man was among those who stayed, and felt a little deflated.

Their intended destination was a small, fragrant rose garden, framed on all sides by high hedgerows that shielded it from the view of the house. The main pathways through the grounds were lit with flickering lamps, but once they'd slipped through the opening in the hedges they were all cast in the faded indigo of the darkening sky. They sat down on cool stone benches, the men chuckling at some joke Georgiana hadn't heard, barely visible to each other in the gloom until someone struck a light.

Georgiana was just wondering what exactly they intended to smoke when a pipe flared into life nearby, and the man who held it disappeared behind a cloud of hazy smoke. She watched, fascinated and a little nervous, as it was passed from hand to hand. A few moments later it was pressed into her own by Mr. Smith, who was sitting on her left. Georgiana had absolutely no idea what to do with it; she had seen her father and her uncle smoke but had never imagined that she might be permitted to do something so singularly suggestive with her mouth. Besides, she wondered wildly, what was so special about this pipe in particular?

She stared at it for a moment, and Jeremiah looked up from where he was sitting with Frances.

"We don't have all day, Miss Ellers," he said, in an uncanny impression of a flinty governess. Frances laughed.

"I'm not sure this is—" Georgiana started, but Frances cut her off with a small smile and a shake of her curls.

"You are certainly not obliged to take it—but I'm sure you'll like it, Georgiana. In fact, I'd bet my life on it. If you don't, I'll . . . Well, I'll give you the keys to my house and you can move in forthwith—how's that?"

Jeremiah laughed, putting a hand on her arm; she turned back to him, obviously pleased, and murmured something Georgiana could not hear.

She turned to Mr. Smith in desperation. "I don't . . . ," she said to him in a small voice. "That is, I haven't . . ."

He grinned at her conspiratorially, and she couldn't help but smile back.

"Just put your lips to it and breathe in," he advised quietly, lifting the pipe to her mouth. "Hold it in your chest for as long as you can before you expel it. Try not to cough," he added sternly, "or you'll embarrass me."

She did as instructed, and although her eyes watered, she managed not to choke before handing the pipe to Miss Dugray on her other side. She watched in utmost awe as Cecily inhaled and exhaled deeply three times and passed the pipe on; she undertook the whole thing as nonchalantly as if she were simply taking in fresh air. She noticed Georgiana watching her and smiled beatifically.

"Frances said you're staying with your aunt and uncle?" she asked. "Are your parents visiting, too?"

Cecily was so beautiful that it took Georgiana a moment to realize that she was expected to respond.

"Ah . . . no. My mother is unwell—headaches—so they've taken to the seaside for a change of air," explained Georgiana. The tips of her fingers felt oddly numb; it was quite pleasant. "Personally, I think they grew tired of the restraints of parenthood."

Georgiana had never voiced this aloud—had barely allowed

herself to think it—and had no idea what had compelled her to do so now, in front of a veritable stranger. She *was* feeling rather light-headed, and deduced that the special nature of whatever was in that pipe was to relax the smoker until they felt comfortable letting all manner of nonsense escape their lips. She dimly registered that from the moment she had taken in a lungful of thick, fragrant smoke, everything around her had felt somehow much less shocking. Women smoking? Fine. Unchaperoned youths ensconced in a garden in the dark, sitting so close that their knees and shoulders kept bumping together? Absolutely run-of-the-mill.

"Oh, you poor thing," said Miss Dugray, shaking her head in what seemed to be genuine remorse. "Here—have some more of this."

It didn't seem like the worst solution; the more Georgiana smoked, the less urgent her problems became, until the idea that her parents had grown bored of their only child and abandoned her in favor of a sea view seemed almost a trifling concern.

Frances and Jeremiah were sharing a bench and speaking to each other in low voices that spoke of mutual affection and confidence; he had her hand in his, and as Georgiana watched, he curled his index finger and stroked gently along the inside of her palm. Georgiana felt a pang of something as she watched—embarrassment, perhaps, for witnessing something so intimate, but also a vague sort of yearning. Frances was so obviously happy, engaged to a man she seemed to love—something that was never guaranteed.

Georgiana dragged her gaze away and looked surreptitiously around at the young men sitting about her. Jeremiah's anonymous friends were good-looking and obviously well-off, but they also had an air of hardness about them, a carelessness that put her on edge. Georgiana had never much bothered with men, and they had returned the favor—the children of her parents' friends had not been promising candidates for courting, matrimony, or any sort of tension that occurred outside a rousing game of cards.

Mr. Jonathan Smith was perfectly friendly, but Georgiana still thought he seemed inclined toward Frances, despite the fact that she was a lost cause; he was currently talking to one of Mr. Russell's friends, but with one eye on Frances at all times. Mr. Crawley honestly alarmed her a little; he kept twirling his mustache, apparently unaware that it was the classic hallmark of a literary villain. Mr. Russell himself was obviously spoken for, currently exploring the underside of Frances's wrist. Georgiana's thoughts drifted back to the curly-haired stranger who had remained at the house—now, *he* was another matter entirely, fascinating precisely because he had simply looked a little morose and said nothing at all. Compared to some of Jeremiah's other friends—one of whom was currently trying to smoke the pipe through his left nostril—this made him eminently promising.

The reality, of course, was that nobody in a hundred-foot radius would ever dream of considering her an equal match. Unless Georgiana's parents had somehow acquired land, inheritance, and titles since she had last seen them, she was of too little consequence to be worth a second glance. Her tenuous friendship with Frances, still very much in its infancy, was as close as she came to having her own connections; even if she did take a fancy to one of the gentlemen present, to make those feelings known would surely only invite ridicule.

After all, she still hadn't entirely ruled out being spat on.

"Who was that man with Mr. Russell by the fountain?" she asked Cecily anyway, trying and failing to sound casual. "The darker gentleman, with the curls?"

"Oh, I think he's a . . . maybe a Hornsley? Horsely? *Hawksley*, that's it. He's a family friend of the Russells, he lives up at Highbourne House. His mother is from somewhere abroad, I can never quite remember—"

"India?" Georgiana asked.

"Oh, that's it! You clever thing. India. From some immensely rich family out there, they did something to do with . . . trade. *New* money, although his father had plenty of his own. He used to hang about with Jeremiah, but I haven't seen him for years. Quiet sort of fellow now, although I'm sure he wasn't always— they say he is outrageously rich, but then, they say that about everyone. And—kind, too," she added as an afterthought. They were interrupted by a flask, passed by Mr. Smith.

Georgiana tried again. "Are the Hawksleys—"

"Hawksley?" One of Mr. Russell's friends cut her off, leaning in and laughing unkindly. "I wouldn't waste your time there, ladies. The word 'fun' left that chap's vocabulary quite a few years ago. The closest he comes to a lively jape these days is when he wears a cravat that doesn't quite match his stockings."

He reached for the flask, claiming it before Georgiana had taken her turn, and then turned back to his companions.

"He does look terribly sad most of the time," Cecily said, frowning. "Like his horse has just died."

"Perhaps it has," said Georgiana.

"I had a lovely horse once," said Cecily wistfully. "She was called Hestia. I told her all my secrets, you know, and I really do think she listened to me. It's so rare to find somebody who truly understands your heart, man or beast."

Georgiana checked to see if she was joking; Cecily had a slightly vacant air about her, but she was also extremely earnest and seemed perfectly serious about communing with her horse.

"What's the difference?" Georgiana replied, as if she had all manner of dalliances under her belt, and Cecily tilted her head to the side and smiled sleepily. Everything about her gave Georgiana the impression that she was speaking to some kind of ethereal princess, imported from another realm. Her only perceivable flaw was perhaps a certain lack of wits, but Georgiana was certainly not in a position to judge at the minute; whatever had been in the pipe was potent, and everything was getting dreadfully muddled.

There was a lull in the conversation, and Georgiana realized that neither she nor Cecily had spoken for what must have been at least a minute. Some subtle change in the atmosphere, most likely fabricated by her pipe-addled brain, meant that Georgiana suddenly felt constrained and crowded among all these people; she had an immediate, fervent desire to be away from the group and closer to the lights at the end of the garden. Lights, she thought, were innately *good*. People, on the other hand, had the potential to be bad.

Excusing herself, she gracelessly exited the hedgerows and stumbled down the gravel path with what she hoped was a look of polite and casual interest upon her face, focusing on the pleasing glow of the lamps, the only bright spots in the darkness.

She was quite alone this far from the house, with the cool evening air keeping most guests confined to it; all conversation was no more than a gentle murmur in the distance.

Georgiana's spirits were buoyed; she had almost made it to her desired destination when some troublesome stone steps appeared as if from nowhere. She noticed them a second too late and tripped quite spectacularly on her hem, hurtling toward the bottom of them. Visions of broken bones and ghastly wounds flashed before her eyes, but she was pleasantly surprised to find that something warm and solid caught her before she hit the ground.

"You have saved me," Georgiana said dramatically, her words indistinct.

Her rescuer gave a short, surprised laugh and gently helped her sit down on the steps. When he sat down beside her, Georgiana squinted at the figure half-illuminated by the lamplight and saw that it was none other than Mr. Hawksley.

"It's you!" she said loudly.

He did not seem to know the proper response to this and simply gave her a slightly strained smile. Up close—and she was *rather* close to him—he was undeniably handsome, although he looked positively exhausted. He had the most extraordinary eyelashes she had ever seen, and in the darkness his irises looked almost black; it was disarming, frankly, to have those eyes focused so intently on her. She almost wanted to shield her face, but luckily some part of her brain registered that it would seem quite insane.

Georgiana realized she had been looking at him in silence for some time.

"Are you enjoying the party?"

"Oh, it's . . . very pleasant," he replied, looking about as if he hadn't realized he was *at* a party. His voice wasn't clipped and polished like Jeremiah Russell's; it was deep and a little hoarse, like worn velvet.

"I'm sure it's nothing compared to the parties you're used to," Georgiana said for some reason. "I'm sure you attend balls hosted by Prussian royalty, where they race pigs and—and eat exotic fruits, and serve turkeys stuffed inside chickens stuffed inside sparrows."

"Sparrows would be in the center," he said evenly. "You can't fit a turkey inside a sparrow."

"Oh," said Georgiana, feeling foolish and wrong-footed. "Well, *you* would know, of course. I'm sure you have fifty acres, and fifteen thousand a year, and an enormous collection of tall hats."

Mr. Hawksley shifted uncomfortably. Georgiana's mouth dropped open.

"You *do,* don't you? You have fifty acres and fifteen thousand a year, and almost as many hats!"

"I don't have anywhere close to fifteen thousand hats. Fifty . . . perhaps."

"Oh," said Georgiana again.

After her initial rush of adrenaline-fueled confidence, she was quite at a loss as to what to say next. She wondered that *anybody* had ever known what to say, in the history of life on earth. After a moment, inspiration struck.

"I'm Georgiana Ellers," she said, holding out a hand.

"Thomas Hawksley," he said slowly, taking her hand in his, "although apparently, my reputation for pig-racing precedes me."

While there was nothing at all clandestine about the brief kiss on the hand one might receive from an overenthusiastic man in a crowded room—often from a gentleman twice one's age, leaving behind an unpleasant smear of spittle that had to be surreptitiously wiped on the furniture immediately afterward—there was something *extremely* intimate about a painfully good-looking stranger slowly pressing one's hand to his lips in a deserted garden, lit only by the flicker of distant lamps.

Unfortunately, said kiss only took place in Georgiana's racing imagination; Mr. Hawksley only cleared his throat quietly, then released her hand as if she were suffering from something contagious.

"Sorry. I don't know what compelled me . . . ," she started.

He had turned to look across the lawn; Georgiana was glad he couldn't see her blushing furiously in the dark. She felt at a natural disadvantage, sitting next to somebody who could so casually lay claim to approximately fifty hats.

"There are just quite a lot of very *well-dressed people* here, have you noticed?" Georgiana said suddenly, and too loudly. "Nobody here looks as if they've ever had to groom a horse, or . . . or . . . tie up their own bootlaces. They probably think horses groom themselves with long tongues, like cats—and the idea of a shoelace has likely never even entered their periphery. They . . . They probably just announce that they're leaving the house, and somewhere far below them a maid does something indecipherable, and then—hoorah, they're ready to go!"

A slightly stunned silence followed this, which Georgiana thought was fair.

"I rather enjoy grooming my horse," said Mr. Hawksley eventually. "I find it quite calming."

"Well, of *course* you do," said Georgiana churlishly. "It's all very *calming* when you can *choose* whether to groom your horse or not. And especially when, even if you do choose to groom him, it's your only domestic task of the day, after which you can retire to the fireside to . . . I don't know, drink a bucket of fine brandy, patting yourself on the back for a hard day's work well done."

"Hmm. Are you in the habit of grooming horses, Miss Ellers?" asked Mr. Hawksley.

Throughout the course of their short conversation he seemed to have somehow unclenched, and was now leaning back against the steps with an informal ease. She watched his hand, which he was absentmindedly running through his hair, and then quickly looked away. It was rather an agreeable hand, but she couldn't really account for the strength of feeling it roused in her.

"Well—no. My uncle has a man who does it."

"Ah, I see. So these are purely ideological leanings in regards to the politics of horse-grooming, with no basis in the realities of your day-to-day life?"

Georgiana said nothing. He was potentially onto something here, but she saw no reason to let him know so.

"I know very little about you, Miss Ellers—not who your family are, or where you live, or how you came to be at this party surrounded by people with whom you seem so unimpressed—" Georgiana made to interrupt him, but he continued. "I can't pretend I don't share some of your qualms about our present company, but it seems to me that you might want to *ask* people if they harbor airs of grandeur, or perhaps even engage them in polite conversation first, before you give them up completely as a bad lot."

He made to get up. Georgiana couldn't help but feel that she'd said something wrong, but in her present state of mind she wasn't quite sure what it was. She really didn't want him to go, now that she was presented with that possibility, but could think of nothing to say to allow her to keep him.

"I'll take my leave of you, Miss Ellers. I believe your friends are looking for you."

Georgiana twisted clumsily to see Frances and Cecily stumbling out of the ornamental garden, loudly hissing her name in stage whispers as they went.

"Incidentally, while I have never seen a pig-chase, I did see someone racing ducks once. It was quite disturbing. They had little bonnets on."

Georgiana turned back, smiling, a response to this halfway to her lips—but he was already gone, casting a long shadow as he strode back up the path toward the party.

Chapter Four

ALTHOUGH MRS. BURTON HAD NO SOLID EVIDENCE THAT HER
niece had spent the evening in undesirable company indulging in
illicit activities—Georgiana had found her aunt and uncle again by
the very respectable hour of ten o'clock—she tutted down Georgiana's explanation that she'd simply had too much champagne
and treated her to a lecture about ladylike behavior (and the importance of chaperones, and modesty, and proper introductions)
for the best part of an hour on the carriage ride home. Georgiana
rested her forehead on the faded interior of the carriage and tried
her best to look innocently intrigued, but only succeeded in looking as if she were suffering some sort of intestinal discomfort.

She arose late the next day with a pounding head, emerging
just in time for luncheon with her aunt and uncle, the former
of whom greeted her loudly and enthusiastically, and then narrowed her eyes suspiciously at her when she winced.

Georgiana still didn't know exactly what had been in that
pipe, but whatever it was, it was certainly not just tobacco; she
had never known her uncle to toddle off toward pretty lights or
start giggling uncontrollably when he indulged in smoking after
dinner, although admittedly he had once shocked her by wan-
tonly undoing the top button of his waistcoat.

The Georgiana who lived with her parents and spent Saturday nights reorganizing her books by year of publication would
have been absolutely horrified at the idea of smoking mysterious, mind-altering substances with near-strangers, but she was

quickly realizing that she didn't have to be that Georgiana anymore. Perhaps this version of herself—the one who could be on first-name terms with Frances Campbell, and keep up with her high-society friends, and be welcomed wholeheartedly into a literal inner circle wreathed in rosebushes—was also the kind of person who acted as if such things were no more out of the ordinary than enjoying a particularly well-brewed cup of tea.

Georgiana was picking half-heartedly at her food when Emmeline came to tell them that someone had called for her and was currently waiting at the door—a pretty, dark-haired someone with a carriage so impressive that it apparently warranted extensive description.

"Oh, my good God! It's Miss Campbell, isn't it?" Mrs. Burton said loudly, her hands flying to her face.

"She can *obviously* hear you," Georgiana hissed back.

The fact that Frances had come to find her—that Frances had discovered her *address*, had gone to the trouble to actually seek her out—thrilled her to an unreasonable extent, immediately accelerating her heartbeat and slicking her palms with sweat, but there was no time to dissect all of that right now.

A momentary and rather farcical panic ensued, in which Mrs. Burton's immediate instinct was to pick up and hide a block of cheese, while Georgiana rushed to pull on her cloak and bonnet. Mr. Burton stayed stoic and stationary throughout, like a mountain in the middle of a hurricane. Georgiana was out of the door with her luncheon haphazardly bundled into a basket for a picnic before her visitor could get a good look inside the house, aided in this endeavor by Mrs. Burton, whose concerns about the propriety of Miss Campbell were trumped only by her horror at someone of Frances's standing seeing the modest and slightly dusty interior of her home.

Georgiana understood; for once, she and her aunt were aligned on the horrors of dust.

Frances seemed politely bemused by the rush to get her away but accepted the plan for a picnic as it was a fine day. She instructed her driver to take them to a spot Georgiana recommended—a country meadow ten minutes from the house, down the narrow, uneven lane. Georgiana had often enjoyed it alone with a good book, a habit that had earned her a sermon from Mrs. Burton on "the evils of reading out of doors." They settled down in the shade, on a rug that had been procured from the depths of the carriage and had the general air of being imported from somewhere.

Frances looked exhausted but happy, reclining nonchalantly back on her elbows, and Georgiana tried to imitate her, as if a million thoughts were not currently rushing through her head—as if she were not so excited to be here, sitting under a tree with Frances, that she felt a little sick.

"How was the rest of the party?" she asked casually, squinting as the dappled sunlight flitted across her eyes, sending pain lancing through her head. The discovery that enjoyable but questionable behavior had consequences, Georgiana mused, was most disappointing.

"It was *marvelous*," said Frances, languidly taking off her shoes and stockings. She was still wearing her green and gold silks from the night before, although they looked slightly rumpled. She stretched, catlike, and wiggled her toes in the grass. "Jeremiah could barely tear himself away. It all thinned out a little after midnight, but he and I were talking well into the early hours. I slept at Jane's—these are her stockings. A little tawdry for my taste."

Georgiana offered Frances a sandwich, which she ate immediately and ravenously.

"I'm expecting a proposal before the summer is over," she said between mouthfuls. "Honestly, God himself couldn't have arranged a more perfect match through divine intervention."

"But . . . you mean to say you're not engaged?" Georgiana said, her own sandwich faltering halfway to her mouth.

She had just assumed Frances and Jeremiah were engaged from the way they'd been carrying on—how *intimate* they had been. Georgiana didn't know what God himself would have to say about erotic hand-fondling before marriage, but she couldn't imagine it'd be anything good.

"Gird your loins, Georgiana, for I am about to shock you to your very core—no, we are not engaged," Frances said, rolling her eyes. "Oh, don't look at me like that. It'll happen any day now. I must say, I would find the whole thing more vexing, but the anticipation is quite frankly . . . *delicious.*"

"He certainly looks at you like you're something he'd like to eat," said Georgiana; she was treated to Frances's most mischievous smile.

"God, I hope he *does,*" she replied, and Georgiana snorted with shocked laughter. "Come, now, I'm not the only one who's been frolicking in Jane's garden—I heard you were making connections of your own, Georgiana. Miss Woodley saw you dallying with our most reticent Mr. Hawksley. You know, he's something of an enigma—but that only seems to make the ladies want him all the more."

"Which ladies?" asked Georgiana, putting her untouched sandwich down.

"Oh, you know," Frances said dismissively, waving a hand. "Everyone. He ignores them all, poor dears. Of course, Jeremiah is highly sought-after, too—many have tried, and many have failed. I can't wait to see the forlorn looks on their poor little faces when we announce our engagement. But come now, don't change the subject—Mr. *Hawksley.* I want all the sordid details."

"There isn't much to tell," said Georgiana truthfully, brushing crumbs from her skirts. "We just talked about . . . you know, the party and the guests, and a little about . . . horses."

She was lying by omission, but she didn't think Frances needed to know how thoroughly she had embarrassed herself in front of Mr. Hawksley, or about her insinuation that someone like Frances wouldn't understand the concept of a shoelace. She had just seen her friend untie her own shoes, after all, so that particular matter was settled in Mr. Hawksley's favor.

It was inevitable, of course, that he had been the subject of female attention in the past—he was wealthy, and mysterious, and had eyelashes comparable to those of a newborn calf—but it still rankled Georgiana, who knew rationally that she had absolutely no claim to him. She wasn't sure why she was so intrigued by him, but for some reason she longed to be in his good graces.

If she was honest with herself, that didn't seem particularly likely, unless he had a particular penchant for being insulted.

"Jeremiah and I were talking of him last night. He actually lives here all year round, you know—he doesn't just summer here like the rest of us. We used to see more of him a few years ago, he was often in among the rabble at parties, but he vanished somewhat mysteriously and has only just reemerged. It's probably the most interesting thing he's ever done, which speaks volumes—I don't think I've actually managed to have a proper conversation with him since. He does have a *staggering* inheritance, and I know he's in charge of his family's business. There was something . . . something about his family that Jeremiah alluded to, but he didn't go into detail—well, he was distracted." She grinned, and Georgiana wondered what exactly Frances had been doing to distract him. "The only trouble is, all that responsibility has made him intolerably dull. I fear that marrying him would be like marrying a particularly well-connected broom handle."

"He seemed tolerable to me," said Georgiana, thinking that he probably couldn't say the same for her.

"Really? Well, each to her own. I certainly can't imagine setting up house and spending a lifetime of parties on the arm of someone so desperately averse to enjoying himself. He barely drinks, he doesn't smoke. His main hobbies seem to be creating uncomfortable pauses in conversation and looking at his hands. He's very polite, of course, perfectly *nice*." She shuddered theatrically.

Georgiana couldn't understand why Frances was so intent on assassinating Mr. Hawksley's character; perhaps she had never been close enough to him to be entranced by his eyelashes.

"Your other friends—they were very kind," Georgiana said, keen to change the subject, finally taking a bite of her lunch.

"Oh, my ladies-in-waiting," Frances said, laughing. "Jane's a tough old nut, but she's all right really. I've known her forever—we were children together. I fear she's getting more and more onerous in her old age, though. She barely seems to enjoy her own parties these days. *Cecily* is a card. She's disgustingly handsome, anyone can see that, but she's not exactly . . . Well, she's not going to be the first woman in government, that's for certain. She's good value, though, always game for anything, and she's got such *beautiful* brothers. All married now, of course," she said with a wistful sigh. "They're all as tall and fair as she is. I thought the youngest might look my way, but their mother tied them up in engagements with some fresh society girls in London as soon as she could."

"Mr. Smith seems very fond of you," ventured Georgiana. "Did you and he ever . . . ?"

Frances looked at her in genuine astonishment, and then threw her head back and laughed.

"Oh, not Jonathan! Poor man, you slander him. He's like a brother to me—and I don't mean to shock you, Georgiana, but I am *very* much not his type. A confirmed bachelor at the ripe old age of twenty-two."

Georgiana had absolutely no idea what she was talking about and didn't manage to arrange her face to pretend otherwise.

"He's a man's man, Georgiana. 'Ladies not permitted,' like at those clubs in the city."

"Oh!" Georgiana said, her face reddening as she finally caught on. "You mean . . . ?"

"I'm pretty sure the last I saw of him yesterday, he was disappearing round the back of the greenhouse with one of Jeremiah's dreadful friends," she said, arching a dark eyebrow.

"*Oh,*" said Georgiana again, her mind racing.

She had heard of such men before—one could not have a basic grasp of classical Greek literature without being introduced to a whole host of them—but as far as she was aware, she had never met one in person before. Mr. Smith hadn't seemed the least bit peculiar or fiendish—or, at least, no more than the rest of them. In fact, Georgiana had warmed to him more than any of the others.

She could only imagine what her aunt would say—his behavior was against the law, after all—but in some ways Georgiana thought it added a certain thrill of romance to him. He was willing to risk it all, to break the law for love—or for whatever exactly it was people did behind the backs of greenhouses.

Frances looked rather pleased at managing to shock her. Georgiana realized she had misinterpreted their closeness, his frequent glances across the rose garden; his was not a look of longing, but rather a watchful protectiveness over his dear *Franny.*

"He's terribly lucky we're all so practiced at looking the other way," said Frances. "We actually pretended we were courting, once, for a time. He was trying to throw the dogs off the scent, and people believed us readily enough. It was all ruined when a group of us walked in and found him completely nude in the billiard room with this terrible Italian at my birthday party." She wrinkled her nose at the memory and then sighed. "He and Christopher are always an inch away from murdering each other. Frankly, I wish Jonathan would just hurry up and garrote him with one of his own ghastly cravats. Christopher is so wrapped up in the idea of being a *ladies' man,* he hasn't noticed that all women find him repulsive. Honestly, that boy is the devil incarnate in garish tailoring. We only tolerate him because he's terribly well connected when it comes to procuring certain *vices* we all enjoy. He's a second cousin of Jane's, or something, and he was at school with Jeremiah. Don't get into a carriage with him alone, and don't drink anything he gives you that he's not drinking himself. Actually, not *even* if he's drinking it himself, he's probably built up a tolerance to fifty sorts of poison by now." Georgiana must have looked horrified, because Frances relented a little. "All right, he's not that ghastly. He just gets a little wild sometimes—but don't we all?"

The wildest night Georgiana had ever experienced had concluded only fourteen hours previously, and had been entirely due to Frances, but she nodded as if she, too, were rumored to have swum half-naked in a stranger's millpond.

"It's not always just the five of us, but sometimes people miss a few seasons or accidentally find themselves married. So far this summer, we seem to be the only survivors. Last year we were eight, and we almost burned down Henrietta King's summer house, so a smaller party is probably for the best. We have acquaintances by the dozen, of course, and there's Jeremiah's set—but I do think it best to have a smaller group of really firm friends, don't you?"

"Yes, of course," said Georgiana, hoping it wasn't obvious from the expression on her face that it was now her dearest hope that their five might become a six. She was sure they could expand to include her without any additional risk of committing arson.

"My parents actually considered going elsewhere for a change this year, but I insisted. By September, Jeremiah will be back in Manchester, and I shall return to London. Two hundred miles by coach certainly does *not* make the heart grow fonder, so it all rides on this summer. But I already think it's going to be one for the ages."

A season that had stretched drearily ahead of Georgiana was transforming before her very eyes into one full of promise. Perhaps, she thought, hers did not have to be a tale of monotony and loneliness as she had once feared; perhaps she was destined for greater things. If a certain amount of impropriety was the price she had to pay in exchange for them, then so be it.

Frances Campbell did not have to know that she had spent all of her previous summers playing chess, reading Chaucer alone, and barely daring to dream that there might be any other way to live. Frances and her friends were quick-witted, and scintillating, and so very *alive*. Georgiana ached to be one of them—for everybody to see her in the company of Dugrays, Woodleys, and Campbells, and for her to make sense among them. She wanted evenings full of laughter, and wild escapades, and invitations that the Burtons simply didn't receive. She wanted to be asked to Frances's house in London, for a friendship that extended beyond summer exploits and into stays at Michaelmas and Christmas. And she *really* wanted to attend parties with curly-haired strangers who refused to laugh at bawdy jokes, had strangely arresting hands, and groomed their own horses just for the pleasure of it.

"I'm sorry about my mother the other night," Frances said, sighing and reaching for another sandwich. "She wasn't always such a prig. She and my father used to throw the most incredible parties. He's been a real bastard lately, always off on trips abroad, and when he is around you can hear them carrying on wherever you are in the house. *Marital bliss*, you know."

"Really, it was nothing," said Georgiana. "If my aunt had been the one to discover us, I'd have been thrown in the carriage and driven to a convent directly."

Frances laughed. "Probably the best thing for us, George, to keep us out of trouble," she said, patting Georgiana's leg fondly.

Georgiana went pink with pleasure at the familiarity and the nickname, then reached for another sandwich in an attempt to hide her face, only to find the basket empty.

"Oh, damn, I've eaten all your luncheon!" said Frances. "You must come up to the house soon, though, and we can see you fed properly. You'll like it—we've got the most darling dogs and the finest horses in the county. Father seems to collect them endlessly, although he rarely takes them out anymore. We can ride out one afternoon. Unless, of course . . . you have other plans?"

It was clear from her expression that Frances had guessed—correctly—that Georgiana had no prior engagements. A moment of understanding passed between them, and Georgiana realized that, although her new friend didn't know the particulars of her former life, Frances was no fool; she knew precisely what she brought to this partnership, and all the ways in which Georgiana was lacking. If she cut her tomorrow, Georgiana would have to spend the rest of the summer—perhaps the rest of her life—embroidering pastel-colored nightmares in Mrs. Burton's parlor, reminiscing about the few glorious days she had spent in the company of the esteemed Miss Campbell.

Frances was knowingly socializing below her station. Georgiana couldn't begin to guess why, but she knew her role: to accept, and to be grateful.

And she *was* grateful. Immeasurably so. Frances could eat all of her sandwiches every day for as long as they were acquainted, and Georgiana wouldn't say a word.

"No. I have no other plans," said Georgiana.

"Excellent," said Frances with a grin, rising to her feet and offering a hand down to Georgiana. "Come on, George. Off with your boots. I saw a stream back there I'm just *dying* to dip my feet in."

Chapter Five

MRS. BURTON'S GENTLE CORRECTIONS WERE ALMOST AS EX-cruciating as her outright scoldings. When unchallenged, she was quite a mild-mannered woman—definitely prone to fuss and bother when it came to matters of parties and propriety, but a person of kind spirit and good intentions. She had, however, made it clear to Georgiana as soon as she had returned from her outing that she did *not* approve of her new friendship. She was not showing any signs of letting up. Mr. Burton, silent behind his paper, let her get on with it.

"In any other circumstance, I'd commend the connection, Georgiana—but your mother and father entrusted us with your well-being, and if they should return from their holiday to find the countryside rife with rumors about the company you keep, I shall never forgive myself."

"It's hardly a holiday, Aunt, unless they sold the house by accident," Georgiana retorted, hanging up her cloak. She made to walk past Mrs. Burton toward the quiet refuge of the library.

"Oh, no, you don't! I understand you long for companionship, I really do, but Miss Campbell is not an appropriate choice. *I* will find someone suitable who is equipped to take you under their wing and show you the benefits of the neighborhood. Clearly at home you are allowed a freer rein—and I suppose I cannot fault my sister, as she has been so distracted of late—but it ends *now*."

Georgiana's urge to roll her eyes was so strong that it actually hurt her head to resist; she settled on looking intently at

Mr. Burton's back as she pulled off her gloves. The stitching of his jacket, she noticed, was coming loose at the shoulder. Her aunt was correct in assuming that her mother and father had never paid particular attention to her comings and goings—they had, in fact, often gone about their business as if they did not have a daughter at all—but Georgiana had grown used to this state of affairs and was certainly not in the market for any additional *fussing* or *meddling*. Mrs. Burton sighed, tutted, then reached for the letters on the table and, riffling through them, discovered what she had been searching for and held it aloft in triumph.

"Aha! Miss Walters is in town! My dear friend Mrs. Walters's granddaughter—around your age. Let's see here—a Miss Betty Walters, a bright young girl, most accomplished at penmanship and needlework. She has been living with her cousins but is coming to stay, perhaps for good. Betty Walters would make a fine companion. I shall arrange something immediately."

"You shall do no such thing!" cried Georgiana, unable to restrain herself further. "I'm sure Miss Betty Walters is a *bright young girl* by your estimation, and I'm sure she's all the more dull for it. I cannot think of anything more excruciating than spending my leisure time with somebody who is most commended for her *penmanship and needlework*. Honestly, if that is all Mrs. Walters can think of to say to recommend her granddaughter—she might as well have said that Betty is accomplished at 'breathing in and out, at regular and most pleasing intervals.'"

Mrs. Burton spluttered, going red, and then faltered. She opened her mouth to speak and closed it again, looking to Mr. Burton for help. His eyebrows had appeared from behind the paper, and Georgiana could see that he was frowning.

"You go too far," said Mrs. Burton finally, before rushing from the room in a whirl of skirts and hurt feelings. Georgiana felt guilt curl in her stomach as she went.

There was silence for a moment and then, to Georgiana's

astonishment, Mr. Burton lowered his paper. He was so averse to conflict or dramatics of any kind that she had honestly expected him to pretend he hadn't heard a bit of it.

"Georgiana," he said firmly, in the deep voice she heard so seldom, "there is such a thing as considering oneself *too* clever. You'd do better to apply that mind of yours to the improvement of yourself and of those around you, rather than letting your cleverness fester into cruelty."

The newspaper was snapped fully open again and put back in place, and Georgiana was left staring at it.

She supposed there was nothing else for it; at some point she would have to make it up to Mrs. Burton by acquiescing to an afternoon with Miss Walters, a girl she had already—perhaps unfairly—decided would be about as much fun as a medicinal bloodletting.

Mrs. Burton was very much not speaking to Georgiana. Occasionally she asked her husband to relay pieces of information or questions to her niece, but as Mr. Burton was so naturally taciturn, they rarely reached their intended destination. As a consequence, Georgiana only found out with a day's notice that she and the Burtons had been invited to a group outing to make the most of the fine June weather—a picnic, with some of the local families who also lived on the outskirts of the town.

Mrs. Burton had taken to talking to the cook, Marjorie, with some frequency now that she couldn't talk to her niece, and this was how Georgiana learned of their excursion while skulking in the hallway. Her eavesdropping bore further fruit as she heard Mrs. Burton going on to discuss who would be in attendance: neighbors and friends who were not even of the slightest interest to Georgiana, and of course, "Mrs. Walters will be there with her granddaughter—I only hope that seeing how a lady *should* behave will knock some sense into a certain *someone* who has been rather bullheaded of late."

Some very childish part of Georgiana thought to dramatically interrupt and restart their quarrel anew, but she knew that no good could come of angering her aunt further; if anything, she should make amends for the sake of poor Marjorie, who had once glanced at Georgiana while her aunt's back was turned and mimed hanging herself to get out of listening to another complaint about a neighbor's roof thatching.

Georgiana returned to her room—she had to try three times to get the door to close, warped as it was in the frame—and then she collapsed into the chair at the tiny desk beneath the window and sighed. She would meet Miss Walters at this picnic. She would be perfectly polite and cordial. But there was no reason why she shouldn't also be allowed to have a little fun of her own design.

Without allowing herself time to think it through and change her mind, Georgiana scraped open the desk drawer and felt around for the pen, paper, and ink that she had pilfered from downstairs while considering writing to her parents. She scribbled a hurried note addressed to Miss Frances Campbell and immediately went in search of Emmeline, insisting it be sent away that very hour.

Surely Mrs. Burton couldn't be angry with her if Frances seemed to appear at the picnic of her own volition—and Georgiana might be spared some portion of the endless inevitable conversations about the joys of good penmanship with Miss Walters.

A few hours after the initial excitement of the idea had worn off, Georgiana began to feel very nervous, pacing about the house and rearranging things at whim. The best-case scenario was now that Frances *didn't* come, and it was simply a terrible waste of a sunny day with dreary companions—because if she *did* come, Georgiana could now imagine all manner of disasters that might befall her. This friendship was newly fashioned and exceedingly fragile; one dull remark from her aunt about bridge repairs might bring the whole thing tumbling down.

The next day, they set off midmorning to the extensive grounds of an estate held by a young earl called Haverton, who, being so rarely at home, had opened his manicured gardens to the public. It was the sort of agreeable day without a cloud in the sky; the glare of the summer sun was tempered by a light, cool breeze. Mrs. Burton made a lot of fuss about setting up their blankets and unpacking their picnic food, but once they were in place, Georgiana found the situation surprisingly pleasant. There was a good turnout of some ten or eleven families, and as they all got reacquainted and the women shared news and gossip about their animals, children, and husbands (in that order), she was left alone to enjoy the birdsong, and the smell of crushed grass, and the gentle murmur of conversation that didn't require her participation. Couples strolled past arm in arm, and over on the ornamental lake a gaggle of aggressive swans were winging each other in the face.

Frances would not come to this picnic, Georgiana reassured herself; in fact, Frances would probably rather be shot in the street than be seen sitting on Mrs. Burton's slightly hairy horse blankets. She could not imagine Miss Campbell making idle chit-chat with the Burtons about the weather any more than she could imagine her aunt and uncle accepting an invitation to engage in illicit drug-taking in the shrubbery.

Georgiana felt extremely relieved to have settled the matter in her mind and was just allowing a small sigh of pleasure to escape her lips when she saw a stout young woman approaching her with purpose, arm in arm with an older lady, whose face was set in a grimace despite the loveliness of the day.

Miss Betty Walters—for it seemed inevitable that this was she—was pleasantly plump, rather plain in the face, and very fair. The only parts of her not the color of straw were her cheeks, which were flushed and pink, and her eyes, which were a thin, watery blue. Her mouth was smiling, but her eyes were full of terror, as if she expected their quiet picnic to be set upon by wolves at any moment.

Despite how vehemently she had argued against this meeting, in her newly relaxed state Georgiana felt it would be charitable to give the poor girl the benefit of the doubt. After all—there wasn't a pen or needle in sight.

Mrs. Burton seemed to conveniently forget that she wasn't talking to her niece and immediately launched into enthusiastic introductions. Miss Walters went even pinker and sat down awkwardly next to Georgiana, after which an uncomfortable pause ensued.

"How are you finding . . . the neighborhood?" Georgiana ventured, to break the silence.

"Oh! Most pleasing indeed!" Betty said, almost gasping in obvious relief at being asked a question she could answer. "Well—I have not yet been into the town proper, but I intend to do so tomorrow. You know, there are such a great many wonderful driveways and fence posts around here—everywhere I look, I think, What a *fine* house must be just beyond this fencing, or—or this wonderful entrance. You cannot see many houses from the road, of course, but you can often tell by—by the quality of the gravel."

Georgiana bit her lip and ducked her head a little so the shadow of her bonnet obscured her expression, which was not particularly kind.

"Yes," she said once she was composed. "Such wonderful gravel, indeed."

"I wonder—yes, I wonder where one gets gravel from, incidentally. I can't imagine it comes naturally from the ground in such small pieces. Perhaps it is—like sand, on beaches? Or perhaps they take a larger rock, and they set upon it with mallets and axes until it is all broken up. Oh, Grandmama—" Here, her grandmother looked up from where she had been conversing with Mrs. Burton. "Do you know from where they obtain gravel?"

"Gravel, dear?" Mrs. Walters said, looking puzzled. "Gravel?"

"Oh, yes, gravel. Gravel, for driveways. Little stones—and pebbles, and the like."

"I shouldn't care to venture," said Mrs. Walters, turning back to Mrs. Burton.

"Ah! Yes." Having failed to bring her grandmother into the conversation to rescue her, Miss Walters looked positively panicked. "In any case, it is often such lovely colors. All shades of gray, and white, and brown—and darker, and lighter browns—"

"I think perhaps we have exhausted the subject of gravel," said Georgiana firmly, wondering how long Betty would have continued her list without intervention. "Have you been to many parties since you arrived?"

"Oh! Not yet—but I hope to do so—I hope very *much* so—I do love parties. At home we have such merry little gatherings— there's food, and drink, and dancing if we're lucky, and everybody looks so well dressed up in their finery, and—we dance, and eat, and drink. I do think it helps to have one very small drink, perhaps a little wine with water—then one doesn't feel so conscious of one's—well, it's a little easier to converse, I think."

Georgiana could not imagine that any amount of alcohol would improve Betty's conversational skills. At least she seemed to find herself almost as ridiculous as Georgiana did; she was blushing even redder now, apparently mortified to hear the things coming out of her own mouth.

Georgiana knew she ought to be sympathetic to her plight, but Miss Walters had such a keen look of longing and palpable urgency to *belong* that she could hardly stand to look at her; it was evident in her clenched fists, the sweat on her brow, the apologetic little grimace she gave once she'd finished speaking. The uncomfortable truth was that had Georgiana not chanced upon Frances in the darkened hallways of the Gadforths', she, too, may have been desperately searching for a friend at this picnic. Admittedly she would never embarrass herself by talking a mile a minute about the virtues of fence posts—she sincerely hoped that she gave a much better first impression in general—but Betty's friendlessness, that quality she and Georgiana might have shared, was all over her like a rash. Looking at her now was like seeing her own past desperation in a mirror, and Georgiana reacted with a rush of revulsion, as if such a thing were contagious.

Miss Walters kept talking, saying nothing at all of consequence, and Georgiana made small noncommittal noises when appropriate and tried not to let the constant flow of chatter distract her from the glory of the day. She let her eyes wander, looking from the vast, lush lawns to the lake, and then the orchard—and then stopped abruptly. Between the branches laden with unripened fruit, Georgiana could see a familiar black carriage pulled by two gleaming horses, which was just coming to a stop. As she watched, five well-cut figures slipped lightly out, linking arms and swapping jokes, their laughter audible from where she sat.

Unless Georgiana was very much mistaken, Frances had defied all reason and decided to attend this lowly picnic after all.

Georgiana was not the only one extremely startled that Frances and her friends had deigned to attend; the rest of the company set about whispering and muttering to one another as soon as they noticed the new arrivals making their way toward the picnic. Georgiana suddenly felt just as bumbling and red-faced as Miss Walters, watching Frances's brows dance as she leaned over to whisper something in Jonathan's ear as they drew nearer.

Georgiana had no idea what they were doing here—what could possibly have possessed them all to give up an afternoon that she was sure they would normally have spent drinking imported spirits on their own vast lawns, or hunting commoners for sport, or whatever it was that extremely wealthy people usually did to while away pleasant summer hours. One thing seemed certain: if Frances saw her speaking to Betty Walters, she was absolutely done for.

Mrs. Burton was looking from Frances to Georgiana with utmost suspicion, but her niece had such a look of genuine astonishment on her face that she seemed satisfied that it was not a plan of her making.

Those of the party nearest rose to meet the newcomers, and after much flustered curtsying and bowing in their direction, Frances and her companions came to stand by the Burtons' corner of the picnic. Everyone else sat down again, but Frances and her friends remained standing. This left Georgiana in rather an awkward position; once she had sat and the others had not, she had to crane her neck and shade her eyes to meet Frances's.

It was all too literal and unfortunate a metaphor.

"What a delightful assembly, Georgiana," she said, taking in the assorted crowd. "We were just on our way out of town, but we thought we'd come and see what constitutes a romp on this side of the bridge."

"Oh, well, of course we enjoy all sorts of things," said Mrs. Burton, sounding harried. "Hunting, dancing, dinners . . . er . . . sleeping—all the usual things, in fact."

Georgiana flashed her aunt a pained smile. *Sleeping,* indeed.

"Oh, I daresay," said Frances, quirking an eyebrow at Mrs. Burton.

She had a very particular way of smiling that seemed almost entirely sincere but threatened to transform into a smirk at any moment; her eyes often sparkled with a barely concealed mirth that did not quite match the situation, and it gave Georgiana the impression that she was always enjoying a private joke that belonged only to her.

The mystery of why Frances and her friends were still standing was soon solved; two servants came rushing over with folding chairs and cushions, setting them up with military precision. Only once they could be elevated a safe distance from the evils of grass and dirt did they all sit, still towering over Georgiana and the others from their vantage points on the ground. A large hamper was brought, and wine was produced with a flourish and carefully poured before the men retreated back to the carriage to care for the horses. Miss Walters looked very impressed—in fact, she was staring at the glamorous newcomers with unadulterated awe. Miss Woodley noticed, and nudged Miss Dugray, who snorted.

Frances continued talking to Mrs. Burton, who was hesitant at first but soon seemed to warm up to her, as Miss Campbell was being her most animated, charming self. Georgiana resisted the urge to listen in, and engaged Jonathan Smith and Christopher Crawley in conversation instead.

"I have to say, I am surprised to see you. I didn't truly expect Frances, let alone the rest of you," she said, trying to sound as if it were only mildly unexpected, rather than the reason she was digging her nails so hard into her palm that she'd likely be scarred for life.

"Oh, well, Franny has a mind of her own," said Mr. Smith, pouring a glass of wine for Georgiana and handing it down to her. "She beckons, and we all come bumbling along like blind little puppies following their harebrained mother."

"Or lemmings," said Mr. Crawley darkly, accepting his own glass and knocking it against Georgiana's. "Cheers."

"Oh—cheers." Georgiana clumsily attempted to raise her wine to him after the fact, before taking a sip and glancing over at Frances, who had one hand on Mrs. Burton's arm as if they were the best of friends. "Well—she is rather hard to resist."

"We are certainly never bored," said Jonathan, although his current expression somewhat contradicted his words. "Occasionally at great risk of *arrest,* but never bored."

Georgiana looked at her aunt quickly to see if she had heard him, but she was laughing slightly nervously at something Frances was saying to her. If Mrs. Burton were to warm to her a little, perhaps she would forgive all crimes of vulgarity—both real and imagined—and stop tensing up like a woman bound for the gallows every time Georgiana spoke the name Campbell.

Jane and Cecily had, unfortunately for both parties, struck up a conversation with Miss Betty Walters; Jonathan and Christopher were now bickering about the choice of wine, so Georgiana leaned over to listen in with some apprehension. It seemed that Miss Woodley and Miss Dugray had prompted Betty to speak and were simply letting her continue. Without any assistance or interruption, she was gathering speed at an alarming rate. It was like a carriage crash; she couldn't look away.

"I have heard such wonderful things about your families, your families both, and the delightful parties you throw, Miss Woodley—and I have often wondered if I might be invited to such a party at some point—not to impose or to ask for an invitation, of course, and not *your* party in particular, just *a* party, something of the party variety—I do have a dress that I keep in case of just such an occasion—it's pink, but not a garish pink, although my grandmama does often say that I look quite ill in pink, quite piggish in fact—I do *like* pigs and would see not much fault in being compared to one, but they do so like to roll in muck and mire, and I don't wish anyone to think of me up to my neck in the mud, ha! I love the countryside but Grandmama thinks I shall like living near the town, too, once I am used to it, and I am so looking forward to—"

Here Georgiana interrupted, for she could not bear to listen to any more.

"Perhaps, Betty, now is not the time to compare oneself to a pig, however fond you might be of them," she said pointedly.

This was the last straw for Miss Woodley and Miss Dugray, who burst out laughing, Miss Dugray pressing her hands to her mouth in an attempt to stop herself. Betty, whom Georgiana had imagined was almost impossible to injure, looked hurt; her forlorn expression was directed at Georgiana rather than the others, which seemed a little unfair. She sniffed and turned away to speak to her grandmother.

Georgiana rolled her eyes at Jane and Cecily, who were still giggling uncontrollably; she had been attempting a *rescue mission*, not an assassination.

Frances extracted herself from Mrs. Burton and pulled her chair toward the others, leaning in close so she wouldn't be overheard.

"Your aunt is a riot," she said in confidential tones, taking another glass of wine from Jonathan, having already drained her first. "She could *not* recommend a Miss Betty Walters enough—seemed quite enamored with her. If I didn't know better, I'd say she was trying to make you an unholy match."

Georgiana laughed and put a cupped hand to her mouth.

"Hush, Frances, don't embarrass me—for the beau in question is sitting just there," she whispered, nodding her head toward Betty.

"Is she?" Frances said, raising her eyebrows and not bothering to lower her voice. "Gosh—I can't say I think much of her dress, George, and she must be at least three or four years your senior. I hope she's fabulously wealthy and well-read, and intends to be a most obliging and *attentive* husband to you."

"Oh, I don't doubt that she'd be an endless source of amusement," Jane cut in, lip curled in a sneer. "She was just telling us how frequently she's mistaken for swine."

This was too much for Cecily, who started giggling again in earnest; this set the rest of them off, including Georgiana, who tried to rein herself in and chanced a look at Miss Walters's back.

She wasn't sure, but she thought she detected a slight stiffening of Betty's posture at the sound of their merriment.

Jonathan and Christopher entertained them all for a time with a story of much debauchery from a party none of them had attended a few weeks previous—they kept interrupting each other, disagreeing about the specifics of *who* exactly had pushed *whom* in the fish pond—the whole lot relayed in low, conspiratorial tones, and punctuated with exclamations and suppressed giggles from the others.

Soon, Frances looked around restlessly and announced that they must be going on to a further engagement. Georgiana felt a pang of longing as she wondered where they could possibly be going and how marvelous it would feel to be among their number. As they got languidly to their feet and the wine and chairs were packed back up into the carriage, Mrs. Burton saw that they were to leave and came over to speak to Frances, dragging Mr. Burton along with her.

"It was a delight to make your acquaintance properly, Miss Campbell. Do send my regards to your parents; I would dearly love to meet them."

"Of course, you must all come to Longview!" cried Frances, clasping Mrs. Burton's hand as if she were in raptures. "Delighted, Mrs. Burton, delighted."

Mrs. Burton genuinely seemed as delighted as Miss Campbell purported to be; long after she had said her goodbyes and the elegant carriage had driven out of sight, Georgiana was still listening politely as her aunt recounted their conversation, and at

length pardoned her friend of all the ill graces and grave misbe-
havior of which she had previously been accused.

"She was most obliging, most obliging indeed—and with
such a family, how could she not be! I think she has been treated
most unfairly, for I cannot now imagine the rumors I have heard
of her conduct to be true. She was telling me of her parents, her
father especially, such a rich history . . . Oh, I do hope they invite
us for dinner, Georgiana. Miss Campbell seemed most sure they
would. A fine family! A fine girl."

Georgiana deemed it best to stay quiet on the subject of her
aunt's rapid reversal of opinion, simply agreeing politely with her
when appropriate, all the while dancing a jig on the inside. As
the picnic came to an end and they climbed into their respective
carriages, Georgiana found herself quite pleased with how the
day had turned out after all.

The only fly in the ointment came as she settled into the seat—
next to a rather sunburned Mr. Burton—and turned for one last
look back at the grounds, awash with gold in the evening sun.

Among the stragglers she caught a brief glimpse of the red,
tear-stained face of Miss Betty Walters.

Chapter Six

A NOTE CAME THE VERY NEXT DAY, INVITING GEORGIANA TO be a guest of the Campbells the following Friday. The invitation did not extend to her aunt and uncle, but Mrs. Burton took this surprisingly well, giving Georgiana her permission at once. She seemed to feel that it would only increase the likelihood of an invitation of her very own at a later date; Georgiana rather thought that this was wishful thinking but admired her optimism.

Emmeline helped her pack her four best dresses—"Four?" cried Mrs. Burton in horror upon seeing her trunk. "*Four* dresses, for one night away? What do you plan to do to the first two—swim in them?"—and Georgiana made the journey early on Friday morning, eager to arrive with plenty of the day ahead of her. She found herself so agitated, so entirely incapable of sitting still, that eventually she sat on her hands just to keep them out of trouble. She still couldn't quite believe that she was to be a guest of *Lord and Lady Campbell;* if she did not have the note right in front of her—if she had not read and reread it a thousand times, checking again as they neared the house that she had definitely been invited and had not somehow misinterpreted a practical joke, or a letter asking her to please *not* come for a visit—she would not have believed it.

Longview was just as unbelievable as everybody had made it out to be. The estate was directly north from the town and sat perched atop the hill, which afforded it the magnificent views that had given it its name. The grounds were large and rambling, the gardens close to the house pruned to perfection, and Georgiana could imagine no finer place to sit and read than by the wild natural lake that they passed on their way up the drive. The house itself was intimidatingly grandiose; it seemed so integral to the landscape that Georgiana felt it must have been standing there since at least the dawn of time. It was rendered in pale gold stone, fronted by neat rows of wide windows that gleamed in the early morning sun.

It made perfect sense that this house had created Frances Campbell.

As Georgiana was exiting the carriage, the front door opened and Frances tumbled out to greet her. She was wearing nothing more than her shift and a peculiarly ornate dressing gown, her dark curls loose about her shoulders. Her uncle's coachman looked away, blushing, as he brought Georgiana's trunk to the door.

"George! You're *here!*" she cried. "You made it all the way up the driveway and everything, you clever thing!"

"Are your parents not here?" Georgiana asked, still a bundle of nerves, looking behind Frances as if expecting them to appear in the doorway in matching dressing gowns.

"No! Oh God, did I not say? They're away. The house is empty—it's ours!"

Georgiana would not have quite described it as *empty;* Frances draped an arm around her shoulders and steered her inside, and they passed at least a dozen servants on their way from the frankly enormous marble entrance hall to the guest bedroom that had been prepared for her. It was vast and high-ceilinged, furnished with an ornately carved four-poster bed, side tables inlaid with mother-of-pearl, and numerous portraits of stern-looking relatives and their even sterner-looking dogs. Georgiana had never been inside such an ostentatious bedroom in all her life. She could have ridden a horse around it quite comfortably.

A maid unpacked her trunk for her, accepting the need for four dresses without question, and Frances left Georgiana to "refresh" herself. The person peering nervously back at her in the over-gilded mirror looked insipid and demure—dressed and ready for any and all excitements that could possibly take place inside a church, or a particularly lively convent. There was nothing to be done about it now, Georgiana thought bracingly. She would just have to wear enough clothes for the two of them.

She almost got lost on her way to the garden and had to ask multiple bored-looking servants for directions. When she got there, she saw Frances sprawled out on one of two well-stuffed velvet chaises that had clearly been dragged outside at her bidding. Her eyes were closed, and she was smoking a pipe. The scene looked like some sort of erotic painting.

Georgiana had been mentally preparing for a visit full of straitlaced afternoon teas and excessively formal dinners; she had been rehearsing witty lines and opinions on various subjects, so that she could thoroughly impress the Campbells with her spontaneous acuity and charm. She had gone so far as to write a list of her favorite works of literature, music, and art, for when quizzed on her preferences her mind always went instantly blank, as if she had never encountered so much as a pamphlet or a tin whistle in her life.

The far more informal reality of the visit actually unfolding in front of her was an enormous relief; Georgiana accepted a draw on Frances's pipe, and a glass of wine when it was offered, slipping off her shoes and reclining on the other chaise.

"George, George, this is the good life," Frances said, sighing happily. "You know, I was rather enamored with a boy *actually* called George, once, on a rather accursed visit to Brighton. He was just so *expressive*. Fancied himself the next Byron. He wrote me my very own poem. It was bloody dreadful—I think he compared me to a wood pigeon—but I told him I'd treasure it forever.

What I'll *really* treasure forever is the memory of how frightfully good he looked in his obscenely tight breeches when he bent over to pick up my handkerchief." Georgiana laughed rather uncouthly into her wine. "What about *you*, George? I sense hidden depths lurking behind those dimples. Have you secretly been corrupted by caddish men? Or have you never admired the beautiful flank of a gentleman in retreat?"

"*Nobody* is quite as thoroughly corrupted as you are, with your particular eye for the fit of a man's breeches," said Georgiana, and Frances gave her a rakish look.

"Don't avoid the question, George. You must entertain me."

Georgiana considered inventing a more intriguing romantic past for herself—illicit affairs, dramatic missed connections—but she simply didn't have the range to make them sound like anything other than tales stolen from her collection of romance novels.

"In all honesty, there has been nobody. My parents were too preoccupied to pay much mind to that sort of thing, so they did not encourage my affections in any particular direction. I *thought* I liked somebody once, when I was seventeen. I tried to talk myself into it, anyway. His name was Patrick Elliott. He was the son of a good friend of my father's, so he was around the house often, and I thought that the proximity would surely breed familiarity and affection, I suppose in the way that you grow fond of a dog or . . . or a much-used hat. He had a little money, too, enough to be quite comfortable, but I'm afraid that was where his list of commendable attributes came to a rather abrupt end. Patrick was encouraged by his parents, who wanted the match, and he started pompously bringing me flowers almost every morning." Georgiana shuddered at the memory, fingers clenching around her wineglass. "As soon as he became earnest and eager, I realized I didn't want him at all. If anything, he started to repulse me. I looked for an excuse to leave the room every time he approached.

I hid—I actually physically *hid* behind a church pew once so that he wouldn't see me, and then realized that of course he could see the top of my bonnet the whole time. He got the hint, in the end."

"Oh, you wicked thing," cried Frances. "I'm sure you quite crushed him. Puppyish creatures they all are! It is a wonder anybody marries at all, honestly. Most men think it's the pinnacle of romance to give you a slightly more pronounced nod of greeting than they give the next girl. And behind all the bravado, there's nothing there—can't hold a sword, can't hold a woman. I had honestly never thought myself the marrying type. I fancied myself a wealthy, *eccentric* spinster—you know, holding extravagant dinners with acrobats and fire-eaters, surrounded by likeminded ladies, pitting all my sister's children against one another for sport at Christmas—and that's what I told my parents, to their deep chagrin. But then Jeremiah started looking so *attractive* last summer, and he's . . . Well, I think he's perfect for me."

She stretched pleasurably and then glanced over at Georgiana in her dress, bonnet, and gloves.

"Oh, George, you can't be comfortable dressed for *dinner with the Campbells*." She clapped her hands together. "Come, let us fetch more wine and you something more appropriate to wear."

She led Georgiana inside, through the endless long, paneled corridors and up the stairs to her own dressing room, where she produced another robe like hers.

"They're French. Spoils of war, I suppose. Aren't they hideous?"

Frances was only satisfied once Georgiana was identically attired in just her shift and the gown, although at the last minute she also looped some long necklaces over their heads, the combined value of which Georgiana was sure could pay for the Burtons' house many times over.

"See, now you are ready to bed a man or bathe in the lake at a moment's notice," Frances said gleefully, reaching over to adjust Georgiana's gown for her, then pinching her cheek fondly.

Georgiana hoped very much that she was joking, on both counts. Hot as it was, the greenish water of the lake was not particularly inviting, and she had recently read that most bodies of water in England were rife with eels. As for bedding a man— well . . .

She'd rather face the eels.

They passed the rest of the morning most pleasurably, aided by Frances's never-ending supply of superior alcohol. Everything felt as if it were moving very slowly—the breeze jostling the silver birches, the scattering of threadbare clouds, and Frances herself, as she leaned too far off the chaise while telling an animated story about her childhood governess and fell quite gracefully onto the lawn. She didn't bother getting up. As it approached one o'clock, a servant with impeccable posture marched from the house to murmur in Frances's ear.

"Luncheon! Oh, I almost forgot. Jonathan is coming for luncheon."

When Georgiana sleepily made to get up, planning to go into the house and get dressed, Frances told her not to bother—so Georgiana stayed where she was, trying to wrap the robe more tightly around herself to preserve what was left of her modesty. Servants brought out chairs and a table, unfurling a tablecloth like a sail and setting three places with polished silverware, utterly straight-faced, as if it were completely unremarkable to host a luncheon party on the lawn halfway to nudity.

"Will they not tell your parents?" asked Georgiana anxiously, once the last of the fine china had been carefully deposited in front of them.

"Ha! No, they certainly will not," said Frances, pouring more wine. "Not because they live in fear of me, you understand—I am not some sort of despicable tyrant. They simply wouldn't bother my parents with such trifles. There is enough discord in this house without adding complaints about my wardrobe or the fact that I like to dine al fresco."

Georgiana could not imagine what sort of discord could exist in a house so large that the inhabitants might go about their lives for a week without bumping into each other, but she didn't think it polite to ask—and a moment later, Jonathan arrived.

"Have I interrupted the two of you in the throes of passion, or are you only just out of bed?" he asked as he came to sit with them at the table, taking off his own cream-colored jacket and removing his cravat immediately. He looked glamorously tired, dark circles under his eyes, his hair a little scruffy. He immediately took out a pipe of his own and lit it.

"Oh, it's not as bad as all that," Frances said.

"It's worse," said Georgiana gravely. "You should not mock us for our state of undress, Mr. Smith, for you have just missed an incident which gave us cause to fear for our very *lives*."

"He has?" said Frances, mildly interested, as she spilled a single drop of wine on the snowy tablecloth and studied it, frowning.

"She's forgotten it, in all the shock," Georgiana said, leaning toward Jonathan. "We were just lighting candles—to *pray* by, you see—when Miss Campbell's dress set alight! I took off my own to beat the flames. Alas, they were both reduced to nothing but ash. A monstrous shame, but as you can see—completely unavoidable. So here we are."

"If *you're* not praying for your souls, somebody certainly ought to be," said Jonathan, smirking as he ran a hand through his hair. "Franny, we've ruined this girl. It feels like just last week she was so young, so fresh . . . so full of hope."

"It *was* last week," said Georgiana.

"She's not ruined, she's just a little . . . I don't know, *saucy*," said Frances, winking at Georgiana.

They ate a four-course luncheon in the shade of umbrellas that Jonathan bade the servants bring—"to preserve my porcelain features, for the good of the populace"—and at length, the conversation turned to Jeremiah Russell.

"I know Christopher is a cad, but I think there was something in what he said about Kitty Fathering," said Jonathan as they ate decadent custard desserts. "I was with her brother playing a few rounds of hazard the other night, and he referenced some dreadful mischief that had resulted in Kitty being sent away to stay with friends in the country. You know what he's like—upstanding military type, he wouldn't say anything more—but she was seen with Jeremiah often enough last summer."

"Well, I consider myself warned," said Frances in a slightly dangerous tone. "If you think I'm as stupid as Kitty, Jonathan, then you must think it's a wonder I ever manage to string so many pretty words together into sentences."

"Don't be like that, Franny. I only mean—"

"I know perfectly well what you mean, and I don't need your veiled warnings. It's petty, Jonathan, all this jealousy. You are not my *brother,* and I don't need protecting, so there's no need for all this fisticuffs-at-dawn nonsense. Besides, the man is besotted with me. It's almost embarrassing! Everybody can see it. You can see it, can't you, George?"

Georgiana nodded in confirmation, mouth full of custard.

Jonathan sighed. "You're intolerable."

"I know," said Frances, smiling now, her tone abruptly shifting. "But *you* tolerate me. I wish you *were* my brother, you know. Perhaps you are—perhaps you're the product of my father's dalliance with some handsome woman abroad. Maybe you were squirrelled away in secret and brought up apart from me. How wonderful that we've found each other, after all this time! I'm sure I have half a locket somewhere that would match up *perfectly* with one of your own."

"How wonderful indeed. Especially as, if that *is* the case, I'll name your father as mine the moment his health falters, inherit Longview, and turn you out at once to live on the streets like the slattern you are."

"I'd like to see you try," said Frances, jabbing her spoon threateningly at him as if it were a dagger, but all was clearly well between them again.

*L*ater, when they had been drinking a lot and talking about very little for quite some time, Frances tipsily entreated both of her guests to join her in the lake to cool off. Georgiana felt it best to stay on dry land after consuming such large quantities of wine, and Jonathan just raised an eyebrow at her and stayed where he was. Frances shrugged, took off her dressing gown, and waded in up to her waist, shrieking and splashing.

Jonathan reluctantly slung his jacket over her shoulders when she got out, to preserve her modesty. Georgiana tried not to look, and failed; Frances didn't seem to care a bit, merrily flicking a fine spray of water at both of them, causing Jonathan to swear quite impressively and threaten to drown her. They lay in a tangled pile on the grass as she dried off, Jonathan between Georgiana and Frances, watching the clouds scurry past overhead as the wind picked up.

"Do you believe in true love?" Frances said, turning her head to Jonathan and squinting at him.

"I believe that money, breeding, and a good set of teeth can conquer all," he replied without much conviction.

"Good God, Jonathan, that's so romantic," Georgiana said, wrinkling her nose at him. "You should write a book."

"*Some* of us can't afford to be romantic," he said pointedly.

Frances reached down and took his hand. Georgiana hesitated for a moment, but then the wine won out, and she took the other.

"We've already got true love, anyway, my boy. You're looking at it," said Frances, squeezing his hand firmly. "And besides, if it all goes to hell, I'm sure George will marry you. She's got absolutely nothing to lose. No offense, Georgiana."

When the last long fingers of summer sun had begun to retreat, Jonathan made his apologies and left, with both Frances and Georgiana crying out after him to stay ("We'll do anything! We'll give you our wealth!" "Our wine!" "Our soft, innocent bodies!"). With Frances too cold and damp to stay outside any longer, they retreated to the fireplace in one of the Campbells' many parlors and played a rousing game of chess in which Frances seemed to be making up rules as she went along. She was just insisting that "horses are allowed to jump over whomever they please, in whichever direction—haven't you ever seen a horse, George?" when they heard a commotion in the hall, raised voices and the sound of dogs' paws scrabbling on marble, and saw servants rushing past the open parlor door.

Frances scrunched up her face in disdain.

"Panic in the hallways can only mean one thing; our liege lord returns. *Damn.* They weren't due back until tomorrow. Quick—if we take the back stairs we can avoid difficult questions about . . ."

She gestured at herself and Georgiana, then snatched up the bottle of sherry they had been drinking and rushed from the room with Georgiana at her heels. They made it upstairs without incident; Frances told Georgiana to dress quickly so that they could make a respectable appearance and say good evening, and then disappeared off toward her own bedroom deeper in the house.

As Georgiana pulled on her clothes and tried to repin her hair, fumbling with alcohol-addled fingers, she suddenly heard voices through the half-open door—unmistakably Lord and

Lady Campbell. Georgiana froze comically in place, listening. It sounded as if they were on the stairs in the entrance hall—the stairs that wound upward and eventually passed right by her bedroom. Lord Campbell was shouting something in hard, furious tones, and she couldn't help but strain to listen.

"I am not a fool. I will not be made to *look* a fool," he snarled in a voice that made Georgiana's blood run cold. "You will *not* undermine me in front of my associates."

"I apologize," Lady Campbell said coolly.

"You *apologize*? But you must do *better* than apologize, Joanna— you must make it right! Do you know what manner of ridicule I opened myself up to when I married you? Do you know how few men of good standing would have put themselves in my position?"

"Yes," said Frances's mother. "Yes, I believe you have made that perfectly clear."

"I did it for *you*, Joanna, for *us*—God help me, I thought you understood what a precarious position that might put me in— and yet this is how you repay me, for everything I have given you. Haven't I been good to you?" Lord Campbell's voice had softened momentarily, as if he were pleading with her to see reason, but when he spoke again he was almost hissing his words. "You know full well that your behavior was beneath you. It was certainly beneath *me*. Everyone was laughing at you, Joanna. And by extension . . . By extension, at me."

Lady Campbell made no reply that Georgiana could hear.

"Are you listening to me? Answer me then, if you can hear me! You certainly had plenty to say earlier—*speak*, woman!"

She did not answer—instead there came the sound of something large and heavy hitting an immovable surface, a shattering of china so loud and sudden that Georgiana flinched as if she had been the one to break whatever had been smashed. She heard brisk footsteps on the marble floor, and then all was silent except for the sound of a dog distantly whimpering.

Georgiana barely dared to move, but she suddenly wanted to be as far away from what had just happened as possible, as if the fury and the violence might seek *her* out, too. She slipped from the room silently to look for Frances, already resolving that there was no need for her friend to know what she had heard.

But Frances was leaning against the wall outside Georgiana's bedroom, still in her shift, her eyes closed. She opened them when she sensed Georgiana's approach and stared at her, saying nothing. Georgiana felt nausea rising in her throat as they both listened to Lady Campbell's echoing footsteps for one long, excruciating moment as she walked away.

Georgiana went to speak, unsure of what was going to come out of her mouth, but Frances immediately turned on her heel and walked off down the hallway. Georgiana, at a loss as to what else to do, followed.

As it turned out, Frances had a very fine fireplace and a chess set of her own in her large, champagne-colored bedroom, which looked out to the west over a vast expanse of hills and trees. They resumed their game, silently at first—but Frances snorted when Georgiana made the queen swoon coquettishly in the face of an advance from one of her knights, and slowly they settled back into mild conversation and moderate-to-heavy drinking. Frances was quick to smile now, joking about Georgiana's serious expression as she moved closer to checkmate; she did not give any indication that she wanted to discuss what Georgiana had heard, or even acknowledge that it had happened at all. The house was so large that ten more arguments could have been taking place at full volume throughout and they wouldn't have heard a word from this room.

They passed the rest of the evening as if nothing untoward had taken place, but when Georgiana became too tired and drunk to keep her eyes open any longer and suggested that she should retire to bed, Frances stopped her.

"Stay in here!" she said quickly, her fingers finding Georgiana's wrist. "You're so far away down the hall. Stay here, and we can keep talking as we fall asleep."

Georgiana was much too exhausted to be good company, but Frances suddenly looked so fierce that she agreed. Maids were called to plait their hair and bring them fresh bedclothes, and to draw the curtains around the four-poster closed as Frances and Georgiana climbed, giggling, into it. The maids departed, leaving only a faint solitary candle burning on the dressing table, light flickering lazily through the gaps in the curtains.

Georgiana's head was fuzzy, and the bed was exceedingly comfortable; she was nearly asleep when her friend spoke.

"Do you ever wonder what it's like?" she whispered. "To go to bed with a man?"

Georgiana was glad of the gloom, so Frances couldn't see her blushing.

"I suppose I have," admitted Georgiana quietly. "Only a little."

"A little! What a saint you are," said Frances heatedly, and Georgiana laughed.

They turned to face each other in the dark, Frances's hand almost touching Georgiana's as she adjusted herself on the pillow. Her features were softened by the curls that had escaped her plait, tumbling across her forehead and brushing her neck, dark against the crisp white sheets.

"I must admit I found the whole thing quite disgusting at first," said Frances, "but my sister, Eleanor, said there reaches a point where you're so close, and you like it, and no longer want to . . . stop. It sounds dreadfully uncomfortable. I *certainly* like the part where I think of Jeremiah in a state of undress, but the rest . . ." She trailed off. "Eleanor won't tell me anything more, that *witch*. It shouldn't be some secret, you know, that married women keep. We should all know, so we can be thoroughly prepared."

Georgiana laughed sleepily. Her thoughts had immediately turned, unbidden, to Mr. Hawksley, who had looked so fine at Jane's party. She tried to imagine him without his breeches on and was immediately so scandalized at herself that she pressed a hand to her mouth. Frances didn't seem to notice the disturbance; her eyes were fluttering closed.

"Good night then, George," she said softly against the pillow.

"Good night, Frances," Georgiana replied.

She was just drifting off when she felt a disturbance, some tiny movement in the bed with her, and she realized that Frances was shaking; her shoulders were shuddering, but in such small increments that it was almost imperceptible. Georgiana was about to ask if she was unwell when she realized what it was—Frances was *crying*.

It seemed so out of character for her to cry that Georgiana had no idea what to do. She wondered wildly if it was best to pretend she hadn't noticed, to preserve Frances's dignity, but then Frances spoke.

"I can't stand it," she whispered bitterly. "It's been dreadful since Eleanor left to be married. Or . . . perhaps it was always this bad, but she managed to shield me from it." She rubbed at her eyes furiously, and Georgiana reached for her arm in an attempt to comfort her. "My father acts as if my mother—as if she *tricked* him somehow, as if *he* didn't pursue *her*. He rages and rages, and he breaks things, and then the next day all is always forgiven. The mess cleaned up, as if it never happened. And my mother is right back on his arm, until some small thing sets him off again—and God forbid anybody get in his way." Another tear escaped, and she brushed it away.

"Frances, I'm so . . . I don't know what to say," Georgiana said uselessly. "Is there nothing to be done?"

"God, no. Who would care? Who would think his behavior unusual, even? They all think . . . They thought he was mad to marry her. No. This is just how it is." Frances took a deep breath to steady herself. She found Georgiana's hand on her arm and clasped it so tightly that when she removed it, her nails had left little half-moon grooves in Georgiana's skin. And then the sheets rustled, and Frances was turning toward her.

Clumsily, in the near-darkness, she moved until her face was almost touching Georgiana's; their noses brushed together, and Frances looked so forlorn and serious that Georgiana leaned forward to kiss her cheek. Her aim was off, and instead she found her lips pressed to the corner of Frances's mouth. She tasted like sweet sherry and pipe smoke, and her cheeks were hot and wet from crying; Georgiana felt a tear that did not belong to her slide down her cheek as she pulled away.

As quickly as it had begun, the moment had passed.

"This is silly," Frances said evenly, as if their conversation had not been interrupted. "Forget—just forget I said anything. I will be married soon, like Eleanor, and away, and none of this will matter." She took another deep, steadying breath. "Jeremiah and I will be engaged before the summer is out."

Georgiana, confused and tired and drunk but wanting to soothe her nonetheless, put an arm around her friend. Frances settled into her, a warm and comforting weight against her side.

"I know you will," said Georgiana. "It'll be all right, Frances."

"It's just . . . ," Frances said, sounding thoroughly worn-out. "It's all so *much* sometimes, George. Everything out there. Everything in here. I am quite tired of it. People look at me and they expect me to be something particular, for better or worse, and I often think . . . it would be nice to just *be*. You know?"

"Of course," said Georgiana, not sure she really understood at all.

"It shan't be like that with us, though," Frances mumbled,

turning her face into Georgiana's neck with a little sigh. "You're not like the rest of them, George. Not at all."

"Am I—am I not?" Georgiana whispered back, tensed for an answer, but Frances said nothing, and within a few minutes, she was asleep.

Georgiana lay awake for a long time afterward. Her arm became quite numb with Frances's weight, but she didn't move it; she listened to Frances's breathing, and the creaks of the house, and eventually fell asleep just where she was.

Chapter Seven

THE NEXT MORNING GEORGIANA AWOKE, STILL CURLED ON her side, to find the other pillow empty; Frances was standing at the foot of the bed, fully dressed and groomed, looking for all the world as if the previous night simply hadn't happened.

"Look alive, George," she said, throwing a dressing gown at Georgiana's head. "The morning is wasting!"

They breakfasted in the garden at a table set up on the back patio, enjoying all manner of breads and pastries and fruit, Frances entreating Georgiana to try little bites of everything. Afterward they walked the grounds, down sweeping lawns and through gated gardens, all the way to the stables some two miles away, with three lean, dark greyhounds following at their heels. Frances showed Georgiana her father's horses, introducing each one by name and pedigree, telling her how her father had come to acquire them without a hint of malice in her tone. Georgiana didn't see hide nor hair of Lord or Lady Campbell, but Frances noted that her father's favorite horse was gone, indicating that he must have gone for an early ride.

She kept studying Frances for any signs of what had occurred the night before; she could almost tell herself that she had dreamed it all—the crying and the hushed words in the dark and the quick brush of her lips—but she knew she hadn't imagined Lord Campbell's fury or the sound of china being thoroughly obliterated against the wall. Frances was smiling while speaking of him and his horses now, and Georgiana couldn't understand—couldn't understand how Frances could laugh prettily while telling some anecdote or link her arm through Georgiana's as if she hadn't gripped it so hard the night before she had left telltale marks. She had expected Frances to mention their strange half-kiss, to make light of it perhaps, but that, too, seemed to have been put aside along with the rest. It occurred to Georgiana in passing that it hadn't felt as odd as it should have.

When the afternoon came and the Burtons' carriage arrived, Frances was still all smiles, bidding her to keep the necklace she had worn last night and saying that she must come again.

"Oh! And before I forget, Christopher Crawley has been planning a little jaunt out into the deepest, *darkest* countryside on the fourth of July. He's invited a whole group of us to stay in this quaint little cottage owned by this dastardly relative of his for a few nights. You must get permission to come, I'll be bored out of my wits if you don't."

"I'll be there," Georgiana assured her, thrilled and somewhat relieved to have secured another invitation.

The carriage set off and rumbled slowly away, Georgiana turning and waving until Frances seemed impossibly small in the shadow of her beautiful, cavernous house.

Georgiana was awoken on Sunday morning by a series of taps on her bedroom door, so light she thought she had dreamed them. She turned over to face the wall, eyes half-focused on the faded floral wallpaper as she tried to will herself back to sleep, but the tapping came again.

Expecting her aunt—although confused as to why she hadn't just burst in, as she usually did—Georgiana forced herself out of bed and flung the door open. It wasn't Mrs. Burton after all; it was Mr. Burton, looking mightily uncomfortable, averting his eyes immediately when he saw that Georgiana was in her nightclothes.

"Your aunt wished me—ah—to bid you good morning, and to tell you it is time for church."

Georgiana hadn't forgotten church; she had just been so wrapped up in a number of relatively unholy thoughts since her visit to the Campbells that it had momentarily slipped her mind. Her parents, it had to be admitted, had been slightly lax when it came to her spiritual upbringing. She had attended the school chapel with them weekly, mostly staring fixedly at her Bible so she could pretend not to notice the mutterings and attentions of the schoolboys around her, but otherwise had not been encouraged to think very frequently of the Lord. It was the teachings of great writers—of Homer and Virgil, Shakespeare and Burns—that were treated as scripture in their house, and that Georgiana might be quizzed on at any moment while simply trying to enjoy her breakfast.

The Burtons approached church differently. They dressed carefully, always had the carriage brought out despite the relatively short walk, and expected Georgiana to treat the whole morning with reverence befitting the occasion. Georgiana found it rather dull and had spent all her Sundays since her arrival somewhat sentimental for the days when her father might point his fork at her and demand that she recite "Address to the Woodlark" from memory.

"I thank *you* for wishing me good morning, Uncle," Georgiana croaked, "as I don't imagine Mrs. Burton really bade you say that part."

"Nevertheless . . . ," said her uncle.

Georgiana waited for a moment, expecting more, but he simply nodded at her and walked quickly away.

Emmeline was called to help her dress, and Georgiana complied, still half-asleep; it was only when she stumbled downstairs and caught sight of the time on the carriage clock that she realized something was amiss.

"Why are we leaving so early?" she asked, befuddled, as Mrs. Burton came rushing down the stairs, swept her up in her momentum, and bundled her out of the door.

"I *told* you, Georgiana, for goodness' sake—the vicar has taken ill, and they could not replace him. We are all to travel out to St. Anne's instead."

Georgiana pretended to recall what her aunt was referring to and therefore could not ask any more questions. The journey to their local church usually took but five minutes by carriage, while St. Anne's clearly necessitated a much lengthier trip. It took them northward, away from the town, mirroring the route to the Campbells' estate and then continuing even farther until they reached a very small village, with only one or two other buildings that were *not* St. Anne's.

"Are we early?" Georgiana asked, seeing only three other families approaching, rather than the usual steady Sunday stream.

"They have to fit two congregations into one church, Georgiana—I am not taking any chances," Mrs. Burton said, straightening her bonnet and squaring her shoulders as if for a fight.

She led them all determinedly through the pleasant, rambling churchyard and into a church so neat and quaint that it looked straight out of a painting. Some of the others already gathered seemed to be friends of the Burtons; they took a well-polished pew near the front and her aunt started talking in hushed, important tones with the family in front of them, while Georgiana attempted to take a small nap without being noticed.

The church began to fill up around them as it approached a more respectable hour, and Georgiana was jolted from her reverie by Mrs. Burton's fingers, which were poking her in the arm.

"What?" she mumbled, receiving a disapproving glare in response.

Georgiana straightened up reluctantly and then turned to see Miss Cecily Dugray entering, with two equally statuesque and blond people she assumed must be her parents. They slid into a pew a few rows back from the Burtons on the other side of the aisle, and then Cecily's gaze alighted on Georgiana, and her eyes lit up.

"Oh, Miss Ellers!" she said, not bothering to temper her voice. "Are you well? You must come and sit with me."

She patted the space next to her; Georgiana glanced at her aunt, who looked slightly flustered but nodded her approval.

Georgiana expected to be introduced to the Dugrays, but they were already talking to another couple on their other side.

"How are you?" she asked Cecily, who was wearing cornflower blue and looking very well indeed.

"Very well indeed," she said, confirming Georgiana's suspicions. "I shot five threes and a seven this morning."

"Five threes and a—?"

"Oh! Longbow," Cecily said enthusiastically. "I shoot targets in the garden—or in the ballroom, if it's raining. I'm dreadful, but I'm getting better."

"But you were shooting already? This morning?" Georgiana said, rapidly trying to keep up with this new information. "It is not yet ten o'clock."

"Oh, I don't sleep much," Cecily said, perfectly cheerful. "It's quite light this time of year, even at six o'clock in the—Oh, here's Jane."

The Woodleys had indeed arrived. If she had realized this was the church favored by all of Frances's friends, Georgiana thought ruefully, she'd have combed her hair a little more diligently.

"Morning," Jane said as she drew level with them. "Good shooting, Ces?"

"Five threes and a seven," Cecily said with a smile, drawing herself up to full height.

"You're improving," said Jane, raising an eyebrow. "Any casualties?"

"Oh," Cecily said airily, "not really."

"Not really?" Georgiana said, alarmed, and Jane seemed to notice her for the first time despite the fact that she'd been speaking over the top of her head.

"Good morning, Miss Ellers," she said, her eyes immediately darting to Georgiana's hair. "Windy in town, is it?"

She was hurried along by her parents before Georgiana could think of how to respond. Christopher Crawley walked past a moment or two later, with a man who must have been his brother; he looked monstrously hungover and stopped only to kiss both of their hands before collapsing into a pew, taking the position closest to the wall and sliding down into what was almost a horizontal position.

"Will Miss Campbell be joining us?" Georgiana said, glancing around to see if she had already arrived without her notice. "Or . . . Mr. Smith?"

"Hmm—unlikely," said Cecily. "Frances doesn't usually make appointments before eleven o'clock, and her parents are often away, so there is nobody to force her. Jonathan doesn't come at all."

"Why?"

"He says he's circumvented God, looped back around, and now only does business with his next of kin."

"What—Christ?"

"No," Cecily said brightly. "The devil."

"Ah," said Georgiana, once again at a loss for words.

"There's Jeremiah," Cecily said, glancing back at the door. "Only, don't stare. Frances gets ever so angry when I do."

It was difficult for Georgiana to follow her instructions; it soon became apparent that Mr. Russell had entered with quite a large crowd, including various family members, some of the men Georgiana had seen him with at Jane's party, and finally—crucially—the tall, dark, and very miserable-looking Mr. Hawksley. The front pews, perpendicular to the rest so that they flanked the lectern on either side, seemed to have been left empty for them; they descended, greeting friends and neighbors as they went, with Mr. Hawksley taking up the rear. Georgiana was prepared to look away and appear uninterested the moment he saw her, but he walked past without noticing her at all.

As soon as they were seated, the rather stout young vicar, Mr. Weatherby, took his place and cleared his throat for quiet, which he mostly received. The sermon began, but Georgiana found herself unable to focus. She was watching Mr. Hawksley's profile—the loose curls that had already slipped from his queue, his slight frown, and the careful journey of his hand as he turned the pages of his Bible. She only looked away when Cecily asked her which hymn they were supposed to be singing next, and she had to explain that she had no idea.

The hymn sung, they took their seats again and Cecily leaned over to whisper in Georgiana's ear.

"That fellow Mr. Hawksley is looking at you."

"Oh," said Georgiana, keeping her eyes fixed on the back of the pew in front. "Well—what kind of looking is it? Is he looking on purpose, or are his eyes just here by accident?"

"I think he looks quite annoyed, actually—have you quarreled with him? He's blinking quite a lot, which seems . . . Oh, no, wait, I think he might have something in his eye. Yes, he's trying to get it out. Goodness, he's really going for it."

"Great," whispered Georgiana despairingly. "Thanks."

"Wait a minute," Cecily said, nudging her. "Now I think he *is* looking this way. He's just quietly asked that gentleman something. I'm sure he nodded in our direction . . . Never mind, he was asking for a handkerchief. And the gentleman—yes, the gentleman does have a handkerchief he can borrow. He has the handkerchief now."

"Thank you, Cecily, really," said Georgiana. "I think you can stop now."

"*Have* you quarreled with him?" Cecily asked—but Georgiana was saved from answering by the announcement of yet another hymn.

The rest of the service dragged, Georgiana's nerves dancing with anticipation of the moment when Mr. Hawksley would walk past and perhaps, this time, notice her. When the time came, she was so focused on trying to look casual, on smiling pleasantly at Cecily so that he might see her looking favorable, that she didn't notice he and Jeremiah Russell were actually standing right next to her until Cecily's smile over her shoulder became overly wide and very pointed.

"Miss Dugray," Mr. Russell said, nodding at her. "And . . . Forgive me, I'm not sure we've been introduced."

"Georgiana Ellers, sir," Georgiana said, feeling herself blush, despite the fact that they absolutely *had* been introduced, and he had clearly immediately forgotten her. He was the sort of handsome that made one feel bathed in a ray of sunlight while under his gaze, even if he did seem to have a very short memory.

"Ah, yes. Well, be good, ladies—God is watching," he said, raising an eyebrow suggestively and giving them another nod of farewell.

Mr. Hawksley had been standing silently at his elbow; as Jeremiah made to leave, he finally met Georgiana's gaze, and visibly flinched as if startled. Georgiana didn't know much about gentlemen, but she was relatively sure that flinching at the sight of you wasn't a good sign.

She and Cecily both looked expectantly at him, and he flashed them a quick, terse smile and inclined his head.

"Good day," he said before walking swiftly away.

They sat in silence for a moment as the rest of the congregation milled past.

"Maybe," Cecily said charitably, "he still had something in his eye?"

"Yes," said Georgiana, getting to her feet as Mrs. Burton made furtive gestures for her to come. "Yes. I imagine that was it."

Chapter Eight

WHEN WORD FINALLY CAME FROM GEORGIANA'S PARENTS, she was sitting in the library windowsill reading in a most unladylike position—hair loose, back against one side of the sill, legs lifted and braced against the other. They had enjoyed shortbread with luncheon, and Georgiana had furtively visited Marjorie in the kitchen afterward and traded a dramatic reading of part of the book she was holding—Henry Fielding, all domestic tragedy and lukewarm adultery—for some more biscuits, which she was enjoying rather messily as she turned the pages.

The letter from her father was delivered directly into her hand by a very curious Emmeline, as her aunt and uncle were out on an afternoon walk, and she immediately gave up her book, shook out the crumbs on her dress, and pulled up her uncle's chair to the small desk to give it her full attention.

Georgiana,

Apologies for the delay of this letter, but we have been setting up the house and making it habitable, and we finally feel settled enough to catch up on our correspondence. Your mother is much improved, taking regular walks and sea baths, and enjoying every part of life on the coast apart from the near-constant cries of the gulls. I have shot five so far, and hope to shoot many more. We regret that you are not with us, of course, but know you are in capable hands. We will arrange a visit later on in the summer, if time allows. Please pass our thanks to your aunt and uncle for taking you into their care.

Additionally, it has come to my attention that I seem to be missing my copy of Richard II. If you are currently its guardian, please have it sent by post at your earliest convenience.

Your father,

Mr. Jacob Ellers

Georgiana turned it over to see if there was a postscript and then checked the envelope again to see if it might be the first of many letters. It was not. She read it again, trying to extract some further meaning from it, and then put it down, overcome with emptiness. All she could do was stare at the desk in front of her and will herself not to cry.

When Georgiana was seven, she had picked up an unsupervised embroidery needle and attempted to imitate her mother, pushing it through a half-finished blanket so forcefully that she had driven it into the palm of her other hand. She had been absolutely hysterical with pain and horror, running through the house screaming for her mother and father, until she discovered them sitting in the drawing room, books in their laps, looking slightly annoyed to have been interrupted.

Upon realizing the source of all the fuss, her father had removed the needle without ceremony, pressing his handkerchief to the puncture wound and attempting to send her on her way.

"I was trying—" Georgiana had explained through hiccupping sobs, "I was trying to—to help Mama, with the blanket."

"Oh, *Georgiana,*" her mother had said disappointedly, picking up her book. "That's not at all the right needle for working with wool."

Georgiana had spent her entire life looking for something more than calm, measured practicality from her parents and was furious with herself for still being surprised when she did not receive it.

I have shot five so far, and hope to shoot many more.

No word for the best part of a month, and her father thought that the hunting of seabirds merited a lengthier mention than any sort of affection for his daughter. He didn't want Georgiana back, not at all—but he was in *desperate* need of *Richard II*.

Sudden, molten fury flooded her veins, and she got to her feet and crossed to the bookshelves, searching haphazardly, almost manically. When she found what she was looking for in the section her uncle had set aside for her books, she pulled it out and stared at it for a moment.

Damn *Richard II*. She didn't even consider it a particularly good play, as the *Richards* went.

Georgiana seized a thick handful of pages and tore them out in one quick motion. She watched as the fine yellowed paper fell to the floor, and then she set about shredding the rest of the book in a frenzy, not stopping when a page sliced a thin cut up the length of her hand, continuing until all that remained was the hard cover and a pile of kindling.

Regret found her then, as was inevitable. Destroying a book felt like sacrilege—as if she had laid her hands on something that ought to have been untouchable. She should have kept it instead and read it often, taking delight in it, enjoying it all the more because she could read it while her father could not.

It was far too late for that now. She sucked the blood from her hand, feeling quite exhausted and very small, only just managing to keep her tears at bay. Picking up the debris helped, focusing her mind on a task, and she was careful not to leave a scrap of evidence behind. She gathered everything up and took it to the kitchen, offering it to Marjorie to be burned. The older woman looked at her askance but said nothing, studying Georgiana's expression for a moment longer before taking the pile of paper and pressing another biscuit into her hand in its place.

When the Burtons returned from their walk, Georgiana was still in a foul mood. She handed the letter to her aunt without a word and went to bed, leaving her to read it for herself.

Mrs. Burton came to find her later, knocking and then immediately pushing open the door with a look of such kindly sympathy on her face that Georgiana wanted to scream. Her aunt sat down on the edge of her bed, which creaked in complaint, and patted her arm fondly.

"Your parents . . . They are not much for words of affection," she said gently.

"You can say that again," Georgiana said into her pillow. "'I seem to be missing my copy of *Richard II*.'"

"Ah. Yes. Well—have you seen it? It doesn't seem to be in the library."

"No," Georgiana said guiltily before sitting up to look at her aunt. "I do not begrudge them the move, Mrs. Burton, and I am glad my mother's head is better and of course I am grateful to be here, but would it have been so difficult to *pretend* they missed me? Just a little?"

"No, it would not," said Mrs. Burton with a sad sigh.

"I imagine if I turned up unannounced, they'd panic and shoot me on sight, like one of those poor seagulls."

"Probably not, dear," Mrs. Burton said unconvincingly, and then she drew Georgiana into a crushing hug. It felt startlingly unfamiliar to be loved this way, so physically, so fussily, and she was embarrassed to find that her eyes were slightly wet when she drew away. "You're not having too dreadful a time here, though, are you? I hope you know that your uncle and I are very happy to have you. We shall arrange some more outings—and you said you had a lovely stay with the Campbells."

"I did," said Georgiana guiltily.

She had given her aunt a very warped version of the truth, telling her that she had spent her trip dining with the Campbells and enjoying rousing games of chess by the fire, omitting the fact that this had all taken place half-dressed and fully inebriated. As kind as her aunt was being, it seemed the perfect moment to bring up the cottage party Frances had mentioned, and she winced internally before adding yet more lies and half-truths to her score sheet.

"Actually, Mrs. Burton, the Campbells are traveling out to the country soon and they wanted to invite me along . . ."

Mrs. Burton listened as Georgiana falteringly—and falsely—explained the nature of the trip, and then smiled, squeezing her niece's hand.

"I think that sounds splendid. Just the thing to get your spirits up. In fact, let's go into town tomorrow and pick out some lace to brighten up one of your old frocks," she said, fingering Georgiana's sleeve.

Georgiana pulled away, nettled at the implication that her dresses needed improving, worrying that perhaps Frances and her friends might think the same. All the guilt at her deception was pushed immediately from her mind.

"Fine, fine," she said to Mrs. Burton, who looked a little crestfallen as she left the room.

As morose as she felt about what a few lengths of lace could possibly do to improve her apparently dismal wardrobe, Georgiana perked up as the carriage traveled into the town; the cottages and hedgerows gave way to rows of narrow houses, pressed so closely together that she couldn't imagine how the people inside them had space to breathe. They were all carved out of matching honeyed stone, with pretty window boxes full of pansies and daisies the only bright splashes of color among all the brown. There were so many people in the streets; they were surrounded by the shouts of street vendors, the smells of sewage and horse dung, and the sight of crowds walking under parasols and dodging carriages like theirs as they crossed the street without a thought for their personal safety.

They spent a very long time in the haberdashery, Mrs. Burton showing Georgiana so many almost identical samples of lace that she started to see intricate patterns on the insides of her eyelids every time she blinked. Eventually her aunt consented to her going to sit outside on a bench in the shade, as long as she stayed in full view of the shop. Georgiana hurried away before Mrs. Burton could change her mind, reveling in the sudden freedom.

The town had two intersecting and well-stocked high streets, meeting in the middle where the most popular shops, the inns, and the imposing assembly rooms were arranged around a wide, cobbled market square. Georgiana had been warned by her aunt during the carriage ride—three times, in fact—that the public house on the very corner of the square was patronized entirely by ruffians and rogues, and that to venture down the length of street that followed was tantamount to a death sentence.

Looking at it now, Georgiana suspected her aunt was exaggerating somewhat; there were a few older gentlemen who looked rather shabby conversing on the corner, and a woman farther down the street who seemed to be begging with little success. As Georgiana watched, a very well-dressed woman partially hidden by a parasol bent to drop a handful of coins into the beggar's outstretched palms; she looked down at the money and then back up at her benefactor, smiling, but then faltered. Her smile became a scowl, and to Georgiana's confusion, she spat at the feet of the woman as she hurriedly walked away.

As the woman drew nearer, a manservant following closely behind with his arms piled high with packages, Georgiana realized with a start who it was: Lady Campbell, her face oddly blank, eyes fixed ahead without seeming to see anything at all.

"Oh," said Mrs. Burton's voice from behind Georgiana, thoroughly startling her. "Isn't that . . . ? Lady Campbell!"

Before Georgiana could stop her, her aunt was waving Frances's mother over. The determined blankness of her expression immediately smoothed over into a polite smile, and she stopped to greet them both.

"We have not met properly, of course, but my Georgiana is quite taken with your Frances," Mrs. Burton said, beaming. "It was so kind of you to have my niece to stay."

Georgiana immediately felt very sick, imagining all her lies laid out before her as if they were being presented in a court of law. She very much suspected that Lady Campbell had no idea Georgiana had crossed her threshold, let alone pulled a drunken Frances from the lake or heard a domestic quarrel that was definitely supposed to be private.

"Please do let us know if we can ever repay the favor in kind."

"Ah . . . yes," Lady Campbell said, frowning slightly as she glanced at Georgiana, who must have looked petrified. "It was no trouble. She can come again anytime."

Georgiana tried not to breathe an obvious sigh of relief and simultaneously attempted to convey silent thanks to Frances's mother, who seemed utterly uninterested; she was already looking beyond them, as if a more arresting thought had occurred to her.

"Well, we shan't keep you," said Mrs. Burton, sensing that she had already lost her audience. "Good day, Lady Campbell."

"Good day," she repeated, already walking away.

Mrs. Burton immediately started to extol her virtues and examine every aspect of their conversation forensically, but Georgiana wasn't listening; she was watching two ladies step aside to allow Lady Campbell into the millinery. They were polite enough as she nodded her thanks, but as soon as she was inside, Georgiana saw them whispering furtively to each other as they hurried away.

Mrs. Burton steered Georgiana back to their carriage, which

was waiting for them five minutes away; when they passed back through the square on their way home, Georgiana glimpsed Lady Campbell through the shop window, sitting upright and expressionless as the milliner brought her hat after hat after hat.

Chapter Nine

THE LAST TIME GEORGIANA HAD VISITED A COUNTRY FAIR,
she had been twelve; it had been held at her father's school, and
a boy called Tommy Hannock had kicked her in the shins and
called her a "slug" because she'd beaten him in the archery con-
test. It seemed unwise to her that he had chosen to insult her
when she was still holding a weapon in her hand, especially a
weapon she had just proven she was far more adept than him at
using—but with regret, she had not shot him.

When Frances had invited Georgiana to the fair on the last
Sunday of June—via a scrawled note on Saturday evening, followed early next morning by Frances herself showing up in her
carriage and asking Mrs. Burton with a wink if Georgiana could
come out "to play"—she had thought it a surprisingly wholesome
activity, by her friend's usual standards.

As it turned out, being an adult at a fair meant that drinking
was acceptable—perhaps even required—and Georgiana entered
in high spirits already, having prepared for the afternoon at Frances's house, along with Cecily and Jane. Lord and Lady Campbell
were both once again mercifully absent. Jonathan sent a note of
apology, saying that he was engaged elsewhere, and that even if
he weren't, he would certainly *pretend* he was to avoid attending a
country fair. Christopher's whereabouts had, in Frances's words,
been "impossible to pinpoint."

"It's a girls' day!" Frances had said happily beforehand as they
sat in her garden drinking something Cecily had concocted that

tasted like rubbing alcohol and elderflower. Jane had been in a better mood than usual and had braided flowers from the Campbells' gardens into their hair, so that the four of them looked like a gaggle of pagan fairies. They had skipped church in favor of readying themselves, and Mrs. Burton probably would have called for a vicar posthaste had she seen them out without their gloves or bonnets, but she and Mr. Burton had set off midmorning to visit his sister some twenty miles away, so Georgiana did not have to worry that they might make a surprise appearance and catch her running about like a fair-weather heathen.

There were a number of stalls and games set up in the grounds of St. Anne's, bordered on all sides by elm trees shedding the last of their papery seeds like confetti. Children dressed in their Sunday best tore up handfuls of grass and threw them at one another, giggling madly and chasing each other between the tables. A strongman was challenging passersby to have a go with his mallet. There was even a band—although calling it a band may have been a little charitable, as they all seemed to have fashioned their instruments themselves out of scraps of wood and tin.

"Jane *loves* the fair," Frances was saying teasingly, and Jane elbowed her in the side.

"I'd love it a lot more if you'd stop *badgering* me," she replied—but she was smiling, and Frances was smiling back.

Georgiana had no idea what had brought this on and found it a little unnerving, but it certainly made a change from Jane's usual dour looks and pessimism, so she endeavored to make the most of it.

"George, I'll give you a pound if you can knock his head off," Frances said, shading her eyes with one hand and pointing with the other at a stall where the primary objective seemed to be to knock apples off things, with the application of slightly smaller apples. The centerpiece was a scarecrow with fruit balanced precariously on his burlap head, and the prize was a basket of strawberries so red and ripe they looked fit to burst. Baskets sat either side of the stall, overflowing with yet more apples for sale.

On the whole, Georgiana thought they had rather overdone the theme.

One pound was an unthinkable amount of money to throw away on a bet, but Georgiana suspected that to Frances, it was such a trifling number that she expected all involved to forget about it immediately afterward. She strode up to the stall and paid a few coins to play, and the boy minding it gave her a little pile of yellowing apples. Pulling her arm back, closing one eye, and attempting to aim, she snapped one at the target and missed spectacularly. The others cheered—Frances and Jane sarcastically, Cecily with all sincerity—and Georgiana felt herself getting a little hot under her dress, shrugging and self-consciously unclenching her mouth.

She missed twice more, getting increasingly frustrated. She could see that Frances was losing interest now, whispering to Jane and looking about for something else to do. Georgiana narrowed her eyes at the scarecrow as if it had personally affronted her and gave the last throw her all; this time she hit it square on, but the apple did not fall. Instead it broke in half, and it became clear that a stake had been driven through it, keeping it firmly in place and making the game completely impossible to win.

Georgiana turned to look at the others in openmouthed disbelief, pointing at the broken apple. For a moment it looked as if nobody was going to take up her cause, but then Frances saw what had happened.

"Cheat!" she cried.

The boy looked up from where he had been idly quaffing ale and eyeing up passersby. When he saw the state of his apple, he quickly removed it, studied it, then put another in its place, driving it hard onto the stake to trick the next unsuspecting customer.

"You can't do that! I want my strawberries!" Georgiana said, alcohol fueling a level of rage that seemed entirely proportionate in the moment.

Frances was now standing beside her with her arms crossed.

"It says 'knock it down to claim a prize,'" the boy said, grinning infuriatingly, pointing to a sign that did indeed say just that.

"But it's impossible to knock it down! It might as well say—I don't know—'fly a lap around the fair to win a prize.'"

"Yeah, well. Doesn't, does it?"

Jane advanced on him, looking menacing.

"How much do I win if I knock *your* head off?" she hissed, and he looked so astonished to be spoken to in such a way by someone like Jane that they all burst out laughing.

"Come on, George. Let's leave this man to his illustrious career as an *apple-herder*," Frances said, hooking her arm in Georgiana's and pulling her away. The boy sneered at them as they went, and Georgiana was gripped by a strong desire to throw every single one of his apples at him.

"He should be . . . I don't know . . . Thrown out of the fair. Banned from—from all apple-related activities for life," Georgiana said, drunk and wounded, and Frances patted her on the arm consolingly.

"Come on," she said. "I know what'll cheer you up."

Cecily and Frances were bartering with the man selling wine. He was around five-and-fifty, a little rounded at the middle, and clearly having the time of his life as they flattered him, fluttered their eyelashes, and employed every last excruciating drop of their womanly charms to get him to hand over a case of his best for half the asking price. Georgiana assumed they must have been doing it just for the fun of it, as they had no need of discounted wine from a man who had scratched his crotch twice since the haggling began.

Jane, meanwhile, was a short distance away, deep in conversation with the man running the pie stand, which was odd in and of itself. Georgiana doubted Jane had ever eaten a pie in her life, and these were thick-crusted, greasy things, with no telling what might be inside them. Cecily and Frances left the wine merchant—blowing him a kiss as they did—and as they all approached Jane, she shook the pie-seller's hand and turned to them with a very serious expression.

"Everyone—this is John Louis."

"John Louis!" they all chorused back, delighted, as if he were a very old and dear friend. Georgiana considered him for a moment.

"Who's John Louis?" she asked Frances quietly.

"Absolutely no idea," Frances replied.

"John Louis is selling us a pie," Jane said slowly. "It's a very *special* pie, and we must go with him to his wagon to fetch it."

"Is she feeling quite all right?" Georgiana asked Frances as John Louis set off toward the trees and they all followed.

The pie in question turned out not to be a pie at all—it was, in fact, a plain wooden snuffbox.

"Bring it back," John Louis said sternly.

Jane nodded, and Frances waggled her fingers in farewell before linking her arm with Jane's as they walked away, with Cecily and Georgiana hurrying to keep up.

Jane led them through the trees, out of the churchyard grounds proper, and to some sort of outbuilding. It may have once housed horses but now was simply three walls and a partially caved-in roof, with hay bales stacked in the only corner that was still covered.

Jane and Frances sat down on a bale, and Georgiana leaned in curiously to see what secrets the snuffbox held.

"It's . . . Is that snuff?" Georgiana asked dubiously when Frances reverently lifted the lid to reveal a light brown powdery substance.

The others all laughed knowingly, and Georgiana felt thoroughly rebuked.

"Sort of," said Frances kindly.

"It's *not*. It's *special* snuff. Snuff plus. You take it as usual," Jane said.

She demonstrated, sprinkling some onto the back of her hand and bringing it to her nose, and then held the box aloft for Georgiana.

She hesitated only for a moment, feeling distantly concerned but trusting that Frances wouldn't expose her to anything too sinister, then lowered her face and sniffed, hard. Her sinuses burned, and she watched through watery eyes as Frances and Cecily took their turns.

"Peasant drugs are the best drugs," Frances sighed happily, wiping her nose. "They have absolutely nothing to live for, and you can really *tell*."

"Jesus Christ, Frances," Jane said, but she was smiling lazily, leaning back on a bale of hay with flushed cheeks. All this smiling was getting a bit alarming.

"Cheers to peasants!" Cecily cried, raising a bottle of wine aloft.

Georgiana winced, feeling a little too close to peasant-dom herself to join them in earnest, but drank all the same. They toasted to country fairs, and hay, and especially to John Louis, until sobriety was a distant dream and the sun was decidedly lower in the sky.

Georgiana had never considered herself a particularly gifted dancer—but today, for some reason, she was *truly excellent* at dancing. Frances had announced that she wanted to see the band and they had all trooped over to the makeshift stage, giggling and tripping over one another as they did, and joined the next dance.

They were by far the most enthusiastic ones there and kept rearranging themselves so they could remain each other's partners even as the other dancers switched around, much to the chagrin of some of the young men present, who were openly staring at them and jostling one another to try to get closer to them. The man playing the pipe onstage seemed encouraged by their energy and started to stamp his foot as he played. They all cheered him on as they danced faster and faster, spinning and turning and clapping in time, while flower petals fell from their hair and were crushed underfoot.

After seven songs in a row in the late afternoon heat, Georgiana needed to sit down. The crowd had grown enormous now, and she could barely see her friends among it; *everyone* was dancing, even the children, swung around on their parents' arms. Whatever had been in that powder, it had made her feel all at once elated, discombobulated, and *desperately* thirsty. She acquired a cool cup of ale and sat down at a table that overlooked the dancers, drinking it so clumsily that about half of it ended up dripping down her chin.

Someone tapped her on the shoulder, and she almost jumped out of her skin, but it was just the man from the pie stall.

"John Louis!" she said weakly, toasting him with her cup.

"Where's your friend?" he asked.

"I don't . . ." Georgiana gestured to the crowd and they both looked around for a moment, before realizing that Jane was nowhere to be seen.

"Tell her I want it back," he said insistently. "Now."

Georgiana nodded and got to her tired feet to demonstrate that she was willing. She thought Jane had most likely slipped away to the outbuildings again, to partake in a little more of what John Louis so urgently wanted returned, and walked off in vaguely the right direction.

* * *

When she finally found the outbuilding—there had been many false starts, including one in which Georgiana had seen a pretty frog and been so distracted that she had stared adoringly at it for at least a minute (the frog seemed unmoved)—she couldn't see anyone in it at first, but heard the rustling of hay and cleverly deduced that it was occupied.

Her first thought upon seeing Jane and Frances was that they were fighting—wrestling each other on a hay bale. This made no sense, of course, but it took a moment for her brain to rearrange the scene into something that did.

They were *kissing*—and these were certainly not the quick, chaste kisses of friendship. Frances was lying lazily back in the hay, watching through heavily lidded eyes and smiling as Jane slowly kissed a trail up her chest, her collarbone, and then finally reached her lips. She had a hand on Jane's waist, and Georgiana could see her knuckles whitening as she closed her eyes and pulled her closer.

Georgiana knew she needed to sneak away urgently, but she was frozen where she stood, and suddenly it was too late— Frances had opened her eyes and looked directly at her. Georgiana expected her to sit bolt upright, push Jane away, pretend it wasn't happening, but instead she kept looking at Georgiana, holding her gaze as Jane kissed her somewhere near her earlobe, smiling at her beatifically.

"What do you want?" Frances asked eventually.

Jane jumped and looked over her shoulder, pushing herself up onto her knees.

"Um, I'm sorry, I . . . I was sent to—but then I—" Georgiana spluttered. They both stared at her expectantly. "I saw a frog," she said feebly, and Jane rolled her eyes.

"You saw a *frog*?" she repeated incredulously.

"Yes, and . . . Oh! John Louis wants his snuff back."

Frances fumbled for it in the hay and then closed her fingers around it, tossing it to Georgiana quite roughly, considering how reverently she had first opened it. Now that she had no further use for it, it seemed it held no worth at all.

"Thank you," said Georgiana, and then she half-ran back in the direction of the fair.

Her head was still reeling with what she had seen. She had never heard of women doing such a thing—of *wanting* each other that way. She didn't understand why her palms suddenly seemed so sweaty, her neck so flushed; it was just so unexpected—that must have been it. Because Frances was in love with *Jeremiah*—so what on earth was she doing literally rolling around in the hay with Jane?

When Georgiana reached the dancers, she looked vaguely around for John Louis, but her mind was thoroughly occupied by the extremely vivid image of her friends on the verge of ravishing each other. It was impressively bold, she thought slightly hysterically, to do so not fifty feet away from a church. She started giggling with shock, her knuckles pressed to her mouth. If *Georgiana* were found horizontal and passionately kissing another woman—and her eyes went wide at the very thought of it, color rising anew in her cheeks—Mrs. Burton would probably make her wear a blindfold for the rest of her life, so that she could not see the soft curve of a woman's cheek or the salacious flash of an ankle and be enticed into committing some indelible sin in a shack that smelled faintly of horse manure.

Georgiana was jolted from these all-consuming thoughts by the appearance of John Louis at her elbow. She handed him the box without a word; he tutted when he opened it briefly to see how much was left, then snapped it shut and slid it into his pocket.

"You want to dance?" he asked gruffly.

"Oh . . . No thanks," said Georgiana.

He didn't seem particularly disappointed, but she felt she had let him down somewhat by not being a good enough sport. After all, an hour previously they had been toasting him with every sip of their drinks.

She was just thinking that she must look for Cecily—did she know about Jane and Frances? Had she even noticed?—when the crowd parted, and she saw Jeremiah Russell striding toward her in his shirtsleeves. Frances *had* said something about him— that he'd meet them later, perhaps, if his schedule allowed—but Georgiana was so distracted that for a moment she was utterly confused by his presence, as if he were a unicorn appearing in her bedroom rather than a man attending a fair. He approached, look- ing terribly good in the early evening light, all golden and artfully undone. She felt a strange sense of pride when he recognized her and called out to her—as if it were such a great compliment to be remembered by a man who had been introduced to her twice, and who should have certainly recognized her by their third meeting.

"Where's Frances?" he asked after kissing her hand, and only then did she realize her conundrum.

"I think . . ." She cast wildly about for something to say. "I think she was getting a pie."

"A *pie*? Frances?"

"Yes. She said—er—she said she was very hungry, from all the dancing, and she must eat something . . . and of course it would not be her first choice." Georgiana was rambling now. "I don't think she's ever been so close to a pie in all her life, but tonight a pie was just the thing—"

"Jeremiah! What's all this about pies?"

Frances's voice came from behind her, and Georgiana felt weak with relief. She was approaching arm in arm with Jane, looking perfectly innocent, but Georgiana couldn't look at them without seeing Frances's dress rucked up—Jane's hand sliding up Frances's bare thigh.

"Miss Ellers was under the impression that you were obtaining one," said Jeremiah jovially.

"Christ, no. They've probably baked their children into them," Frances retorted.

She unlinked herself from Jane to go to Jeremiah and allow her hand to be thoroughly kissed. He offered her his elbow and she took it, nestling in close. Georgiana risked a look at Jane. Her face was thunderous.

They danced a little more, but Georgiana had become accustomed to partnering with Cecily—who seemed to have ascended to a different plane of existence and was dancing with almost no awareness of the people around them—which now left Jane the odd one out. She kept getting stuck with strangers who looked mildly frightened of her—and rightly so, for she was positively glowering. Jane couldn't stop looking at Frances; almost everyone was. She and Jeremiah were the very picture of young love, laughing and savoring every touch.

Jane looked as if nothing on this earth would make her happier than driving the strongman's mallet into Jeremiah's skull.

As the last of the glorious sun vanished behind the trees and the dancers came to a sweaty pause, Georgiana suddenly found Frances at her side, pulling on her sleeve and giggling.

"Come on, come on," she said in a stage whisper, and Georgiana went with her.

Their destination turned out to be the apple stall where Georgiana had been so egregiously cheated out of her winnings. It seemed nobody had won the strawberries, for they were still sitting on the table—but the boy in charge of them was nowhere to be seen.

"Claim your prize!" Frances said, nudging her forward, and Georgiana seized the basket triumphantly.

She looked around surreptitiously and made to walk away,

thinking they would exit the scene as quickly as possible and sneak off to celebrate with the others, but Frances wasn't finished yet. She winked at Georgiana, then turned and kicked over one of the baskets of apples for sale and started to stamp on them, pounding them into the dirt as they bruised and split beneath her feet.

"Don't let him get away with it, he's a . . . a *bad apple*," she giggled drunkenly to Georgiana, who looked around to see if anybody was watching. Her instincts were telling her to run for it, but Frances was gesturing expectantly for her to join in.

"But . . . Should we really . . . ? I mean, surely this is his trade?" Georgiana said weakly, and Frances laughed.

"His *trade* is cheating innocent young girls out of their money, Georgiana. He's a thief! And we are avenging all those who have come before us, who deserved strawberries just as much as you or I! It's time to take a stand—to rise up against this apple tyrant!"

Roused by this speech, Georgiana joined her. They got rather carried away, knocking down the fence posts, kicking the scarecrow into the mud; Georgiana certainly did her part, and yet was quite shocked when she looked up only ten or fifteen seconds later and saw how much devastation they had wrought.

"Quick, quick!" Frances cried.

She grabbed Georgiana by the hand and hurried her away. As they heard people approaching they broke into a full run, and they arrived back with the others, laughing, gasping, bent double as they tried to recover themselves.

"What on *earth* were you two doing?" Jeremiah asked, raising an eyebrow at Frances mischievously.

"Strawberries!" Georgiana said breathlessly, holding up the basket, and the others all exclaimed in delight and helped themselves. A shout of genuine anguish went up from the direction of the apple stall, and Georgiana caught Frances's eye.

"What's he so upset about?" Cecily asked mildly.

Frances and Georgiana laughed silently, covering their mouths as strawberry juice ran through their fingers.

"Nothing," said Frances eventually. "Eat your strawberries, Ces."

Chapter Ten

THE FRIDAY OF THE TRIP TO THE COTTAGE FINALLY CAME, and Georgiana was ready to leave a full hour before it was strictly necessary. She sat dressed and perspiring with nerves, waiting for the rumble of a carriage on the road. Mrs. Burton came to sit with her for a while but found her niece far too distracted to be good company (when asked about the book she had been reading, Georgiana found herself unable to provide its title, a summary of the contents, or even the vaguest indication that she understood what a book was).

When she at last heard a commotion outside, Georgiana ran in a very ungainly fashion to kiss her aunt goodbye and then rushed to exit before Mrs. Burton had a chance to come out with her and notice that the carriage did not contain any variety of appropriate parental supervision.

The driver took Georgiana's trunk from her, and she climbed into the grand covered coach to find a party of sorts already under way within. It was a very good thing indeed that her aunt was only just reopening the door to wave them off as the horses turned back onto the road, for Frances, Cecily, Jane, and Jonathan were already drinking, and smoking, and cheering raucously at the sight of Georgiana with absolutely no regard for the fact that it was only ten o'clock in the morning.

Georgiana felt suddenly very dull, sober as she was. She took a deep swig from the glass Jonathan passed to her, which had the unfortunate effect of making her feel instantly nauseated. She pushed through and took another sip, thinking that it would not be in the spirit of the thing to vomit before they had even reached their destination. Frances, who was wearing a beautiful gown of deepest green and looked frankly effervescent, held her own glass aloft.

"A toast! A toast to friends, and to the country, and to Christopher's naughty, naughty uncle for the gift of Bastards' Cottage!"

They all hurrahed and clinked their glasses clumsily as the carriage threw them about.

"Bastards' Cottage?" Georgiana asked once she had taken another drink.

"You do look *scandalized,* George. We named it so because Christopher's uncle bought the place to raise his bastard children away from prying eyes. They've all grown up now and gone off to spend their hush money and plot how to kill his true-born children, so he lets Christopher use it."

"I hope he's had it cleaned," said Jonathan pointedly. "I can't *imagine* what Christopher uses it for when we're not around, but I'm sure it involves copious amounts of unseemly bodily fluids."

The girls squealed and exclaimed in disgust, and Cecily hit him playfully on the shoulder.

"What? He's filthy! I'm sure we'd all have a much better time of it if we were being hosted by one of those good, honest bastard cousins."

"Hear, hear," said Jane darkly.

She seemed in low spirits again, but at least now Georgiana thought she might have some inkling as to why. Frances had barely looked her way at the fair after Jeremiah arrived, and had even gone so far as to shake Jane off when she attempted to take her arm on the walk back to their carriage. Georgiana had winced at the sight of it and had attempted to catch Jane's eye with an expression of sympathy, but the other girl had stormed ahead and fumed silently the whole way home.

Georgiana had replayed moments from the last month over

and over again in her head since that day: Frances pulling off a pair of borrowed stockings; her eyelashes wet with tears and far too close in the dark of her bedroom; Jane standing alone on her patio at the first party, refusing to go one more step with Jeremiah Russell. It was all starting to form a complete picture in Georgiana's head, although she had to entirely rewrite what she thought she'd known of their characters for it to make sense. The experience had been jarring, although it felt less so by the minute. Georgiana looked at Frances now, beautiful and elegant even as she frowned at Jonathan, her glass dangling precariously from her hand. *Nothing* had changed, really; this was who she had been all along, even if Georgiana was too blind to see it.

Frances rolled her eyes. "If you could all keep your opinions about Mr. Crawley to yourselves for a few more days, please, you ingrates. I'd like to enjoy my holiday without being cast out onto the moors due to your abominable manners, thank you very much."

The weather was very fine. Sun filtered through the trees and flashed intermittently through the windows as the carriage traveled farther from town, and they drank steadily, their stories getting wilder and ruder as the bottles of wine at their feet grew emptier.

Georgiana was flushed and giddy with pleasure at how *easy* it all felt; nobody seemed to see her as an outsider or an unwelcome addition to their party. For the first few weeks of her friendship with Frances, she had almost felt as if she were taking part in an audition—an attempt to earn her place, to prove that she belonged—but no longer; she had won the part, she had *arrived*, and she could enjoy herself freely without worrying that they might spontaneously tire of her and abandon her at the crossroads with her trunk to await the evening's post.

Toward the end of their journey, the toasts grew increasingly ridiculous ("To the vine that gave us the grape that produced this wine!" "To the dogs that pissed on it!"). Georgiana was absolutely starving and judged it to be well past lunchtime as they traveled up a very uneven track to the house and then fell over one another as they tried to exit at once. A mostly empty bottle of wine rolled out after Frances and smashed, but she just laughed and stepped over the mess, throwing her arms wide as if she were presenting the cottage to Georgiana.

It was much larger than she had anticipated—at least as large as the Burtons' house, and she'd never have dared call that a cottage in her aunt's earshot. It seemed as if it might be whitewashed under its dense covering of wisteria and ivy. They were surrounded by trees, and turning around, Georgiana could barely make out the track they had traveled up to get there. Once the coachmen had unpacked their luggage and made for town, they'd be quite on their own.

It was the kind of place that should have been exquisitely peaceful—but of course, there was nothing remotely like peace on the agenda.

The front door opened and Christopher emerged with a violently lavender shirt half unbuttoned, a bottle of wine in each hand, his arms raised high in greeting. As their trunks were brought in, they followed him through the small entryway and down a narrow passage to what turned out to be the kitchen, already strewn with empty bottles. On the table there was also an assortment of platters: thin cuts of meat, tarts, cheeses, and breads all laid out and ready to eat.

"There's a modest estate about half an hour east that's almost always empty, so I have employed their staff to keep us alive. They'll bring us three square meals a day, fresh water, ale—and besides that, the cellar will keep us well lubricated." Christopher motioned with one of the wine bottles to an open trapdoor, which he seemed to have recently ascended from. "I'm afraid they don't do much in the way of housework, so you'll have to be self-sufficient. Try not to faint from the shock, Smith. Dress yourselves, bathe yourselves. Wipe your own arses."

They all helped themselves to plates of food, and Christopher passed up more bottles from the cellar, making sure they were all carrying one before leading them through the back of the house and into the grounds. These were not quite the vast, manicured gardens of Longview; there was simply a long, narrow lawn bordered with fragrant flower beds, with a thicket of trees to the rear.

The grass was already occupied by Mr. Russell, along with a couple of other familiar faces from Jane's party. Georgiana scanned them quickly and noted that Mr. Hawksley was not among them. She hadn't truly allowed herself to hope that he might be, the general idea being that it would help her weather the disappointment a little better, if it came.

It hadn't worked.

The men looked as if they had started a game of pall-mall and then suddenly found themselves too fatigued to continue and fallen where they stood, as they were lounging on blankets among the hoops, jackets off, some of them still holding their mallets as they laughed and drank. Frances held the bottle of wine over her head like a trophy as she made a beeline for Jeremiah.

Mr. Russell's hangers-on turned out to both be called James, and Georgiana immediately christened them James I and James II, based on their proximity to her. They didn't inconvenience themselves by looking up from their discussion about the various virtues of their horses to greet the newcomers. As she had no interest in competitive horse bragging, she seated herself with Cecily, Jonathan, and Jane, and ate with them in a companionable silence for a while until the rising volume of equine conversation interrupted their peace.

Jonathan nodded his head ever so slightly in the direction of both Jameses and rolled his eyes at them.

"I'll bet you five pounds they're secretly fucking their beloved horses," he said in a stage whisper.

Jane snorted. Georgiana, who had never heard such obscene swearing in all her life, felt hot with embarrassment for a second before remembering to smile.

"I can't take you up on that," Jane replied dryly. "The odds are tipped far too heavily in your favor." She leaned toward him and continued, sounding bored, "I'll wager you one further—I bet they're fucking their horses, and I bet their horses are all named after their mothers."

"He is handsome, though, Jane," said Cecily earnestly, seeming not to have heard them. She was gazing at the taller James, somehow immune to the embarrassment of admiring a man they had just named a horse-fucker.

"Don't let us hold you back, Ces, I'm sure he's as rich as God," said Jonathan. "Just give him a nip from me if he tries to feed you a carrot."

"Yes, or if he insists on keeping you in the outbuildings," added Jane.

"Or if he hits you with his *crop* when he wants you to move a little faster . . ."

Cecily was already gone, smoothing her dress and hair as she went to see if she could prove herself more interesting than a horse. James II looked her up and down appreciatively as she approached.

"You can hear what he's thinking," said Georgiana in a low voice. "*Sixteen and a half hands, strong teeth, back nicely curved and positioned for a saddle . . .*"

She and Jonathan fell about laughing, and Jane smirked. Jonathan opened his bottle of wine and drank straight from it, so Georgiana followed suit, knowing that if her aunt could see her now—lounging on the grass drinking with men she didn't know, unescorted, instead of flanked by responsible parents for a few days of brisk walking and high tea—she would promptly and quietly die of shame.

"This tastes like piss," Jonathan said, wincing.

Georgiana couldn't have told the difference between good and bad wine if her life depended on it and bore them all equally without really enjoying them. Jonathan's tastes, apparently being much more refined than hers, clearly could not be satisfied by what they had. He abruptly got up and walked back into the house in search of something with a better vintage, muttering something darkly about Christopher's taste as he went.

Left alone with Jane, Georgiana felt instantly uncomfortable. She struggled to make conversation with Frances's least loquacious friend even when part of a group; now, with what she knew—and what Jane *knew* she knew—she was unable to look her in the eye. She wanted to offer some variety of sympathy but somehow didn't imagine that would go down particularly well. The constant underlying air of hardness, of distance, made sense to her now; Jane seemed genuinely enamored of Frances— perhaps as much as Frances admired Jeremiah—and it must have been terrible to watch the two of them constantly engaged in what was tantamount to an upper-class mating ritual. Georgiana had always felt as if she had somehow garnered Jane's disapproval, but it occurred to her now that perhaps it was *life* that had disappointed her, causing her to find almost everything and everyone barely tolerable.

They both reached for their bottles of wine and drank deeply to fill the silence, and although it didn't breach the awkwardness of the moment, Georgiana felt bolstered by the thought that Jane might be experiencing some of the same discomfort she was. Any evidence of Jane's humanity was welcome at this point.

"I suppose this all seems terribly exciting," Jane said eventually, and Georgiana looked up.

"Oh! Yes, I suppose it is," she replied, trying very hard to look as if this weren't in fact the most exciting day of her life so far.

"Mmm," said Jane, clearly not fooled. "You do seem like a nice sort of girl." Somehow this didn't sound like a compliment.

"Thank you?" said Georgiana.

"I don't say so to flatter you," Jane said flatly. "I say so to *warn* you. You aren't from money—certainly not any significant money, anyway. This is all new to you. You should be sitting in a drab little parlor somewhere, keeping company with local girls until you're married off to a modest man with modest land, who keeps an elderly cook and one spotty maid to dress you and put pretty paste earrings in your ears."

Now Georgiana knew she was being insulted. She made to speak, but Jane continued.

"Again, please do not mistake my meaning. I don't say this to do you harm. I am simply laying out the facts. You would not be unhappy, I think, with an ordinary life befitting your station. Here—now—you have truly stumbled into the lion's den. The potential for unhappiness here is vast. Nobody here will be shamed or cast out for the many sins I'm sure they'll commit before Monday. There is almost nothing we can do that will not be excused because of our wealth, our standing. Our parentage. Can you say the same?"

Jane had delivered the entirety of this speech in a straightforward, confident tone; Georgiana felt like a scolded child, tears springing to her eyes unbidden, embarrassingly upset in the face of Jane's impassive expression. Whatever inner turmoil plagued Jane, Georgiana thought, it certainly did not excuse her being such a *toad*. Perhaps it came from a place of jealousy; Frances had been paying her far more attention than she did Jane, of late. After all, it was *Georgiana* Frances had come to call on to discuss the party, *Georgiana* who had been invited to stay at the house. She had learned Frances's secrets, and shared her bed, and held her as she cried in the dead of night. Perhaps their intimacy felt like a threat to Jane—a laughable and misplaced notion, considering that Frances was standing and giggling with Jeremiah Russell this very moment, letting him murmur things in her ear, wriggling with pleasure when he pulled an errant blade of grass from her hair.

Before she could begin to think of how to respond to this tirade, Frances was calling to her, approaching them radiating joyful exuberance.

"Come and play with us, George! We need another girl to make up the teams. Don't let our Jane bore you to death."

Georgiana let her friend pull her away and felt a jolt of cruel satisfaction at the thought of Jane watching them leave her behind.

The game that Frances needed her to join was so ridiculous that she was sure they must have invented it on the spot. The ladies were to climb onto the backs of the gentlemen, riding them as if they were ponies in cravats, and continue their game of pall-mall. When Frances demonstrated with Jeremiah, Georgiana saw with horror that it required the men to wrap their arms around the ladies' legs, and the ladies to grip the men between their thighs in return. Even through protective layers of skirt and petticoat, Georgiana blushed to see Jeremiah hoisting Frances so nonchalantly. Nobody else seemed the least bit shocked; Jeremiah looked exceedingly pleased with himself. Georgiana was beginning to suspect that this game was designed solely to give everybody involved a socially acceptable excuse to feel one another up.

Cecily was to ride her preferred James, and Georgiana realized with a sinking feeling that Frances intended Christopher for her steed. He reached out his arms to her and raised his eyebrows, and Georgiana shrank away involuntarily.

"Oh, come on, little Georgie," he said in a condescending voice that made her skin crawl. "I shan't misbehave, I'm broken in."

"I think . . . I'm actually still quite hungry, I think I'll go back inside—"

Georgiana's excuses were cut off by an exasperated Frances.

"Come on, George, don't be a stick in the mud. We can't very well play with just two pairs."

She was pouting, and Georgiana felt all eyes on her as they waited for her verdict. She didn't think it fair that *she* was being made out to be the ridiculous one, for not wanting to play a game in which a grown man was to pretend to be her horsey. Regardless, she didn't really have a choice in the matter; she sighed with frustration and felt thoroughly mortified as she walked over to Christopher and clumsily mounted him.

Georgiana had never had a man's hands on her legs, let alone on her thighs. She felt extremely hot under her dress, and her heart was beating so rapidly that she was sure Christopher must be able to feel it against his back. Cecily and Frances didn't seem at all perturbed and were laughing prettily as James II and Jeremiah rushed about the garden "practicing." The others were drawn in to hand up dropped mallets and keep score, and they played a quick, dirty game that seemed to have few to no rules.

It was a clear, warm day, and Georgiana could feel heat radiating through Christopher's back and see beads of sweat forming on the back of his neck above his collar. It was jarring to share a moment of such intimacy with somebody she hardly knew—especially when she so little liked what she did know about him.

They played miserably, mostly due to the fact that she was trying to touch Christopher as little as possible. When he tried to hitch her up more securely onto his back by grabbing higher, she gave him a swift knee to the ribs and he dropped her with a grunt.

"For God's sake, it's just a game!" he said, trying to sound jovial. There was an edge to his voice that made it clear that he felt she was not being a particularly good sport about it.

"It is just a game, isn't it, Christopher?" Georgiana said crossly. "And we seem to have lost."

While the others were distracted arguing over points and fouls, she dropped her mallet, picked up her bottle of wine from where it sat abandoned on the grass, and walked quickly away.

Chapter Eleven

THE NUMBER OF GUESTS AT THE COTTAGE SEEMED TO QUA-
druple between the hours of seven and eight o'clock in the evening. Georgiana lost track of names and faces; it had something
to do with the fact that she had drunk her entire bottle of wine
and made great headway with a second. They had whiled away
the afternoon so thoroughly that she was now sleepily off balance, struggling to distinguish between where her hand ended
and the sun-warmed lawn began. She had never before experienced inebriation like this—being too drunk to walk in a straight
line, or to mind that Jane was definitely still glaring at her, or to
take offense at the increasingly bawdy jokes of the men around
her, who thoroughly outnumbered the women.

As the sun finally went down, some of the more spirited gentlemen with energy to burn started challenging one another to
races. Georgiana sat up by the house and watched with Cecily,
who kept sighing and telling her about droll things James II had
said throughout the afternoon ("Oh! And he showed me his
pocket watch. He said it fell from a general's coat at Waterloo—it
even had a bit of French blood on it, it was lovely"). Georgiana
smiled and nodded—keeping her opinions about the utter medi-
ocrity of Mr. Russell's acquaintances to herself—as she surveyed
a garden dipped in the liquid gold of a sunset and felt a deep
sense of satisfaction at her current circumstances. She slipped
her shoes off, marveling at the fact that it didn't feel at all strange

to go stocking-footed among a party of strangers, like some kind
of . . . well, some kind of wild animal in stockings.

The only dampener was the lack of anybody attempting to woo
her with a blood-soaked French timepiece. Even Miss Woodley
had been spotted deep in conversation with a short, determined-
looking fellow who kept self-consciously adjusting his cravat in a
way that indicated that cantankerous, intimidating women were
his particular poison. She had asked around about Mr. Hawksley's attendance, once drunk enough to do so without embarrassment or subtlety, and had received a mixed response, so it
did not seem wise to hinge her enjoyment of the evening on the
anticipation of his arrival. Besides, she reasoned with herself, she
didn't need a man to have fun. She was having plenty of fun already, pretending to listen to Cecily.

She was *still* talking about James, and twenty minutes later,
Georgiana felt that the subject had been thoroughly exhausted.
She made vague excuses to Cecily that were hardly words—her
friend didn't notice, as the object of her affection had joined the
races and was currently bent into a most advantageous starting
position—and then she wandered into the house, looking for
something more to drink. She expected to find it empty, the evening too temperate for indoor activities, and paused when she
heard low voices emanating from farther down the narrowed,
darkened hallway.

"I know," somebody—*Frances*, Georgiana realized—was
murmuring. "I know. No matter what you may think of me, you
must know that I feel the same—but we can't do this now."

She stepped backward into Georgiana's eyeline, still looking
at whomever she had spoken to as she moved away from them.
When a hand reached out to stop her, Georgiana expected to see
Jeremiah at the other end of it.

It was Jane.

"When *shall* we do it, then?" she said, sneering and dismissive, her hand holding on to Frances's arm a little too tightly. "Let's just go. I don't want to be here. Come with me."

"Come on, Janey," Frances said gently, leaning in close and touching her fingertips to Jane's chin, her voice softened by wine. "We can't go over all this again. Just for fun, let's be realists."

"Let's not," said Jane fiercely, but Frances had pulled herself free and disappeared through a doorway. Jane followed her like a shadow.

Georgiana stumbled into the empty kitchen, barely remembering why she had sought it in the first place. Then she spotted the trapdoor that led to the wine cellar still open, the glow of a lamp below reassuring her that she wouldn't be descending into total darkness. She hitched up her skirts awkwardly to navigate the ladder and almost slipped as she felt her way down, swearing softly and then sighing aloud with relief when her feet hit the cool, rough flagstone floor below. She turned to inspect her options, wondering if Christopher's uncle's cellar might offer something with a less prodigious vintage but more palatable taste to wash down the conversation she had just overheard—and then let out a scream.

She wasn't alone in the cellar. A tall figure had emerged from the darkness almost as soon as she had alighted on the ground. He advanced into the lamplight—and was transformed.

Mr. Hawksley, summoned as if by sorcery by her thinking of him with such frequency, was standing before her, looking quite alarmed.

She clapped her hands over her mouth to cut off the scream that had issued from it and stared at him, hardly believing he was really there, raising his dark eyebrows at her. Having imagined him at least three dozen times since the church, she was surprised to find him a little shorter and less supernaturally beautiful than he had been in her mind. Nevertheless, he was still very pleasing to the eye, and more importantly, he really did seem to be standing there in front of her. He put his hand on her arm very briefly to steady her and she felt the solid warmth of him, proving his existence.

"My sincere apologies—I was sent to select something for a friend—I thought it best not to call out to you and startle you while you were . . . clambering."

He removed his hand. Georgiana missed it immediately.

"I wasn't clambering," she said with as much dignity as she could muster for a person who had been shrieking like a banshee moments before. "I was making a . . . a controlled descent."

"Ah, of course," said Mr. Hawksley politely. "My apologies. It looked for a moment like a clamber."

Georgiana suddenly remembered how thoroughly she had embarrassed herself during their last conversation and decided it might be best not to talk at all. She tucked a loose lock of hair behind her ear and walked past him with a wobbly determina- tion that wouldn't have been out of place on a moving ship. The shelves were lined with hundreds of bottles and casks of wine, and she pretended to cast a critical eye over them. She was keenly aware that she should not really be alone with a gentleman—even one of Mr. Hawksley's standing—in Uncle Crawley's sex cellar, of all places. Her heart was thrumming in her chest, but she could not pretend it was out of any sort of anguish at the impropriety of the situation.

The sounds of the party were muffled here, the lamplight flickering across the walls and dancing in the glass of the bottles, and Thomas Hawksley was watching as she ran her hand over a label to rid it of dust and squinted at hand-scrawled names and dates that meant nothing to her. She felt his gaze on the back of her neck like a physical touch.

"My apologies again for disturbing you," he said, his voice just as pleasantly deep as she remembered.

She looked back to see that he had already put a foot on the lowest rung of the ladder and was making to leave. He looked a little defeated, and Georgiana wondered if he had come down here to be alone.

"No," said Georgiana loudly, before she'd decided what to say next. "Er . . . Do you know anything about wine?"

"I know a little," he said, stepping back down, one hand still resting on the ladder as if he hadn't decided whether to stay.

"Excellent," she said, putting an arm to the wall to steady herself. "That means you know at least twice as much as I do and can rescue me from the shame of choosing something squeezed from . . . from inferior grapes, and bottled by some sort of terrible incompetent."

He smiled at this and came to stand next to her, arms crossed.

"What are your usual requirements, when it comes to wine?"

"Something light and not too heady," said Georgiana, feeling both of those things herself. "Something with the taste of . . . fruit, perhaps, or something floral."

"So essentially, you want something that tastes as little like wine as possible?" asked Mr. Hawksley, raising an eyebrow. "Have you considered a fruit cordial? Some light ale? Or perhaps some water? I can provide you with a delightful vintage, bottled from the well down the road yesterday. It has a light, watery bouquet followed by a pleasant, watery finish."

"You mock me, sir," said Georgiana, not minding a bit. "I am wounded."

"You are drunk," said Mr. Hawksley bluntly, and now Georgiana did feel a little hurt.

"Are you not?" she replied.

Before he answered, he, too, began to look through the shelves, running his hand lightly over the bottles as he searched. Georgiana felt the fine hair rising on her arms; it would be rather agreeable to be a bottle of Uncle Crawley's merlot at this particular moment.

"No," he said eventually, bending to look closer in the gloom. "I have had exactly two glasses of wine—very good wine, it must be said—but I have no need for a further, especially if I am to be climbing ladders, assisting ladies in their choice of libations, et cetera."

"Oh," said Georgiana, giving up any pretense of looking for wine herself and instead watching him as he explored. "I have had . . . more than two glasses."

She found herself admiring his hand again. Large, with short, even nails, the pads of his fingers perhaps a little gently callused from riding—but most attractive in the surety with which it traveled.

"Yes," said Mr. Hawksley, as if there were no need for her to state something so obvious.

Georgiana swayed a little on her feet again and struggled to right herself.

Mr. Hawksley looked round at her and frowned. "Miss Ellers?"

Hearing him say her name was so deliciously distracting that she almost forgot to reply.

"Oh . . . I'm fine. Just getting my sea legs, you know. This is only perhaps the third or fourth time I've continued past the bottom of a bottle."

"Ah," said Mr. Hawksley, as if this explained a lot, looking at her for a moment longer before turning back to the wine. "And have these occasions happened to coincide with time spent in the company of Miss Campbell?"

Georgiana narrowed her eyes at him. "And what if they did?"

Mr. Hawksley found a bottle that seemed to hold promise and pulled it from its resting place, blowing gently to dissipate its fine shroud of dust.

"I only ask because I have observed that she and her friends often seem to be operating under the influence of various . . . substances."

"It is not some sort of requirement of her friendship," said Georgiana, frowning.

"Yes. Well," he said, presenting her with the bottle. "It is none of my business, of course. I just thought you seemed like you might be in need of . . . Anyway, this is a white wine, from Bourgogne."

Georgiana reached for the bottle, but—her hand-eye coordination being more than a little off—managed to drop it immediately. It hit the floor with a thud, and they both looked down to see if it had broken. It seemed intact. In unison, they bent to pick it up, and in a last-ditch attempt to avoid colliding with Mr. Hawksley's head, Georgiana veered wildly to the side and ended up hitting him anyway and knocking them both to the ground.

The air was forced from her lungs by the impact of her chest against Mr. Hawksley's shoulder, and for quite a few seconds all she could do was wheeze attractively. He let out a little pained huff of breath, sat up quickly, and grasped her gently by the upper arm and the small of her back to help guide her into a sitting position. For what felt like a deliciously long moment his hands held her, and she felt strangely hot at every small point of contact, as if he had taken them straight out of a furnace to touch her.

She'd been touched before. She'd been steered into rooms, walked arm in arm, shared chaste—or at least, *mostly* chaste—kisses. Christopher had just been touching her *legs,* for goodness' sake, and it also wasn't as if she had never felt Thomas Hawksley's hands on her before—unfortunately, she was making a habit of performing ill-advised amateur acrobatics in his presence. Despite all this, somehow this touch—alone in the cellar, in the semidarkness, with wine on her tongue and scuffs on her dress—was nothing like any of the ones that had come before it.

Even if *she* had abandoned all sense of propriety long ago, he had not. He looked quite mortified by the prolonged contact, retracting his hand from her bare skin and starting to mutter apologies. Too drunk to restrain herself from her baser instincts, too desperate to know how it would feel, Georgiana reached out and took his retreating hand in her own.

He did not resist. His palm was cool and dry, but she could feel the calluses she had imagined before, an infinitesimal amount of drag against her skin. They were sitting extraordinarily close together—she could have counted each of the long lashes that framed his dark eyes. She was still winded, which accounted for her erratic breathing; he had not been winded at all, so there was no logical explanation for the rapid rise and fall of his chest. She could actually *feel* his breath, hot against her cheek.

It occurred to Georgiana that she very much wanted to kiss him, and she was horrified to discover that she actually might follow through; she felt thrilled to her core and slightly sick all at once just thinking of it. She tugged gently on his hand to pull him toward her and close the gap between them—and then suddenly a shout came from above them and she pushed away from him, feeling as shocked and ashamed as a rutting dog doused in cold water in the street. There were more shouts—they were more distant than they had seemed at first but still far too close for comfort—and, the wine forgotten, Georgiana sprang to her feet and pulled herself shakily up the ladder, not daring to look back to see if Thomas Hawksley was following as she went.

Chapter Twelve

GEORGIANA EMERGED INTO THE KITCHEN AND FOLLOWED the source of the commotion until she reached the doors that led to the garden patio, where Christopher, not sounding entirely serious, was shouting, "Is there a doctor in the house?" while waving a lit candle above his head like a distress beacon.

"What on earth has happened?" asked Georgiana as he passed her.

"Ces is dying," he slurred, alcohol thick on his breath. "It's . . . most unfortunate."

"What?" cried Georgiana in alarm, looking about. "Where is she?"

"She's in the parlor, poor duck," he said. He squinted at her and leaned a little too close to her face for comfort. "Are *you* a doctor?"

"No," said Georgiana firmly, pushing him away and heading back inside to the small parlor at the front of the house.

Cecily did indeed seem to be in a state of some distress. She was lying on the sofa in a tangle of long, pale limbs, pink muslin, and golden hair, which had come partially undone throughout the course of the evening, and she looked frightfully gray. Jane was sitting by her side, holding what seemed to be a chamber pot. Horsey James, Georgiana noted, was nowhere to be seen—and neither was Frances.

As she watched, Jane put a comforting hand on her friend's

forehead and stroked her hair away from her temple. This tenderness still seemed so out of character to Georgiana that she hardly knew what to think. Jane leaned down and muttered something in Cecily's ear; Cecily responded by pitching suddenly forward and retching into the proffered chamber pot, instantly demonstrating its part in the proceedings. Whatever was coming out of her mouth was so dark it looked black, which wasn't a particularly encouraging color for somebody's insides to be.

"She's poisoned herself," said a voice from behind Georgiana's left ear.

She jumped but recovered quickly. Mr. Hawksley had come into the room after her. She imagined that he had probably lingered a little longer in the cellar for the sake of decency, both to allow her time to climb the ladder without accidentally getting a glimpse up her skirts, and so that nobody saw them exiting a confined underground space together.

"Poisoned?" asked Georgiana, unable to meet his eyes.

"Yes. By the consumption of large quantities of alcohol," he said, similarly unable to meet hers.

She noticed that he was holding the bottle of wine she had abandoned; it seemed inappropriate, given the circumstances, and he placed it awkwardly on a side table.

"Well deduced," Jane said sarcastically, wincing as Cecily demonstrated the point by vomiting again. "She usually gets it all out of her system on her own within a few hours."

"She needs a doctor," said Mr. Hawksley firmly. "She's unwell. My carriage is outside, I hadn't intended to stay long. I will take her."

"You?" Jane asked sharply. "She's *my* friend, and to be quite honest, I don't really know you."

"I can assure you that she will be in safe hands. There's a doctor in the village—it's but half an hour from here. I will deliver her myself."

"Fine," said Jane. "I'm coming, too."

"Fine. Will you . . . ?"

He gestured at Cecily's limp form, and Georgiana hurriedly stepped forward to help Jane. Between them, they managed to heave Cecily to her feet and maneuver her outside, where Mr. Hawksley did indeed have a man and a carriage waiting. Having deposited her friend and given a half-hearted wave goodbye to Jane and Mr. Hawksley—both of whom ignored her—Georgiana stood in the dark driveway watching them pull away with a strange sense of anticlimax. She eyed the hazardous front step of the cottage and briefly considered tripping over it to necessitate her own visit to the doctor, but then sighed and went back inside, her mind fixed on the bottle of wine awaiting her in the parlor.

Now that there was no chance of another surprise encounter with a certain dark-haired gentleman—and with the dramatics of Cecily's poisoning behind her—Georgiana's interest in the party was beginning to wane. This could have been easily remedied if she could locate Frances, but her friend had been missing in action for quite some time now. She felt a little abandoned; Frances, after all, had invited her here, and there was this nagging feeling of being left out of the *real* fun if she was not by her side. Frances radiated a kind of energy that drew all around her closer, made her the center of every party, every conversation, every orbit. Without her, Georgiana was left adrift.

She wandered between scattered groups, clutching the bottle of white wine, taking little sips from it and treasuring this small connection to Mr. Hawksley. She *did* like it, and in her well-lubricated state this made her feel as if he must truly understand some key facet of her being.

It must have been past midnight when she was called over to a group by name, and she didn't hesitate to join them, feeling flattered that her presence was being specifically requested. When it turned out to be Christopher who had called to her, the feeling abated a little, but Jonathan was there, too, so she took her place in a circle of partygoers who seemed to be engaged in some sort of drinking game.

"The game is Confessions," Jonathan explained. He wasn't slurring his speech like Christopher, but he was still clearly very well liquored. "Somebody confesses something *dreadful,* and if you, too, have partaken in the dastardly deed, you drink."

A pretty redheaded girl next to Christopher was taking her turn.

"I confess to . . . er . . . breaking a family heirloom. And passing the blame to my mother's maid."

Everybody around the circle drank. Georgiana's wine was left untouched.

"Oh, come now," said Christopher, sounding scandalized for the wrong reasons. "Is that the worst you've got? Absolutely *pathetic.* I 'borrowed' my father's favorite horse when I was twelve and broke the poor beast's leg on an ill-advised jump. Father shot it himself—closest I've ever seen the old bastard come to weeping. I blamed it on a servant's boy. I thought he might shoot the gormless little lad, too, but he just dismissed them both."

Everyone laughed. Georgiana did not.

"All right, Georgie, it's your turn," said Christopher, and she had the uncomfortable feeling of every eye on her, greedily awaiting something salacious. Her mind was completely, impossibly blank; luckily, Jonathan saved her.

"Leave the poor thing alone, she's new to this," he said crossly, probably just for the joy of berating Christopher. "*I* confess to stealing an afternoon of kisses from a pretty little thing who works in the Campbells' stables. The smell of horse shit, though pungent, did nothing to dampen our ardor."

Everybody laughed, and Georgiana wondered how many knew that the Campbells only employed stable boys.

"Stolen kisses, then—come on. Drink up, you miserable harlots."

To her surprise, almost everybody drank—even the women. Georgiana was once again astounded at the extent to which the rules *really* did not seem to apply to these people. To kiss somebody you were not engaged to—somebody whom you were not in any way promised to beyond that night—and flaunt it so flagrantly would have been the end of her at home, or in her aunt and uncle's regular circles. She had always imagined that the same rules applied to all, that all characters were judged equally, but she supposed that some sort of agreement of secrecy existed among this particular class of people. They did not seem to think any less of one another for it. After all, if *everybody* had been running amok, kissing whoever they pleased—how could they? And how could you ever restrict your potential future partners to those who had remained ideologically pure and not engaged in any of this illicit kissing, if it were as common as catching a cold?

Christopher had noticed that she wasn't taking a drink.

"Goodness, a *saint* walks among us," he drawled unkindly. "I'm sure we can find someone to remedy that tonight, Georgie."

"Has anyone ever told you that you sound *exactly* like those men who sit in the back of brothels, leering and sweating and parceling out the women to scabby customers?" Jonathan said scathingly.

"What were *you* doing in that sort of brothel, Smith?" Christopher spat back. "Trying to cure yourself of your terrible ailment?"

The mood thus ruined, the game abruptly ended, and Georgiana was back on her feet again, now simply looking for a place to hide until it was quiet enough to go to bed. It was strangely claustrophobic to have her bedtime dictated by the whims of other people. She was feeling the unsettling combination of drunk and sick that comes from imbibing over a long period of time and would have swapped all the wine in the cellar for a quiet, comfortable place to rest her head.

Eventually she found an uninhabited corner of the garden where she could sit on a stone wall with her back against a tree trunk, mostly obscured, and watch in a detached sort of way as the party dwindled. It was not lost on her that, even surrounded by precisely the right people, at a party she never could have imagined in her wildest dreams just a few short weeks ago, she was once again hiding and hoping to remain unbothered.

If she couldn't be alone with Mr. Hawksley, she could do the next best thing and be alone with her *thoughts* of Mr. Hawksley. The rational part of her mind, which had been absent for most of the evening, told her that a man like him could never truly be interested in her. He was too kind to snub her outright, as others at this party might, but that did not indicate anything more than basic good manners. It *certainly* did not indicate attraction. Even if he *was* attracted to her—and Georgiana had really believed for a moment there, as they sat together in the near-dark of the cellar, that her feelings might be reciprocated—perhaps despite his moralizing about drunkenness and his outward displays of geniality, he was really just the same as his wealthy peers. Perhaps he would have kissed her, or let himself be kissed, and then forgotten it the next day, or moved on come the next party—just a story to be retold during the next round of Confessions. But it was no use obsessing over the meaning of a kiss that hadn't even happened. She hardly knew the man—even if he did have excellent taste in wine.

She was deep in thought when somebody sat down next to her, jolting her mentally and physically out of her reverie. She thought it must be Frances and felt pleased at being discovered—but when she turned, she saw Christopher Crawley leering at her, his shirt now almost completely undone and hanging from his frame.

"Hiding, are we?" he slurred, leaning toward her and putting his hand on her thigh.

Georgiana moved away from him, but only succeeded in backing herself farther into the corner.

"I'm not interested, thank you, Christopher," she said, attempting to remove his hand from her leg.

"It's not a proposal of marriage, Georgie." He smirked at her, half of his face lit by the nearby lamps and the other half in darkness. "There's no need to take it so seriously."

Sluggish as she was, Georgiana was starting to feel panic flaring in the recesses of her mind. They were quite well hidden, and Christopher's grip on her was surprisingly strong for somebody so drunk. He was leaning in closer to her, but somehow she felt she could not cry out—she could not make an embarrassing fuss, especially as she was at *his* house, surrounded by *his* friends—but he smelled so strongly of whiskey and pipe smoke and pungent perfume that she thought she might vomit. Her heart was pounding uncomfortably, which felt ridiculous; he wasn't hurting her— her life was not at stake—and yet she felt as if it were, her every nerve screaming at her to run as she sat frozen in his grasp.

Just as she thought it was actually going to happen—she was going to be kissed by this repellent man who had laid claim to her so casually—she saw Frances staggering from the house, and called out her name.

Frances turned toward the sound, and Georgiana could immediately tell that something was terribly wrong. Her face was contracted in a horrible rictus, her eyes unfocused as she stumbled toward them. Christopher had been surprised enough by her exclamation to let go of her, and she took the opportunity to push past him and rush to her friend's side.

She reached her at the same time that Jonathan did, and they both saw that Frances was shivering uncontrollably. He immediately removed his jacket and put it around her shoulders, steering her back to the corner Georgiana had just vacated; mercifully, Christopher had disappeared.

"What on earth, Franny?" Jonathan asked with genuine concern. "Have you taken something?"

"No. I mean, yes," she slurred. "But that's not . . . I . . . Something happened—but I need your help, I need . . . Oh *God*, we must go back inside." She was suddenly insistent, sounding almost frightened, but still smiling that terrible, stiff smile.

"All right—inside? We can go inside," said Georgiana, exchanging a confused look with Jonathan. "Where inside, Frances?"

"I'll show you," she said.

Jonathan put an arm around her, clearly holding at least half her weight as they walked. Frances directed them upstairs and along the narrow landing to a bedroom lit by a single lamp, where they helped her to sit down on the edge of the four-poster.

Frances did seem very drunk, but this wasn't unusual. What was genuinely alarming was the fact that she looked half-dead and completely stunned; Georgiana was reminded of descriptions she had read in books of those who had seen battle. It was so strange to see her light thus dimmed that Georgiana could think of nothing to say, simply rubbing her arm as Jonathan left to fetch her a drink, returning with gin in one hand and ale in the other. He handed them both to Georgiana and firmly shut the door behind him.

"Go on," said Jonathan, taking the ale and pressing it insistently into Frances's hands. She looked at it, barely seeming to comprehend what it was. "What is it? What happened?"

"You mustn't tell anybody," she said. Suddenly her expression grew fierce, and she looked at them both in turn. "You must swear it. You must not let it leave this room."

They both agreed. Frances let out a sigh.

"I was with Jeremiah. He said he didn't want to waste his time in the company of anybody else. He only *came* because he knew I'd be here. I thought he truly cared for me, but now I am sure of it—oh, I suppose he's my fiancé now!"

"Oh, Frances!" Georgiana cried. "How wonderful! He proposed?"

"Well . . . not in so many words, exactly," Frances replied, smiling down at the hands that clasped her cup of ale. "But that's a formality. We are promised to each other now."

Jonathan, who had been sitting next to her on the bed, got up at these words. He looked suddenly furious, and Georgiana could not understand why.

"Franny—look at me." She did not. He reached down and took the cup from her hands, and she looked up then, still smiling that strange, pained smile. "What *happened*?"

There was a long silence. The feeling of wrongness—that something terrible had happened—weighed heavily on Georgiana, but she didn't yet understand what was causing so much apprehension. They were almost engaged? They were *promised* to each other? What was so bad about that?

"Jonathan, don't look at me like that," Frances said, and Georgiana was horrified to see tears gathering in her eyes and spilling slowly and steadily down her cheeks, her voice cracking even though her tone was light. "We'll be engaged by Sunday! It's all going to be *fine*."

Her hands were shaking so much that Georgiana gathered them both up in her own, just so she didn't have to see them behaving so pitifully.

She still didn't understand.

"Where?" asked Jonathan, in a voice like thunder. "*Here?*"

"No." She nodded toward a door Georgiana hadn't noticed before, opposite the bed. "That's why . . . I need your help. There was some—well, I tried, but I couldn't get it out. I don't know why."

She laughed suddenly, and it sounded harsh and strange with tears still wet on her face. "But my damned hands won't stop shaking." She stopped laughing abruptly. "He said . . . He said he wanted us to be *together*."

"Is that what you wanted?" Jonathan replied. He certainly wasn't laughing.

"Perhaps . . . Perhaps not now. Not like this. But it did seem silly to make a fuss, Jonathan, when we know what we plan to do. He said so, Jonathan. He said we'll be married soon, so what's the difference?"

Georgiana looked at her in genuine horror. Comprehension was finally dawning on her. Jonathan crossed the room in a few strides and opened the adjoining door. It was dark beyond the doorway, so Georgiana picked up the lamp and followed him inside, the flickering light illuminating a very small dressing room.

There was blood smeared on the edge of the dressing table. Splashes on the white marble of the tabletop—small drops soaking into the floorboards and the rug. Georgiana could see where Frances had tried to remove it but had only succeeded in spreading it around. Three bloody fingerprints on the mirror. Georgiana put the lamp down on the windowsill, fighting a wave of nausea, and Jonathan left the room without a word, returning quickly with cloth dark enough to disguise any marks and a pitcher of water that had been left by the bed.

Georgiana and Jonathan worked quickly together in silence, scrubbing the surfaces, doing what they could for the deeper stains until they were just anonymous smudges of indeterminate color. When they were done, Georgiana took the lamp and they went back into the bedroom to find Frances curled up on the bed fast asleep, looking far smaller and more breakable than Georgiana had ever seen her.

Jonathan sighed heavily, sitting down on the floor at the foot of the bed and taking a deep swig from the untouched gin. He handed it up to Georgiana, who sat down beside him.

"She's living in a fantasy," he said quietly, leaning against the bed, looking exhausted. Georgiana didn't know it was possible to convey such venom with a whisper, but somehow he managed it. "He's not going to propose. He's a conceited little shit with a reputation. She likes to think she's special, that it's different for her, but it's not. She's just another silly girl in a long, long line of silly girls."

Georgiana felt this was rather unsympathetic for a man who had moments before been cleaning up his best friend's blood.

"She seems . . . shaken," she whispered back. "What if she truly didn't want this, Jonathan?"

Jonathan exhaled sharply through his nose.

"Even if she didn't, who would believe it? Who's going to believe she didn't want him, unchaperoned at this party, alone with him in an upstairs room? What if she's *with child*, Georgiana?"

Georgiana stared at him hopelessly.

"I suppose . . . I suppose if she isn't, there's a chance she'll get away with this," Jonathan said, closing his eyes and scrubbing a hand across his face. "Jeremiah may talk, but it may not go beyond schoolboy bragging. Perhaps people will think he's lying. She might even be able to marry someone else before it gets out, if she acts fast. She's not some *farm girl*, Georgiana, she's . . . She's *Frances Campbell*. Jesus *Christ*."

"And if she *is* with child?" Georgiana breathed.

"Then I very sincerely hope I'm wrong, and Jeremiah Russell isn't an unendurable fuckwit, and he's left posthaste to ride through the night and prise his grandmother's ring from her finger so he can come back and propose tomorrow."

When Jonathan phrased it like that, the prospect did not seem particularly likely.

"What do we do?"

"We say absolutely nothing to absolutely no one. We hope that Jeremiah Russell is shooting blanks, and we pray very hard that he takes an unfortunate tumble off his horse tomorrow and isn't found for at least twenty-four hours," he said darkly. "Come on. I'm going to see if he's still here."

"I'll stay," said Georgiana, not wanting to leave Frances and suddenly exceedingly tired of everyone and everything. Jonathan shrugged, patted her shoulder distractedly, and then exited.

Georgiana lowered herself onto the bed as gently as she could and arranged her limbs so that she would not disturb Frances, whose face was pressed into her clenched fists, thinking she'd almost certainly be lying awake until dawn, and then falling asleep almost at once.

Chapter Thirteen

GEORGIANA WOKE UP LATE THE NEXT MORNING WITH A pounding headache and a very strange, bitter taste in her mouth. She sat up fully clothed, looking around through bleary eyes to find that Frances was no longer in the room. She entered the dressing room, trying and failing not to think about what had transpired there the night before as she cleaned her face and combed her hair through with her fingers, attempting to pin as much of it back up as she could by herself. She couldn't help but stare at a dark stain on the rug by her feet.

What had it been like? Had he used force? Was it usual, that amount of blood? Had she enjoyed it? Had *he* enjoyed it? Had she led him in here herself, given in to her instincts like Georgiana nearly had in the cellar? Had it felt just like that—pleasant sparks of sensation, shortness of breath, a racing heart? Or had she been trapped like prey, pushed into a corner, leaving a trail of blood behind like a wounded animal?

Her brief toilette complete, Georgiana went downstairs in search of Frances. She was surprised to see everybody up and dressed; most of the guests had departed during the night, leaving just a handful behind. They were sitting at a long table in the garden, eating a large array of breakfast foods that had clearly arrived just before Georgiana had. Most surprisingly of all, Cecily and Jane were with them, Cecily looking drawn and exhausted but smiling nonetheless as she picked at a boiled egg. Christopher, she noticed, wasn't eating anything at all. He had his head in his hands and looked barely conscious, but she sat down as far away from him as was possible anyway.

"Are you all right?" Georgiana asked Cecily as she took a place opposite her. She also wanted to direct the same question at Frances, who was currently laughing at something Jeremiah was saying as if nothing at all had happened between them.

"Oh, yes," said Cecily. "Thomas found me a doctor. Jane said he pounded on every door until he found the right one, and went and woke the poor man up. I don't remember that part. He made me eat something ghastly, and I got up whatever it was that was making me so ill. I had a *terrible* stomach upset."

"Yes," said Jane, rolling her eyes. "A stomach upset. Must have been something you ate."

"Oh, hush, Jane. Thomas was wonderful. He was due somewhere else today but he stayed with me at the doctor's until I was feeling better, and then he brought us back here just before dawn."

"Careful." Frances's voice cut across the table; Georgiana hadn't realized she was listening. "You'll make poor George jealous."

"Don't be silly," said Georgiana, attempting a laugh.

Truthfully, she *was* a little jealous. Of course it was wonderful that Mr. Hawksley had taken care of Cecily. Of course he should have stayed with Jane and Cecily until the latter was feeling better; he could hardly have left them alone at a strange doctor's house in the middle of nowhere. And of course Cecily could call Mr. Hawksley "Thomas" if she wished, even though the easy familiarity made Georgiana want to grind her teeth into dust.

The real issue was that Cecily was so beautiful that Greek gods probably would have thrown themselves willingly onto pikes for the chance to see her unclothed shoulder, and there was absolutely no chance Mr. Hawksley hadn't noticed. Even in the midst of copious vomiting, she'd given off an air of grace and delicacy that Georgiana couldn't have mastered in a thousand years of trying. Perhaps Mr. Hawksley liked his women pale and sickly, fainting against him at the doctor's, instead of obstinate and bold in the wine cellar? Perhaps it was alluring, to look as Cecily had last night—as if you were already laid out at the mortuary, ready for embalming.

"I'm glad you're all right, Cecily," Georgiana said with some effort, reaching for the eggs herself.

She caught Jonathan's eyes across the table—they were really only half-open as he leaned on his elbow, looking as if he hadn't gone to bed at all—and he rolled them in Frances's direction before tucking into his own breakfast.

Everybody was rather subdued all day. Cecily seemed to have given up on her previous conquest, and both of the Jameses sat with Christopher and Jeremiah in the shade of an apple tree for most of the afternoon, playing cards and losing outrageous amounts of money to one another. Georgiana could tell that Frances wanted to go over to Mr. Russell and engage him in conversation or invite him to be alone with her elsewhere; she kept laughing a little too loudly at things that weren't particularly funny and shooting sidelong glances at him from where they sat on the patio. He ignored all of this, only responding when she spoke to him directly, and doing so with perfect, painful cordiality.

Frances did not seem outwardly concerned, but Georgiana noticed that her fingers kept beating a drum on whatever surface they alighted on, a sure sign that she was keenly aware of his absence. Georgiana desperately wanted to speak to her alone but did not manage to do so all that afternoon; Frances and Jonathan were inseparable, and drinking again, making up limericks and being insufferable to all but each other. Instead, she had to sit and listen to Cecily extolling the virtues of her dear friend "Thomas," until she wanted to go back down to the cellar and scream where nobody could hear her.

"He is just what a young man ought to be, don't you agree, Jane?"

Jane gave a "Hmmph," which could have signified agreement or disapproval. She had been stony-faced and impressively dead behind the eyes all day.

"So thoughtful. So kind," Cecily went on. "I know he can be a little dull, but I think what happened with his brother has given him a sort of sensitivity—and an inclination to be *sensible*—that so many men seem to lack."

"What happened with his brother?" asked Georgiana, torn between wanting Cecily to shut her perfectly formed, beautiful mouth and wanting to know anything more there was to know about Mr. Hawksley.

"He died just a few years ago—he was the younger brother. James told me yesterday. Oh, he was making some terrible snide remark about how it had made Thomas *boring*—such a dreadful thing to say. So sad, to lose family so young."

"How did he die?" asked Georgiana, trying to sound no more than casually interested.

"You know, I'm not sure. James didn't say. An illness, I think. I'm sure it must have affected Thomas quite keenly."

Georgiana, never having had a sibling, could not ever understand the loss of one. It had been bad enough losing her parents to a better climate, but at least they might return, or invite her to tea, however unlikely either possibility seemed at present; death was so unsettlingly permanent. She could not begin to imagine how it might affect her to lose her family forever—how "boring" she might become to those around her.

"Anyway, he knew there was a doctor in the village because his house actually isn't too far from here. I've heard it's magnificent, I wonder if he would ever—"

"Are you *still* talking about bloody Mr. *Hawksley*?" Frances asked, distracted from giggling with Jonathan. "Did he *give* you his carriage, Ces? Did he catch your vomit in his cupped hands, so as not to waste a drop? Did he pull down his breeches and show you his solid gold—"

"All right, all right, I was only saying," said Cecily reproachfully.

Georgiana laughed along with the others, grateful to Frances for putting a stop to Cecily's endless exclamations of admiration.

They passed the rest of the day quietly. At one point almost everybody fell asleep, woken only when Christopher slipped from his chair and hit the ground with an angry shout of fear, which roused them all in a panic that quickly turned to laughter. He did not seem to enjoy being mocked and stalked off into the house to nap somewhere else. Georgiana felt some part of her unclench as he went, still feeling his hand on her thigh as if he had bruised her.

He hadn't. She'd checked.

It was much more pleasant to reminisce about Mr. Hawksley's hands on her—although the more she did, the more she came to realize she had practically thrown herself at the poor man, who had probably volunteered to take Cecily just to get away from her brazen advances. In the pleasant space halfway between wakefulness and sleep as they all dozed in the garden, Georgiana carefully rewrote the narrative; she imagined that he might return to the house later that night, ostensibly to check on Cecily's wellbeing, but really to see her again. He'd catch her eye and tell them all that he was going for another bottle of wine—code that only she would understand—and she'd steal away to meet him in the darkness of the cellar, his hands on hers the moment she set foot on solid ground. He'd tell her he could not stop thinking about her, that the musty smell of a cellar would make him burn for her for as long as he lived. He'd say that Cecily was beautiful, but a touch *too* pretty, and that he much preferred brunettes of average height with a tendency to let their mouths run away from them. The frisson she had felt between them the night before would return—real, not imagined—but this time there would be no interruptions. He'd take her in his arms, and brush her hair aside, and kiss her.

And then what? She could not imagine what would happen next. Certainly not what had transpired between Frances and Jeremiah. And she couldn't imagine a proposal, either. No—the fantasy ended there, and she had to start again from the beginning. Luckily, replaying it was not too much of a hardship; the part where they kissed was a particular favorite of hers.

When evening came and they all went upstairs to wash properly and dress for dinner, Georgiana seized her chance and followed Frances into her room, closing the door behind them.

"Are you—how are you, Frances?" she asked, sitting down on the edge of the bed as Frances crossed to the adjoining room, sat down at the dressing table apparently without self-consciousness, and considered herself in the mirror. The sun was setting and the room glowed pleasantly, the pinkish light burnishing Frances's dark curls.

"How am I? I'm fine," Frances said casually, unpinning her hair and beginning to comb it out carefully in short, even strokes.

"But . . . are you upset, about what happened? Do you want to talk about it?"

"Upset? Why should I be upset? You sweet thing, George. I know Jonathan hates him, but Jeremiah isn't the cad he makes him out to be. He's good, you know. He's honorable. He simply doesn't want to propose surrounded by this dreadful rabble, and I can hardly blame him. Imagine agreeing to be his wife at *Bastards' Cottage*." She put the comb down and uncorked a bottle of a sweet-smelling oil, rubbing a little between her fingers before smoothing it through her hair. "In all honesty, I think Jonathan may be a little jealous. It's sad."

"Jealous?" asked Georgiana. "But I thought—"

"Oh, not in *that* way, of course. But he and I are thick as thieves and have been for a long time. You've seen how we are together. I think he sees Jeremiah's gain as his loss. I can hardly be gallivanting about the countryside with Jonathan if I'm Mrs. *Jeremiah Russell,* can I?"

"I suppose not," said Georgiana, watching as Frances expertly twisted her hair up and pinned it into place. "Frances, I . . . What about Jane?"

Her friend stiffened minutely, then placed her hairpins down on the table in front of her.

"What about her?" she asked slowly.

"You know I saw you, Frances. I'm sorry, I didn't mean to, but . . . I did. And I don't know what it was, or what it means, but I do know that Jane—she seems quite upset."

Frances laughed, shaking her head. "Georgiana, what do you think you saw? Have you never had a friendship like that? We're young. It's summer! We were drinking, we were . . . It doesn't *mean* anything."

Georgiana wasn't quite sure that they could write off all of their behavior as youthful summer indiscretions anymore past the age of twenty but held her tongue.

"It's a little tradition of ours, the fair—mine and Jane's, I mean, since we were children. But that is all it is. A bit of . . . summer nostalgia. Jane, *upset.* Imagine." She was pinning her hair again with firm precision. "What a thing to think of, honestly—especially now, with everything that's happened with Jeremiah . . ." She trailed off, studying herself in the glass with a smile that didn't quite reach her eyes.

Georgiana came to stand behind Frances, looking down at her hands so she would not see her reflection as she spoke.

"What was it . . . *like* with him, Frances?"

She had been trying very hard not to ask this question but found it impossible; Frances was now the oracle of what went on beyond locked doors with handsome young men.

Her friend was opening a small pot of carmine now and applying it to her lips with a light hand. When she was finished she turned her head from side to side, admiring the effect in the glass.

"It was . . . Well, I can't tell you *everything*," she said with an air of worldly knowledge. "You have to experience it to know. Parts of it were . . . awkward—you should have *seen* the expressions on his face, he looked positively *possessed*—but I felt very close to him. Very exposed, but . . . But I feel now that I can trust him completely. And he *was* kind, after. He only left me because I told him to go, so we wouldn't be discovered together. You needn't look so worried, and you certainly shouldn't pay Jonathan any mind—I'm not sorry it happened. He really is a gentleman, George."

"If you're sure," said Georgiana, hoping dearly that Frances was right and Jonathan wrong—that they would both dance at her wedding before the year was out. The alternative was too terrible to consider.

"I'm sure. Sit—I'll do your hair," Frances said kindly.

Georgiana took her place on the stool, enjoying the intimate feeling of deft fingers in her hair and the gentle pull of the comb as Frances worked.

"Cecily was in raptures over your Mr. Hawksley," she said as she brushed. "Christ, you'd think he'd personally brought her back from the dead, the way she carries on."

"He's not *my* Mr. Hawksley," said Georgiana, but her tone of voice betrayed her true feelings, and Frances laughed.

"Don't take it to heart—poor Ces is just too foolish to know better. She doesn't realize she's hurting your feelings. I don't think anyone has ever managed to hurt hers, so she can't empathize.

She seems to float through life, absorbing its blows, bouncing off to the next thing when something falls through. It's charming, in a way—but extremely aggravating when you're collateral damage."

Georgiana had thought Frances a little unkind to Cecily in the past, but this assessment of her character was cheering her mightily. Whatever Mr. Hawksley was, he certainly wasn't a fool, and she didn't think he'd suffer foolishness in a partner. Even one as tall and slender and helplessly beautiful as a tree sapling.

"I'm not sure he likes me at all," Georgiana said aloud. "It's so hard to tell. And then, even if he did . . . Well, I'm hardly a catch."

She was reluctant to draw too much attention to this; after all, she imagined that her friendship with Frances relied entirely on her friend not thinking too hard about how much she outranked her.

"Oh, I don't think that matters," said Frances dismissively.

They both knew this to be patently untrue, but Georgiana was happy to pretend otherwise, both when it came to any imagined relationship with Mr. Hawksley and her current, very real relationship with Frances, who was currently putting the final pins in her hair.

"There. You're as pretty as a show pony. Go and change your dress and we can play a drinking game at dinner—take a *very* big sip every time Cecily says the name *Thomas*."

The rest of the trip passed without incident. They drank quite a lot with dinner on Saturday, and Jonathan treated them to a performance of increasingly filthy stories as the evening drew on, but they were too exhausted to do much more than laugh at him and sporadically refill their glasses. Christopher left Georgiana alone, nursing such a terrible hangover that he constantly wore an expression of acute pain. Frances's reprimand had worked, and Cecily did not treat them to verse twenty-seven of the many virtues of Mr. Hawksley.

Georgiana staggered up to bed that night feeling tired but on the whole rather happy. The niggling worries and concerns that had plagued her all day were nothing compared to the feeling of belonging—the memories of her friends laughing at her jokes and refilling her glass, of being enclosed on all sides by people who truly wanted her.

On Sunday, after a late breakfast, the carriages arrived. The front drive was suddenly a busy metropolis, with servants crossing back and forth carrying trunks, and horses snorting and stamping their hooves, impatient to be away. Georgiana lingered on the threshold of the cottage, wondering if she was crossing it for the last time or if it would become familiar to her, part of the tapestry of summers to come—until Frances grew tired of waiting and called for her to hurry up. While the others slumped down in their seats, clearly settling in to sleep all the way home, Georgiana craned her neck to look back, watching as the house grew smaller and eventually disappeared.

Chapter Fourteen

GEORGIANA'S HEAD WAS SO FULL OF FRANCES AND THOMAS Hawksley and everything else that had happened at the cottage that she barely heard Mrs. Burton when she told her that they were soon to receive visitors at the house.

She had tried to say as little as possible about her trip away while still satisfying Mrs. Burton's endless curiosity, and in the end had invented a headache that had theoretically kept her in bed for most of the past two days; Mrs. Burton was sympathetic and a little disappointed, as if Georgiana should have tried a little harder *not* to be ill, if only to provide her with interesting stories.

This phantom ailment also meant that Georgiana was allowed to languish in her bedroom for days to properly nurse her prolonged hangover, only surfacing for meals and to fetch new books from the library; she was therefore in quite tranquil spirits until Wednesday, when her aunt reminded her at breakfast that they were to entertain Miss Betty Walters and her grandmother for tea.

She did not want to complain and ruin her position in Mrs. Burton's good graces, so she said nothing, and when the time came was readily dressed and waiting downstairs for the Walters to arrive. When they did, Georgiana resolved to be as pleasant as possible. Her resolution was almost immediately undone when Betty opened her mouth.

"It feels such a long time since we last met, Miss Ellers—I

don't know if you recall—everybody looked so fine at the picnic, I thought—it is the outdoor light, perhaps, it means you can see everyone so clearly—and Miss Campbell especially had on such a pretty dress. I was not sure of her friends at first, but then, one's first impressions can be wrong—I am wrong frequently, so I'm sure we shall get on just wonderfully if our paths cross again—we have been invited to a party at the Gadforths' on Friday—I believe they have just bought a delightful new dining set and wish to show it off to their friends—will you be there, Miss Ellers?"

She seemed to have forgiven Georgiana for whatever wrong-doings she had previously attributed to her at the picnic; Georgiana wondered if she was very kind or if she simply had an extraordinarily short memory, like an octogenarian or a goldfish.

"I regret I shall not be there," said Georgiana, regretting nothing. "I shall be at another party."

"Oh! With whom? We have been dining with all manner of local people of late—I have met so many new acquaintances—but you shall be with Miss Campbell, I imagine? And Miss Woodley? Miss Dugray? Mr. Smith? Mr.—"

"Yes," Georgiana said quickly. "Yes, Miss Campbell and her friends."

"Hmph," said Mrs. Walters suddenly, and they all looked at her in surprise. While it seemed Betty would not stop talking even if held at musket-point, Mrs. Walters was usually quite taciturn. "I can't say I think much of the Campbells."

"Oh, but they are so kind to our Georgiana!" cried Mrs. Burton, at once leaping to defend these people she barely knew. "Only recently they had her to stay, and then they took her along on a little holiday, and nursed her when she fell ill! I cannot imagine two more agreeable people."

"Lord Campbell is a funny sort of man," said Mrs. Walters, ignoring her. "I knew him as a boy, and I never liked him. Joined the militia when he was still just a scrap—I must say, I do feel sorry for any troops he came up against. I recall I once found him trying to drown a neighbor's kitten. He said he was just giving it a wash, but I know a drowning when I see one."

Mrs. Burton was aghast. "Lord Campbell is a fine man! Is he not, Georgiana? The very picture of a doting father and husband!"

Georgiana could not disagree with Mrs. Burton now, after all her intricately embellished lies about their trip away together.

"Yes, Aunt. A fine man," she said without emotion.

"Hmph!" said Mrs. Walters again. She was looking at Georgiana, wispy eyebrows raised. "I feel for his wife, you know." Georgiana was momentarily stunned by her astuteness—but she lapsed back into silence, and Betty took up the conversation again.

"Have you read a great deal of good books lately, Georgiana? I must say, your aunt has told us all about your reading, and I am very impressed! I have only finished a few in my time—they contain such a multitude of words—a multitude! I think myself not half as clever as you are, with all the words you must know—is there a favorite word you have come across? A word that has surprised you, perhaps?"

Georgiana bit back her instinct to scoff and genuinely considered this question for a moment.

"You know," she said, lifting her teacup to her lips and taking a sip, "I'm not sure. I always struggle to identify favorites of anything, when asked."

"I like 'bum-fodder,'" said Mrs. Walters, so suddenly that Georgiana almost choked on her tea.

"Bum-fodder, Mrs. Walters?" Mrs. Burton said, sounding a little faint.

"Oh, I've never—what does it mean, Grandmama?" Betty asked, all wide-eyed innocence; Georgiana would have believed her entirely, had she not noticed the corner of Miss Walters's mouth twitching ever so slightly as she awaited the answer.

"Newspapers," Mrs. Walters barked, "that are good for nothing but wiping your arse with."

Georgiana couldn't look at Mrs. Walters, who was entirely straight-faced, or Mrs. Burton, whose expression had frozen in a polite grimace; she stared determinedly into her teacup and, when she glanced up, saw that Betty was doing the same, biting her lip and looking almost tearful in an attempt to control herself.

Thankfully, the conversation moved away from the subject of arses, and when Mrs. Walters asked for a little nip of sherry with her tea and then promptly fell asleep midsentence, Mrs. Burton whispered to Georgiana that she should give Betty a tour of the house.

A little confused, as there wasn't much house to demonstrate, Georgiana nevertheless agreed. She led Betty through the hallway and toward the library on instinct, and was surprised when she opened the door to find her uncle sitting within, reading the paper and smoking a pipe. Usually so stoic, he looked somewhat guilty, his mustache bristling as he pursed his lips.

"Mrs. Burton said you were asleep," Georgiana said curiously, and the mustache-bristling intensified. "She said you were taking a nap, and not to disturb you."

"You know," said Betty brightly, "perhaps—well, maybe we did not visit the library straightaway. Maybe we walked in the garden first, and lingered for a time?"

"Yes," said Georgiana, catching on immediately and exchanging a quick look with Miss Walters. "I imagine we were so enthralled by the flowers that we didn't have time to discover who may or may not be smoking in the library."

"Right," said Mr. Burton, clearing his throat. "Indeed."

"I *also* imagine that when we did reach the library, somebody had kindly left a pipe and a considerable amount of good-quality tobacco on the desk," Georgiana said, aware that she was trying her luck.

"They had not," said Mr. Burton flatly.

"Alas," Georgiana said, shrugging. "We must have been confused—seeing things—dazzled by the begonias, Uncle."

She and Betty left the library, giggling, and did in fact venture out into the garden. It was small and haphazardly paved, with a few well-pruned borders stocked with flowers and shrubs arranged in unnaturally neat rows, as if to make up for the failings of the paving stones.

"Oh, I do love dog roses, don't you?" Betty said happily, taking one in her hand and stroking the petals reverently. "I know people say they're common, and I suppose they aren't half as pretty as a *proper* rose—less dignified, I imagine, although I can't imagine what a *flower* could do to get itself into somebody's bad books—incidentally, I wonder who it is that decides which flowers are good and which ones are ugly? What separates the weeds from the prizewinners? I often—"

"Betty," Georgiana said wearily, sitting down on the slightly rusted bench at the back of the garden. Her hangover seemed to be making a surprise reappearance.

"My mother loved dog roses," Betty said, finally getting to the crux of the matter. "She liked dandelions, too, and slow horses, and pigeons—she always said she liked the least-loved things the best, because it always took her by surprise, the unfussy beauty of them. Nobody's surprised if you like a proper rose—of *course* you like a rose, who wouldn't like a rose? You can accidentally like a rose without even meaning to—but to love something like a dog rose is something else entirely—you simply can't love it by accident."

"That's . . . That's really quite lovely, Betty," Georgiana said, confused to find herself genuinely moved.

"Have I told you about the time a pigeon flew down our chimney and died?" Betty asked brightly, ruining the moment entirely.

"No," Georgiana said, and when Betty started to speak again, she added, "Please don't."

"Probably for the best," Betty said, leaning to smell some honeysuckle and then sighing. "We didn't find it for a week, and Mama was dreadfully upset. Do you mind if I pick some?" She gestured to the honeysuckle.

"Be my guest," said Georgiana, shrugging. "Where is your mother now?"

"My mother and father died when I was ten," Betty said, coming to sit next to Georgiana with two freshly picked blooms clutched in her palm. "There was a terrible carriage accident. I was in the carriage, too, but I sort of . . . bounced free of it all. You do that, when you're small, I'm told."

"I'm so sorry," Georgiana said. Betty patted Georgiana's palm in response, and when she took her hand away, she had left one of the honeysuckle blossoms behind. "It must have been terribly hard to lose them."

"It was," said Betty thoughtfully. "But then, I have some lovely cousins, and I lived with them for many years. I have an uncle in Scotland who writes me very jolly letters. And I have Grandmama, of course. And her dog. He bites, but he doesn't mean it."

"I like dogs," said Georgiana, brushing her thumb over a honeysuckle petal.

"Oh! Careful, Miss Ellers. You don't want to lose the nectar."

"The what?"

"But—you've never tasted honeysuckle before? Oh, you *must*. Just pinch the end off—like this, you see? I always feel as if I am hurting flowers when I pick them—silly, of course, as I don't imagine they have feelings—yes, very good! And then you pull out the little—well, I don't know what it's called, the long part, the leg. See the little droplet? Oh, yes! That's the nectar. Try it!"

Georgiana hesitated for a moment before pressing it to her tongue; it was so delightfully, unexpectedly sweet that she laughed, and then held her hand out to Betty to ask for another.

When Mrs. Walters awoke and announced it was time to leave, Mrs. Burton actually had to come and find Georgiana and Betty in the garden to deliver the message. Her aunt kept smiling broadly at both of them as they said their goodbyes, as pink-cheeked and proud as if Georgiana had announced she was engaged.

With the taste of nectar still lingering on her tongue, Georgiana told Betty that she was welcome to come back another time as they bade farewell, and even went so far as to actually mean it.

The door had barely closed when Mrs. Burton threw up her arms in delight and exclaimed, "I knew it, Georgiana! I knew you'd make the best of friends, I just knew—"

"Don't labor the point, Mrs. Burton," Georgiana said, sighing. "You shall put me off her just as I've begun to like her."

Mrs. Burton held up her hands in surrender but went off into the house humming to herself; she was so pleased with her niece that at dinner that night she kept on giving her extra helpings of pudding, until Georgiana had to push away her bowl and beg her to stop.

Chapter Fifteen

To WALK INTO A PARTY WITH FRANCES AND HER FRIENDS
went a little something like this: They would enter, and the music would pause for just a fraction of a second before starting
up again. A hundred small murmurs and whispers would burst
into life from all corners of the room. Heads turned; glances were
thrown sidelong. Once, a fat little dog-in-arms sensed the subtle
shift in mood and immediately urinated all down its owner's
gown. They did not take any of it personally.

Jeremiah had not come to call since the cottage. Frances
didn't say this, but Georgiana did not have to ask to know it. She
was invited to drunken card games in Frances's solarium, long
evenings in the parlor at the Woodleys', dances at the small and
rather crowded assembly rooms, and every other manner of
gathering that the town and surrounding hills had to offer—and
at not one of them did they see Jeremiah Russell. Frances would
be restless every time they entered a parlor or a ballroom, never
wanting to stay in one place for more than a quarter of an hour,
constantly insisting that there must be far more interesting people in the next room.

They threw themselves into society with such ferocity that
Georgiana got persistent blisters on both feet, and her lips were
perpetually stained with the carmine she borrowed from her
friends. She would call farewell to them on a Sunday morning
at five o'clock after a night of revels and then give them a pained
wave from across St. Anne's Church only a few hours later, while

Mrs. Burton sniffed disapprovingly at her obviously delicate state. Frances attended services once or twice, craning her neck to look back at the door frequently until the vicar began to speak, and Georgiana knew it was not due to some sudden burst of piety.

When Christopher was with them, Georgiana navigated around him as if he were a venomous snake, always aware of exactly where he was in any room, never allowing herself to be alone with him. Sometimes he was absent—he had a hearty gambling habit and often disappeared to indulge himself—and she could relax.

To Georgiana's eternal relief, Cecily bumped into horsey James again one night at the assembly rooms; he asked her to dance, and then kept asking, and it seemed to drive all talk and thoughts of Mr. Hawksley from her mind. Georgiana thought a little unkindly that James's chief advantage was in being the last man of interest Cecily had encountered—his position in her affections primarily achieved by being the freshest face in her memory.

Mr. Hawksley was never to be found. Georgiana didn't stop looking for him.

On one occasion when they didn't return home from the assembly rooms until seven o'clock the next morning, Georgiana stumbling from Frances's carriage with only one glove on, Mrs. Burton cornered her in the hallway and implied that she was displaying behavior befitting a stray cat or an industrious prostitute.

"I've only been to a late party, Mrs. Burton," Georgiana replied, aching for her bed. "Not signing on at the bawdy-house."

"One often leads to the other," Mrs. Burton replied, sounding quite stern.

Georgiana dutifully stayed at home for most of a week to demonstrate that she had not found gainful employment in the arms of strangers, until Frances grew tired of sending urgent notes and simply showed up to take her out. She sat for tea, smiled winningly, and made polite, witty conversation with Mrs. Burton for the best part of three hours, until her aunt had no choice but to approve, waving them off to have fun.

Georgiana and Frances waved back with the utmost sincerity until they were well away, and then fell into each other's arms, laughing hysterically.

The party they were attending that night was at Cecily's house. Georgiana had never seen it before; it was farther away from the town than any of the others and looked exactly the sort of fairy-tale castle Cecily would belong to, with great turrets and spires and a curving stream that Cecily insisted wasn't really a moat.

The golden-haired Dugray brothers were in attendance, with their wives—it seemed to be some sort of birthday party, although whose birthday they were celebrating was somewhat lost in translation—and Georgiana found them to be just as fair and strapping as Frances had described them to be. Lovely as they were, they could not distract her friend from the fact that not one of the grand, well-tapestried rooms contained Mr. Russell— and so, unable to find the company she craved inside the house, within a few hours Frances had somehow convinced them all to go up onto the roof.

It had been a painfully humid August day, the clouds pressing down on them and making everybody miserable, but as they sat looking out over the hills, something magical happened—first, forked lightning in the distance, then a rumble of thunder, making them all cry out with joy and terror. The storm was too far away to be any real threat, and it did not begin to rain, so they sat in awed silence for a while, listening to the booms that reverberated around the valley and pointing every time the sky lit up, as if they were not all watching the same spectacle together. Georgiana had never experienced such a storm—but then, she had never watched one directly after smoking one of Christopher's mysterious pipes, either.

"It makes me think of a poem," Jonathan said, waving his hand at the general landscape.

"Which poem?" said Frances.

"Oh, I don't know. Any of them."

"*Soon as the sun forsook the eastern main, the pealing thunder shook the heav'nly plain,*" quoted Georgiana without thinking.

Jonathan clapped a hand to her shoulder, thoroughly pleased with her.

"My God, do you just keep all that in your head?"

"I'm sure it's taking up valuable space," Georgiana said, smiling self-consciously. "My father used to have me memorize them so I could perform them at the dinner table."

"Who wrote that one? About the thunder?"

"Er . . . Phillis Wheatley Peters."

"Which one is she?"

"She was a slave," Frances said coolly. Georgiana flinched; she had never heard Frances use that word before and had gone out of her way not to use anything like it in her presence, as if avoiding the subject made it any less real. "She has a particularly good one about her glorious and benevolent masters' civilizing her—it's in our library. Father reads it out sometimes, but I'm not sure he quite grasps the irony. Come on, George, don't hold back—I'm sure you must know it off by heart, too."

"I don't want to," Georgiana said quietly.

"Well, well, let's see what I can remember." Frances rotated her wineglass in her hand so that it threatened to spill with every turn. "*'Twas mercy brought me from my Pagan land* . . . Something about God, and saviors, and how diabolic her skin was. Hard to remember, really, because that's the part where my mother always starts crying."

There was a long, uncomfortable silence. The clouds roiled on, the only sign of rain the blurring of the darkening horizon.

"I wonder what makes it do that," said Cecily eventually. "The sky, I mean."

"It's *electricity*, Ces," said Christopher pompously, loosening his cravat.

He had tried to sit next to Georgiana when they first arranged themselves across the rooftop, and Georgiana had pretended she had something very urgent to say to Frances so that she could shuffle clumsily away from him. He had never acknowledged what had happened at the cottage, and neither had Georgiana, but sometimes when he looked at her she thought she saw a glint of something in his eye—the thought of what he might consider unfinished business.

"Well, what good does it do me to know that?" Cecily replied, raising an eyebrow at him. "You may as well tell me it's . . . I don't know . . . *physics*."

"Christ, Ces, surely you know what *physics* is?"

Frances's mood so easily tipped over into irritation right now, and apparently Cecily's lack of basic scientific knowledge was good enough reason to gripe.

"Why should I? It's hardly relevant," Cecily replied, shrugging.

"All right, so you just need a real-world example. A practical lesson."

Frances snatched up Cecily's silky gray reticule from where it had been sitting abandoned beside her and walked to the edge of the roof. While it wasn't raining, the wind was a little too strong to be standing so close to what was perhaps a fifty-foot drop.

"You don't want me to let this slip through my fingers right now because of *physics*."

"Give it back, Frances," Cecily said, pouting. "It's my best one!"

"Don't blame me—blame physics! Physics will make it fall.

Physics will dash it to the ground and ruin it. Come on, Ces, it's not difficult."

"Physics is a cruel mistress," Jonathan said with a sigh.

"As is Frances," muttered Jane, getting to her feet.

Georgiana looked sharply up at her; her expression was unreadable.

Cecily had risen waveringly and gone to fetch back what was hers, but Frances narrowed her eyes and grinned, skipping out of her friend's reach and dangling the bag over the edge, where it swayed in the wind.

"Do you understand it now?" she said insistently. "Say you understand!"

Cecily gave a little scream of frustration. "Fine, fine, I understand!" she said. "Give it back *now*."

Frances didn't move, so Cecily leaned forward to snatch the reticule from her hands. Frances opened her fingers and seemed to let it drop, and Cecily grabbed wildly, losing her balance and almost pitching forward off the edge of the building and to her certain doom.

Jane was at her side in an instant, pulling her roughly back so that they both fell safely onto the roof with a heavy thud. Frances had not really let go of the bag; she had simply let the main heft of it slip from her hand while holding on to the drawstrings. It was still dangling from her fingers.

"For the love of *God*, Frances, was that really necessary?" Jane spat. "You could have killed her!"

"Always with the amateur dramatics," Frances replied, rolling her eyes. She dropped the bag into Cecily's lap. "Come on. Jonathan? Christopher? I need another drink."

She swept away from them all toward the entrance to the stairwell, and Jonathan raised his eyebrows at Georgiana before shrugging and following. Christopher lingered, as if he didn't want to appear to come when called, but eventually stretched, got to his feet, and ambled after them.

"Bloody *hell*," Jane said, glowering after them once they had disappeared.

Georgiana was rather wishing that Frances had called *her* to heel, too; she had generally avoided speaking directly to Jane since the cottage and had no wish to do so now. She stood up, hovering awkwardly.

"Are you all right, Ces?" she asked.

"Yes, yes, don't worry, George—it was just a joke," Cecily said charitably, checking her reticule for any signs of its ordeal.

"Oh yes, really *funny*, if you'd fallen off the roof," Jane said, furious. "I'd expect to see it satirized in tomorrow's paper. *Local woman plunges to her death to appease bored aristocratic sociopath.*"

Georgiana laughed, and then stopped abruptly.

"I'm sorry, it's not funny really," she said, fetching Cecily's wine and bringing it to her.

She, of course, knew why Frances was so frustrated, but she had been sworn to secrecy. Cecily and Jane understood who Frances was searching for when she pulled them through busy rooms and quiet parlors, but they didn't fully comprehend why she did so with such urgency and in such an ill temper. Not that it excused attempts at rooftop manslaughter, of course.

"Well, cheers then," Jane said, "to somehow still being alive despite the many times Frances has nearly killed us."

They all clinked their glasses solemnly. Jane wasn't looking directly at Georgiana, but she wasn't ignoring her, either, or saying anything directly terrible to her—which seemed an improvement.

"How often can one be in mortal danger at house parties and dinners?" Georgiana asked.

"Oh, you'd be surprised," said Cecily brightly. "One time we were at a party in an underwater ballroom—" Georgiana tilted her head quizzically—"Oh, sorry, it's, er . . . It's like a big glass dome under a lake. Big enough to dance in. *Wonderfully* atmospheric, if a bit damp. Anyway, Frances and Jonathan had a *monster* of a fight, really going at each other, and she took this cane he had and tried to smash one of the glass panes. They had to stage an emergency evacuation."

"That wasn't even the worst one," Jane said. "What about that thing at the races?"

"Well, to be fair to her, she didn't know that would happen—"

"All those poor *horses*."

Georgiana decided she didn't want to know.

"Of course, our Miss Dugray is very forgiving," Jane said with a significant look at Cecily.

"Oh, not this again," she said, sighing sadly and shaking her magnificent blond ringlets.

Jane took a very large swig of her drink.

"Ces took a liking to one of the Campbell cousins when we were fifteen and Frances . . . Well, she put a stop to it. She doesn't like to feel outdone, our Franny, or as if our attentions are divided."

"I didn't like him *that* much," Cecily said.

"You were writing to him every night! You couldn't think about anything else! If that's what you do when you don't like someone *that much,* the next man who does take your fancy will need military protection."

Georgiana was silent, taking all of this in. It was a surprise to hear them speaking poorly of Frances. They couldn't think too badly of her; they were still out with her every night, holding her drinks, following her onto rooftops even if she might threaten to hurl their favorite belongings from them.

"But Frances doesn't mean it," Georgiana said to Cecily. "Surely?"

"Hard to say. But it doesn't matter. Not that *you'd* understand," Jane said dismissively. "I've known her since infancy. Our families . . . Well, we grew up together in every sense of the phrase. Sometimes she pushes us to the very limits, but in the end . . ."

"That's just Frances," Cecily finished.

Georgiana opened her mouth to reply—but suddenly, finally, it started to rain. There were no small drops of warning; one moment they were utterly dry, and the next they were instantly soaked, great sheets of water plastering their skirts to their thighs and their hair to their heads. Cecily screamed; Jane spluttered, spilling her wine and swearing as she clambered to her feet.

Georgiana couldn't help but laugh as they all rushed back to the stairs, sprinting for cover as if their lives depended on it, despite the fact that it was already far too late.

Chapter Sixteen

WHEN GEORGIANA GOT BACK TO THE BURTONS' IN THE EARLY hours of the morning, she found it quite a struggle to make it from Frances's carriage to the front door. She was sure that the garden must have been rearranged somehow—the flowerpot she nearly lost her kneecaps to certainly hadn't been there just a few hours before—and it also seemed much larger, her journey taking five minutes when it should have generously taken five seconds. Thankfully, it was no longer raining.

She heard muffled laughter from behind her, and muted cheering when she finally placed a hand on the door; she turned to give the carriage a salute, grinning wildly, and then squinted back at the door handle, which presented a new challenge.

After the rain had started at the Dugrays', she and the other ladies had reunited with Frances, and despite a certain amount of stiffness on the latter's part at first, they had all ended the night in good spirits. *Very* good spirits, in fact; Cecily had gone to her father's drinks cabinet and returned with plundered treasures aplenty. Georgiana had held back from indulging for as long as Christopher was at her elbow, jostling her and attempting jokes as if they were on excellent terms; as soon as he'd left, blowing them all a kiss that Georgiana pretended not to see, she'd joined the drinking in earnest.

It had seemed perfectly reasonable at the time, but now she had forgotten the fundamentals of doors.

Once she had figured it out and navigated herself into the house, she stripped off her soaked gloves and bonnet and left them dripping in the hall; slightly stale bread was obtained from the depths of the kitchen, and then she took up a candle and wandered into the library, leaving a trail of crumbs in her wake.

Mrs. Burton had clearly been writing her correspondence, as there was a pen, a pot of ink, and a stack of paper neatly squared off at the corner of the desk. Georgiana found a letter in her aunt's hand a few seconds later, on top of the pile of outgoing post. On closer inspection, Georgiana realized that it was addressed to her parents.

She immediately wanted to break the seal and peruse the contents but managed to restrain herself at the very last moment—there was no way she would be able to keep the intrusion from Mrs. Burton, even if she were sober. In this state it seemed unlikely she'd even remember she had opened the letter at all, come morning.

Georgiana attempted to file this information away for the morrow and then sat down at the desk. A very dangerous idea was beginning to form.

She picked up the pen.

Dear Mr. Hawksley—

That was hideous. Georgiana tore a strip off the top of the paper to remove the offending words and crumpled it into a ball.

Dear Thomas—

Good God, that was so much *worse*. She couldn't call him "Thomas" as if they were already ten years married. She might as well send the man a nude portrait of herself and be done with it. She tore that away, too, and resolved to forgo a name entirely.

There were a few more false starts, until all that was left was a small strip of paper only fit to hold a few short lines.

> *Sir,*
> *I write to thank you for taking such great care of my friend Miss Cecily Dugray during her hour of need (incidentally she is doing well, and has not been a bit put off the drink), and also to say that I enjoyed the wine you chose for me very much. Was previously much inclined to think Christ a trifle foolish for changing perfectly good water into wine; can now support him in his endeavor as long as he looks to you to choose the vintage.*
> *Respectfully,*
> *Georgiana Ellers*

She sealed it with a drop of candle wax, scrawled Mr. Hawksley's name on the front of it, and tucked it neatly into the pile of post in the hall. Feeling satisfied and only pleasantly devious, she went to bed and fell asleep almost the moment her head collided with the pillow, while the clock distantly struck four.

The next morning, Georgiana was sitting at breakfast squinting blearily into her porridge, pointedly ignoring Mrs. Burton's tutting, when Mr. Burton happened to mention that his sister had written to him.

Georgiana's head shot up; her uncle clutched a letter, and a small stack of unopened post sat next to his place.

"The post has come, Mr. Burton? And—and you sent your correspondence away with it?" she asked, her stomach roiling.

"Evidently," Mr. Burton replied.

"*Shit,*" Georgiana breathed without thinking.

"*Georgiana!*" her aunt cried, absolutely aghast.

Mr. Burton looked as if he were tempted to drop under the table and take cover.

"I'm sorry—I'm so sorry, Mrs. Burton, I didn't—I shall take myself to my room."

Georgiana flung her chair back and ran from the dining room, rushing up the stairs two at a time, slamming her door, and throwing herself dramatically onto the bed. Mrs. Burton followed her a moment later, but upon hearing what sounded like her niece screaming into her pillow, she retreated; when Georgiana finally emerged after hours of staring at the ceiling and regretting the day she'd learned how to use a pen, her aunt seemed quietly impressed by how cowed she was, and satisfied that she must be very sorry indeed.

Georgiana was just beginning to hope that the letter may not have reached its intended destination—perhaps it had been deemed undeliverable without a proper address, or it had been dropped in the lane, or the post had crashed and all had perished in a great and powerful fireball that consumed everything it touched—when a reply came.

She was sitting at the breakfast table a few days later when Mrs. Burton handed it to her, and when she broke the unfamiliar seal, opened the letter, and saw his signature, she dropped it immediately as if it had burned her fingers; she managed to finish her food, although she kept her gaze fixed warily on it at all times. Once she had picked it up again and retreated to her room, it took every ounce of her strength and fortitude to open it and read what he had written.

Miss Ellers,

Your ruminations on the Christian faith are somewhat disturbing, but I am glad to hear that in some roundabout way, I brought you back to the light of the Lord.

I am also pleased to hear that Miss Dugray is well; a small price to pay in exchange for the lining of my very best hat.

Faithfully yours,
Thomas Hawksley

Georgiana laughed, and then read and reread "*Yours*" until her vision blurred and the word lost all meaning.

Sir,

The loss of your hat is devastating; please send my condolences to its forty-nine siblings, for they must be feeling it almost as keenly as you yourself. Take solace in the fact that you were very much the hero of the hour, the day, and the week (although we do not come into contact with many honorable gentlemen, so do not take the compliment too much to heart).

Faithfully yours,
Georgiana Ellers

Miss Ellers,

It is a wonder you so readily refer back to our first meeting, as your impertinence on that occasion—and your suggestion that I might be unable to tie my own shoelaces—would give any wise man cause to cease all correspondence immediately.

I would never consider myself a hero; I put my breeches on one leg at a time, just like everybody else.

Yours,
Thomas Hawksley

Sir,

In that case, I am glad indeed that nobody could mistake you for a wise man.

Yours,
Georgiana E.

Miss Georgiana,

I cannot pretend your observations are unfounded. I often find myself sitting in meetings, or reading endless ledgers, or being asked extensive questions about different varieties of cloth (I confess I have no particular feelings about fabric—but when one's family has made a habit of importing it, one is expected to at least make a good show of pretending), and feeling exceedingly stupid indeed.

Not because I don't understand the task at hand, but because despite understanding it, and knowing how important it is that I pay attention, nothing would bring me greater pleasure than abandoning it all and instead whiling away the hours at the pianoforte like an elderly eccentric, fortune and fabric be damned.

I write to you now, in fact, sitting at the aforementioned instrument; it grows dark, and I must conclude this letter before my candle burns out and I upset the inkwell I have balanced so precariously somewhere near E♭.

Yours,

Thomas

Sir,

I would lament with you upon the difficulties of managing a great many responsibilities but unfortunately I am not even trusted to go to town alone in case I fall down, ill, or in love with a passing down-and-out and throw it all away for him on a girlish whim.

I wouldn't worry about the pianoforte. I am sure you have a spare.

Yours,

Georgiana

Georgiana,

I am inclined to believe that your letters are so short because you deal *primarily in petty insults. It is not becoming for a lady to address a gentleman thus, or in fact for anybody to have to suffer your faint grasp on the ancient practice of written correspondence; you should write about the weather, the company you have been keeping, pleasant developments in your garden, &c.*

You should ask who I have seen, inquire after my business transactions (fabric, I hear you cry! But it is my very favorite subject—please, tell me more about wefts and weights and market value, for I long to hear it!), and pretend to take great interest when I tell you I have had many quiet, respectable dinners at home of late without even one solitary altercation with a drunkard in a cellar.

I will not allow any disparaging remarks about the pianoforte; it is, I'm afraid, my closest companion and confidant.

Thomas

Dear Thomas,

My apologies—please do expand on the endlessly fascinating subject of wefts. Did you always know that you wanted to be a man of the cloth?

All my love to your pianoforte,
Georgiana

Georgiana,

My father met my mother while working in India. They were both great lovers of literature, and apparently they fell in love during a heated discussion about a poem by Mirabai. They returned man and wife, but their partnership also extended to a thriving business through her family connections—a business which has now somewhat crumbled at my hand.

All this to say, it was entirely hereditary, and therefore rather difficult to misplace or give away.

I refuse to write any more when you remain so taciturn. Please urgently reacquaint yourself with the usual standards and traditions of letter-writing and provide something of a decent length so that I may respond in kind.

Thomas

Dear Thomas,
Paper is expensive.
    Yours,
    Georgiana

Chapter Seventeen

"Get in, Georgiana. we're going shopping."

Georgiana had only been roused from her bed by her aunt tapping incessantly on her door twenty minutes previously and was still a little confused. She had been up late the night before, writing and rewriting her reply to Thomas's latest note, until she gave up entirely and sent just the one line on a narrow strip of paper, hoping to at least make him laugh. Frances and Jonathan had arrived without warning and then waited impatiently while she dressed, calling up to her from the drive every few minutes and threatening to leave without her, while Mrs. Burton watched out of the window and sighed in a long-suffering sort of way. Now Georgiana was finally clambering into the carriage, squeaking with surprise as Frances tapped her lightly on the backside with her fan.

"I can't believe you haven't been shopping yet," Jonathan said pityingly. "You've been here for *two* months, George."

"I did venture into town once to watch Mrs. Burton fondle ribbons, but she's very particular about the use of the carriage," said Georgiana, leaning her head on the plush interior of the coach and closing her eyes, still feeling half-asleep. "She chiefly uses it to travel half a mile down the road to visit our elderly neighbor so she can experience the dreadful potholes, giving them something to complain about together for the entire afternoon."

"Gosh, it's always a party at the Burtons', isn't it?" said Frances, and Georgiana kicked her very gently. "Watch it, you cad. This dress is Italian."

"What are we shopping for, anyway?" Georgiana asked, eyeing Frances's impeccable sartorial choices. It occurred to her that she had never seen her in the same dress twice.

"Oh, everything. And nothing. I've exhausted my stock of party dresses so I need something new for the end of the season. I do love shopping for an *occasion,* don't you?"

The last occasion Georgiana had shopped for before the Woodleys' party had been a distant relative's funeral. Otherwise she relied on the same tired rotation of frocks, mostly sewn by a friend of her mother's. She had worn the new dress she'd bought for Jane's party far too many times now, in fervent denial about the fact that no new ribbon or shawl could make it look truly different.

It was jarring to hear Frances mention the *end* of the season— she had known, of course, that they weren't all going to stay forever, but September had been creeping ever closer without her notice. She could only hope that by the close of the summer it would feel entirely natural for her friends to extend an invitation to London at once, so they could continue their escapades uninterrupted.

She must have looked a little concerned, for Jonathan patted her knee fondly. "Don't worry, George, Frances will steer you right. She's like a hurricane with a purse caught in it when she gets going. She just starts flinging coins and notes of credit at people pell-mell, they're lucky to escape with their lives."

"Oh, shut up," Frances replied.

It had not really occurred to Georgiana that she might be expected to shop on this trip, too, and the implication *was* something of a worry. She had hoped to simply trail after Frances and give her advice about which fabrics looked most becoming and which gloves might veer toward the tawdry; the money Mrs.

Burton had pressed into her hand as she hurried out of the door would not be enough to buy so much as a bonnet, unless there were rogue cut-price milliners in the more shady part of town.

They pulled up outside an establishment that purported to sell "hosiery, hats & delights" and all climbed out. A man who looked rather down-at-heel shambling past tried to catch their attention, and Frances let out a little huff of contempt and put a protective hand on Georgiana's shoulder as they entered the shop.

Georgiana sensed immediately that everything in sight was out of her price range and resolved not to touch a thing, lest she mark something dreadful with a spot of dirt—like the hat topped with a rabid-looking ferret eating an apple—and have no choice but to purchase it for approximately the price of a new horse.

"Oh, look at it, George, isn't it lovely?"

Frances had immediately found the most expensive-looking thing in the shop, a white fur shrug frosted with a beautiful hue of bluish-gray, and she slung it around her shoulders with apparently no concerns about dirtying it.

"It's still got a head," said Jonathan dubiously.

A middle-aged, mustachioed, and bespectacled man came rushing over, his navy dress coat easily grander than anything Georgiana had ever owned, a thin gold tape measure slung about his neck.

"Arctic fox, Miss Campbell," he said, bowing deeply.

Of *course* he already knew Frances. She had probably already purchased the rest of the fox's extended family and was back to complete the set.

"It's just the thing, Basil. What do you think, George?"

The fox's glassy eyes seemed to be staring directly at her.

"Well . . . it's summer," Georgiana said weakly.

"Yes, and after summer comes autumn, and then it shall be winter. It's pretty reliable, that way."

"Ignore her, George," Jonathan said. "It's best to agree with her on all things accessories or risk becoming one yourself."

He did a startlingly accurate impression of the fox, going limp and dead-eyed, his tongue sticking out for effect.

"Send the bill to Longview, Basil," Frances said, ignoring him. She handed the fur to the obliging Basil and immediately moved on. "Look at *this*, George, this is just the thing for you."

She was pointing to the most beautiful necklace Georgiana had ever seen. It was formed of delicate gold link and flashing red stones; in the center they had been arranged in the shape of a flower.

"Yes, yes, a lovely bit of paste," said Jonathan, rolling his eyes.

"No, sir! Not paste." Basil seemed deeply affronted. "These are *garnets*. Allow me, miss."

He took it from the display, the links of the chain falling softly from his hands like water, and hung it about Georgiana's neck, steering her to a mirror before she could protest.

The necklace looked so much finer than her dress that she almost felt ridiculous, but she could not deny how well it looked against her collarbones. Her hair, which she normally felt rather let her down by being so dull, seemed warmer and richer, her skin much more rosy and pleasing to the eye. She instantly wanted it more than she had ever wanted anything in her life. Even Jonathan gave a long, low whistle at the sight, and Frances reprimanded him ("We are not in a public house, Jonathan"). As soon as Georgiana realized how much she desired it, she had to begin the painful process of refusing it.

"It is gorgeous," she said sadly, fumbling with the clasp to undo it, "but . . . it's not quite right."

"Nonsense," said Frances. "It's perfect. Buy it, or I shall."

"I'll not stop you," Georgiana said, attempting to sound indifferent.

She wanted that necklace so much it burned in her chest, but short of offering to sweep Basil's shop for a thousand years in an exchange of goods for services, she had absolutely no way to pay for it.

"Fine, fine. I'll take it," Frances said, almost as if it were an inconvenience to her.

Georgiana had never begrudged her friend her wealth, but shopping with her was bringing to light all sorts of feelings that would have been better left buried.

Frances led them out once her purchases had been wrapped up, and they stepped back up into the carriage and went on to their next destination, Georgiana suddenly wishing for the day to be over as soon as possible.

In the next shop, it was a fan. In the one after, pearls—strings and strings of pearls, enough pearls that Frances probably could have wrapped them all the way around the perimeter of her house and still had some to spare. Jonathan wasn't quite as bad, but he bought two hats at the millinery and teased Georgiana when she wouldn't even entertain trying on gloves with lace so delicate that it looked as if they'd be torn asunder by a medium-sized sneeze.

At the jeweler's, Georgiana grew bored of watching Frances try on ring after ring and drifted to the window, where she watched an old man sitting in the neighboring doorway raising his hands to beg from passersby with no success; eventually Georgiana went outside to give him a meager handful of Mrs. Burton's coins. Jonathan and Frances did not seem to notice she had gone; when she returned, she saw that Frances had happily parted with more than fifty pounds in her absence.

Frances seemed to wear herself out in a few hours, having gone on to purchase six different types of fabric for dresses and then insist on the driver carting it around after them until she could find six hats and pairs of gloves to match. She directed the carriage to the assembly rooms for some luncheon, and the man receiving guests almost tripped over himself in his haste to get her situated when he saw her coming. The room was grand but hot and airless, with circular tables crammed with people taking up every inch of space and the sound of laughter and chatter echoing around the domed ceiling.

"Oh, it's nightmarish in here this time of year," Jonathan said, wrinkling his nose in disgust. "Have them seat us outside, Franny."

"We'll get dusty," Frances protested, but Jonathan would not give in, and Georgiana was so overwhelmed by the noise that she backed him.

They ended up sitting on a covered terrace that looked out across the square. The public house at the other end was very lively, and Georgiana found herself watching a group of young men and women of about her age standing outside. They did not have fine clothes or hats—she was sure that present company would find them deeply uncouth—but they all seemed rambunctiously happy, sharing jokes and laughter and drinks, while she sat self-consciously in a dress half a decade out of fashion and listened to Frances talking about the differences between *sapphire* and *royal blue* satin, as if it mattered one jot.

"Have you ever considered," Georgiana said suddenly, interrupting Frances midsentence, "the plight of the poor in town? You don't see it so much out near us, but look—here, poverty is everywhere. We could do something about it. Start a collection, perhaps, or raise funds through an event. Do you not think it our duty?"

They both looked at her for a long moment.

"No," said Frances, and that was that.

They were just finishing up with luncheon and making to leave when Jonathan, gazing out over the square in the natural lull that followed a hearty meal, put his glass heavily down on the table and clapped a hand to his mouth as if he had seen something dreadful. Frances had not seen his face change, but Georgiana foolishly asked, "What, Jonathan?"

"Nothing. *Nothing,*" he said unconvincingly, shooting her daggers.

"What is it?" Frances asked, following his gaze, which kept flicking back over to the public house seemingly against his will.

It took a moment, but then Georgiana realized what he had seen. Jeremiah Russell had just exited the pub, and he was not alone. There was a tiny, pale blond girl on his arm. She was not richly dressed—far from it, she looked poorer even than Georgiana—but Jeremiah was looking at her as if she were the loveliest thing he had ever laid eyes on. She had a round face and enormous eyes, and when she widened them, as she was doing now while Jeremiah whispered in her ear, she was a delight to behold to all—except the three of them watching in horror from the balcony.

Frances was gripping the flat top of the stone railings with both hands, looking as if she were about ready to launch herself over them. She took a deep, pained breath and let go, sitting back in her seat.

"Are you . . . Franny, are you—"

"Am I what? It doesn't mean anything, Jonathan. For all we know that's a cousin, or . . . or a family friend, or his *shoeshine*."

Georgiana did not imagine it was customary to meet one's attractive female shoeshine in a pub in the middle of a Monday afternoon, and from the expression on Frances's face, she didn't really believe it either.

They couldn't help but look back, and therefore saw Jeremiah saying his goodbyes to the girl with a kiss to her hand, lingering for far too long. She stood and watched him as he stepped up into his carriage and was borne away through the streets, and then she turned and went back inside.

"Do you think—do you think she's a whore, Franny?" Jonathan asked gently.

"Oh, there's no doubt in my mind that she is, regardless of her chosen profession," Frances spat back, gathering her things. "Come on." Her tone did not allow for argument.

Jonathan and Georgiana followed in her wake, darting nervous glances at each other as they pressed through the crush of the assembly rooms. Once they had exited, she headed straight for the public house.

"Is this really advisable?" Jonathan asked, dashing in front of her and pressing a hand to her arm.

"Get out of my way, Jonathan."

There was no stopping her. She shrugged him off and stormed into the dingy establishment, looking around with the utmost disgust, as if she had entered a well-inhabited plague house. It all seemed rather inoffensive to Georgiana; there were small groups, mostly men, drinking ale and talking idly at tables and at the bar. Now, of course, they were all staring at their new and vastly overdressed company.

"You," Frances said imperiously to the barman. "Have you seen a ratty sort of blond girl? She just passed through here."

"A ratty . . . ?" He looked positively bemused, and Frances rolled her eyes.

"A young lady," interjected Jonathan before she could do any further damage. "About yea high, in a gray dress. Have you seen her?"

"Well . . . that sounds like Miss Annabelle Baker. She's taken a room upstairs."

"Annabelle Baker," Frances repeated, as if the name were something sour in her mouth.

She turned on her heel and marched back outside as if she were steam-powered, leaving Georgiana to call out feeble thanks to the man before following her.

The silence that followed was excruciating; Georgiana could almost feel it, a tangible and suffocating presence in the air between them. Once in the carriage, Georgiana tried to reach for Frances's hand but was rebuffed. She asked if she wanted to talk about it.

"No," Frances snapped, turning to look out of the window.

She must have been hurt, but the only evidence of it that Georgiana could see was the rigidness of her frame. Jonathan did not even attempt to get her to speak.

Georgiana did not know how to help somebody who so thoroughly did not want to be helped; none of them spoke another word the entire carriage ride home.

Chapter Eighteen

THE PROSPECT OF A DINNER PARTY THAT THURSDAY WITH friends of the Burtons should have been an excessively dreary one, but Georgiana was secretly a little glad of the reprieve from Frances and her silent fury, and besides, she felt she owed Mr. and Mrs. Burton one—or two, or ten—so she tried to bear it without complaint, only rolling her eyes once or twice as a small treat to herself when Mrs. Burton rattled through the prospective guest list all the way through both breakfast and luncheon. Mr. Burton escaped at the last minute by claiming stomach trouble, refusing to meet Georgiana's eye when she attempted to give him a sharp look, and so the women of the house set off alone.

The estate they drew up to was not as large as some of the houses Georgiana had seen of late, but it was classically built and rather beautiful, and Mrs. Burton had led her to believe that their hosts for the evening—and more importantly, their sons—had the potential to be somewhat tolerable. Georgiana's parents had not attempted to make matches for her, apparently assuming that at some point Georgiana would simply snare a passing man in the street or perhaps spontaneously evaporate instead, and it seemed that Mrs. Burton was trying to make up for lost time.

The Taylors had three sons. One was married, with his wife on his arm, but the other two were bachelors, and the younger kept trying to catch Georgiana's eye from the minute she entered the front hall. He was not overly handsome, but not some sort of gargoyle, either; what was uniquely alarming about him was how fervent and frequent his gaze was. She felt he was somehow already conveying the most lamentable parts of his personality from a distance, without needing to say a word. Any moment he would gather up the courage to cross to them and be introduced by his parents, who were currently engaged in conversation with Mrs. Burton, so Georgiana took the opportunity to flee before he could set his mind to it. She walked with purpose down the hall and stumbled upon the darkened dining room, where places were set for at least twenty.

Guests were still arriving and mingling in the hallway and the parlor, but the clamor was reduced to a pleasant murmur here. She closed the door behind her and then turned to press her back to it, sighing with relief—and was surprised to find that she was not alone.

A man of around sixty sat at the table, reading a book by the light of a single taper burning dangerously low, clearly not without trouble; he was squinting down at the words, totally engrossed, and didn't seem to notice her enter.

Georgiana was just turning to leave quietly when he spoke, making her jump.

"Before you go, my dear, would you bring me another candle?" His voice had been weakened a little by age, and he spoke with kindness rather than command.

"Of course," said Georgiana, rushing to do so.

As she set the candle down, she noticed a robust walking stick by his chair and thought she understood why he may have chosen to sit down to dinner before called to.

"Ah, thank you," he said with a sigh of contentment, pushing his glasses up his nose with gently quavering hands. "It is a love story, you see. It's rather hard to understand whose heart is pounding with ardent desire if you can barely make out the words."

Georgiana laughed out loud in surprise, then quickly stopped herself, to avoid the risk of seeming rude.

"Is it your preferred genre?" she asked, not wanting to butt in but simultaneously not wishing to leave the peace and sanctity of the room a moment sooner than necessary. "I greatly enjoy romances but have yet to find a man who'll admit to feeling the same."

"I must confess, I *am* rather fond of them. I flatter myself that I'm quite a prolific reader, but I often find that tedious philosophical musings on the meaning of life leave one a little cold. Life is difficult enough, after all, without dissecting it and agonizing over the pieces. You can *count* on a romance. The path to a happy ending is often littered with scorned and deceased lovers, of course, but if you stick at it, you're usually rewarded with a wedding in the end."

"May I sit?" asked Georgiana. "I don't mean to intrude. If you tell me you are far too caught up with your reading I shall not be offended in the slightest and shall leave you to your imperiled lovers."

"No—of course, of course, sit." She drew up the chair next to him. "I take it as a great compliment that a young lady should choose me for her companion when I am sure there are many diverting gentlemen vying for your attention out in the hall."

"If I may speak frankly," Georgiana said, sighing, "I am here to *avoid* such attentions. I should much prefer to sit with you and discuss the love affairs of others than risk the horror of starting one of my own."

He laughed. "Then tell me, Miss . . . Oh, forgive me, I haven't asked your name."

"Miss Georgiana Ellers, sir."

"Ah. Do tell me, Miss Ellers—who is your favorite heroine? And after her many terrible and inevitable mistakes, did she get what she deserved in the end?"

* * *

When the time came for dinner, Georgiana and her new friend had been happily discussing books for so long that she had almost forgotten their true reason for being there. A few people began to enter the room, but she didn't notice; she was still talking enthusiastically about the literary works of Samuel Richardson when a hand fell onto her neighbor's shoulder and she looked up midsentence.

"Mr. Hawksley?" she cried, unable to contain her surprise, and her companion beamed at her.

"You are acquainted with my son! How wonderful," he said, clasping Mr. Hawksley's hand with his own.

"Your son?" Georgiana repeated stupidly.

She was not sure why she was so surprised at the discovery that this man was Mr. Hawksley's father—they did not look alike, although there was a certain air of quiet contemplation about them both. She couldn't help but instantly recall in vivid detail all the daydreams she'd indulged in recently; the *letters,* so improper between two people who had never so much as been formally introduced. Faced with a flesh-and-blood father in front of her very eyes, it all suddenly seemed inappropriate in the extreme. She was sure that the gentle, genial Mr. Hawksley senior would be horrified if he knew what she had been picturing every night as she struggled to fall asleep. She blushed, and the older gentleman gave her a knowing smile, which instilled a very illogical, but no less pressing, fear in her that he might be able to read her mind.

"Ah, yes—I am Mr. *James* Hawksley. Miss Ellers and I have been discussing literature, Thomas. But I have taken up far too much of her time—I see it is time to be seated for dinner, and our hosts have gone to such efforts to mark our places." He gestured to a meticulously calligraphed name card, and Georgiana wanted to kick herself for not noticing sooner that his identity had been clearly labeled right in front of her the entire time. She thanked him, very flustered, and left them to find her place.

Of course, when she did, she realized with a start that the name card to her left read *Mr. Thomas Hawksley* in careful, slanting script. Her heart started to beat indecently fast, seeing his name in such close proximity to hers. This revelation was marred only by the fact that Marcus Taylor, the youngest son she had been expertly avoiding, had been seated on her other side. Mrs. Burton was practically miles away, down at the other end of the table.

Mr. Taylor immediately introduced himself, and Georgiana turned to him and tried very hard to focus on what he was saying, painfully aware of Mr. Hawksley's presence behind her as he took his seat. Unfortunately, Mr. Taylor was not a particularly gifted or subtle conversationalist.

"I do like your dress," he said, not pausing to swallow his mouthful of soup before speaking, which resulted in some unseemly dribbling. "Mother told me all about you, of course, and she was right—you are not unpleasant on the eye."

Georgiana could have sworn she heard a quiet exhalation of laughter to her left, but it quickly seemed to turn into a politely cleared throat.

"Thank you, Mr. Taylor. This house is lovely."

"Oh, yes, yes—it won't ever be mine, though," he said, suddenly glum. "I won't fare badly, but yes, youngest of three, you know. Still," he added, brightening up considerably, "my eldest brother, Samuel, *will* inherit, but he also has the most frightful wife, so there you go. You cannot have it all. With the right sort of wife, one might not notice the dreariness, or the lack of grounds, or . . . or the small cupboards of one's house."

"Yes," said Georgiana. "You have quite a lot of soup on your chin, Mr. Taylor."

"Oh! Do I indeed?"

He dabbed ferociously at himself with a napkin, and Georgiana was relieved beyond measure when the woman seated on his other side asked him what was in the soup he had so thoroughly decorated himself with. She took the opportunity to turn to Mr. Hawksley, who also seemed to be enjoying his soup; he was currently smirking into it.

"It's not funny," hissed Georgiana in an undertone.

"It *is* funny," he said quietly, taking another spoonful of soup.

Georgiana noticed that he seemed to have no problems feeding himself without spillage, and then wondered if her expectations had been far too drastically lowered by previous company.

"Your father seems wonderful," she said, eager to change the subject.

To her dismay, his expression turned quite serious, and he studied his spoon thoughtfully for a moment before looking up at her and answering.

"He is. I have not seen him laugh with someone as he was with you for quite some time."

"Is he . . . ill?" asked Georgiana, hoping this was not too much of an intrusion.

"Yes. He will not leave us for a while yet, though, I am happy to say. It is not the ailments of his body that truly plague him. I think"—he stopped himself and gave a little shake of his head as he lowered his voice—"I think the young Mr. Taylor is *bursting* to speak with you again."

"Please," whispered Georgiana urgently, her eyes wide, "he will go on about *cupboards,* and I do not wish to wed someone who wants to pledge himself to me purely to distract himself from his inferior storage space."

He laughed, as Georgiana had hoped he would, and continued in a low voice so they could not be overheard.

"We shall have to pretend as if we are deeply engaged in a conversation of utmost amusement and importance."

"Are we not?" Georgiana replied.

His eyebrows raised infinitesimally, and she had to bite her lip and turn away lest she blush.

"I was glad when you—I was glad to hear that Miss Dugray did not suffer any lasting ill effects, after our last meeting."

"She did not. Miss Woodley says it is only a matter of time before the performance is repeated, however."

Reminded of wine, even in such an unflattering light, Georgiana picked up her own untouched glass.

"*You* have not been drinking tonight, though." It was stated as a fact.

Georgiana frowned. "I have not. I imagine it would be considered bad manners to get foxed past the point of reason at an extremely respectable dinner party. If young Mr. Taylor accosts me again, though, I will certainly be driven to drink." She put her glass back down. "You seem rather concerned about my drinking, or lack thereof."

"No, no, I don't mean to give the impression . . . I mention it only because it is impossible to ascertain a person's true character when you only encounter them very drunk," he said, lifting his own glass and taking a sip. "But—ah—I seem to have offended you."

"You just seem very quick to pass judgment," said Georgiana. "*You* attend the same parties as I do. *You* keep similar company. You drink! You are literally drinking this very second. Why is it that I am not permitted to enjoy myself, to indulge in the same vices as you and the others? Do you dislike it only . . . only because I am a woman? Would you prefer that I left every party at nine o'clock, and never touched a drop of alcohol again, and . . . and excused myself from company every time I had a somewhat impure thought?"

"Certainly not," he said quietly, and the low cadence of his voice sent a pleasant chill up the length of her spine. They shared a brief look, and Georgiana wondered if he, too, was thinking of the wine cellar, the current setting of all her most obscene thoughts. "I will admit, I do not personally enjoy drinking to excess. It is, of course, your choice what you do with your leisure time. But I *am* enjoying having a conversation with you in which you have not fallen over even once. A rare pleasure."

Georgiana blushed thoroughly this time, unable to hide it. Although she was not overly fond of falling over, she *was* quite keenly interested in what happened when she fell over in his presence—chiefly, that it was a very good excuse for rare and stimulating physical contact.

"Whatever you think of me, Mr. Hawksley, even *I* would struggle to fall from a sitting position," she said, smiling at the man who took away her untouched soup and replaced it with the next course. They sat in charged silence until all the servants had retreated and the conversation around them had swelled again.

"You wrote to me," he said.

There was a strange intimacy to these words, spoken quietly, a tiny oasis in this crowded room. Georgiana was so startled by them that she couldn't think of a witty response.

"Yes. Er—sorry," she said awkwardly.

"Don't apologize."

He was looking at her—really looking at her, holding her gaze with intensity—and then suddenly his face went blank and impassive, and he picked up his knife and fork to eat.

Georgiana realized why a split second later; Mr. Taylor was clearing his throat with increasing volume to try to get her attention. She sighed with frustration and then fixed a smile on her face as she turned to find out what he wanted.

Chapter Nineteen

DINNER DRAGGED ON FOR AN AGE, WITH MR. TAYLOR COM-
pletely unwilling to release Georgiana from his particularly dire
company. She was glad when it was over and she could sit with
the other ladies in the drawing room, half listening as her aunt
talked to the offending gentleman's mother. Another summer
storm had begun outside, and she focused on the raindrops
beating steadily against the windowpane as she willed time to go
faster. From her position near the door she could hear the men
engaged in whatever mysterious rituals they undertook after dinner, and was so eager for the chance to see Thomas again that she
almost knocked Mrs. Burton's glass of sherry from her hand at
the mere suggestion that the two parties should merge.

When the men entered, Mr. Hawksley was deep in conversation with his father, a hand resting on his arm. The youngest Mr.
Taylor spotted her immediately, and as she had no polite means
to avoid him, Georgiana could not pretend she had not heard his
suggestion that she play something for them on the pianoforte.

"You're too kind; I'm afraid I am not a particularly accom
plished pianist, Mr. Taylor," she said, suddenly wishing she *had*
managed to get far more drunk, no matter what Mr. Hawksley
might think of her.

"Nonsense! You have such pretty hands, I'm sure they make
beautiful music," Marcus replied plummily, undeterred.

Georgiana reflexively clasped her hands behind her back, out
of his sight.

"I'll play," said Thomas abruptly from across the room. He strode over to the piano before anybody could protest.

"Very good, very good," said Mr. Taylor, his smile wavering a little. "I must admit, I'd have preferred to hear Miss Ellers play—not to say that you don't have handsome hands yourself, Mr. Hawksley, eh!" He laughed far too heartily at his own joke. Georgiana smiled to herself for entirely different reasons.

Mr. Hawksley sat down, paused for a few seconds to indulge in just the slightest flex of his fingers, and then began to play, softly at first, but gaining momentum, until the piece became violent and jarring and all-consuming. Georgiana had never seen a man play the pianoforte and was immediately entranced. Thomas played with a confidence—almost an aggression—that should have been ugly but was instead mesmerizing. Most music, Georgiana thought, followed familiar patterns; you could make an educated guess at what the next note might be, and it lulled you into a sense of safety. This, whatever it was, did precisely the opposite. She felt as if she were constantly teetering on a musical precipice, grasping for something to hold on to that made sense, only to be hit suddenly with a discordant run of notes or a minor chord—and then all bets were off as to where it was going next. Conversation ceased, and all eyes turned to watch him. This was not music you spoke over or that you drank tea to; it demanded to be heard. After just a few minutes, he stopped abruptly.

"But you must play more, Mr. Hawksley! You have such a talent!" cried a young lady breathlessly from the other side of the room.

"I'm afraid I cannot." He shrugged apologetically, rising from the piano. "It is a partial transcript, sent by a friend in Vienna. I have only learned a little."

"Why—you must teach our Georgiana, Mr. Hawksley!" said Mrs. Burton. There was a manic glint in her eye that made her intentions so clear that Georgiana wanted to kick her shin under the side table. "You are by far the most accomplished player I have ever heard, and she needs a little encouragement in that direction."

Mr. Hawksley looked at Georgiana, who rolled her eyes back.

"There's no time like the present! Nobody else wants to play anyhow, do they?" Mrs. Burton waited only a split second, to ensure that nobody had time to protest. "Good, then that's decided." She beamed at both of them.

Mr. Hawksley's expression was unreadable as he gestured to the piano. Georgiana walked over to it and took a seat at the stool while he pulled up another chair. Luckily, conversation had resumed around the room; she did not particularly fancy displaying her musical ineptitude in front of a large audience.

"Play something," he said quietly. His leg was almost touching hers beneath the piano.

As lightly as she could, with one foot firmly pressed on the soft pedal, Georgiana played the opening bars of Mozart's *Sonata facile*. She felt herself getting hot with embarrassment; after what Mr. Hawksley had just performed, she sounded like a child at her first lesson.

"It's no good," she said. "I'm a hopeless case."

He smiled. "You're coiled as tightly as a spring. Sit up a little straighter."

He put a careful hand on her shoulder blade to help correct her posture, and she didn't breathe until he had removed it again. A burst of laughter made her turn quickly to see whether they had been observed, as if she had been discovered doing something far more illicit than brief shoulder-touching. The others had gathered together by the fireplace to play some sort of parlor game involving rhyming, and Georgiana could hear Mrs. Burton struggling to think of something to rhyme with "blossom." The elder Mr. Hawksley was alone in the corner by a lamp, happily absorbed in his book once more.

"Try it again. Play it with certainty; you might get it right by accident, and then it will sound as if you always meant to."

Georgiana laughed, and played again with a little more confidence. It *did* sound better. She missed a note but continued, and Mr. Hawksley smiled encouragingly.

"Your father seems to have the right idea about how to pass an evening," she remarked quietly as she played.

"Ah—yes. He does not particularly enjoy spending time outside the house, but I encourage him to do so."

"He doesn't?" Georgiana looked up at him, surprising herself when her hands kept moving and hitting almost all of the right keys without her keeping a watchful eye on them. "He seems so pleasant, so amiable. I cannot imagine such a man deciding to shut himself away and deprive the world of his company."

"He tires very quickly," said Mr. Hawksley, frowning down at the piano. "You must curve your hands—imagine you are holding an apple in each of them, like this." He demonstrated with his own. Georgiana attempted to copy him. "No, do not let your wrists become rounded. Here." He reached over and corrected them—and then he stopped for a long moment, his hand resting beside hers. "My brother, Edward, died two years ago, very suddenly," he said, so quietly she could barely hear him. "My mother, shortly afterward. It has been hard on both of us, but my father especially . . . Well, he has not recovered, and I do not think he ever will."

"I'm so sorry," said Georgiana, her hands pausing on the keys as she took in the full weight of his words.

To lose a brother was bad enough, but to be so closely followed by his mother—she could not imagine the depth of his despair. Before she could think better of it, she reached out and gently squeezed his hand. He did not pull it away at first, and she marveled at the warmth of his fingers, the press of his knuckles against her palm—but then suddenly he was up, pushing back his chair, muttering something about getting some air before he vanished.

Georgiana looked around. Nobody had noticed his swift exit. No one was looking at them at all; they were all too engrossed in their game.

She sat for a moment at the piano, listening to their laughter, and then decided to be bold. She abruptly got to her feet and followed him, noting as she went that Mr. James Hawksley had glanced up from his book and then returned to it with a small, private smile.

She walked down the hallway in the vague direction of the back of the house, unsure of where exactly Thomas had gone, and then she saw him; one of the French windows to the garden was open, and he was standing just outside it under the shelter of the upper balcony, unable to go any farther due to the driving rain. Both of his hands were fists, curled tightly at his sides as he looked out over the surrounding grounds.

Georgiana walked to the doorway and paused for a brief moment with her hand on the glass before stepping through it.

"I'm sorry."

He did not turn around.

"You *must* stop apologizing," he replied hoarsely.

She could only just hear him over the rain; it seemed to have increased in ferocity the moment she crossed the threshold.

"I just wanted . . . I just wanted to thank you for telling me. What you told me, I mean. If it were me, I don't know how I'd go on. I—er—I know that's not a particularly helpful thing to say. But you can talk to me, if you need to. I know you don't really know me, but the offer is there, so . . . if you need to say it, I want to hear it." She paused to take a breath, and in that brief moment all of her bravado left her. "Anyway, I . . . I've intruded. I'll leave you." She made to go back inside.

"Don't," he said.

"I'm sorry?"

"Don't leave me. I mean—you haven't intruded." He put a hand to his brow as if his head pained him. "I enjoy your company. Stay."

"I thought—I'm sorry, I thought I had upset you."

Georgiana moved to stand by his side. She studied his profile with concern as he massaged his temple and then put his hand to the stone pillar next to him. He looked bone-weary all of a sudden, barely keeping himself upright.

"No. I find you a pleasant escape from the things . . . from the things that do."

He took a deep breath, clearly trying to pull himself together. They were quiet for a moment.

"I know . . . I know you are a man," Georgiana began, rushing to finish her sentence when she realized that she had left it in a rather ridiculous place, "and there are probably all sorts of rules about how you're supposed to feel, and how you're meant to behave—but I hope you know, you don't have to pretend that you don't have feelings. At least, not for my benefit."

He finally looked at her; she was not prepared for the naked and unguarded hurt she saw in his eyes, the sadness that had clearly taken root in him. It speared her through the chest. She was surprised at the intensity of her feelings—surprised to find that this sudden moment of vulnerability did not alarm her one bit. No hero in any romance she'd read before had been allowed to feel anything other than righteous anger, any sorrow turning immediately to swift and red-blooded retribution. She was glad that he was going off book; she could tell that anything less would have been a lie.

As if in a dream, Georgiana moved closer and reached for his face; he did not try to stop her. Her thumb brushed his cheekbone and he closed his eyes, his face softening at last, relaxing into her touch as a single tear escaped from between his lashes.

She was going to kiss him. She wanted to tell him that however foolish it was, she already liked him a great deal—that it pained her to see him hurt—that he bore too much on his shoulders. The kiss would say it all for her. She tilted her face toward his, and he opened his eyes, his gaze suddenly fierce—as if daring her to be repulsed by his pain and back down.

When it became clear she would not, he shifted suddenly, one hand reaching for her waist, pulling her a little roughly toward him, and then—

"Miss Ellers," said a voice from behind them, with the sort of timing that Georgiana couldn't fathom outside of a Shakespearean farce. They sprang apart.

A tall, slightly disapproving-looking servant was standing in the doorway, his gaze pointedly averted.

"A Miss Campbell is here and wishes to speak with you." He gestured inside the house.

Georgiana swallowed her adrenaline and followed him back into the hallway, not daring to look back at Thomas. The moment she left him, she was half-convinced she had invented the entire thing; had she really touched him? Had he really laid himself open to her—looked at her that way—*wanted* her?

The servant's words caught up with her as she hurried along behind him. She had no idea how Frances could have found her, or what could have brought her to a stranger's door at ten o'clock at night.

When they arrived in the entrance hall and Georgiana saw her, she gasped; her friend's gown was wet through, her bonnet clutched in her hand with its ribbons trailing dejectedly on the floor. Her hair was ruined. Makeup was smeared down her face, and she was openly weeping.

"Frances! What on earth?" cried Georgiana. Another servant came rushing down the stairs with a blanket, and Georgiana helped to pull it around Frances's shoulders. "Are you ill? Should

I ask the Taylors to call for a doctor? Or, dear God—they can have somebody draw you a bath, you're soaked through."

"No, no," mumbled Frances, choking back another sob. She waved the maid away and half-staggered over to the staircase to sit down heavily on the bottom step. Georgiana followed suit. "I came to see *you*, George. I needed to . . . I needed somebody who would understand."

Her eyes were very pink, and Georgiana could smell the alcohol on her; it seemed to come not only from her breath, but from her very pores. Georgiana put a comforting arm around her damp shoulder. She could still hear shouts of laughter from the drawing room and prayed that nobody would come out and discover Frances in such a state.

"How did you find me?" asked Georgiana as Frances pushed a wet curl out of her eyes.

"Oh, that. It wasn't hard. I was with Cecily and Jane, but I haven't *told* them, and I needed to talk to somebody who *knew*. I can't tell Jane, I just can't, so I went to your house, and Mr.—Mr. Burton told me you were here. He did look terribly funny, in his nightgown," she said, with a snort of laughter—but this quickly turned into a sob. "Oh, George, he hasn't written. He hasn't called on me. He certainly hasn't spoken to my *father*. It's been over a month. Bloody Jonathan was *right*. It's all such a mess, I can't—I just *can't* . . ."

Georgiana put a hand to her mouth and then spoke tentatively through her fingers.

"But . . . might there be some kind of . . . arrangements to be made? He must tell his family, or make plans, or—"

"Or," said Frances, angry now and slurring her words, "he never *meant* to propose. He never meant to! And I'm just as stupid as every other . . . every other *stupid* girl who's ever crossed his path. Except even more stupid, even stupider, because I—because we . . ."

She collapsed onto Georgiana's shoulder, crying in earnest again now. Georgiana hushed her and smoothed her damp hair, her fingers catching in the tight whorls of it.

"That girl. *Annabelle Baker.* She's not a whore, George. She's nobody. She's nothing. Just the daughter of some merchant. But he's been seeing her for months. Clandestine meetings in that pub. It was all paid for in his name—her room, board, everything."

"Oh *God,* Frances. How did you find out?"

"What? Oh—I had our lawyer look into it. Jeremiah must think I'm just some . . . some common harlot. He thinks *I'm* nothing. But I'm not, George. Whatever I am, I'm . . . I'm something. I'm *someone*." She was shaking uncontrollably against Georgiana's side.

"Maybe . . . Maybe this isn't the end," Georgiana said carefully. "He's a little wild—but so are you, Frances, that's why it *works.* Perhaps he just needs to get it out of his system."

"How can I want him now? It would all be a lie. And I can't think of him without seeing her. That *slut*." Her voice was rising in volume and Georgiana looked nervously in the direction of the dining room.

"Come on, Frances. You must go home. Get some rest, and I'll call on you tomorrow, and we can talk this through. He's a rat—he's an absolute *rat,* I can't believe he's done this—but it'll be all right, you'll see. You just need to get to your bed."

Frances stiffened and wiped her eyes with the corner of the blanket, suddenly glowering at her.

"Oh, my apologies, am I *embarrassing* you, George?" she asked, a touch too loudly for comfort. "In front of most esteemed friends of the *Burtons*?"

"No! *No.* You're just having a bad night, that's all," said Georgiana hurriedly. "Everything always seems better in the morning than it did the night before, you know that. I'm sure it will stop raining tomorrow, and I'll come to the house for a drink, and we can talk and play chess and . . . and we can work it all out."

She had no idea how exactly this situation could be "worked out," but that was a problem for tomorrow's Georgiana. Whatever paltry comfort she could offer right now, Frances was not in any state to hear it.

"Fine," said Frances crossly, clumsily getting to her feet. She rubbed her eyes, her fingers coming away dark with makeup, and then froze, looking at something over Georgiana's shoulder. "Oh, well, if it isn't *Thomas Hawksley*."

Georgiana turned to see that Thomas had indeed come out into the hallway behind them. All traces of what had passed between them were gone from his face; he looked completely inscrutable and blank, as if they were no more than passing acquaintances.

"Miss Campbell," he said by way of greeting, with a stiff half-bow. "Miss Ellers—I simply came to see if you were . . ." He seemed to suddenly notice Frances's thoroughly bedraggled state. "Miss Campbell, are you quite well?"

"*Quite*," Frances spat back, bristling like a very wet and agitated cat. "I'm in no need of rescuing, Mr. Hawksley, so you can rejoin your little party."

"Frances," said Georgiana nervously, "he's only asking."

Frances narrowed her eyes at him, eyebrows slanting with derision.

"Oh, *really*, George. He's just looking for another chance to play the hero. I'm sure he thought Cecily would want to thank him most *thoroughly* after what he did for her at the cottage, and now he's after somebody else to ply with sob stories and . . . and sink his hooks into."

This was such a terrible assessment of Mr. Hawksley's character that it left Georgiana speechless.

"I can assure you, Miss Campbell, I wouldn't dream of such

a thing," he said forcefully. "Miss Ellers knows I have only the highest regard—"

"Oh, *bore off*, Thomas. We're not in the market for tragic recluses. All that moping and misery shan't win you any points here—she's not going to fuck you just because your brother died and she feels sorry for you." Thomas's mouth opened, but he did not speak. "*Miss Ellers* is far too . . . far too interesting to waste her time on someone as dull, someone as dry, someone as tiresome—"

"Good night, Miss Campbell," Thomas said, in a voice as brittle as bone.

He turned abruptly and disappeared back toward the party.

Georgiana stared after him, aghast. How could she have been so pathetic? So spineless? She had said nothing at all while Frances had attacked his character. After all he had done—after what he had shared with her that night—he had watched her sit there and say nothing in his defense. She was furious with Frances, and she wanted to abandon her on the stairs and rush after Thomas to make sure he knew so—but Frances was crying again, attempting to put her bonnet on with trembling fingers. Georgiana pushed down her anger and helped her, feeling oddly detached, and then accompanied her to the doorway.

"We'll . . . We'll speak in the morning," she said.

Frances looked totally lost for a second, silhouetted against the rain, and then threw herself forward to pull Georgiana into a brief and tight embrace. Georgiana didn't quite return it, her hands dangling uselessly at her sides, but she did lift one in a pale attempt to wave goodbye as Frances stepped up into her carriage, still clutching the Taylors' blanket to her shoulders. The coachman raised his whip, and they sped off into the night.

Georgiana reentered the drawing room with trepidation, but nobody seemed to have noticed her absence. She sat down beside her aunt, trying to catch Thomas's eye, but unsurprisingly he would not meet her gaze—and just ten minutes later, he and his father abruptly began saying their goodbyes. She noticed that the latter looked rather relieved.

Mr. James Hawksley grasped her hand and wished her well when he reached her, but Thomas gave only a curt nod in her direction, his eyes fixed on the wall above her, before assisting his father from the room. Words rose up and then caught in her throat as she watched him leave.

Mrs. Burton, who had been making great headway with the bottle of sherry, did not seem to notice that her niece's insides were at this very moment being shredded like tissue paper. She was still playing the parlor game and leaned sloppily over the arm of her chair to ask for assistance.

"Georgiana, my dear—can you think of a rhyme for 'dishonorable'?"

Georgiana picked up her aunt's glass and knocked back a mouthful of sherry.

"Yes, Mrs. Burton. 'Intolerable.'"

Chapter Twenty

GEORGIANA DID NOT CALL UPON FRANCES THE NEXT DAY.
She couldn't stop thinking about the poisonous words Frances had spat at Thomas—the fact that every single barb had seemed to find its target—the expression on his face as he bore it all, as he absorbed every blow without argument, not looking for one second as if he expected Georgiana to defend him. The fact that, to her endless shame, he had been right.

After all Frances had done—after the moment Georgiana had so long waited for had been ruined—she found that she felt quite uncharitable toward her friend. No matter how distressed she had been, it did not excuse her outright cruelty.

She continued to feel disinclined to reach out to Frances as she spent the next few days drifting around the house, swapping surprisingly scandalous romance novels with Emmeline and eating ferociously, writing to nobody and receiving nothing in return. Occasionally she wandered to her uncle's desk, but every time she thought of Thomas—of the moment they had nearly kissed, and the moment Frances had ensured they probably never would—she put off writing to Frances for another day. She felt that Frances surely owed her some sort of apology and should therefore be the one to write first, to provide it. Georgiana had never had a close friend, had never really cared for anybody before or felt cared for in that way, so had equally never had the chance to feel hurt or let down. She was certainly *not* going to ask her aunt for advice on how to proceed, which meant that the only guidance she had came from her books—and she had yet to discover one in which a heroine had to navigate the repercussions of a drunken, emotional outburst at a quiet Thursday night dinner party.

Georgiana found herself in a very irksome and restless sort of mood. One morning when she and Mr. Burton were alone at the breakfast table, as Mrs. Burton had gone into the town to see about some wallpaper, she attempted to make conversation with him. Her uncle quickly disappeared behind his newspaper, as was customary. She felt she had been quite charitable in trying to engage him when she was feeling so dour, so did not take the rejection well.

She was eating an apple, and in the silence the crunching of it was all she could hear. Experimentally, she took a bite that was so loud as to be indecent. Mr. Burton was not roused. She tried again, this time smacking her lips. The newspaper trembled. She waited a full minute to lull him into a false sense of security and then took another enormous bite.

The newspaper was lowered, and Mr. Burton's eyebrows bristled over the top of it.

"Georgiana—" he began, but Georgiana cut him short.

"George. It's George now."

Mr. Burton looked perplexed. "George?"

"Yes, I would like to be addressed as George. That is what my friends call me, in any case."

"I can't call you George," said Mr. Burton incredulously. "The king's name is George, for goodness' sake!"

"Never heard of him," said Georgiana, taking her apple with her as she left the table.

Mrs. Burton, who had lately taken to watching Georgiana closely like a sort of disappointed bird of prey, invited her firmly into the parlor after dinner that evening. Once she had Georgiana trapped inside, she picked up her hideous embroidery and began to work.

"You've been spending quite a lot of time with Miss Campbell," she observed, needles clicking.

"Yes," Georgiana said, not sure if she was being told off or congratulated.

"Are you forgetting your commitments to *other* friends, Georgiana?"

Told off it was, then.

"What other friends?" Georgiana asked, a touch bitterly.

"Well! You know I am fond of Frances, Georgiana—but I'm sure you promised Miss Walters another visit, unless I'm very much mistaken," Mrs. Burton said, embroidering even harder.

"Right, yes." Georgiana felt suddenly guilty; she had not spared a thought for Betty Walters in quite some time. "I'll send her a note, Mrs. Burton, I promise."

"Very good," said Mrs. Burton with a knowing smile. "I did see you getting on *frightfully well* with Mr. Hawksley at dinner, Georgiana. And at the pianoforte."

If she knew just how well they had been getting on, Georgiana thought, she'd probably embroider a hole in herself from the shock of it.

"Yes, well—he's very good with his hands," Georgiana said carelessly. "Er—with the piano, I mean."

But her aunt did not seem to have noticed; she probably assumed that Georgiana knew of no other uses for a man's hands.

"I don't mean to *pry*," she pried, "but goodness, he is rather handsome, Georgiana. And he's . . . Well, it would be an advantageous match."

"He's rich enough to buy us all, you mean."

"Oh, honestly, must you always be so uncouth?" Mrs. Burton sighed and put her embroidery down in her lap. "I'm just saying that if you *do* like him, it might be wise to let it be known. With subtlety, of course. But not *every* subtlety."

"He's not interested, Aunt," Georgiana said firmly. "I am certain of it."

The truth—that she thought he *had* been interested, that they had recently come within inches of kissing, that she felt she had thoroughly ruined her chances with him by being an unforgivable coward—was far too complicated to explain. Georgiana got up to leave, waiting to see if Mrs. Burton would protest; she did not. As she reached the doorway, however, she heard her aunt clear her throat.

"You should mind me, Georgiana. Handsome, wealthy, *kind* young men aren't that easy to come by. Especially not ones who are . . . *good with their hands.*"

Georgiana rushed away before she could think too hard about what exactly that meant.

The next morning, an unfamiliar carriage arrived at the door; its owner became evident when Jonathan leaned casually out of it and called, "Hop in, bumpkin—we're going to Cecily's for luncheon."

The luncheon in question had been arranged in the shelter of a large, ornate gazebo, for the day was startlingly hot; Jane and Frances were already seated, although they seemed to be turned fractionally away from each other, as if they had recently been arguing. Georgiana avoided Frances's eye as she sat down, wondering not for the first time if Frances might be angry at her for not writing or coming to call, and then determinedly resolving not to care.

Cecily, at least, seemed delighted, kissing Georgiana on the cheek and offering her a plate of food.

"There's going to be a *party*," she said, cheeks flushed with excitement.

Georgiana was confused. "There's *always* going to be a party," she replied, cutting a slice of cheese and eating it while Jane laughed dryly.

Frances was oddly silent and unresponsive, gazing down at her plate without seeming to see it.

"Not like this," said Cecily, popping a grape into her mouth and sighing dreamily.

"The earl who owns Haverton House is back. Where you had that queer little picnic," said Jane, reaching for her wineglass. "He usually hosts the last big event of the season. I'm convinced he doesn't care if we burn that house to the ground, as he has nobody to leave it to."

"Oh, it'd be such a waste to burn it," said Jonathan. "It's like some sort of shrine to decadence. The interiors are wall-to-wall red velvet and gold leaf, and stuffed to the brim with the most outrageous and obscene art. And his parties—you haven't *lived* until you've been to one of Lord Haverton's parties."

"Have I really been dead, all this while?" Georgiana said, but her curiosity was piqued. "Are all invited? Family—chaperones? I can't imagine Mr. and Mrs. Burton on a backdrop of red velvet, admiring pornographic sculptures."

"Oh, it's *strictly* unchaperoned," Cecily replied, skewering more cheese on the end of her knife. "Only for the under-thirties. That's one of the rules. But he's an *earl*, isn't he, and his uncle tends to be there, so my parents are more than happy for me to go. I think they're still hoping I might catch his eye. Jonathan might have more luck there."

Jonathan threw a piece of bread at her, narrowly missing her glass of wine. She scowled at him.

"That won't work on the Burtons," said Georgiana thoughtfully, moving Cecily's glass out of harm's way. "If these parties are as infamous as you say, I think Mrs. Burton may put her rather immovable foot down. I shall have to think of something."

"His uncle is just as bad as he is, if not worse," said Jonathan. "Last year I'm convinced I saw him disappearing into the orangery at about half past three in the morning, wearing nothing but his hat, and loading his pistol as if he were off to commit a little moonlight homicide in his birthday suit."

"Nobody turned up dead, as far as I can remember," Cecily said, shrugging.

Georgiana shot a parody of an alarmed expression at Jonathan, who snorted into his wine.

"Haverton should just marry someone tolerable and get on with things," said Frances, finally breaking her silence. "It's so selfish. The house will end up going to some very distant relative that nobody around here has ever heard of."

"Perhaps his hopes for marriage extend beyond loveless practicality and the logistics of his real estate holdings," Jane replied.

It was innocuous enough but for her tone, and Frances immediately rose to meet it.

"Why don't *you* marry him?" she snapped. "I'm sure your parents will be thrilled to be rid of you."

Georgiana's hand tightened around her glass of wine as Jane flinched. It could have passed for a joke, but nobody laughed—instead, Jonathan turned to Georgiana and pressed a beseeching hand to her arm.

"I've been agonizing over what to wear—you must advise me. If I have to think about it for a second longer, I'm afraid my brains might start leaking out through my ears."

"It's a costumed ball," Cecily explained to Georgiana, who frowned immediately.

She didn't have a single thing suitable for a costumed ball and, unlike the rest of them, did not have endless resources that would allow her to throw something together in less than a week.

"What sort of costumes?" she asked Cecily.

"Oh, whatever you want, really, but the theme is 'nymphs and dryads.'"

"Right, so whatever I want, as long as I look like a creature from Greek myth. Very helpful."

Georgiana mentally rifled through her wardrobe and came up short.

"I might eschew clothes altogether and simply paint myself water-nymph blue," Jonathan mused, arching his brow at Georgiana. "Join me in my depravity—just drape a sheet over yourself and say you're a nymph of the bedroom."

"I'm sure that'll give just the right impression at an unchaperoned party where apparently we'll all be lucky to escape without being shot by an elderly man in the nude."

Everybody except Frances laughed.

"James is going to be there," Cecily said, absentmindedly dropping a grape into her wineglass and watching it bob about with a beatific smile. "I saw him the other night—he said he was going to buy me a *horse*. You know, I think he might propose."

"Cecily! That's wonderful," Georgiana said with genuine delight as Jonathan clapped Cecily on the back. "I think it truly baffling that you weren't married the moment you turned eighteen. You must have been beating suitors off with a stick."

"Well—I *was* engaged to be married a few years ago," she said quietly. Georgiana's mouth fell open. "Only it went . . . Well, it all went quite badly wrong."

Frances gave a dry huff of amusement. "Always so unlucky in love, aren't you, Ces? Showed up at the wrong church, did you?"

"No," Cecily mumbled, looking slightly embarrassed.

"Oh, ignore her," Georgiana said, a little more harshly than she had intended. "*I* want to know."

Everybody seemed to take a collective breath, holding it as they waited for Frances's response, but she only slumped back in her chair; Georgiana pretended not to see the significant look that Jane exchanged with Jonathan across the table.

"I liked him quite a lot, actually. He was the first person I liked after . . . well, the first person I had liked for quite some time," Cecily said, ducking her head. "He was going to be a duke. His family weren't hugely pleased with me—they wanted him to marry somebody titled, you know—but they had come around. Then he got cold feet, just before the wedding. Said he liked another girl, too, of much higher standing, and he was loath to choose between us." She sighed. "I told him . . . I told him to follow his heart, and that if it was too hard to choose, I would bow out. I hate to make choices, they're terribly hard—sometimes it takes me an hour to decide what I want for breakfast, so I truly did feel for him—and I knew his family would be so pleased. It would have been hard to marry him thinking I was hurting his prospects, you know, and they were all so thrilled with the other match."

Georgiana didn't know what to say. She reached out and squeezed her hand.

"You are a sweetheart, Cecily. Far too good for this world. Any gentleman would be lucky to have you."

"Oh, I don't know about that," she replied, blushing.

"If he doesn't propose, I'll marry you," Jonathan said.

Jane made a little noise of derision.

"No, I mean it," he continued. "I've been thinking about it, and I think we'd have a perfectly jolly time. I'll rescue you from the looming specter of spinsterhood. You can romp about in the countryside and shoot your arrows, I'll entertain gentlemen while you're out; it'll be the perfect modern arrangement. For me, at least. No more clandestine meetings in churchyards and gardens. No more pining and wasting away and secrets."

"Oh, but isn't that sort of romantic?" Georgiana said.

She immediately knew she had said the wrong thing when Jonathan winced.

"Not really, George. It doesn't feel quite so poetic when it's all you can ever have. I am afraid it's not some fairy-tale story where all the pain is worth it in the end. You just get the delightful part with all the pain."

Georgiana wasn't sure if she was imagining it, but the tension between Jane and Frances seemed to have suddenly intensified.

"God, I'm sorry, Jonathan. That's dreadful," she said quietly.

Jonathan wrinkled his nose at her and shrugged.

"No need to cry about it. There are worse lots in life than mine—case in point, imagine being *Christopher*."

Georgiana laughed.

"I want to know," Frances said suddenly, "when we all got so bloody *boring*."

She was sitting up in her seat again now, eyes fixed on Georgiana and narrowed in some sort of unreadable challenge. The heat of the day suddenly seemed to have caught up with Georgiana, the rail of the chair burning into her back where the sun had crept in under the gazebo, but she held her ground.

She didn't acknowledge Frances. Nobody did. And Georgiana experienced an odd feeling—a sudden, unexpected twist of grim satisfaction—when she realized that instead, they were all looking expectantly at her.

Chapter Twenty-one

GEORGIANA THOUGHT LONG AND HARD ABOUT HOW TO raise the subject of Lord Haverton's party with Mrs. Burton, but in the end her salvation came in the form of a letter from Betty Walters. She felt a faint stab of guilt as soon as she saw the name signed in neat, round script; she still hadn't written to her, and clearly Betty had grown tired of waiting. Luckily, it seemed she was much more concise when writing rather than speaking.

Dear Miss Ellers,

It is my most ardent desire to enjoy your company once more after the tea and conversation we shared last month. I could hardly believe so many days had gone by, but then I counted on my hands, and there they were! I understand that you have been busy, and therefore I write to ask if you are attending the ball at the Haverton estate this week. I have been reliably informed that he throws the most fascinating parties! Grandmama will not come, of course, but if you will escort me, she will assent to my attending. I propose that we meet at nine o'clock at the west entrance—that is, if you do not wish me to collect you in our carriage—for I would not be bold enough to go it alone! Please write back at your earliest convenience.

Yours affectionately,
Miss Elizabeth Walters

"You see? Betty needs me to go," Georgiana said, brandishing the letter like a weapon as soon as Mr. and Mrs. Burton had finished their supper.

"They haven't even cleared the plates, Georgiana, you're going to get butter on it."

Mrs. Burton rescued the letter from its buttery fate and peered at it. She showed it to Mr. Burton, who gave so quick a perfunctory nod that there was no way he'd been able to read it.

"I don't know, Georgiana. Lord Haverton has always seemed like quite a peculiar fellow. I don't like this. I don't like this at all."

"I think . . . I think he's monstrously misunderstood," Georgiana cried, clutching at straws. "He is just lonely, that's all. Imagine having such a big house and hardly any family to fill it."

"Well, I suppose, if Mrs. Walters was not concerned . . ." Mrs. Burton was wavering.

"Betty needs me. She cannot attend alone, Aunt, you know that. We will care for each other, and make sure we stay far away from anything out of the ordinary. And . . . And Lord Haverton needs us, to stave off the terrible shadow of loneliness!"

Georgiana thought she might be laying it on a bit thick now, but it seemed to be working.

"Very well. But you must be home by midnight, Georgiana. And look after Betty, won't you? She's a sensitive soul. She'll be taking Mrs. Walters's carriage, I expect—have her come and call for you, so you can arrive together."

Dear Betty,
Thank you most kindly for your letter, it brought me more joy than you'll ever know. I will certainly be attending the ball at Haverton House—I shall see you there!
Yours, Georgiana Ellers

In the end, Georgiana *did* have to wear a bedsheet to the party. It was one of Mrs. Burton's best; she had no idea how she would explain all the holes she'd had to make in it to pin it in place, but she began concocting wild stories of pernicious mice in the bedrooms as soon as she decided to steal it, and reasoned that she'd sort out the details later. She made sure to whisk it away when the Burtons were out, and when the day of the ball came, she told Mrs. Burton she was going to have a "quiet lie-down" before the party, then locked her door and fashioned herself something akin to a dress. It wrapped around her waist and then carried on over both shoulders, and was inclined to bunch unattractively if she did not adjust it every few minutes.

A clean getaway in costume would rely on careful timing. Mrs. Burton had retreated to the parlor after dinner and Mr. Burton had gone for his evening walk, just like clockwork, but if her aunt sensed even a hint of movement, she'd come rushing out to see Georgiana off and say good evening to Betty. As Georgiana had in fact arranged for Cecily and Jonathan to pick her up—Betty would have stopped in to be polite, and Mrs. Burton would certainly have banned Georgiana from taking one more step toward Haverton House if she saw her dressed in bed linen—she needed to ensure a foolproof distraction.

When Georgiana finally heard the quiet rumble of a carriage approaching, she rushed to the back of the house, where an ugly vase sat on the windowsill above the stairs. The windows were usually closed, but Georgiana had opened them a few hours earlier so as not to arouse suspicion. She hesitated for a second, then winced and gave the vase a good shove. It dropped like a stone and then smashed spectacularly on the patio, shattering so loudly that Georgiana gasped, despite the fact that she had been the one to push it to its doom. She heard Mrs. Burton's exclamation immediately and waited for a moment, listening.

Sure enough, her aunt was hurrying to the back of the house, calling out to her to ask if she had heard anything amiss.

"Oh *no*, what a mess! It must have been the wind—and the windows! Open! Who left the *windows* open?"

Seizing her chance, Georgiana took the stairs two at a time, almost tripping over her sheet in her haste. She was almost free when she came skidding to a stop—Emmeline was standing in the doorway to the dining room, holding the silver she had been polishing, staring at Georgiana in shock.

"Please," Georgiana mouthed, widening her eyes pleadingly.

For a second it looked as if Emmeline might object, but then she just sighed and shook her head, bemused, and followed the sound of Mrs. Burton's complaining into the garden. Georgiana completed the final phase of her escape and climbed into Cecily's carriage, breathing hard.

"You *are* a nymph of the bedroom!" Jonathan exclaimed, handing Georgiana a bottle of wine before she had even finished sitting down.

"I am! Ces, we'd better get away quickly," she panted, looking furtively back at the house.

"Oh! Done a runner, have you? Say no more." Cecily leaned her head out of the window. "Drive on, Simon! Make haste!"

They took off at speed, and Georgiana could finally relax against the seat and knock back a fortifying gulp of wine as she took in her friends' attire.

Cecily was dressed in green, with what looked like real foliage woven through her hair. She had acquired a shawl of mossy fabric patterned with leaves, so light it seemed to float about her shoulders and never settle. There were emeralds in her ears, and she had even painted her décolletage with greens and golds to complete the effect. She looked so ethereal that Georgiana had no trouble believing that she was from a completely different realm from the one she, a woman wearing a bedsheet, was currently inhabiting. Jonathan had thankfully decided to wear clothes, and was sparkling in a frock coat in shades of cerulean.

Georgiana was alternating wildly between nerves and excitement as she took another pull on the bottle of wine and tried to listen to Cecily talking about axe-throwing, a new hobby she had apparently picked up in the past week. Georgiana could not be sure what awaited her at this party, but it somehow felt more significant than any of the others that had come before it. It had not escaped her notice that Cecily had offered her carriage without prompting, and that Frances was absent—that she had somehow become essential to their plans *without* Frances's invitation. If Frances did not ask Georgiana to stay in London come September—an outcome that currently looked all too possible, if this coolness between them persisted—surely, she reasoned, Cecily or Jonathan would instead?

By the time they had traveled up the length of the enormous driveway, her palms were damp and her head was light, but Georgiana knew with certainty that she was exactly where she was meant to be.

They had to wait in a queue of carriages before they could pull up to Haverton House, and when Georgiana stepped out she was greeted by the sight of towering gray walls, pillars the width of ancient tree trunks, and an audience of leering gargoyles and stone unicorns gazing down at her from the balustrades. The wide steps that led to an enormous oaken door were flanked by flaming torches and costumed servants holding trays of drinks— Jonathan insisted that they stop multiple times on their way up to refresh themselves for the final ascent.

The interior of the house also did not disappoint. It gave the impression of a pawnbroker's shop visited only by the incredibly eccentric and insultingly wealthy, with miscellaneous clutter adorning every wall and surface. In the hallway they were greeted with the sight of an enormous model ship, with a figurehead that

Cecily explained was quite a good likeness of Lord Haverton, if a little more generously lithe and muscular. An entire wall was given over to hundreds upon thousands of knives, forks, and spoons, which had been arranged in careful patterns as one might display military swords. On their way through the house, they passed what looked like a model village; on closer inspection, it was a reproduction of their own town, and they exclaimed with delight and pointed out their respective houses (Georgiana tried not to be offended that the Burtons' was represented by a tiny, anonymous brown box).

Guests were packed into the ballroom, which had been decorated with what looked like living trees; water features had somehow been installed at regular intervals and were trickling away prettily. It was like stumbling into an enchanted wood—the light strangely green, the room's inhabitants all painted and costumed and otherworldly. Frances and Jane were already standing by one of the fountains; Jane spotted them and beckoned.

They were both just as exquisitely costumed as Cecily and Jonathan, and Georgiana tugged at her sheet self-consciously, hoping she didn't look quite as foolish as she felt. Jane was draped in warm autumnal reds and browns, a crown of poisonous-looking berries on her head; Frances was also in flowing white, but her dress looked a thousand miles away from Georgiana's bedsheet. The fabric was so fine that it cascaded around her like water.

It was immediately clear that Frances had started the evening long before the rest of them—perhaps even before breakfast. She was swaying on her feet, her dress in constant danger of being splattered with wine from the glass that she could barely hold upright.

"You're here," she said slightly redundantly when they approached.

Jane deftly swiped the glass out of her hand before it fell, as Frances abandoned it completely and threw an arm around Jonathan's shoulders. Georgiana had been braced for conflict and was pleasantly surprised by how amiable she seemed, even if it was clearly chemically induced.

"Is she all right?" Georgiana mouthed to Jane once she had been released from Frances's sweaty grasp.

Jane rolled her eyes and shook her head briefly, placing the glass out of sight on the other side of the fountain before Frances could pick it up again.

"Christopher said he had something for us," Frances slurred, leaning a little too far into Jonathan before being subtly righted by him. "We're to meet him."

"Did he, now?" Jonathan said, grimacing. "I can't say I'm much inclined to acquiesce to that invitation."

"Oh, don't be . . . Don't be *clever*, Jonathan," Frances said irritably. "It doesn't suit you. Come on, Ces, Janey."

Nobody moved.

Georgiana saw it hit Frances, saw the surprise and fury twist her expression—she was too drunk to conceal it. Whatever power she usually held over them all seemed to be unexpectedly faltering. She opened her mouth again, and Georgiana decided to avert disaster.

"Better to go now," she said, shrugging, "and meet him while we've still got most of our wits about us. Harder for him to pickpocket us or sacrifice us to Bacchus if we're still standing upright."

"Who's standing upright?" Jane said, cutting her eyes toward Frances—but when the latter pushed away from Jonathan and started across the room, they all followed.

They ducked and weaved past the other partygoers, Frances leaning over to snatch another glass of wine from the tray of a waiter dressed like a faun, and then squeezed down a packed corridor until they reached a scarlet parlor, filled to the brim with all manner of taxidermied creatures. Christopher, looking the epitome of an ill-intentioned Greek god and flanked by four other similarly dressed men, was lounging inside it, smoking something that had filled the room with a thick, pungent fog. He had apparently decided that wearing a shirt was optional, and Georgiana looked everywhere but at him, her skin prickling with discomfort.

"Ah! Miss *Georgiana*," he called languorously.

Georgiana realized that he was in fact leaning on a vast, dead striped cat—it could only be a tiger, although she had never seen one in person before. She nodded and gave him a tight-lipped smile, thinking that he seemed far too slow-moving at the minute to pose any real sort of threat.

"Come to sample some of my *many* delights, have you?"

"Alas, if only we could identify them," said Jonathan, but Frances was already at Christopher's side, holding out a hand for the tiny dark bottle he was dangling from his fingers. He grinned at Georgiana as he handed it over, but then turned sharply to Frances when she clumsily removed the stopper.

"Careful," he snapped, grabbing her wrist, his previous practiced cool nowhere to be seen. "Don't *spill* it. You only need a drop or two."

Frances focused long enough to deposit two heavy drops of liquid into her glass of wine and then drank the whole thing down in one go.

"What is it?" Georgiana asked dubiously as Frances handed the bottle to Jane.

"Blood of innocents," Jane said seriously, but she followed suit and added some of whatever it was to her own drink, wincing as she swallowed it.

"It's a *special concoction* of mine," Mr. Crawley replied, which was perhaps even more alarming than being given no information at all.

Nevertheless, Georgiana would not be left behind on the wildest night of the year; she took her turn, drinking deeply from her glass and then passing the bottle to Cecily, coughing and spluttering when the bitterness of the tincture hit her tongue.

"A little much for you, is it?" Christopher sneered, reaching out to rub her back while she was incapacitated.

"Don't touch me," she spat back, shrugging him off.

The room was already spinning around her, and she had the strangest suspicion that her hands were no longer at the end of her arms. She put them out in front of her and observed that she was still fully intact—but when she flexed her fingers, they seemed to move with a few seconds' delay. It should all have been faintly disconcerting, but she couldn't bring herself to feel anything but pleasantly detached.

One of Christopher's friends passed his pipe around, and it traveled lazily from hand to hand; when Cecily took her turn she blew smoke rings, much to the delight of everyone except Frances, who rolled her eyes and waved a hand through them so that they dissipated around her.

"I feel very observed right now," Jonathan said.

He gestured around at the many stuffed and mounted heads, the antlers above the fireplace, the pile of seemingly extraneous animal hides thrown over the back of one of the sofas. Now that he mentioned it, Georgiana felt there were a few too many leering, glassy eyes peering at her through the gloom—Christopher's chief among them.

"Oh, God. I feel as if they're looking directly into my soul," Georgiana said, holding up a hand that suddenly seemed semitranslucent to try to shield herself from the gaze of an extremely judgmental zebra.

"What soul?" said Frances; her tone was intentionally light but entirely unconvincing.

"Come on, George," said Cecily, her hand alighting on Georgiana's shoulder. "You haven't had the grand tour. Anybody else? Jane?"

Jane eyed Frances, who was now stroking the ears of a wolf-skin rug as if it were still alive to enjoy it, and shook her head.

Georgiana allowed herself to be pulled gently from the room. The air outside it was mercifully fresh, despite the crush of guests, and Georgiana found herself taking deep breaths of it as if she had just emerged from a cave or been pulled from the bottom of a well.

They struggled through the raucous crowds, ricocheting off anybody who got in their way and giggling as they went, and then stumbled up a grand staircase until they reached a long, expansive hallway that was far less populated. Cecily tried a door handle at random and found it locked; the next she attempted to throw open dramatically, clearly expecting similar results, and they both squeaked in shock when it did in fact swing open to reveal an elderly man in a very revealing toga. He was standing in the middle of the room on top of a wooden chest while three women, lounging on large cushions, appeared to be painting him. The inhabitants of the room all turned to look at them, and Cecily quickly shut the door, trying to smother her laughter.

The next door she approached slowly, putting a finger to her lips with an exaggerated "*Shush*" as she opened it just a crack so they could see what was happening inside.

At first, all Georgiana could see was movement—then it became a mass of *something*, something writhing, some vast creature that had many arms and many legs moving independently—and then it fell into place and she realized they were *bodies*. Georgiana clapped both her hands over her mouth in shock, blinking rapidly. They were naked human bodies, seemingly completely unashamed of their nakedness and of the fact that they were touching, kissing, *fornicating*—

"Oh," Cecily said faintly. "Oh *my*."

"But they're . . . What are they *doing*?" Georgiana whispered, steadying herself against the wall.

Cecily let the door fall closed and turned to her with wide eyes.

"Well—certainly not painting! Oh, goodness. I think Lord Haverton might have been in there somewhere, but I didn't dare look too closely."

"I—I can't believe it," said Georgiana truthfully.

She had thought herself beyond shock now—had imagined that she had seen the most scandalous of what this world had to offer—but clearly for some people, the limit did not exist. She knew that she would never be able to unsee it; the image was imprinted in her mind indelibly and would probably haunt her for years to come.

"Goodness, it's like we're in *hell*," Cecily said, sounding quite pleased. "Quick, quick!"

She was pulling Georgiana down the corridor again, this time with purpose.

"Oh, God—what now?" Georgiana asked with genuine apprehension, trying to steady herself as they reached another door.

"Don't worry. I know what's in this one, and it's lovely," Cecily said, pushing it open.

They were immediately hit with the smell of manure. Georgiana put her hand over her nose and mouth, fearing the worst—and then her eyes adjusted to the dim light, and she understood why it smelled so strongly of shit.

It *was* shit. The room was piled with straw, and in the far corner, flicking its ears in an interested sort of way toward the intruders, stood an enormous black horse.

"Is this . . . ? Is this his *horse's bedroom*?" Georgiana asked incredulously, her qualms forgotten.

"Yes!" Cecily cried gleefully. "If you look in the corridor on the way back you can see . . . You can see these little dents in the floorboards, all the way from downstairs. He leads it up here whenever he comes to stay, so it can be close to him. Is it not the most wonderful thing you've ever seen?"

"It's the most *ridiculous* thing I've ever seen. This horse has a finer room than I do. It's a *lovely* horse, though."

She approached with her palm out flat, and the horse whickered gently, rubbing its velvet nose over her fingers to see if she had anything for it to eat. When it found she did not, it went back to grazing from a basket that had been suspended from the wall. She scratched it behind the ears, and it bore her attentions without complaint. Looking around, Georgiana saw that every painting in the room was of a horse. She felt faintly hysterical.

"Are those the horse's ancestors?" she choked out, pointing at a very solemn-looking portrait of a similar horse, framed in the finest gilt.

"Yes," came a smooth voice from behind them. Georgiana and the horse both jumped.

A short, dark-haired man dressed only in a loose red robe and with elaborate horns protruding from his head had entered the room and was observing them with his arms folded. Cecily dipped into a quick curtsy, so Georgiana did the same.

"Incidentally, his name is Atlas. The horse."

"Oh," said Georgiana nervously, wondering if they were about to be thrown out of the ball, "what a beautiful name."

"You may visit with him—he likes company—but please, do not bring him down to the party. He is *terrible* when he drinks."

Georgiana bit her lip to keep from laughing, but the man who must have been Lord Haverton did not seem to be joking.

"We won't," Georgiana reassured him. "In fact, ah—we'll just be going."

She carefully clambered over the straw toward the door, trying not to get any manure on her shoes or the very white sheet.

"Hang on—let me look at you."

Georgiana stopped next to Cecily and turned to face him. He leaned back with his hand under his chin, assessing them silently for a moment.

"Superlative. Glorious, both of you. You"—he gestured at Cecily—"are an angel among mere mortals. And you"—here he pointed at Georgiana—"I *love* your take. Minimal, stripped back. Just as gods would have walked the earth. Go forth and get up to some mischief!"

He shooed them away, and they turned to leave, giggling.

"Have fun, ladies!" he called down the corridor after them. "And if you see a fire, whatever you do—don't put it out."

They only made it as far as the top of the stairs before collapsing to the floor, both laughing so hard that their eyes were shining with tears.

"Oh, he's an odd man," Cecily said when she was able, which seemed a very generous sort of understatement.

"He's brilliant," Georgiana said, wiping her eyes. "I love him. I'll propose to him and put Frances's fears about the house to rest, if any wife of his would be treated half as well as that horse."

"I wish Frances wouldn't needle Jane so about him," said Cecily, sighing. "She keeps on about marriages of convenience, but Jane has never been the sort to . . . well." She suddenly seemed to think she had said too much.

Georgiana kept her expression entirely neutral.

"Frances has a needle for everybody right now. We're starting to look like so much embroidery."

"She has been dreadful, hasn't she? Much worse than usual. I think perhaps she'll feel better now that Annabelle—*oh*. God, I wasn't supposed to say."

"Annabelle?" Georgiana said, confused. "Annabelle who? Annabelle *Baker*?"

"I imagine so. The girl, you know, from the public house. Jonathan wasn't supposed to tell me, but of course, he told—and anyway, she's gone now, so I suppose it doesn't matter." Her pale eyebrows were knitted together in consternation. "You won't tell that *I* told, will you?"

"I don't know what I've *been* told," Georgiana said truthfully.

"Oh, it's a silly thing, really. Frances found out who her father was. She wrote to him to tell him what Annabelle had been up to with Jeremiah, and now I suppose she's been . . . sent somewhere."

"Sent somewhere? *Where?*"

"Oh, I don't know. A school? The convent? Wherever they . . . you know. *Send* people." Cecily didn't seem at all disturbed by this.

Georgiana's mouth had dropped open. "But, Ces, she didn't . . . Did she even *know* about Frances? And what if Jeremiah had spun her some tale about getting married, or . . . or—"

"You are sweet," Cecily said, patting Georgiana on the nearest part of her she could reach, which happened to be her foot. "I wouldn't worry about it. I'm sure it's a very nice convent. Oh!" She suddenly seemed to be struck by a thought, and she got unsteadily to her feet, holding a hand out for Georgiana. "We must go downstairs. It's almost time for the dancing."

"The dancing?" Georgiana asked dubiously, her head still full of Annabelle Baker as she was hauled to her feet by a surprisingly strong arm. She barely dared to imagine what kind of dancing would take place at a party like this one.

"Yes, George, of course! What sort of ball would it be without *dancing*?"

Chapter Twenty-two

THE GUESTS WERE ALREADY LINING UP AS CECILY AND GEOR-giana reentered the ballroom, and they joined in with the applause as the musicians struck up a rousing song and the dance began—thankfully, it seemed to be of the ordinary sort and did not involve any abnormal levels of nudity or manure.

"There you are!"

Jane had spotted them; she had one hand on Frances's back, and judging by the state of the latter's current equilibrium, it seemed integral to keeping her upright. Cecily exclaimed in delight and kissed Jane on the cheek with an enthusiastic flourish, as if she hadn't seen her for weeks, rather than half an hour. Or—perhaps it had actually been hours? It was hard for Georgiana to keep track; the minutes were blending into one another, simultaneously seeming to last an eternity and disappear in an instant. She felt a little sick from the rapid motion, as if she had lost the reins on a horse and was galloping out of control.

Jonathan appeared suddenly at Frances's shoulder, leaning in to be heard.

"He's here," she heard him mutter in Frances's ear. It took Georgiana a second to parse who exactly "he" might be. "I saw him in the entrance hall just a few minutes ago."

Frances's expression tightened, but she nodded in return, biting her lip with a look of extreme determination. Without another word to any of them, she turned and shouldered through the crowd, back toward the front of the house.

Georgiana watched her leave and then turned to Jonathan to ask him if they should really be letting her go alone—but he was already gone. He seemed to have spontaneously dematerialized, and Jane had vanished with him. Before Georgiana could voice her concern, Cecily grabbed her by the hand, pulling her into the next dance. They whirled around each other in the chaos, buffeted on all sides by people. Georgiana was barely able to keep Cecily in focus, momentarily forgetting her worries as the room blurred and her feet stumbled in time with the music, throwing her head back with closed eyes and laughing at the ridiculousness of it all.

Halfway through the song, the crowd parted for a moment and Georgiana saw a tall, curly-haired figure dressed entirely wrong for the occasion, his back stiff and flush with the wall as he watched the dancers with a guarded expression.

She tried very hard not to run toward him and hoped she was managing a casual, dignified pace as she abandoned Cecily and pushed her way to him. Thomas saw her before she reached him, which put her in the awkward position of needing to do something vaguely normal with her facial features. She settled on watching her feet as she walked, a necessary precaution even as the immediate effects of whatever had been in Christopher Crawley's bottle started to wane a little.

"You're not in costume," she said when she reached him, raising her voice to be heard above the merriment.

"No," Thomas replied, still watching the dance. He did not seem to want to look at her.

"Would you—would you like to dance with me?"

Georgiana wasn't convinced she was a particularly skilled dancer at this moment, but dying in a freak ballroom accident was preferable to being utterly, furiously ignored.

"No."

Georgiana was frustrated now. Not at Thomas, but with herself—she wanted very much to make things right between them again, but it felt beyond the limits of her cognitive function.

"Will you come outside with me? I need to . . . to say something," she said quietly.

He didn't hear her at first, and she had to lean in to repeat herself, overestimating the enthusiasm required and feeling a lock of his hair brush her cheek as she asked him again. She was almost certain he'd repeat his denial, but instead he nodded curtly and followed her out onto the patio. It was full of people drinking, screaming, laughing—the party spilling out into the night. The fresh air had a slightly sobering effect, and Georgiana realized she couldn't very well have a serious conversation with him while people staggered past, fully absorbed in the bacchanalia.

"Come with me," she said, exercising boldness of character she didn't know she possessed and taking him by the arm. Surprisingly Thomas did not resist and allowed himself to be walked out across the grounds toward what Georgiana could only assume was the famed orangery.

It was warm and dark and fragrant inside, lit with candles that must have been a terrible fire risk—but then, it probably wasn't considered romantic to think about fire safety, and this was certainly an area of the party designated for romance. Trees were growing wild and unchecked, with branches crossing and bending above their heads to make a sort of canopy. She heard giggles and the scuffles of shoes against the path through the leaves but couldn't see who they belonged to—and then the sound of a distant door opening and closing again, followed by silence, told her that they were alone. She sat down on a stone bench, trying to gather herself.

Thomas was still standing, looking at her warily, as if she might be about to attack him. She supposed that she essentially had; bodily dragging a man away from the company of others and into a darkened greenhouse might be considered a little forward, even at this party.

"All right. Well . . . firstly I just wanted to apologize," Georgiana said haltingly.

He gave a curt half-nod.

"We did not part how I had wished us to, the last time we met, and I . . . Well, I have no excuses. I was dreadful. Frances is a very difficult person to contradict sometimes, but I should have said something. She was completely out of order. And I hope you know that I really did appreciate what you shared with me. I know that it might have been . . . difficult for you to say it."

He was regarding her solemnly, and Georgiana felt a rush of affection toward him for the way his brow wrinkled when he frowned, and then shook her head slightly to try to regain her focus.

"There was no truth in what she said about you—we both know that. She was just angry and hurt and . . . anyway. You don't have to forgive her. You don't have to like her. *I* hardly like her some days. But she *is* my friend, and that's important to me."

"Fine," Thomas said, crossing his arms.

"Listen, I know I must seem a terrible disappointment—but I don't think you understand. Coming here was like being *reborn*, Thomas. I had resigned myself to the notion that life would pass me by—that there would be no great adventure, no close companions, no tales to tell. I would be nothing—nobody of importance to anybody in particular." Georgiana stopped to take a breath, surprised by the sudden force of her feelings. "I never dared dream of a life in which I might have friends like Frances, and places to be, and *consequence*. Perhaps it's unforgivable vanity, but now that I have had a glimpse of this world, I don't know how I could retreat into my old life and be content."

Thomas approached her—warily, as if there were some chance she might be rabid and he didn't want to get within biting distance—and took a seat next to her on the bench.

"I wouldn't have any of it, if it weren't for Frances. I was so very alone before I met her. Perhaps it sounds like a poor excuse for even poorer behavior, but I just wanted . . . Well, I just wanted to say that. To explain myself. Because I care very much what you think of me, although I have done a bad job of showing it. I have liked you from the moment we met."

"Georgiana—"

"Perhaps I make myself foolish by saying it aloud," Georgiana said, her words coming out in a panicked rush, "but—I *want* to be foolish. I've never been allowed that, until now."

"Georgiana—"

"I'm sorry for everything, Thomas, I really am; if I made you feel like you didn't matter, then that was the worst sort of lie imaginable."

She felt a solitary tear spill over her lashes; she couldn't look at him and stared at her hands instead, curled tightly in her lap.

"Are you quite finished?" Thomas asked, still sounding very serious.

"Yes," Georgiana said in a small voice.

"Are you going to look at me?"

"No," Georgiana said, just as quietly.

"Why not?"

"Because I'm afraid you think me an unforgivable fool."

Thomas sighed, and she felt him shifting on the bench next to her.

"You're not a fool," he said, his voice much closer and softer than she had expected. "Or at least—if you are, then I must be twice as foolish and more besides."

She felt a shock go through her as he placed a warm hand on her jaw, his thumb brushing against the corner of her mouth. She thought maybe he was reaching to wipe away her tear—but then he was leaning toward her, cradling her face in his hand, pressing the gentlest of kisses to her lips, as if he were afraid he might break her. And she felt he had, in a way; some part of her mind had clearly detached from the rest of her, because abandoning all inhibitions, all concerns that this was a line she could never uncross, she reached out to pull him properly to her. He looked almost pained in the second before she closed her eyes, but his lips parted to meet hers, and for a glorious moment she allowed her body the closeness it had been desperate for since she had first met him. His hand traveled along her jawline and behind her ear, stroking her hair, fingers tangling in it as he attempted the impossible and tried to bring her even nearer—and then suddenly he pulled away, breathing heavily, eyes closed and brows furrowed as if something had gone terribly awry.

"I'm sorry. I'm so sorry," he said, getting up and actually walking away from her.

"No, don't say that," Georgiana said breathlessly. She had no idea how he was able to coordinate himself to stand, let alone think of leaving. "Please. Stay."

He stopped in the doorway, apparently unable to look at her.

"No, this is . . . We both know this is wrong. You're incapacitated, you're upset, and I have taken advantage of you, and—"

"Taken advantage of me?" Georgiana felt a little indignant now. "*I* brought *you* here! I—I practically *dragged* you into the shrubbery. And I can assure you, I did not know this would happen, but I'm glad it has. Thomas, I *want* this, drunk or sober—I would have kissed you before, at the Taylors'. I would kiss you any time you'd have me."

"Please, don't just—you cannot want this," he said agitatedly. "We are not engaged—we haven't even made a passable attempt at *courting*. You have spent too much time around these people, these people with no regard for consequences. You don't want—"

"No. No! Do not tell me what I want," said Georgiana, getting shakily to her feet and crossing to him. "Look at me."

He turned toward her but closed his eyes and sighed with frustration, shaking his head.

"Georgiana, I—"

"Thomas. Please. *Look* at me."

Finally, he did. He looked at her as if he were afraid of her, and of himself, and of every possible thing that could happen next. She put out a hand and slowly pushed away a loose lock of his hair, as tenderly as he had reached for her the first time. He shivered very slightly at her touch, his eyes fluttering closed again—and then she kissed him, hard, pushing him back against the door frame, feeling his breath catch as he pulled her into his arms. His hands were at her face again, and then the nape of her neck, the curve of her back. He was kissing her as if he *needed* to, as if he'd die if he stopped, and all she wanted was to be closer to him, even though surely they were already as close as they could be in every possible way—even though she could feel every con-tour of him against her as his hands traveled down her back again and clutched at her waist, burning everything they touched—

Georgiana pulled away from him herself this time, reaching out an arm to steady herself against the glass of the wall. Her body was betraying all logic, breaching all the parameters set in place to keep her safe; in this moment she *wanted* him, in every sense of the word, more than she had ever wanted anything in her life. There was no real danger—somehow she doubted he'd pull her down into the damp soil beneath the orange trees and make passionate love to her then and there, even if she begged him to—but just the realization that she wanted more, that even *kissing* him wasn't enough, was a distinctly sobering thought.

They looked at each other, as wild-eyed and rumpled as if they had just been pulled apart in a fight, and then Thomas broke the tension by laughing quietly. He scrubbed a hand across his face and then took her by the hand, leading her wordlessly back to the bench. They sat side by side, both still a little out of breath, silent for a moment as they considered their sins.

"Georgiana," he said quietly, "let me . . . let me try to do this one thing right. I have come to care for you. Obviously. I wouldn't have . . . Anyway, look, I don't want you to think this is nothing to me. And I don't want you to be dishonored, in any way, by my behavior. I will speak to your aunt and uncle. I will send word to your parents—"

"You'll—what? You don't have to *propose* to me because you feel *bad* for me," said Georgiana, horrified. "Or out of any sense of—I don't know—of propriety. You don't have to get down on one knee for every girl who confesses that she likes you, or . . . There's nobody *here,* Thomas. Nobody saw us. I consider my honor thoroughly intact."

Even as she said it, she felt she was betraying herself. She did not think he owed her anything, but that did not mean she did not long for it, all the same.

"You think I feel *bad* for you? Of all the things I feel, that's not . . . God, this isn't coming out right at all." He put his head in his hands, and Georgiana watched him miserably, waiting. "The truth is that I have been fascinated by you, and honestly a little *frightened* of you—you say exactly what you mean, drunk or sober, and you seemed to demand that same honesty from everybody else. And you made *me* want to do it. To be honest. To be open with you, even if it scared me. I love . . . I love being near you, but then there's always—"

He sat up and looked at her, and she was astonished to see that he looked truly upset.

"'There's always what?" Georgiana asked with great trepidation.

There was a pause. Thomas cast about, as if he didn't know where to begin, and then bit his lip and tried.

"You know, if . . . if my brother, Edward, were still alive, no power on earth could have kept him from this party. We were very close when we were children. He never forgave me for being the eldest, he seemed to take it as a personal slight—I think he truly believed that if he tried hard enough he might be able to make up those three years and close the gap. Everything I did, he had to do, too. Sometimes he tried to anticipate what he *thought* I'd do, just so he could get to it first." He smiled, although it seemed to pain him to do so.

"He must have loved you very much," Georgiana said gently; to her horror, she saw him swallow hard, as if to keep himself from tears.

"I believe he did. I certainly loved him. It's funny—I never actually told him that. I thought I knew what it was to be a man—to be a brother, a son—but now I think I got it entirely wrong."

"I'm sure that's not true," said Georgiana.

"You only say that because you don't *know*," he said, shaking his head. "Edward was seventeen when he died, Georgiana. I don't know what rumors you may have heard—what stories people tell about us to fill in the gaps—but this is the truth of it: he drank himself to death. He went out one night, to some party, and it was the end of him. He made it home, God knows how, but then—" Thomas's voice broke and he took a second to compose himself. "He died alone, in his bedroom, while I slept down the hall. A stupid thing—he got very ill, and he was asleep on his back. Every day I think . . . I think of him by himself, choking, perhaps afraid for a moment, and then just—gone. Every day I think of how things could have been different. What I should have done to prevent it."

Georgiana found herself crying. "But . . . But it wasn't your fault."

"If the fault lies anywhere, it's with me. I mean, I was supposed to *be* there. I don't even remember why I didn't go to that party now, some headache, or some . . . Well, it hardly matters. I was his brother, and I was meant to be with him, and I wasn't. But it's *more* than that. Everywhere he went, all the choices he made—he was just following my example. Back then Jeremiah and I were always pushing things too far, always sailing too close to the wind, and Edward was just trying to keep up. To prove he could be just as much of a man as I was. And now he's dead, because I realized far too late that . . . that I was no sort of man at all."

"Thomas," Georgiana said helplessly, pressing a hand to his shoulder. "No. It was an accident. A *terrible* accident, but an accident nonetheless."

"If I had done things differently, he might still be here. My mother, too. I don't know if it's truly possible to die of heartbreak, but I believe she did. She was so full of joy before, so full of life— she was the one who made everything work, the business *and* our family—but the loss of my brother was too much for her to bear. Family was everything to her, and she had lost so much already by coming here and leaving most of hers behind. After Edward died, she couldn't eat, nor speak. My father gave everything he had trying to keep her alive, to keep her anchored here, but it wasn't enough—and once she was gone, he was completely adrift. We . . . We lost *everything,* and all because I thought that all of this"—he gestured around him, at the party in general—"was what really mattered."

"I don't believe that," Georgiana said fiercely. "I don't, Thomas. You must know that there isn't another version of this story where you did everything right and all was well. There is only what happened. If it hadn't happened that way, it might have just been the next night. The next party. You might have told him to change his ways, and he might have gone out and done exactly the opposite, because he was young and headstrong. There is no way of knowing, and there is nothing about this that you can change now if you just . . . if you just *blame* yourself hard enough."

He closed his eyes tightly, tears finally breaking free, and then lifted a hand to brush them away. They were quiet together for a while, the only sound the gentle drip of condensation from the glass roof and the distant sounds of revels.

"I'm sorry," he said eventually. "To burden you with all this. I don't even know why I'm telling you, we never really . . . I don't speak of it. Jeremiah was there for the worst of it, but we don't talk like that, and I think he expected I'd soon be my old self again. He is disappointed, I think, to find me changed. He's changed, too, or perhaps—perhaps I just couldn't see him clearly before. These parties, this scene—there is nothing for me here anymore. Yet here I am, trying to cling to the threads of my old life, trying to remember how it was to be—" He broke off, and Georgiana squeezed his shoulder in support. "God. I'm sorry. You must think me mad."

"You *must* stop apologizing," Georgiana said gently through her tears, smiling weakly at him. He attempted to return the gesture, and when he couldn't, she took his face in both hands. "Thomas, not for one second have I ever thought you mad. You are in *mourning* for all that you have lost. And no matter what you choose to believe about yourself, please know that you have been unable to convince me that you are anything other than good. A good brother. A good son. A good man."

She pushed his hair back from his face and kissed him gently on the forehead; he let himself lean into her, and she could feel his shoulders shaking with sorrow that he had held back for far too long. When he pulled away, his eyelashes were wet with tears. He opened his mouth to speak again—but was interrupted by an earth-shattering boom from somewhere outside the orangery. They both jumped, looking up to see fractured light exploding across the night sky, their view warped through the glass.

Somebody was setting off pyrotechnics on the lawn.

Thomas shook his head, bemused, and then they both laughed shakily through their tears.

"I meant what I said before," Georgiana said, wiping her eyes, when the fireworks came to a polite pause. "That you're not . . . You are not obligated to me. But in the interest of honesty, I can't pretend that I don't want that. Want you. I mean, *clearly*, as I can't be trusted to be around you without accosting you in a cellar, or a greenhouse."

"I can hardly blame you," Thomas said, smiling faintly. "There is nothing more attractive, of course, than a gentleman . . . a gentleman kissing you and then *crying* on you in a stranger's garden."

He clearly meant to sound jovial, but she knew he was embarrassed. She shook her head at him, smiling fondly.

"You are exactly correct," she said, interlacing her fingers with his. "Nothing gets a lady going like a bit of late-night weeping."

He laughed, then put her hand to his mouth and kissed it.

"I'm not sure you can call it that. Evening weeping, at most— it's barely eleven."

"Oh." Georgiana hadn't actually noticed the time passing; in all honesty, she had momentarily forgotten they were even at a party. "Eleven? I suppose . . . I suppose I should catch up with my friends."

She had suddenly thought of Frances—jaw set, shoulders squared as she set a course for certain disaster. Now that she knew Thomas was not angry with her, it was much easier to be forgiving, and she felt a pull of guilt in her friend's direction. As dreadful as she had been, this was not a night for Frances to be alone.

Thomas, she noticed, was attempting to conceal a grimace.

"You don't have to come with me," Georgiana said quickly, and he looked instantly relieved. "I'll find you again, after."

"All right," Thomas said, clearing his throat and getting to his feet, offering her his hand to help her up. "Find your friends. I shall return to the party, where I shall be the life and soul— leading every dance, spinning every yarn."

"No, you shan't," said Georgiana.

"No, I shan't," Thomas agreed as they made for the exit. "But I think I could stretch to fetching us both a drink."

Chapter Twenty-three

GEORGIANA'S FRIENDS SEEMED TO HAVE BEEN SWALLOWED up by the party. It was a living thing, swelling and retreating as it reached into every corner of the house, quietening to a murmur in places and then suddenly roaring to a crescendo in response to stimuli Georgiana couldn't pinpoint. In the crush of the ballroom, a woman dressed like a scarlet bird knocked hard into Georgiana's side, then kissed her cheek with her false beak by way of apology and rushed to join the dancers. Some of Christopher's half-naked friends had filled one of the water fountains with wine and were lapping at it like thirsty puppies. The hallways, when she reached them, were full of giggling couples and groups of friends shrieking hysterically together as they fumbled for doorknobs and disappeared into rooms that Georgiana did not dare enter.

She made her way back outside, having seen nobody she knew within, and wondered for a moment whether she was hallucinating or there really were now people in full military regalia—armed and everything—squaring up against each other on the back lawn. A crowd had gathered to watch, and when a horn sounded, the two rows of party militia ran toward each other, screaming like banshees, swords aloft. She saw a girl who seemed to be dressed as an acorn standing alone at the edge of the spectators and approached to ask her what was happening.

"Oh—they're fighting for Lord Haverton's favor," she replied, as if this should have been obvious.

Sure enough, the man himself was sitting in a sedan chair, watching with a rather bored expression as the sound of swords clashing together began to fill the night air.

"They're not really going to kill one another, are they?" Georgiana asked, wincing as a sword flew so close to one gentleman's face that it trimmed a little of his facial hair. Clearly, they had not been blunted.

"Oh, probably not," was the girl's rather concerning reply.

"Have you seen—do you know Frances Campbell?" Georgiana said, raising her voice over the sound of drunken battle cries, but the girl just shrugged.

"Miss Campbell?" said another girl, glancing back over her shoulder. "I just saw her with some blond dandy in the sculpture garden. She asked me to leave. She was quite rude about it, actually."

That certainly sounded like Frances. Georgiana thanked her and walked away, keen not to be present when people started sustaining their inevitable horrifying injuries. She had no idea where the sculpture garden might be, but she made her way around the house in what seemed a promising direction until she found herself wandering through an extravagant and alien grove. Greek statues towered above her on white marble plinths, and the many topiaries were sheared into strange, bulbous shapes—she was just studying one to try to work out what it could possibly be when she heard a disturbance up ahead.

Moving closer, she heard a tremulous voice through the bushes that seemed vaguely familiar; as it got louder, she realized that it was Frances. Georgiana hadn't recognized her at first because of her tone; it was rapid, frenetic—almost manic. It immediately gave Georgiana the impression that she was eavesdropping on something very personal. She ducked behind a particularly girthy topiary and, peering around it, saw that Frances was talking to Jeremiah Russell. He was leaning back on a bench with practiced ease as he listened, although even from this vantage point, Georgiana could see that his fingers were tapping out an endless, agitated rhythm into the stone.

Frances was not even attempting to appear calm. She was standing before him, gesticulating with her arms outstretched as she spoke. Georgiana was reminded of the illustrations she had seen of courtrooms, of defendants pleading their cases while impassive jurors looked on. She knew she should leave, but there was something about the way Jeremiah was leaning away from Frances, the desperate tone of her voice, the way he wasn't meeting her eyes; it gave her such a deep sense of foreboding that she decided to stay put.

"I'm not stupid, Jeremiah," Frances was saying, but somewhat gently now, as if she were trying her utmost to be understanding, "I know you've been avoiding me. Just . . . Whatever it is, we can talk about it. Perhaps it was all too much too soon, perhaps—let's *court*. Let's do things properly. Why not! We can have chaperoned dinners, I can . . . I can spend time with your parents."

Jeremiah sighed and rubbed his temple.

"What is it that you *want*? I thought we understood one another," Frances continued, clearly attempting to sound perfectly in control of her feelings, but with a shake in her voice that even she could not disguise.

After what felt like an age, Jeremiah finally spoke.

"Please don't make this more than it is, Frances," he said.

Georgiana took a sharp intake of breath. Frances seemed to have done the exact same thing.

"More than . . . ? We were both *there*, Jeremiah. Did I dream it? We were in that damned cottage, and you said . . . You said you couldn't *wait*, you couldn't *wait* until we were married. What could have been *more* than that? How could I—how could it mean anything less than it did?"

Jeremiah looked sightly uncomfortable. "I'm sorry if you feel I have wronged you, Frances. But . . . come *on*. Every time I turned around, there you were. Sitting as close to me as you possibly could, drinking from my glass, practically climbing on top of me at every opportunity. I think we both knew where it was leading. That night—that was just the . . . the natural conclusion."

"The *natural conclusion*?" Frances hissed, and Georgiana could practically see the rage radiating from her. "The *natural conclusion* when one talks of marriage—when one makes *promises*—the natural conclusion is a *wedding*, Jeremiah."

"You're drunk, Frances. You're out of your mind—and you *always* are. You think I want you to spend time with my *parents*? Are you *mad*? 'Oh yes, Father, please meet my fiancée, she's been at the laudanum, and the opium, and Christ knows what else—'"

"*Coming from you?* Where do I get half of it, Jeremiah—"

"Yes, but we drink, we smoke—we do it to have *fun*. We know when to stop. We're not all quite as desperate to escape reality as you are, Frances. You're completely out of control. I know what you did to Annabelle, I know you hunted her down and found her father—what right had you to do that? If you really want to get married, if you want a good match, you need to settle down and stop behaving like a spurned child. At this rate I can't blame your father—"

"*Fuck* you," said Frances, and her voice cut clear through the night. It seemed to leave a ringing silence in its wake.

"Well, there you are. Just proving my point. My father certainly warned me this would happen—told me to set my sights on a nice, traditional girl—"

"I *am* a nice girl," Frances said, but all the fight seemed to have gone out of her.

"Oh, come on, Frances. You're not *nice*, and you know it. God—there's no talking to you when you're like this." Jeremiah shook his head, getting to his feet. "I really am sorry, Franny. It just wasn't . . . It just wasn't like that, for me."

There was a shout from close by, and Georgiana jumped. Two of Jeremiah's friends came swaggering through the bushes, crying out to him in greeting. Georgiana bit her lip, her eyes on Frances. She was shaking but standing her ground. Incredibly, she was not crying.

"Jeremiah," she said softly. "Please."

"Oh, *please*, Jeremiah," parroted one of his friends in a cruel falsetto.

Georgiana expected Jeremiah at the very least to reprimand him—to apologize, to do anything other than let Frances stand there in total humiliation while they smirked at her—but he didn't. He *laughed*. He laughed, and then he got languidly to his feet and walked away.

He didn't look back.

Frances collapsed onto the bench he had vacated as if she had been shot.

Casting aside the awkwardness of her sudden appearance, Georgiana rushed to her side and reached for her arm.

"Frances, are you all right? I saw him leave, I heard him—"

She was cut off by Frances's expression; instead of despairing, she looked outraged, as if *Georgiana* had said something to offend her.

"Keep your hands to yourself," she said coolly, and Georgiana froze with one hand hovering ridiculously over Frances's shoulder.

"Oh, come on, Frances, you don't—"

"No." Frances got to her feet with both arms wrapped around herself as if she were cold. "I don't need your help."

Georgiana gaped at her. "Why are you angry with *me*?"

"Oh, don't pretend you're so *innocent*," Frances spat. One of her ivory gloves had a large red wine stain on it, and Georgiana found herself watching it as Frances raised her arm to point at her. "You like to pretend you're so good all the time, such a great friend, but when there's the slightest risk that I might embarrass you in front of some second-rate *man* you like, suddenly I'm not your friend at all."

"Hang on," Georgiana said, feeling herself growing hot. "Wait. That isn't—that's not what happened, Frances. You were terrible to Thomas. He was just trying to help, and you were—"

"*I* was terrible?" Frances said, still trying to keep her voice level but wavering with the effort. "I came to you because I needed . . . *God*, I thought you understood! I thought you were different. I waited for you the next day, Georgiana. You said you'd come, and I believed you. And then when you didn't call, you didn't write—I didn't understand *why*."

"I just *told* you why—I was waiting for an *apology*, Frances, I was waiting for—"

"No," Frances said, shaking her head with a grim smile, as if nothing Georgiana could say now would change her mind. "That wasn't it, was it? Because when I saw you at Cecily's, I knew. You don't want to be my *friend*. You want to feel important. You want to come to nice parties and drink the best wine and have people point at you and say, 'Look, there's *Georgiana Ellers*, isn't she something?' You wanted my friends, my position, my influence. Well, I hope it's everything you wanted, *George*. I hope it makes you very, very happy."

"You're wrong," Georgiana said, hearing how pathetic her rebuttal sounded. "That's not—"

"Oh, thank Christ, here you are." Jonathan was suddenly there, stumbling through the trees, and a few seconds later he was followed by Jane and Cecily. If he sensed the tension, he decided to ignore it. "I thought maybe the French had nabbed you. Come on, stop lurking about in the garden—let's go and find the *party*."

"Yes," said Frances, her eyes fixed on Georgiana. "Let's."

* * *

"*U*h-oh," Jonathan said half an hour later, looking up from the straight gin he had been pouring himself, his glass precariously balanced on the edge of one of Lord Haverton's ornamental fountains. He nodded very slightly across the ballroom. "Natural disaster incoming."

"Oh, *Christ*," Jane said immediately, rolling her eyes. "Just . . . don't look at her, and maybe she won't see us."

Frances, who had been unnervingly silent since the scene in the garden, snorted into her drink.

It was too late. Betty Walters, red in the face and adorned with a few drooping flowers in her hair, was approaching with purpose.

"Georgiana?" she said. "Miss—Miss Ellers?"

Georgiana winced, exchanging a pained look with Jonathan before she rearranged her features into a more neutral expression and turned to look at Betty.

"Can I help you, Betty?" It came out a little less warmly than she had intended, gin sharpening her tongue, and Georgiana heard Jonathan choke on a laugh behind her.

"Well, it's just—we had arranged to meet," Betty said, going even more red.

Georgiana felt something drop in the pit of her stomach. She had forgotten. She had forgotten entirely.

"We had said we would meet, you know, outside the front of the party, and I thought—well, I arrived at nine as we had agreed and I waited—I thought perhaps you had been waylaid or you had forgotten something and had to go back for it, and I didn't want to go anywhere else in case you pulled up and I had vanished—so I waited, you see, I waited for an hour or—perhaps it was two hours—but eventually I thought maybe you weren't coming, so I came in to see if I had somehow missed you, and I met some very interesting people but none of them were you. I thought you might have come in at the wrong entrance, or be waiting for me elsewhere, or—"

"Betty," Georgiana said, attempting to abate the flow, knowing that Betty was due an apology but feeling incapable of doing so sincerely while she could hear Jane laughing openly at her shoulder. To her horror, Betty looked precariously close to tears.

"I just thought—we agreed to come in together, you said so in your letter, and so I thought it must have been some kind of mistake—it is a mistake, isn't it? Because I thought we had such a pleasant time when I came to tea, we had such fun—"

There was an unpleasant feeling rising in Georgiana's throat. The more Betty spoke, the more hot and embarrassed she became. She could feel the eyes of her friends burning into the back of her head, feel them jostling and laughing and likely losing all respect for her by the second. The gin she had poured generously down her throat to cope with the awkwardness of standing next to Frances, as if nothing were wrong between them, seemed to be poisoning her from the inside out.

Incredibly, Betty was *still* going.

"—I was going to have you over to our house, Grandmama told me to invite you, she said it's only polite when we came to you, and that if you are to be my special companion—"

"*Betty*," Georgiana said with enough force that Betty finally did come to a pause. "Don't you *ever* grow tired of listening to yourself talk?"

Betty looked, for a moment, as if she were trying very hard to find some charitable reading of this sentence that might mean she had not been insulted; when she failed, her entire face seemed to crumple inward on itself.

"I thought—I thought we were friends," she said quietly.

Georgiana's mouth felt very dry; she raised a hand slightly, as if she might be about to reach for Betty and apologize, but she found herself unable to move it any farther.

Betty took one last look around at the faces behind Georgiana and then tearfully fled.

"Oh *dear*," said Jonathan when Georgiana turned back toward him, not sounding the least bit sorry. "I think you've broken her poor heart, George."

"God, something about her puts all my teeth on edge," said Jane.

Frances laughed humorlessly—but Cecily was frowning.

"Oh, I feel sorry for her," she said, shaking her head slowly. "She can't help being so ridiculous. And it is a *party*, after all. Nobody should be crying at a party."

"Nonsense," said Jonathan. "One of the main purposes of a ball is for people to cry on the outskirts of it."

Cecily still looked rather disappointed.

"I think we should go and make a peace offering," Frances said suddenly. Georgiana shot a confused glance at her, but she seemed sincere. "In the spirit of the party."

"Oh, please do," Cecily said. "Otherwise the image of that sad little face will rather ruin my evening."

"We should take her a drink," Frances said; she raised her own glass of gin.

"I'll do it," Georgiana said quickly, taking it from her with dubious coordination. "I'm the one who upset her. I'll take it."

"You are a dear," Cecily said, patting her on the shoulder as she went.

The room was far too loud, too bright, too hot; Georgiana must have bumped into upwards of twenty people as she crossed it, but this seemed inconsequential, as if all strangers had become part of the furniture and required no acknowledgment or apology when nudged or tripped over. She paused and shook her head slowly in an attempt to clear it, and only succeeded in loosening more of her hair, which was dropping from its pins at an alarming rate. She distantly wondered what the sheet formerly known as her dress now resembled; if it was covering all of her vital organs, it would quite frankly be a miracle.

She discovered Miss Walters outside, sitting on a bench, looking excruciatingly heartbroken as she gazed forlornly into a rosebush.

"There you are," Georgiana said, and Betty turned her pink, tear-brimmed eyes to Georgiana. "Betty, listen, I've had far, far too much gin to give you the proper groveling sort of speech you really deserve, but just . . . Here—please, have a drink. From me. Well, from all of us, really."

It was a poor attempt at an apology, but Betty was easily mollified and took the glass from her.

"I'm sure—I'm sure you didn't mean to be so cruel," she said in a tremulous voice.

Georgiana felt guilt roil in her gut. She knew she didn't deserve so benign a judgment, but she shouldn't have expected anything else from Betty; she was unable to be anything other than too kind and forgiving.

"And, well—I don't drink beyond a few fingers of wine, ordinarily—Grandmama says that's quite enough to lubricate one of an evening. But when in Rome, I suppose . . ." She took a sip of gin, wrinkling up her face in disgust as soon as it hit her tongue. "This is—oh, this is quite horrible!"

"It is, isn't it? You get used to it," said Georgiana, wondering if she herself had perhaps become a little *too* used to it.

Betty bravely endured a large gulp and then put down the glass, sniffing and wiping her damp eyes with her gloved hands.

"You forgot to meet me, didn't you? It's all right, you can tell me, it's not the first time it's happened to me—I did wonder, when you weren't there, because of course the mind does go straight to the disappointments of the past, and one always lives in horror of repeats—"

She stood up, clearly attempting to rally, but then her expression became quite strange.

"Betty?" Georgiana asked nervously, watching as Betty seemed to sway on her feet and then sat abruptly back down again on the bench. She had gone very pale and suddenly clapped both hands over her mouth as if she might be in danger of imminently vomiting. Georgiana moved away instinctively.

"What is it?" she asked.

"I feel—I feel very odd," Betty said, eyes wide.

"Oh. Are you—er . . . Are you ill?"

"I'm not—I'm not certain." She tried to get to her feet once more but had to hold on to the bench to achieve something resembling an upright position. "Oh, Miss Ellers, I've come over so queer—I think I may be dying!"

Georgiana was too unsteady on her own feet to be of much use, but she stood and held out a supportive arm anyway. The sudden shift of weight when Betty tried to take it proved too much for her in her current state, however, and she lost her balance, sending Miss Walters tumbling quite spectacularly to the ground. Some guests nearby exclaimed at the disturbance, a few making to come to their aid.

"Oh, Christ, Betty. I'm so sorry—"

They were interrupted by a sudden burst of laughter, and Georgiana looked up to see Frances watching them, her eyes narrowed.

"Not much of a drinker, are you, Miss Walters?" she said.

Georgiana looked from her friend to the half-drunk glass of gin beside them; Frances had something small and dark clutched in her hand, and with an unpleasant lurch of her stomach, Georgiana recognized the horrible, potent bottle of *Christopher's finest*.

"What have you *done*?" said Georgiana in consternation as Betty struggled to get to her feet, "She's not well, I really think we ought to—"

"Miss Walters?"

Georgiana froze. She knew that voice.

She turned to see Thomas was standing behind her, two glasses of champagne in hand, frowning at the scene in front of him.

Georgiana could not have devised a worse situation for him to walk into if she had tried.

More people were beginning to gather around, to see what was the matter; Betty was swaying, almost swooning on her feet, and seeing this, Thomas put down the champagne and rushed to steady her before she fell again.

"Are you all right? Do you need a doctor? What happened?"

He looked from Betty to Georgiana in concern, clearly baffled by Georgiana's lack of action.

"Oh, Mr. Hawksley," Betty gasped, tears streaming down her cheeks. "There was something in—in my drink—I thought she was really sorry, I thought she wanted to make amends, but instead she—she's *p-poisoned* me."

"Who's poisoned you?" Thomas said insistently, his arm around her shoulder.

Georgiana felt sick to her stomach as Betty raised a shaking hand and pointed directly at her. She put up her own hands, pathetically trying to indicate her innocence.

"*Georgiana?*" he said, his tone disbelieving.

"Oh, it was only a very *small* poisoning," Frances said dismissively. "We all know it would take more than that to bring you down, Betty."

Georgiana looked at Frances in horror as she so casually damned her; Frances just laughed. Thomas was gazing at Georgiana with utmost shock and revulsion, as if she had disappointed him even beyond his lowest expectations.

"She told me she would meet me, so I wouldn't have to come in alone, and then she left me there—she just left me standing all by myself, it was horrid." Betty sobbed into Thomas's shoulder. "And then when I found her she was so *rude* to me, and I thought—I thought she was my *friend*."

Georgiana tried to interject, attempted to say something in her defense, but only managed a spluttered "No!" before she was being bustled out of the way by guests coming to help, offering Betty their carriages and drivers. Two of them took her from Thomas and put a shoulder each under her arms to bear her away to safety; only once she was being carried over the threshold of the house with a small crowd in tow, her sobs still audible as she went, did Thomas turn back to look at Georgiana.

"What happened?" he asked her, his tone flat.

Frances snorted.

"Leave us, Frances," Georgiana muttered, and Frances pressed a hand to her chest in mock affront.

"I'd rather stay and watch the show, if you don't mind."

"Miss Campbell, this is none of your concern." There was not an inch of give in Thomas's voice, which was rough with fury.

"Hmmm . . . Not entirely true, I'm afraid, but I'll leave you to your lovers' tiff." Frances picked up both abandoned glasses of champagne and saluted them as she went. "Good luck, George."

Georgiana's hair was half undone. Her sheet was listing off one shoulder, exposing part of her shift. Her lips were stained with wine, her mind foggy with gin, and an excruciating head-ache was beginning to pick away at her left temple.

In contrast, Thomas seemed perfectly sober—upright and re-splendent in his anger. The only fault she could find with him was that one curl had fallen out of place, and despite his expression, all she wanted to do was push it back behind his ear.

"I didn't poison her," she said, her head finally forming the words and transporting them to her lips.

"Then what *happened*?"

"It's not . . . It's not *poison,* Thomas. It's just something Frances took—*I* took. She's not *dying.* She'll be all right."

"I'm sorry," Thomas said, pressing his fingertips to his forehead as if he had a headache just as hideous as Georgiana's. "Let me get this straight—are you saying that you *did* slip something into her drink?"

Georgiana did not seem to be explaining herself very well, but her grasp on their conversation was so insubstantial; all she wanted to do was lie down right there on the patio and sleep, or die—whichever happened to come first.

"No! No. It was Frances. Frances did it, she told me to take it to her, I just gave her the drink—but I didn't *know* there was something in it."

"So it didn't seem at all suspicious to you that Frances Campbell wanted you to give Betty Walters a drink, out of . . . What? Out of the kindness of her heart?"

"No!" Georgiana said, but he was right—how could she not have seen it? "You're not *listening* to me. It wasn't me. It was Frances's fault, it was all *Frances*—"

"So Frances forced you to stand Miss Walters up, and leave her alone, waiting for you, at a party at which she knew next to no one? Frances held you at gunpoint, I suppose, and forced you to say dreadful things to Betty when clearly the poor girl has been nothing but kind to you?"

He didn't just look angry anymore; he looked disappointed and hurt, which were both infinitely worse.

"No," Georgiana said, desperately. "No, but if it weren't for Frances—"

"You can't blame Frances for all the world's ills, Georgiana—and nor for all of yours. Betty Walters is extremely upset and might be gravely hurt, because she was abandoned and belittled and—and let down, by somebody she considered a friend. And it wasn't Frances, Georgiana. It was you."

Tears coursing down her cheeks, Georgiana tried to speak—stopped—opened her mouth again, then realized she had absolutely nothing to say in her defense.

Thomas shook his head and then left her standing there without another word.

Chapter Twenty-four

GEORGIANA COULD NOT IMAGINE THAT ANYBODY IN THE world was more pitiful than she was at this very moment. She thought vaguely that plague-stricken orphans might have come close to feeling this destitute—but then, they had probably never been to a party, and perhaps it was better to have never been to a party at all than to have experienced one as disastrous as this. She could hear all manner of merriment taking place around her, but she was so thoroughly miserable that not an ounce of it could raise her spirits; if anything, it irritated her further to know that others were still enjoying the night, without worrying that they had angered almost everybody they held dear in the course of one short evening. Tears fell freely as she staggered through the house forlornly, feeling like the drunken ghost at the feast.

She wanted to leave immediately, but there was the small matter of transport to deal with. She had arrived in Cecily's carriage, but so far, Cecily was nowhere to be found. She spotted many fair and golden heads among the dancers, but none of them belonged to her friend. She wasn't playing cards with any of the suspicious-looking men and women in the drawing room; she wasn't in the horse's bedroom; she wasn't swimming in the lake half-dressed or harassing the swans, although quite a few people were.

Georgiana almost tripped over a huge form lying across the grass by the patio and went to apologize tearfully to whomever she had almost kicked, before realizing that it was not a horizontal drunkard; it was an absolutely enormous dog. It did not seem at all perturbed by the goings-on around it and was looking up at Georgiana quite calmly, its head resting on large brown paws. She looked around for an owner and saw none. She assumed this must be part of Lord Haverton's menagerie, probably dislodged from its palatial kennel by people looking for a clandestine place to hide.

"Good evening, dog," she said, and more tears sprang to her eyes.

She sat down beside it and buried her fingers in its thick, musty fur. The dog gave a little sigh of contentment.

"Everything has gone so terribly wrong," she whispered in its ear.

The dog did not judge her, and it did not get up and walk away. It seemed to accept her completely, no matter how dreadful a person she was starting to suspect she was, and she spent a while enjoying its quiet, sighing company and petting it by way of thanks.

When she finally got up to leave, the dog giving her a gentle farewell lick on the hand, inspiration struck; she had seen Cecily eyeing up horsey James earlier, and the orangery was still glowing attractively in the distance. If they had gone looking for somewhere more private, surely that would have been their destination? Georgiana set off across the garden with purpose, swearing under her breath each time she stumbled over the end of her sheet, which was occurring rather frequently as it became more hem than dress.

The orangery was vast, and beyond the entryway where she and Thomas had spoken earlier there was a small wooden slatted path, which wound through the trees and presumably continued on to the other side. Branches and leaves pressed against her as she walked along it; the heat only intensified the farther she went, and the smell of citrus was so overwhelming that Georgiana felt as if she had genuinely been transported to some tropical locale. She pushed past a rather obnoxious tree that had almost cut off her route and turned a corner to find another circular clearing.

It was occupied. Not by Cecily and James, but by Jeremiah Russell, who seemed to have ridded himself of his friends and was smoking moodily, his shirt half-undone, the leaves that had adorned his hair rumpled and mostly lost to the exploits of the evening.

He turned to look at Georgiana with mild interest as she knocked some dirt off her glove, and she felt a rush of fury and indignation at the sight of him.

"That's probably bad for the oranges," she spluttered angrily.

She had quite a lot she wanted to admonish him for, and smoking something pungent was the least of his sins, but she supposed she had to start somewhere.

"It's probably bad for me, too, but that doesn't seem enough to stop me," he replied.

He did seem genuinely morose and withdrawn compared to his usual self, but if he was at all upset by how things had turned out between him and Frances, then that was entirely his doing.

"Well . . . good. I hope you keel over and . . . and die of consumption," she said, crossing her arms and scowling at him. "I heard what you said to Frances, you know."

"Oh, did you indeed?"

He got to his feet and Georgiana suddenly realized how inebriated he was—even more so than her. He wore it differently—he did not stumble or fumble his words—but his eyes were so bloodshot they looked crimson in the low light, and every movement was undertaken in slow motion, as if he were wading through water. He still walked with purpose despite it all, while she trembled with exhaustion, feeling that her legs might give out at any moment.

"I did, and I think it was foul. *You* are foul. You can't pretend you didn't know what you meant to her, Jeremiah, and we all saw how you were together. You don't understand—"

"No," he said, and his voice was suddenly a lot less languid. "*You* don't understand. You are not the sole heir to a vast estate, Miss Ellers. You are not . . . There are things I cannot . . . I know you think it's all terribly *glamorous,* terribly *easy,* but there are responsibilities upon my shoulders that you could never dream of. When I marry, it will not be a matter of love or attraction—it will be a matter of business. You cannot enter a partnership with someone . . . someone irresponsible, someone constantly on the verge of passing out in a hedgerow, someone who has no *limits.* She's simply not the right sort, Georgiana. But then"—he narrowed his eyes and sneered a little as he cocked his head to one side to consider her—"you cannot see the difficulties—you, I imagine, being heir to . . . what . . . ? A single cow? A single cow and a lightly used box of your father's chewing tobacco?"

"How can you stand there with a smile on your face and be so atrocious!" Georgiana suddenly had no idea what she, or Frances, or Annabelle Baker, or anybody at all had ever seen in this arrogant, pompous arse. "You . . . You utter bastard!"

"Oh, don't be like that, *George.*"

He was suddenly standing much too close to her, although Georgiana hadn't even really seen him move. The smell of alcohol on his breath was so potent that she felt dizzy just from the fumes. She was uncomfortably aware of how truly alone they were—how entirely concealed from view. It made her shiver, even in the warm, humid air, as Jeremiah looked her up and down. He seemed to be seeing her for the first time—noticing how precariously wrapped her dress was, how disheveled and unsteady she looked.

"Don't call me that," she said weakly, taking a step back and self-consciously pulling the sheet up so that it covered more of her chest. "*You* don't get to call me that."

He laughed, and the sound grated against her nerves. She felt desperate panic beginning to constrict her lungs; it felt ridiculous to run, to scream, when he hadn't *done* anything. He was just drunk. Maybe this uncomfortable moment would be over in an instant.

"Christ, what are you wearing? Come here," he said, his voice a low, dangerous rumble.

Georgiana took a small step backward. "No."

"Come *here*," he repeated sharply—and this time Georgiana did try to run.

She didn't take her dress into account, and her legs tangled in it immediately; she braced herself for the impact of the ground, but it didn't come. Instead he caught her painfully by the wrists and dragged her upright. Still, she thought wildly—perhaps he was just steadying her. Perhaps this was all a misunderstanding, and any second now he'd let her go. She tried to pull away, but his hands gripped her like a vise, and she felt all the breath go out of her in her shock. She realized she had been waiting for something to interrupt them, for somebody to come to her rescue, as Frances had inadvertently back at Bastards' Cottage when Christopher had cornered her—but it didn't come.

He pulled her to him and kissed her, hard. She froze in place, hoping that it would discourage him, but her lack of reciprocity did not seem to inconvenience him in the slightest. One hand still held her tightly by the wrist, but the other went to her neck, ignoring the fact that she shuddered at his touch, tracing down to her collarbone, then gripping her so hard that she wondered distantly if he had broken the skin, leaving her shot through with wounds the exact size and shape of his fingertips.

His hand started to move farther down her chest, and she gasped indignantly against him as she felt his fingers move under the fabric of the sheet and grope wildly at her. Some part of her mind reassured her that this *could not* be happening—but the pain insisted that it was. He pulled at her sheet one-handed and it occurred to her that he might be trying to take it off. She took a deep breath so she could scream—so she could try *something,* anything—and then suddenly, mercifully, she heard the sound of someone crashing through the trees behind them. Whoever it was, they were moving away, but it was enough of a distraction that Jeremiah loosened his grip for a moment, whipping around to see who might have discovered them.

A moment was all Georgiana needed. She picked up what remained of her skirts and ran clumsily in the opposite direction, unable to feel relief even when the night air hit her, unable to stop until she had put some distance between her and the smell of the orange trees. One of her shoes caught on the lawn and fell off, and she paused briefly to kick off the other, sprinting in her stockings until she couldn't run any farther.

She had made it close enough to the house to be within shouting distance of other people, and that point of relative safety was where she finally collapsed. She sank onto a low wall, trying to breathe, her sobs catching in her throat.

Jeremiah did not seem to have followed her. She couldn't see him—he wasn't at the door of the orangery, wasn't coming back up the slope toward her—there was no imminent need to escape. She couldn't quite imagine his running after her, trying to grab her in full view of the guests, but then he was so well respected and well loved by all; perhaps they simply would have watched, silently, as he dragged her away.

This thought, however irrational, made her blood run cold. She got unsteadily to her feet, anxious to be home, wishing more than anything that she had arranged for the Burtons' carriage to provide her an easy exit. Her chest felt constricted, and there was something urgent and searing rising from her stomach as if she might vomit at any minute; no matter how hard she tried to breathe evenly, she couldn't stop taking rough, gasping gulps of air instead.

She thought of Cecily and her carriage again, immediately exhausted at the prospect of having to resume the hunt but wanting to be as far away from Jeremiah Russell as possible. She knew that in time, she would be angry beyond words—she could feel it curled up inside her, just out of reach—but now that the worst of her fear had begun to abate, all she could feel was nausea and fatigue.

She was so very *done* with this night, and by extension with everybody here. She could not bear to experience one more thing, one more inebriated person or inane conversation or glass of wine; she needed her house, her bed, and the familiar sound of Mr. Burton's snoring through the wall to lull her to sleep.

It was strange to feel claustrophobic on an estate that must have spanned seven or eight hundred acres. She looked back compulsively over her shoulder as she walked, to make sure there was still no shadow behind her, no footsteps gaining on her—and instead, she saw Frances.

She was quite a distance away, standing at the edge of what had been the makeshift battlefield, looking out over the sloping lawns that led down to the lake; but it was unmistakably her, the moonlight picking out the delicate outline of her white, flowing dress.

Georgiana thought for a moment that perhaps she should go to her. Not to try to unravel the mess of their friendship, all the necessary apologies and arguments and explanations—she was too far past the point of exhaustion to even know where to begin—but because it was dawning on her that Frances might be the only person who would truly understand. She remembered the dreadful expression on Frances's face when she and Jonathan had run to her aid back at the cottage, and all at once knew with grim certainty what Jeremiah had truly done.

She realized with a wilting of her shoulders that she could not find the words to speak to Frances tonight. Her wrist was raw and red, her neck smarting where Jeremiah had gripped it. It would all have to wait until the morning. She was utterly spent.

"You look *dreadful.*"

A voice jolted her from her thoughts, and she looked up to see Lord Haverton standing there, magnificent in a new costume of what looked like real leaves coated in a thin veneer of gold. His tone was not accusatory or cruel, he was simply stating a fact.

"Yes," she replied, knowing she sounded wholly defeated.

"You're not having fun," he added. This was not phrased as a question.

"Er . . . No, not really," Georgiana said, thinking that this was the understatement of the century.

"You must go home, then. The party is over for you."

Georgiana smiled at him weakly. "I have no carriage," she replied. "I cannot find my friends."

He studied her for a moment.

"*I* have a carriage," he said. "I want it back, mind. I'm quite fond of this one. *And* the man who drives it."

Georgiana felt such overwhelming relief that she took a clumsy step forward and hugged him. She realized a second too late that this was probably a vast overstep, and began to apologize as she let go, but he just patted her fondly on the head as if she were an unruly dog and then sent her on her way.

His handsome carriage driver did not question her, did not even look at her askance when she climbed into the ornate white vehicle looking as if she had crawled out of her own grave; he simply asked for her address, and then they were away.

She was extremely grateful to him for this small kindness, and for his continuing silence as she lay back against the cushions and closed her eyes, happy to be putting distance between herself and the most hideous night of her life.

Chapter Twenty-five

GEORGIANA ARRIVED HOME LONG AFTER THE BURTONS HAD gone to bed, and awoke early the next morning with a deep sense of unease, courtesy of a lurching stomach and hours of disjointed nightmares. She kept returning to the terrible images of Betty, hurt and betrayed; Frances's hands, shaking in her bedroom at Bastards' Cottage; Jeremiah, leering at her through the dark; Betty, tricked and poisoned and sobbing hysterically as good Samaritans carried her away.

The sun was only just rising; even the soft pink light of it was vaguely offensive to her pounding head. She dressed quickly and quietly, then went downstairs to request the carriage be brought around in hushed tones, before her aunt could awaken and forbid it.

Of all the people Georgiana had ever encountered on earth, Miss Walters deserved cruelty the least. Her mind was still in disarray, but she knew that if she was going to put anything in her life right, she had to start with Betty.

She was surprised upon arrival to find that the Walters' house was beautiful—tasteful and well-kept, not too large or small, with a flourishing garden full of an array of sticky, sweet scents. It looked quite old but had clearly been well cared for over the years. Being even farther out of town than the Burtons, Mrs. Walters had ample land and had made it look very agreeable indeed.

After her admittance to the house, she waited nervously in a cool, neat parlor while a friendly-faced maid went to announce her arrival. A man appeared from upstairs, looking in and giving her a brief nod before exiting holding a large leather bag, and Georgiana realized with trepidation that he must have been the doctor. Eventually she heard slow footsteps on the stairs, and Mrs. Walters entered the room with Betty—who looked pale, but fortunately quite a bit more alive than Georgiana had feared—on her arm. A small scruffy-haired dog followed close at their heels, looking up anxiously from Georgiana to its mistresses and then back again.

"Good morning, Miss Ellers. Let's go into the garden." Betty sounded monstrously tired, but there was more surety in her voice than Georgiana had ever heard before. "It's all right, Grand-mama."

She took Georgiana's arm instead and together they walked slowly out into the back garden, where they sat down surrounded by a multitude of roses of every variety and color. They were si-lent for a minute as they listened to the sound of birdsong and sleepy bees bumbling about them, until Georgiana could bear it no longer.

"You look *well*, Betty—as well as can be expected, I mean," she said, the words tumbling out of her. "Here—I brought you some lace that Mrs. Burton was saving for me, and some dog roses and honeysuckle from the garden, and cordial—only, I'm not sure what gift you give to say 'I'm sorry I poisoned you.' I really am so *dreadfully* sorry, though, Betty. It was an accident. Well . . . it wasn't an accident, of course, but *my* part in it was accidental. Frances put something in your drink, and I had no idea she would go so far—I mean, I should have thought, I should have known, but I just . . . didn't." She ran out of air.

Betty considered her thoughtfully. "It was dreadful, you know. I have never felt quite so—disconnected, from my own body," she said gravely, and Georgiana nodded, wincing. "Once I was done feeling faint and sick I got quite high-spirited—by the time they had brought the carriage around, apparently I thought I was a real fairy, a nymph, and the Salisburys—the lovely couple who were helping me—had to catch me, because I was dashing about the place saying that I was 'spreading my magic.'" Georgiana nodded again, attempting to keep a straight face at this last. "I was violently ill by the time I got home. I actually vomited on Grandmama's Dandie Dinmont terrier."

Georgiana worried she might laugh and hurt Betty's feelings; to her relief, Betty did first.

"I'm so sorry, Betty. I know it's not funny really," Georgiana said, attempting to compose herself.

"No, no," said Betty mildly, "it really *is* quite funny. As soon as I'd done it, the poor thing took one look and turned around and vomited, too, all over the rug."

They both giggled weakly, but then Georgiana's expression became serious again.

"I forgot to meet you, Betty. I forgot what I had promised you, and then instead of giving you the apology you deserved, I was terrible to you. I know you are always inclined toward forgiveness, but my behavior was truly unforgivable, and nobody would think badly of you if you never spoke to me again. If you'll let me, though, Betty, I want to make it up to you."

Betty sighed and then leaned over and patted Georgiana's hand.

"I cannot say all is forgotten, for it isn't—but even in remembering it, I can't find the strength today to feel vexed. Perhaps you are lucky I didn't sleep a wink, but I think I can give you another chance. And besides—nobody has ever brought me dog roses before."

Georgiana felt a little of the weight leave her chest; Betty's kindness was a balm, even if she knew she did not deserve it.

"Thank you, Betty. Truly. I'm sorry about Frances—she has behaved so poorly, although I cannot pretend the fault is entirely hers. I behaved just as badly as she. God, I wish I could turn back the clock and decide to stay home from that wretched party. It was a nightmare from start to finish."

"She is . . . She is a bit of a *rotter* sometimes, isn't she?" Betty said, and the fact that it was such a struggle for her to find a bad word to say about somebody who had literally poisoned her caused Georgiana to feel a forceful rush of affection toward her.

"Well . . . so am I," Georgiana said ruefully.

Betty smiled. "What was it that made the rest of the evening so dreadful for you, if you don't mind my asking?"

Georgiana was going to deflect again, for this hardly felt the right time or place to talk about herself, but something about Betty's kind eyes, or their peaceful setting—or perhaps the newly acquired knowledge that Betty and her grandmother weren't going to run to the constable and have her charged with attempted murder—put her so much at ease that she found herself telling Betty the whole story.

To her credit, Betty gasped at all the right moments—particularly when Georgiana got to the part where she and Thomas had kissed, although she rushed quickly through it in the retelling so as not to shock Betty back into her sickbed. She was intentionally vague about what she thought had transpired between Frances and Jeremiah, and she stalled a little when she reached her own encounter with him in the orangery.

"I don't imagine there's a soul at that party who would believe me, but I went in there looking for Cecily, I didn't arrange to *meet* him or anything. He was so drunk, Betty, so . . . Well . . . let's just say that whatever he'd taken didn't quite have the same effect on him as it had on you. He wouldn't let me leave." Her hand went to her wrist, though it bore no marks. "He kissed me, and he tried . . . I think he would have done far more, had we not been interrupted."

She felt a hardness in her throat, a solid mass that threatened to choke her, but still, she did not cry.

"Oh, Georgiana, I'm so sorry. He is beastly. Simply *beastly*," Betty said, aghast. "If I were—well, if I were a man—I'd run him through!"

Georgiana laughed shakily. "Would you really, Betty?"

"Well . . . no, I suppose I wouldn't, as I don't much fancy prison. Grandmama says they only let you wash once a month, and without any soap at all! But gosh, I'd certainly give him a good talking-to."

"I do believe you would," said Georgiana, smiling.

It felt cruel to think that she liked Betty because there was no pressure in her company—no urgent need to impress—but then again, perhaps it wasn't a bad thing to be so at ease. Perhaps it was a sign that one was in the presence of a true friend.

"To be frank, Betty, I am at a loss as to what I'm supposed to do now."

"I think—if I may be so bold as to offer a little advice—I think honesty is the best policy, Miss Ellers. Tell Mr. Hawksley what really happened—tell him how you feel. Only you can decide how to proceed with your friendship with Miss Campbell, although I must say, if I have a vote, I would prefer her to be in prison without any soap *or* any friends." This came out of her in a rush, but then she paused and seemed to reconsider. "Or, perhaps, no, that is too unkind—she may have one or two friends, of the criminal sort—I imagine one must make friends for life during incarceration, so that could be quite agreeable for her—"

"You're right, of course, Betty," interrupted Georgiana, before this got out of hand. "I must put things right. I only hope . . . I hope I haven't ruined all of my friendships here beyond repair."

Betty patted her hand where it lay on the bench and smiled.

"Well, whatever happens—you have me, Georgiana. I may not be quite as much fun as the rest, but I am rather good at cards, and so far there has been no need to call a doctor to any of my games of loo."

It was almost lunchtime by the time Georgiana returned to the Burtons'; the previously clear sky had clouded over considerably, and it had begun to drizzle. She was hunched over to escape the rain as she rushed for the front door.

Before she could open it, somebody else did.

Frances was standing in the doorway, immaculately dressed, seemingly midway through saying her goodbyes; she turned to smile benignly at Georgiana, who simply looked confused in response.

"Frances? Are you . . . ? I was out, but if you want to talk—"

"Oh, don't worry, George, I've been having a *wonderful* chat all morning. I'm all talked out. I'll let you catch up."

She nodded her head in farewell, still sporting the same unnervingly calm smile, and then walked back down the garden path at a leisurely pace. Her carriage pulled up to receive her with impeccable timing.

This exchange only left Georgiana more confused, and she hurried inside the house, hanging up her hat and taking off her gloves.

"Mrs. Burton, I—"

She heard a throat being cleared; when she turned around to see who it belonged to, she almost dropped her gloves in shock.

Mrs. Burton was visible through the open doorway, hovering awkwardly by the dining table. The figures sitting opposite her, rigid in their seats and staring at Georgiana over two cups of untouched tea, were none other than her parents.

"But you're . . . What are you doing here?" Georgiana said, feeling for a moment as if she had fallen out of time.

She had absolutely no idea why they were here; she hadn't

even thought of them for weeks, and they made absolutely no sense to her now, sitting at the same table she had breakfasted at every morning for the past three months.

"Your parents were on their way to London, Georgiana, to arrange some of their affairs . . . well, and I had written to them, you see," Mrs. Burton said, twisting a napkin tightly in her hands. "To ask them to visit you, as I knew you were missing them—and so they thought to stop in on the way, and—and here they are."

Mr. Ellers, dressed all in brown and with a neat mustache to match, looked thunderous. Mrs. Ellers, who looked almost exactly as Georgiana suspected she would herself in twenty-five years, had a few more gray hairs salting her tightly pinned hair and wore a very pinched expression. If the sea air had indeed done her good, there was certainly no evidence of an improved temperament on her pale face.

"Here we are indeed," said her father, through clenched teeth.

"I don't understand. Frances was here? And you—"

"I would hold my tongue if I were you," said Mrs. Ellers sharply.

Georgiana flinched so hard she moved almost a foot backward.

"Sit down."

She did, with a sinking feeling in her stomach so strong that it threatened to pull her directly through the floorboards.

"Your friend Miss Campbell has just informed us of your absolutely reprehensible behavior. She told us that you have been engaging in . . . engaging in . . ." Her father was so furious that it seemed to be a struggle to get each word out.

"Engaging in what?" Georgiana asked in a voice barely above a whisper, her mind accelerating rapidly as she tried to keep up.

It was true that she had been engaging in plenty of things that her family would not approve of lately, but she could not believe that Frances would make the trip to her house to make idle chit-chat with her parents about her drinking habits. After all, it was usually Frances handing her the bottles.

"You have been engaging in . . . *intercourse,* Georgiana!" her mother cried, grimacing away from the word as she spoke.

Georgiana was so shocked that she was speechless for a moment. Of all the things she might have expected her mother to do after so much time apart, shouting the word "intercourse" at her had not been one of them. She had never seen her parents display so much emotion in all her life. She threw a panicked look at Mrs. Burton, but her aunt wouldn't meet her eye.

"I most certainly have not!" Georgiana said indignantly, her anger rising to match her mother's.

"Miss Campbell seemed quite distraught, in two minds about whether or not to say anything, but frankly, thank God she did," said her father, slamming his hand down on the table so that the teacups rattled nervously. "You are out of control, Georgiana. And it ends now."

"I don't *understand,*" Georgiana said, looking beseechingly between them. "What is it exactly that I'm supposed to have done?"

"Miss Campbell said that you've been off cavorting with a man," Mrs. Burton said quietly. "Lying to us, Georgiana, lying to me, about the chaperones at events, about where you have been— pretending you are with the Campbells, when really you're off with that Woodley girl and her friend—"

Georgiana's heart broke a little, hearing the betrayal in her aunt's voice.

"Mrs. Burton, please, I can assure you—"

"No! Not another word," her mother snapped. "Miss Campbell was to be engaged, she said, to a Mr. Russell—honestly, how could you do such a thing to a girl you claim as your friend? She said you had been flirting with him, behaving most inappropriately, and then you two had . . . Good God, Georgiana! We shall all be ruined."

Georgiana was still trying to make sense of this—flirting, with Jeremiah? *Sleeping* with Jeremiah? What could have possessed Frances to fabricate such a thing?

"Mr. *Russell*?" Georgiana turned to her aunt again. "Mrs. Burton, please, I will admit that I have been keeping company you would not entirely approve of—and it is true that I have been to some . . . some parties, some outings that were not entirely appropriate, but I have never looked at Mr. Russell that way in my life, and I—"

"Don't deny it, Georgiana," said Mr. Ellers gravely. "Miss Campbell said you disappeared off with him at some cottage. There were no chaperones, she said, her parents away, she thought your aunt knew. She says you made it quite clear to her that you had gone upstairs and done something unspeakable with him."

"In the cottage? That was *Frances*, Father. It was Frances! Why she wouldn't want that generally known is perfectly clear to me, but why she would instead claim that it was *I*—"

"She said she tried to help you, even to forgive you, but you are beyond forgiveness, Georgiana," said her mother, shaking her head. "After all she has done for you, she says she saw you kissing this Mr. Russell again last night."

"Georgiana, she said you tried to hurt Miss Walters," Mrs. Burton said sadly. "That you slipped something into her drink, just to be cruel."

Her mother was saying something else, but Georgiana could not hear her, a strange ringing in her ears obscuring all. A lot of things were suddenly falling into place. Of course. Of *course*. *Frances* had been the one to interrupt them. She had seen what Jeremiah had done to her in the orangery. She had seen his fumbling hands, seen them pressed together in that close, hot darkness, and had come to her own conclusions. As furious as Georgiana was, she understood, and she was also distantly impressed; she could not have calculated such perfectly executed revenge herself in a thousand years of trying.

"I do not blame my sister," Mrs. Ellers was saying stiffly. "I could never have imagined that you had this in you, Georgiana, or I would have taken great pains to keep you out of trouble. I can only hope that it is not too late. Pack your things at once—I'm sure the Order of St. Lucy will take you, until we decide what to do next."

The Order of St. Lucy sounded suspiciously like a convent. That fact cut cleanly through all the noise in Georgiana's head.

"No," she said quietly.

Her father was shaking his head.

"It's already decided."

"No. No! I won't, Father. I won't go. I am guilty of poor judgment, I am guilty of lying—I have lied to you, Aunt, and I am dreadfully sorry for it, you did not deserve it—but I am *not* guilty of the rest. I have not been out *fornicating*. I did not poison Betty Walters. Even Betty herself does not believe that! I have just come from speaking with her now, and she has shown me every kindness. And I will *not* be sent away—I will not go!"

"Perhaps . . . ," Mrs. Burton said to her sister, her voice clouded with tears. "Perhaps it might be best to give her a chance to—"

"No," said Mrs. Ellers, getting to her feet. "Your reputation is in tatters, Georgiana. And ours will be, too. We must act for the good of all involved. What will we do with you now? How can we hope for any sort of match? Who would possibly have you?"

"Oh, I don't know!" shouted Georgiana recklessly, getting up to match her mother in stature and anger. "You didn't seem particularly interested in having me before, so why should that matter now? You can't ignore me when I'm good and quiet and do everything you say without complaint, yet try to play at parenting now when I'm finally living my own life. If you're just trying to get a return on your investment, why don't you take me down to the docks and sell me to a passing pirate? I'm sure they have at least five thousand a year, even if it is in stolen goods!"

"This is not a laughing matter, Georgiana," said Mr. Ellers, rising so that they were all standing around the table. "You will come with us now, without fuss, and we will—*Where do you think you're going?*"

But Georgiana was already gone. It was clear that nothing she could say would convince them, and she wasn't even sure she wanted to anymore. Her only regret was the look on Mrs. Burton's face as she fled; she was the only one there who was owed an apology, and the truth.

She needed to move quickly, but of course she could not call for the carriage; she thought frantically about where to go, and her mind flew to Betty's house, even knowing that it must be at least eight miles across country. Betty knew the truth and could help clear her name. Betty would offer her refuge. Even if Mrs. Burton directed her parents there at once, they would *have* to listen, with Betty by her side, and then perhaps they would begin to understand.

The rain was picking up, but Georgiana had no choice now but to go on; she put her head down and began to run toward the Walters' house, as fast as her tired legs could carry her.

Chapter Twenty-six

It was quite easy to determine which way was north-west when standing in a familiar front garden, but after two hours of walking in the driving rain, Georgiana couldn't have navigated herself out of a puddle—and she was, unfortunately, currently ankle-deep in one. Her dress was plastered to her body and her hair was a mess of heavy, saturated tendrils that she had to keep pushing out of her eyes in order to see. If she had followed the road, she would have made it somewhere familiar eventually, but in her panic she had rashly decided to take a more direct route to speed up her journey and avoid detection. She had taken short walks through the meadows and wooded lanes that surrounded the Burtons' house before and knew there to be many pathways and easily traversable routes, but this far away from civilization, all she could see for miles around was undulating moorland.

It was not an encouraging sight.

The weather that Georgiana had taken for a quick summer storm was showing no signs of abating, and although her hurt feelings and fury had propelled her for the first twenty minutes of her journey, they had turned irreversibly to despair around the time she realized she could run no longer. Since then, she had been trudging through the mud with the increasingly unsettling feeling that she had made a terrible mistake. Chiefly, she now had to admit that she had no idea where she was.

Occasionally she could just about make out the faint glow of sunlight through the thick cloud and used the position of the sun to reorientate herself—but come to think of it, she wasn't entirely convinced that Betty's house was actually due northwest in the first place. It was at least west-ish, or west-adjacent, but she was quickly learning that this wasn't enough pathfinding knowledge to justify a solo expedition without even a bonnet to keep off the rain. She had planned a quick getaway, imagining that by now she would be with Betty and that all would be explained; instead, she had managed to get thoroughly and completely lost on the moors.

There was nothing to be done except walk, and nothing to do while walking but think.

Georgiana understood why Frances was so angry. She could only *imagine* how bad it had all looked to her, and how betrayed she must have felt. It was perhaps taking things a little far to go to Mrs. Burton before asking Georgiana to explain—to try to ruin Georgiana's life with lies and scurrilous accusations, and in front of her parents, no less—but Frances had been hurt, and hurt badly. Georgiana longed to see her so that she could make her understand; to tell her that she now knew exactly what kind of person Jeremiah was, and what it had cost her to find out.

Her parents could not have picked a more fantastically ill-timed moment to pop in for a cup of tea.

Georgiana wasn't concerned, she decided, about disappointing them. It was quite freeing to admit to herself that really, *they* had been disappointing *her* for a very long time—it was only fair to return the favor. In one summer, the Burtons had managed to be more involved in Georgiana's life than her parents had ever been, and it was Mrs. Burton that Georgiana pictured now, hurt and bewildered and stunned in the corner of the dining room.

Her parents could go to hell, for all she cared.

If she ever made it to the Walters', Betty would tell Mrs. Burton what had really happened at the party. Even if her parents were determined to lock her away, at least the Burtons would know the truth, and perhaps they would be able to persuade her mother and father not to behave quite so medievally. Georgiana thought guiltily that she would have to be *almost* entirely honest with Mrs. Burton if their relationship were to ever recover, and just live in hope that she considered a bit of drinking and smoking—and perhaps some illicit kissing, if Georgiana could bring herself to admit to it—to be less horrifying than fornication and attempted murder.

Thoughts of said illicit kissing should have brought her great joy but now only sent icy fingers of regret and anxiety skittering across her chest. It was hard to untangle it all: the scent of oranges; the feeling of Thomas's gentle hand on her jaw; the expression on his face over Betty's stricken form; the pain of Jeremiah's fingers pressing harder and harder into her skin. She wanted to tell Thomas what had really happened, to find and pull at the singular thread of truth, but that also meant telling him what Jeremiah had done. It had been hard enough to tell Betty.

It was, Georgiana thought desperately, a complete and utter mess.

The Georgiana of just three short months ago would have been both impressed and appalled at who she had become this summer. Out on the moors, with seemingly endless time and space to consider what had led her there, she finally felt the true weight of it hit her. She had not been a good friend to Betty, who only wanted a companion. She had not been a good friend to Frances, who had behaved badly, yes—but who had also come to her for comfort, needing support, and been forsaken by Georgiana when she was at her very lowest. Frances had been right— Georgiana *had*, just for a moment, dared to imagine herself a person of consequence in her own right. She had pictured herself among London society come the autumn, such a success that nobody would ever recall that she had no right to be there in the first place. She had imagined all that power and status almost within her grasp, as laughable as it felt now. She would never be able to replace Frances Campbell—and becoming the sort of person who lied and schemed and abandoned people outside balls wouldn't change that fact.

Everything Thomas had said about her had been entirely, dismally true.

All of this self-reflection was, of course, immaterial if she was going to die right here on the moors from a potent combination of exposure and a severe lack of common sense. The thought of how hard she would need to work to make things right should have been enough cause for her to give up, flop facedown in the grass, and resolve never to get up again—but she gritted her teeth and soldiered on, with no idea where she was heading, but the faint hope that it might be something like the right direction.

When the lightning started, Georgiana had almost made it to a small copse of trees; they were groaning with the effort of staying upright in the gathering wind, thrashing about as if under attack. With the lighting came thunder, rolling through the dark sky above her and making her gasp with how close it seemed. She was sure she had been told that it was unsafe to be the tallest thing on the landscape when lightning struck—but then, perhaps it was also deeply unsafe to take shelter *under* the tallest thing around, and she eyed the trees that she had previously considered her salvation with utmost suspicion. Deciding that she would likely drown if she did not, she determined to entrust herself to the trees, finding the least wet knot of roots beneath them and sitting down to rest her aching legs until the weather let up. It smelled like moss and damp earth, and she breathed deeply, the relative stillness welcome after hours of feeling as if the howling wind were snatching the air from her lungs. The thunder rumbled on, the rain continued to fall, but the air was thick and sticky

with summer heat, and despite her sodden dress she found herself nodding off against a rough pillow of bark, feeling as if she
had expended every ounce of physical and emotional strength in
her reserves.

She awoke in a panic when a large thunderclap seemed to
shake the ground beneath her, and opened her eyes blearily just
in time to see more lightning streak through the sky not too far
from where she sat, followed by another earsplitting boom. She
was shivering—it was much colder now—and to her horror she
realized that it had grown dark around her.

Incredibly, it only now occurred to her that she should truly
be afraid; if it had been impossible for her to find her way by
daylight, how would she manage by night? And how could anybody else find her, when she herself had absolutely no idea where
she was? All she could do now was sit in her misery, wait for the
light of morning, and hope earnestly that she was remembering
correctly that there were no wolves left in England. If she'd had
the strength to do it, she might have cried. She supposed it was
at least a rather dramatic way to meet her doom. She had, after
all, always wanted to play the leading role in some grand, exhil-
arating story.

Admittedly, not one that ended like this.

She wasn't quite asleep, but she wasn't quite awake either
when she heard a curious sound that didn't seem to be part of her
dreams. It was getting louder, and once she realized what it was,
she was scraping her hands on the roots in her haste to get up, staggering to her feet to meet it. Dawn was attempting to break, and in
the unreal, rosy gloom a chestnut horse was cantering toward her
across the moor, splattered with mud up to its flanks, its rider bent
low over its neck.

She raised her arms feebly and tried to call out but found that
her voice had died in her throat. Luckily the rider seemed to need
no encouragement; they came straight for her and pulled up in

a rearing halt just before the trees, disembarking in one swift movement and ridding themselves of the hat that had obscured their face on the approach.

"Oh," said Georgiana stupidly. "*Oh.* It is . . . absolutely ridiculous that you are here."

Thomas Hawksley was dripping wet, caked in mud, and sporting an expression of such deep concern that it utterly obliterated whatever meager resolve had been holding Georgiana together until now. She took a deep breath, made to say something ridiculous (she was considering "Come here often?"), and then instead burst into loud, mortifying, unquestionably ugly tears.

He walked toward her, already opening his arms, and she sank into them, her body shaking with cold, exhaustion, and instantaneous relief.

Thomas didn't let go for a very long time; when he did, it was to take off his ruined coat and wrap it carefully around her shoulders. She pulled it tightly around herself, retreating back to the knot of roots so that she could collapse shakily onto them as he quickly attended to his horse.

Every second he was not touching her now felt like a terrible loss, and when he returned to sit next to her, she wordlessly reached out a shaking hand. She could have expired with joy on the spot when she felt his warm, gloved fingers interlace with her own. She met his gaze, and for a moment all the complications fell away; it was simple and right and good to just sit here and hold his hand as dawn broke over them. As filthy as he was, she knew that in comparison she must have looked like a garden statue that had been left to mold; she turned away, suddenly self-conscious, and he seemed to read her mind, offering her his handkerchief to wipe her red, tear-streaked face.

"How . . . ? How on earth did you find me?" she asked, once she had composed herself and abated the attractive flow of mucus from her nose.

"You are sitting underneath the only trees for miles around. The only distinguishable landmark, really. It would have been harder *not* to find you, once I was in the right sort of area."

"Oh. Right," Georgiana said. "But . . . why are you here at all?"

"Unfortunately Mrs. Burton was under the impression that you might be dead. I called on Miss Walters this morning to inquire after her health, and your aunt was there with two people who purported to be your parents—they said you had been missing for many hours, and they had taken the carriage to the Walters' to see if they might find you there. Betty and your aunt were quite . . . hysterical." He looked a little pained at the memory, and then his expression became serious. "You are exceedingly lucky to have a friend as forgiving as Betty Walters."

"I know," Georgiana said, taking a deep breath. "I was dreadful to her, Thomas. I know I was. I've told her how very sorry I am, but it's not enough—I shall keep telling her and showing her until she knows it to be true. You were right at the ball. Betty Walters is a true friend, and I have behaved like a complete and utter cad. I displayed unforgivable weakness of character. I will do everything in my power to make sure that doesn't happen again, because that . . . that is not the sort of person I want to be."

"Well," Thomas said, sighing, and then smiling weakly at her as if she were an idiot he had accidentally become partial to, "I'm glad to hear it. I had just recently made up my mind to be very fond of you, and it would have been a shame to reverse the decision so soon."

This was such a relief to hear that Georgiana felt fresh tears threatening to brim over. She blinked them away with a tremulous smile.

"I can hardly . . . Well, I can hardly blame you for thinking ill of me. I have done everything so terribly wrong. Were they—was Mrs. Burton very angry?"

"No, just . . . concerned," he said. "We were all concerned."

"My parents?" Georgiana asked, seeing the answer in his frown before he replied.

"Ah . . . yes. Well. They did seem a little angry."

"I wasn't trying to . . . I don't know—*do away* with myself or anything," she said sheepishly. "I was in a bit of a predicament and I didn't know what to do. I was actually on my way to see Betty, but I . . . Well. I'm not particularly good with directions."

"Where do you think you are right now?" he asked, and she looked around, as if the moors might hold more answers today than they had yesterday.

"Er . . . about five miles northwest of the Burtons'?" she asked hopefully.

He laughed, but not unkindly. "You're only about two miles from home. You must have gone back on yourself; if you had carried on this way, you would have only encountered moorlands for at least another day."

Georgiana shuddered at the thought and was glad that she had spent an uncomfortable night in the embrace of a tree rather than stumbling in the darkness toward her inevitable annihilation.

"*Thank you.* For coming to find me, I mean. Despite . . . well, despite everything."

"Seeing as you can hardly make it to the far end of a garden or into a wine cellar without almost falling to your death, I felt someone should attempt to recover you before you walked off a cliff," he said, squeezing her hand. "Why were you in such haste to return to Miss Walters? Your aunt did not manage to explain that part."

Georgiana took a deep breath, and then everything came out in a rush.

"Frances got . . . Well, she got the wrong end of the stick about something. She thought I'd done something to hurt her, and instead of asking me about it, she decided to go straight to the part where she exacted her revenge. She told terrible lies to my aunt, to my parents. They want to send me away, because they think . . . they think me utterly ruined. I know why Frances is angry, I really do understand, but I wish she'd just given me five seconds to explain. She thinks I'm entangled with *Jeremiah,* of all people, of all the ridiculous . . . Well. If only she hadn't seen me with him in the orangery—"

"The . . . orangery?" Thomas said gently, apprehension in his voice.

Georgiana tried to brace herself to say it all out loud; she knew that Jeremiah was the villain of this story, but she still dreaded telling it. Especially, it occurred to her now, the part where he had forced himself on her just a few feet away from where she and Thomas had shared their kiss. She did not want him to get the impression that she was some sort of serial orangery-kisser.

"I was looking for Cecily, but I found him instead, and I didn't realize how inebriated he was—I should have left, really. But, *no* . . ." She shook her head. "He shouldn't have done it. I tried to get away, I did try, but it was too late, and he grabbed me, and . . . well. He wouldn't let me go."

"He . . . what?" Thomas said slowly.

Georgiana winced. "I know it's nothing really in the scheme of things—a stolen kiss, I'm sure it happens a thousand times a day, but . . . Well, I didn't *want* to kiss him, Thomas. And I don't think he wanted to stop there. He hurt me, he was insistent, and we were interrupted, thank God, but it was truly . . . It was frightening. It wasn't like it was . . . well. Like it was with you."

Thomas had gone very quiet, staring down at their hands. She wanted to prompt him to speak, feeling more nervous the longer his silence went on, but held her tongue.

"I'm going to kill him," he said quietly into his lap.

"No, you're not," Georgiana said, pressing her thumb lightly into his palm. The contact seemed to help him come to his senses.

"No, I'm not," he said, sighing and shaking his head before finally looking at her, "But good God, Georgiana, somebody ought to. Are you . . . ? Are you hurt? Are you all right?"

"A little. I don't know. If I'm not all right now, I think I will be," she said, unconsciously touching her fingers to her collar and hoping it was true.

"I knew he was lost," Thomas said wretchedly, "but not *this* lost. Perhaps it was right in front of me, and I did not—or did not care to—see it. Somebody needs to do something—to knock some sense into him."

"Please don't," said Georgiana, trying to lighten the mood. "Really. Betty says there's no soap in prison."

He didn't laugh. He was looking at her intently, checking her for signs of damage, and as she watched, his gaze traveled down to the neckline of her dress. With excruciating gentleness, he reached out and lifted the fabric an inch or so away from her skin. Georgiana had not yet checked for bruises blossoming there, had not wanted to see herself marked by Jeremiah's hand, and yet she could tell from Thomas's thunderous expression that she was.

She felt embarrassed for some reason, self-conscious, as if this was evidence of some failing of hers—but when she looked at Thomas he seemed close to tears. She put a hand to his face, trying to offer him some sort of comfort, and he gently gathered it in his and pressed a kiss to her fingertips.

"I'm sorry," he said.

Georgiana bit her lip and thought for a moment before speaking again.

"He went to bed with Frances, you know," she said quietly. "I don't think . . . I don't think she wanted to do it. Not really."

He took a sharp intake of breath, then let it out slowly.

"I should have . . . If I had been paying attention, looking outside myself, perhaps I could have prevented this. You, Miss

Campbell . . . How many have suffered, because I couldn't see him for what he had become?"

"Suffered because of *him,* Thomas," Georgiana said. "Not because of you. It is not your responsibility to save everybody." She reached out to touch him gently on the arm. "Although today you've certainly done a remarkably good job of saving me. Now if I can just convince Mrs. Burton that I haven't really been out rutting indiscriminately across the countryside . . ."

He laughed briefly in shock at this, as had been her intention.

"I have no doubt that Betty is trying to clear your name in earnest this very minute, although she may struggle. When I left, the poor woman was quite incoherent with worry."

"We should put her out of her misery," Georgiana said.

Thomas nodded; he seemed to be about to get to his feet, but then he hesitated.

"Georgiana, I must warn you—I can't waste any more of my time on this damnable scene. I can't watch people lie and drink themselves half to death and urge each other on to new and more terrible heights—it's too much for me to bear. I cannot . . . I see my brother, Georgiana. Every time. I see everything I've lost. I thought that if I broke off from Jeremiah, from my old friends, I'd lose the last shred of myself I was clinging desperately to, but I see now that it's no loss. I'm finished with the man I was, and I'm not going to shame Edward's memory by pretending otherwise. I shall . . . I shall have to learn how to get on with things on my own terms."

He looked slightly anxious, as if Georgiana might be about to proclaim that she could think of nothing worse than giving up the parties and the melodrama and the vast carelessness of high society that had already worn her down to the bone.

"Do you know, I'm rather tired of it all," she said. "I confess, nothing would make me happier than to see out the end of the summer playing cards with Betty, if she'll have me, and taking very long naps, and enjoying a little peace and quiet."

"I can't imagine anything better," Thomas said, relief softening his expression.

"I might have the occasional glass of wine with dinner, you understand," Georgiana warned. "I might even get a little drunk, if I have to listen to one of Mrs. Burton's stories about parsnips. But . . . really, Thomas. You needn't worry."

"Not an easy feat, as you are frequently extremely worrying," he said.

He took both of her cold hands in his, his thumbs grazing her wrists where her pulse fluttered, and she wondered briefly if she might faint from the sheer pleasure of it before deciding that would be an utterly absurd thing to do.

"Of course, my intentions hardly matter if my parents are to succeed in dragging me away to repent properly for all of my sins," she said instead, sighing.

Thomas pulled her to him, and she leaned heavily against him, marveling at the fact that the sheer volume of mud on both of them was not in the least bit off-putting.

"I'd like to see them try," he said, his lips brushing her forehead as he spoke. "Come swords or hounds or hellfire, I won't let them take you."

"Well, steady on," Georgiana said, smiling. "I shouldn't think it'll come to all that."

Chapter Twenty-seven

GEORGIANA RETURNED TO THE BURTONS' SOAKED THROUGH, filthier than she had ever been in her life, and steeled for battle. She wasn't sure exactly what she would say to her parents, but just having Thomas with her—helping her down from his horse, standing at her shoulder as she opened the front door—helped calm her nerves and brace her for whatever was waiting inside.

She needn't have worried, however; the moment Mrs. Burton saw her, exhausted and muddy with eyes swollen from crying and pale tear-tracks decorating each cheek, she rushed to pull her into a crushing embrace.

"Oh, Georgiana, I'm so glad you're *safe*," she cried into Georgiana's damp hair.

Georgiana knew she couldn't be a particularly pleasant person to hug right now, and squeezed her aunt back as tightly as possible to demonstrate how grateful she was.

Perhaps Mrs. Burton expected similar displays of affection from her parents; instead they stood awkwardly in the hallway, watching her with matching frowns, a tic twitching away in her father's temple. Mr. Burton, clearly wishing to be as far away from this conversation as possible without actually leaving the house, was standing in the parlor doorway, looking relieved but apprehensive.

"Be that as it may," her mother said, "this little distraction is over. No more delaying tactics, no more hysterics. You're coming with us."

"Distraction?" Mrs. Burton said, releasing her grip on Georgiana and gaping at her sister. "She could have fallen! She could have died!"

"She wanted our attention, and she has it," Mrs. Ellers said evenly. "This changes nothing."

"If I may," Thomas started, "there are certain circumstances that you may not be aware of—"

"I am perfectly aware of what happened, or of what *this girl* claims happened." Mr. Ellers waved his hand toward the open dining-room door, where Georgiana saw Betty Walters standing with a handkerchief clutched in her hands. She had obviously been crying but was attempting a wavering sort of smile in Georgiana's direction now. "Perhaps there are a few discrepancies between the story Miss Campbell told and the one Miss Walters has just relayed, but the fact remains that our daughter has been attending unchaperoned parties—drinking—making herself vulnerable to advances from all manner of knaves and rogues—"

"Mr. Ellers," Thomas said stiffly, perhaps aware that he was also being implicated in this speech, "I can assure you—"

"And who are you?"

"My name is Thomas Hawksley, and I must say that I object in the strongest terms—"

He stopped speaking abruptly, because Mrs. Burton had reached out and patted him on the arm.

"Don't worry, Mr. Hawksley," she said, turning to Georgiana's parents and pulling herself up to her full height. "I'll handle this from here."

"You'll *what*?" said Mrs. Ellers coldly. "I am afraid this is no longer your concern."

"You will listen to what my wife has to say," Mr. Burton said suddenly. Everybody turned to look at him, distracted for a moment by the very fact that he had spoken.

"Yes. *Yes.* You heard me, Mary," said Mrs. Burton, buoyed by her husband's support. Georgiana exchanged a startled look with Betty, whose hand had flown to her mouth. "I'll not deny that Georgiana has displayed questionable judgment, and I blame myself for not keeping a better eye on her. No, no, Georgiana, it's true—I know you're not a child anymore, but I am still your guardian while you live here, and I failed you. I did. But I will not stand here and allow you"—she pointed at Mrs. Ellers, whose mouth had dropped open in shock—"to blame her, and shame her, and try to have her punished, when Miss Walters has just told us what that hideous man Mr. Russell did to her. She's not a criminal, she's not the devil, she's just a young woman who has made some mistakes and has suffered very badly for them—and I won't have it. She needs to *rest*. She needs someone to look after her. She needs to buck up her ideas, yes, and she has a lot of hard work to do if she ever wants to be trusted under this roof again— but I won't let you take her anywhere, and if you still want to try, you're going to have to come back here with all the militia in England. I'll fight the lot of them. I mean it, Mary."

"This is ridiculous," Mr. Ellers said, taking a step toward Georgiana. "She's *our* daughter. We will decide what's best for her— how best to deal with this."

"I believe," Thomas said, putting a protective hand on Georgiana's shoulder, "that has already been decided. Georgiana?"

"I'm staying here," Georgiana said, a little teary. "For as long as my aunt and uncle will have me."

"Right," said Mrs. Burton, crossing her arms and glaring at Mr. and Mrs. Ellers as if they were two interloping rats in her hallway, rather than very close relatives. Georgiana thought that her parents had never looked quite so small. "That's that, then."

The rest of the day passed in a strange, surreal blur. Georgiana's parents departed, with a few more choice words exchanged with

Mrs. Burton on the garden path. Thomas stayed long enough that Mrs. Burton stopped fretting and started shooting Georgiana knowing little smiles, at which point Georgiana rolled her eyes and told him to go home and get some rest.

Betty wouldn't budge, cheerily waving Georgiana upstairs and saying she would wait for her in the parlor and work on her penmanship—"Grandmama doesn't need the carriage anyway, today is her napping day, so really I can stay as long as you need me"—and Mrs. Burton instructed Emmeline to draw her niece a bath.

"I'm so sorry, Mrs. Burton," Georgiana said wretchedly as her aunt helped her upstairs. "I really am. I promise to do better. All you have ever done is show me kindness, and I have behaved monstrously."

"Oh, hush. I shall be angry with you later, Georgiana, but I can't quite work myself up to it now," her aunt said, wiping her eyes and then sending her niece off to bathe.

Georgiana received the warm water like a benediction, feeling it loosen every muscle that had been pulled taut as she soaked in it. She expelled so much mud that she felt as if she had been encamped in the wilderness for weeks, not one measly night.

The bruises on her collarbone were blossoming in ugly clouds of purple, yellow, and green; she ran her fingers over them, wincing, and finally turned her thoughts to the hand that had made them.

Thomas believed that he could have stopped Jeremiah Russell, had he known just how far he had fallen; Georgiana now found herself in the uncomfortable position of not only knowing but having experienced for herself how utterly out of control he was. In the safety of her home—for it *was* truly her home now, she thought tearfully—her wits thoroughly worn out, she was tempted to close the book on him. To stop speaking of it. To cross it out and try to forget.

She could not, however, rid herself of the thought that he would just go on to do the same again—and worse. Frances was unlikely to tell another soul what had transpired between them in the cottage that night—at fault or not, she *would* be ruined—but perhaps Georgiana could tell and still keep some piece of herself intact. Even if she was labeled a harlot, a liar—even if half the county took his side—perhaps it was worth it, to sow the seed of doubt; perhaps ladies would keep their distance, parents would think twice about leaving their daughters in the company of Jeremiah Russell. She might be whispered about in polite society; she might struggle to find another man to have her, if Thomas took another look and changed his mind—but there was more than one way to be considered ruined, and Georgiana had realized which of them mattered to her the least.

She knew, now, how she wanted this particular story to end.

She slept briefly after her bath but could not let her guard down completely and spent the rest of the day in a state of intense agitation, unable to explain herself to Mrs. Burton, who probably put it down to general nervous exhaustion.

Betty had been invited to stay for dinner; Georgiana did not eat much of anything, despite all of her aunt's fussing, and Betty kept throwing her worried sidelong glances as she tucked into her pie.

Afterward, when she finally found herself alone with her friend, Georgiana pulled her to the side and whispered conspiratorially in her ear, laying out a plan that had begun to form somewhere between the pie and her untouched pudding. Betty looked a little nervous but nodded gamely. A few hours later, once the Burtons had retired to their beds and Betty had supposedly gone home for the night, Georgiana was once again sitting by the door and listening intently for the sound of hooves on the road. When the carriage arrived, she climbed in as quietly as possible, gazing out of the window wordlessly as they set off, not realizing how tense and still she was until Betty reached out to pat her hand reassuringly.

"Thank you, Betty," she said quietly once they had reached their destination. "Please, if you don't mind—I think I must do this alone."

Georgiana got out and walked up the last stretch of the enormous drive, shivering a little, although whether it was from nerves, the night air, or fatigue, she couldn't tell. Despite the lateness of the hour, many rooms on the ground floor of the house were still lit; Georgiana hesitantly knocked on the door, half-praying that it wouldn't be answered and she'd be able to slip away as if she had never been there at all.

A servant opened the door and went away to convey her message while she stood uncertainly on the threshold. When he returned, however, he was alone. His mistress, reportedly, was "indisposed." Georgiana considered asking more emphatically—considered, very briefly, pushing past him and running into the depths of the house—but instead she thanked him and gave him every impression that she was leaving.

Instead of returning to the carriage, she glanced about and then walked quickly around the side of the house, hoping she would not be spotted by some eagle-eyed groundsman and shot on sight. She reached the back gardens, the familiar lawn, and through the closed French windows she saw what she had been looking for.

Frances was sitting inside, eating supper with her friends. She looked sullen and exhausted in the candlelight, her hand clutching a full glass of wine, her dress falling carelessly from her shoulders. Jonathan was speaking to Jane; Cecily was listening to Christopher, who was gesticulating with his fork as he spoke. They took on a sort of supernatural glow as they sat ensconced in the candlelight, but the scene that Georgiana would have once been desperate to be a part of looked a little different to her now.

She did not see youth and vivacity and glamour; she saw people old beyond their years, people who seemed unhappy more often than not, people with desires and wants and needs so often unmet. Even now, despite everything, she could not be angry at Frances; her friend looked so thin, so thoroughly worn down, the light casting shadows in the hollows of her cheeks. Georgiana thought she understood some of that feeling after just a few months trying to keep up with her; she couldn't imagine the toll an entire lifetime would take.

She was staring at them all, for a moment still captivated by them, when Frances looked up and their eyes locked. She thought that Frances would pretend not to have seen her, or perhaps send for her father's hounds and have her run out of the grounds rather than talk to her. Instead she got up unsteadily and walked to the doors. The rest of her friends turned to look as she pushed them open and stood staring down at Georgiana.

"What?" she asked bluntly.

"Frances . . ."

Georgiana did not know where to begin. She had felt resolved in the carriage, but now her voice was shaking. Jonathan got slowly up from his chair and came to stand behind Frances, saying nothing, his expression wary.

"I came to tell you that what you saw—what you *thought* you saw between Jeremiah and me—it was not some sort of romantic embrace. Had you not interrupted . . . Well, I dread to think what he would have done. I am grateful that you were there. You saved me, however inadvertently. I promise, I did not go looking for him, I did not seek him out, I was looking for Cecily and then . . . he *attacked* me, Frances."

Frances took a deep breath as she absorbed this. She did not speak, but Georgiana saw the comprehension in her eyes—the sagging of her shoulders as some of the anger went out of her. For a moment, she felt relief. Frances *believed* her. She was sure of it. Jonathan looked as if he did, too; his eyebrows had shot up so high they were almost concealed by his hair, and he was studying Frances's face carefully, as if looking for cues.

"And I wanted to say . . . I wanted to say that I'm sorry. I haven't been a good friend to you, when you really needed one. I don't think that quite excuses what you did to Betty, or what you tried to do to me, but I understand why you did it, even if I sorely wish you hadn't. And . . . Frances," Georgiana continued, quietening her voice to almost a whisper, "what happened last night, it made me realize . . . back at the cottage, I believe that Jeremiah attacked you, too."

The change in Frances was instantaneous, even though the individual adjustments were minute; she straightened up, squared her shoulders, tilted her head very slightly as she considered Georgiana.

"You have absolutely no idea what you're talking about," she said, her voice cold and clipped. "And I wouldn't go repeating that little fantasy you've concocted, if I were you."

After all that she had endured already, it surprised Georgiana that these words still cut her to the quick.

"Frances, I am not saying this to hurt you. I mean, you tried to *ruin* me, you hurt Betty, and I should be furious—I *am* furious— but this is more important. Why else would I come to you now? Please . . . just . . . you don't have to be alone in this."

"This pathological need to be at the center of everything is wearing thin," Frances said, sounding almost bored. "You're not the *protagonist* of our lives, Georgiana. You're not even particularly interesting. I can see why you'd invent something like this, why you'd project all of your melodramatics onto me—"

"I haven't invented anything," Georgiana said, feeling her cheeks flare red with frustration. "He . . . I am *bruised,* Frances." She yanked down on the fabric of her dress. Frances watched her without a word, but she saw Jonathan start at the sight, glancing back over his shoulder to where Jane, Cecily, and Christopher sat, watching silently. "That's the sort of man he is. We both know it. Whatever has happened between us—I *care* for you. I think . . . I think that he must be brought to some sort of justice. I want to tell people what he did to me. I will not tell your story for you, or ask you to speak, for that is your decision and yours alone. But I need my friend . . ." Her voice broke, and she tried to swallow it down. "I need to know I have your support in this."

She knew Frances abhorred weakness, but it couldn't be helped; she *felt* weak. She had not slept properly for two days. She felt raw and exposed, and the longer Frances stared coldly at her as if she were mad, the harder it became to form coherent thoughts.

"I have nothing further to say to you," said Frances.

Georgiana knew then that she had lost her; it was an all-consuming and violent hurt, like being shot through the chest. A whole summer of friendship—everything they had shared—extinguished in one day.

"Why?" she heard herself asking, and she hated that it sounded like a desperate plea.

"Why?" Frances said mockingly. "*Why?* Did you really think you could latch on to me, on to all my friends—play at being rich and well connected and important forever? This was never your world, Georgiana. You were only visiting. You were here because you amused me—you no longer amuse me. I do not derive an ounce of enjoyment from associating with girls who try to usurp me and then find they cannot keep up—who want all the fun and all the glory, but throw accusations around when they get in over their heads—"

"He hurt you, Frances!" Georgiana shouted. "We both know it. *Jonathan* knows it. And you must know that I am telling you the truth. Whatever happened, you were not at fault—he's *dangerous*, and I'm sure he's done it before. What about that girl

Kitty, from last summer? What about Annabelle Baker? He'll do it again. He . . . Jonathan?"

She turned desperately to him for help. He was pale, his jaw set; he seemed almost as if he was about to say something, but then he shook his head sadly, looking to Frances, who met his eyes with grim determination.

They were all in this together, Georgiana realized, and now that she was not with them, she was against them. Whatever Frances said would be the truth; Jonathan would not contradict her. They would live in this lie forever, and make their peace with it.

Georgiana could not. She pushed past them both. She stood in the dining room, tears of frustration wet on her cheeks, looking to Cecily. To Jane.

"You know I'm telling the truth, don't you? Why don't you *say* something? Why don't you do something for once? You were my friends," she said pathetically.

Cecily was crying, a hand pressed to her mouth, but would not meet her eye. Jane would, but her face betrayed nothing. Christopher had the audacity to smirk.

They made Georgiana feel like a child throwing a fit. It was as if she had stepped into a nightmare—or rather, that she had woken up from a long dream in which they had actually cared for her and been faced with the reality in front of her.

"Get out of my house," Frances said, her arms crossed.

"Please, Frances—"

"*Get out of my house,*" she said again, each word enunciated clearly.

Georgiana glanced around the room one last time—she looked at Jonathan, whom she had believed was a true friend, but he only cast his eyes down at the floor—and then she gave up.

She walked from the room, barely able to see her feet in front of her through her tears. She heard Christopher's laughter behind her—cruel, careless, dismissive. She had almost made it to the driveway when she stumbled and fell into the stinging gravel, exhaustion and distress overwhelming her. She kneeled sobbing where she had landed, making no attempt to get up, feeling that her legs would not be able to hold her steady. The noises coming from her sounded almost animal; she clapped a hand to her mouth to try to quieten them, but something inside her had been shaken loose, and she could not stop.

She had expected anger, and upset, yes—but some very foolish part of her had imagined that she would be able to have it all. To say it aloud and still keep Frances in some small way.

But Frances could not face what Jeremiah had done to her, and Georgiana could not turn away from it. The ways in which they could survive this were incompatible; their realities had diverged. To accept Georgiana into any part of her life would be to accept that it had all truly happened just as Georgiana said it had—and that wasn't something Frances was prepared to do.

Georgiana was still choking out sobs into the ground when she heard footsteps crunching on the gravel; suddenly Betty had her, was pulling her into her arms, shushing her, stroking her back as if she were a sickly infant.

"There, there," she murmured, letting Georgiana cry, patting her slightly clumsily on the head. "It'll be all right, you'll see. What's that saying? It's always darkest before . . . something. Oh, gosh, what is it? Darkest before the light? That doesn't sound— well, anyway, the point is that it's rather dark now—but it won't be dark forever."

Chapter Twenty-eight

THE NEXT MORNING GEORGIANA AWOKE CONFUSED AND
puffy-eyed after sleeping for twelve long hours. She sat for a while
at her tiny dressing table in a patch of midmorning sun, gathering her resolve. Things had veered quite spectacularly off track,
but it was within her power to take charge of the rest of her story.
It would simply require her to do something that she had been
avoiding for almost the entire summer: telling the truth.

The first step was to talk to Mrs. Burton.

"He is a scoundrel. A *cad*. I cannot believe he did such a thing
to you, you poor dear," her aunt said tearfully, after Georgiana
had recounted the entire tale of what had taken place between
her and Jeremiah. Mrs. Burton had heard it before, but second-
hand and rather abridged from a distraught Betty; the extended
version seemed to affect her deeply, and Georgiana found herself
in the strange position of having to comfort Mrs. Burton, rather
than the other way around.

"I'm all right, Mrs. Burton. Or . . . I will be. But you're right,
he is a scoundrel. And the thing is . . . I think everybody else
ought to know it, too."

"Are you sure?" Mrs. Burton said, reaching for her hand.
"Once it is out, Georgiana, it can't be put back in."

"I know," Georgiana said grimly. "But that's as true for him as
it is for me. I might lose the good opinion of everybody in this
town, but if he does, too, it will all be worth it."

"All right," said Mrs. Burton bracingly. "All right. I shall write . . . Well, I shall write to every decent person I know. And . . . and I shall write to his *mother*."

She sounded so fierce that Georgiana was inordinately glad to have her in her corner. Her aunt could have gone against her, could have asked her to keep it all under wraps to protect them from shame and ridicule; the fact that she had not, when she lived and died by what the neighbors thought of her, was bravery and loyalty beyond what Georgiana had dared dream.

"I must warn you—people will certainly talk, Georgiana, and I have no doubt that they will say many terrible things about you in return. He will not let this go unanswered, and his family will defend their name to the end. But *we* shall know that we are right. I hope it will bring you some solace. I know it certainly will for me."

True to her word, Mrs. Burton dedicated herself to her letters for almost the entire day, bent over her husband's desk writing and rewriting for hours until she was happy with what she had crafted. Mr. Burton was banished outside for a very long walk; Georgiana thought he seemed quite pleased to go. She came in for paper and ink of her own at one point and kissed Mrs. Burton affectionately on the head, causing her aunt to startle a little and make a funny sort of shrieking sound.

Upstairs in her room, Georgiana wrote her own letters; she wrote to Jonathan, and to Cecily. She even wrote a letter to one Miss Annabelle Baker, and on a hunch addressed it to the Order of St. Lucy. It seemed utterly hopeless, but she could not rest until it was done. She did not expect a single reply. She could only hope that something in her words might appeal to a secret, soft part of them that wanted to do good—or at least the part that hated Jeremiah Russell almost as much as she did.

The last letter she wrote was the easiest.

Dear Thomas,

First, I must thank you once again, and also send my sincere thanks to your excellent horse.

Second, I think it is fair to say that Frances and I have severed ties for good. I regret the manner of our parting—but never fear, for Betty and my aunt have taken good care of me; they have perhaps been over-attentive, if there is such a thing. I have been made to eat lots of fortifying bread and cheese, and take many long baths.

It is probably scandalous to tell you so—about the baths, I mean—so I hope you are satisfactorily scandalized.

I have decided to tell the truth about Jeremiah. I hope that you will understand my reasons for doing so and not feel tainted by your association with me. Even if you do, I must pretend to be strong in my convictions, pretend not to mind what you think and tell you that I do not care an ounce if you disagree. Frances has chosen differently, but I cannot think badly of her for it. There is no right way, I think, to do this—only what is right for me.

Please call soon. I long to see you, and I don't think my aunt will ever let me leave the house again. Left to her devices I may shortly expire, smothered to death under a pile of bread and cheese.

Yours—really, truthfully,

Georgiana

The reply came that very evening.

Georgiana,

It would be a monstrous shame for you to die after I went to so much trouble to fetch you heroically from the moors. Please do not undo all my hard work at once; endeavor to stay on this mortal plane for at least a little while longer.

I hope you know that I will, of course, support you in this. I find I am the sort of fool who will support you in anything, unconditionally. If you ever feel inclined toward becoming prime minister, I will ignore the mockery of my peers and paper the town with posters of your face, persevering even when they begin to throw rotten fruit and vegetables, &c.

I will come to call urgently, if only to pry the bread and cheese from Mrs. Burton's benevolent hands.

I am politely ignoring the part about the baths.

Yours unreservedly,

Thomas

Mrs. Burton was a little anxious when an invitation came for Georgiana to join the Hawksleys for dinner. She could not blame her aunt and did not resent the time she spent reassuring her that Thomas's father really would be in attendance, and that she had nothing to fear at all from her visit. For a while it seemed likely that she might be banned from going at all, as recompense for her outrageous behavior over the summer, but by supper Mrs. Burton had relented, for she was a romantic at heart.

Once she had been talked round and her qualms had been settled, Mrs. Burton actually seemed to take delight in the whole thing, and helped Georgiana get ready with enthusiasm, even lending her some of her finest jewelry.

Georgiana felt sick with nerves all the way there. She had attempted to prepare herself for the sight of Thomas's house, feeling that months of parties in the most decadent of surroundings may have numbed her to the extravagance of large buildings, but it took her breath away all the same. They reached it by way of a long, winding driveway, enclosed on all sides by trees, creating a lush archway that opened up to reveal a grand estate. The house was cut in worn cream stone, smothered prettily by the ivy that grew unchecked. A small flock of servants descended on them to make sure the carriage, horses, and driver were well taken care of, and just the sight of them was enough to intimidate her, but then Thomas was striding out of the door, his smile unrestrained, and all of her fears melted away.

"I feel I could have asked them to carry me to the house and they would have held me aloft and not put me down until I reached the dining table," she remarked as he took her hand and helped her down out of the carriage.

"Nonsense—they only do that for me. *You,* they would drop."

Mr. Hawksley senior was thrilled to see her, kissing her hand with much aplomb. The three of them sat down to dinner in a large, airy dining room that could have easily seated sixty. Thomas watched, smiling, as she fell back into an easy discussion about literature with his father. Eventually, after the main course, there was a break in conversation, and Mr. James Hawksley cleared his throat.

"I recently received a letter, Miss Ellers, from your aunt; it laid out some shocking facts about our friend Mr. Russell."

"No longer our friend," Thomas said forcefully. "I only regret it took me so long to see it."

"Oh, Thomas. You're too hard on yourself," his father said. "You are not responsible for all the ills of the world."

Thomas sighed and shook his head, as if he refused to believe it.

"I'm afraid to say that I have *also* already received a letter from Mrs. Elizabeth Russell, who was once a good friend of mine, as Jeremiah was to our Thomas. She is determined to spread the word that Jeremiah is a good man, from a fine, upstanding family, and that any accusations that indicate otherwise are of a scurrilous nature. She did not paint a particularly pretty picture of you, it must be said, although she did not use your name. Would you like me to pass on the letter?"

"No, no. That's quite all right," Georgiana said quickly.

No good could come from reading that letter. She had known,

of course, that this might be coming, but had perhaps naively hoped that the Russells might be too embarrassed to address the rumors directly.

"I know it may not seem it, but I believe it is a good sign, Georgiana," Thomas said earnestly, reaching for her hand. "If it had not reached them many times, through many respected channels, they would have simply ignored it. That they feel they must write to defend him means that some people—people whose opinions they respect—must believe *you*."

"I suppose that is so. I'm not sure it makes me feel much better, though, knowing I am being slandered across the county." Georgiana felt too hot and took a calming sip of her wine. "Sometimes I feel I am making too much of a fuss over this, and that many people must think so."

"No. You are perfectly in the right here, my dear," Mr. Hawksley said firmly. "There will always be those who do not believe you—or those who *do* believe you, but who dismiss the entire affair as harmless, boyish fun—but I doubt there is a person among them who would wish to be harmed as you were. And there lies the truth of the matter—you *were* harmed."

Georgiana's hand reflexively twitched toward the bruises at the base of her neck, browning and starting to fade, although the real harm Jeremiah had done had left no discernible mark. She suddenly felt she was going to cry and dug her fingernails firmly into her palm to try to stop herself. Mr. Hawksley seemed to notice.

"Thomas, will you please go and request the port? In fact, you may fetch mine, from my study. You know where the key to the cabinet is kept."

Thomas glanced at Georgiana but got to his feet obediently and left the room.

"Miss Ellers, I cannot pretend to imagine what you are feeling at the moment," Mr. Hawksley continued, "but I assure you that you have the support of the Hawksley men. Then again, I'm sure I don't need to tell you that—Thomas seems quite besotted with you."

He said it with such a roguish glint in his eye that Georgiana laughed, despite herself. His expression became serious again.

"I know I have put far too much on Thomas's shoulders. I may seem like a *delight* to be with now, but I assure you, I have dark days. Very dark days. Thomas has weathered them all, despite the same losses weighing heavily on him. I'm sure he has told you, of . . . ah . . . the misfortune we have encountered, as a family. I have not seen him enjoy the company of others for a very long time. He has hosted no friends here at Highbourne. When Rashmi—my late wife—was alive, this house was always so full of joy. She was used to having family around. I know she felt very cut off when she moved here, so she tried to be everyone and everything to her boys. She didn't want them to miss out on anything—we celebrated Diwali and then went straight into preparations for Christmas. It always confused the servants, but by God, Edward and Thomas loved it." He sighed. "That boy who was so full of laughter has been absent for a very long time. He rattled around the house, went for long rides, spoke very little. He only went out into society to serve as my chaperone, to keep me from moldering away in my study." He smiled sadly. "It has not been fair on him. He has fathered me, when it should have been the other way around. I do not say this so that you may pity him, or to put undue pressure on your shoulders—but it is *wonderful,* Miss Ellers, to see him light up again. You have given him the possibility of happiness—the knowledge that it might still exist for him. I am inordinately thankful to you for that."

"I worry . . . ," Georgiana said quietly. "I worry sometimes that I am more trouble than I am worth. I have not behaved very well this summer, Mr. Hawksley. I try not to blame myself for what happened with Mr. Russell, but sometimes I wonder if I didn't deserve it, after all I have done wrong. And—and I do not wish to cause Thomas more bother, when he has already been through so much."

"Oh, dear child, I cannot comment on what has come before or how outrageously you may have acted, but I know with complete certainty that you could never be at fault for the actions of Jeremiah Russell, and I know this—Thomas is not a man to shy away from something simply because it is difficult. You are not a problem; you are not trouble. You are someone my son has taken a liking to—I am rather fond of you as well, although I daresay not *nearly* as much as he is—and whatever it is you face now, if it is right that the two of you are together, you will face it as one."

"I . . . Thank you, Mr. Hawksley."

Georgiana was so overcome she hardly knew what to do with herself, but she contented herself by getting to her feet and kissing him on the cheek.

"Of course, of course," he said, blushing and waving her away, looking pleased.

"Thomas has been rather a while looking for the port, has he not?"

"Yes," he said mildly. "He would be. It has been nigh on four months since I lost that key."

Chapter Twenty-nine

MR. BURTON WAS STILL AS TACITURN AS EVER, BUT TO demonstrate his support for his niece he had formed the habit of giving her reassuring shoulder-squeezes whenever he passed, which perhaps said more than words anyhow. Georgiana visited the library one morning to find a small stack of new books, tied neatly with string as if they had only just been delivered. Mr. Burton would not confirm or deny that he had procured them, but as Mrs. Burton only sighed and rolled her eyes when Georgiana questioned her, she knew that her uncle had guessed at another way to lift her spirits—and had succeeded magnificently.

Although Mrs. Burton had largely forgiven Georgiana for her behavior over the summer, she would not relent over the matter of church. Georgiana dreaded the journey to St. Anne's the following Sunday, and the possibility of seeing Cecily or Jane or—God forbid—Frances herself. Mrs. Burton was convinced that her niece needed to show her face and look respectable, as by now word of what had happened between her and Jeremiah was very public knowledge; Georgiana did not think that a high neckline and extra white ribbons in her bonnet would tip public opinion in her favor, but she put up with Mrs. Burton's fussing anyway, knowing that it came from a place of kindness.

Thomas would be at church to support her, and she knew Betty would be in attendance as well; with Mrs. Burton scowling by her side (and Mr. Burton looking vaguely embarrassed by the whole thing but sticking by both of them nonetheless), she would have a tiny army of rather unconventional soldiers ready to defend her honor.

They arrived early. It was a lovely day, although Georgiana barely noticed. The already bright August sun was offset by a gentle morning breeze, and the church gardens were ablaze with a cacophony of wildflowers.

Georgiana kept her gaze on the ground as they entered and found their seats, feeling eyes boring holes in the back of her head as she did so. Her aunt had insisted that they sit toward the front, to demonstrate that they had nothing to be ashamed of, but Georgiana had pleaded with her to choose a less conspicuous place and had won that particular round. Now that she was seated, she felt able to watch the other churchgoers as they arrived and chatted in the aisles and over the backs of pews. Thomas had not yet appeared; Betty was there with her grandmother and gave her a very enthusiastic wave from across the room.

When Cecily walked in, Georgiana felt her breath catch in her throat; she braced herself for impact but needn't have worried. Cecily walked past as if she hadn't seen her—perhaps she genuinely hadn't—and took a seat toward the front. When Jane entered, she threw a quick sidelong glance in Georgiana's direction and kept walking. Christopher was the only one to acknowledge her; he caught her looking and gave her a lecherous, unfriendly wink that was clearly intended to make her feel cowed—and succeeded.

Mrs. Burton was keeping up a low running commentary of those she had written to and who had responded but had the good sense to direct this toward her husband, knowing that her niece was not in any state of mind to hear it. Georgiana chanced a look back toward the door just before the service began and then froze, her heart in her mouth; Frances Campbell was standing in the entryway, dressed in her Sunday finery, looking a little bloodless and uncomfortable.

The vicar was taking his place, riffling through his Bible, but still Frances did not take a seat, looking behind her as if she were expecting someone. Just as some of the last stragglers were entering—Thomas was not among them, Georgiana noticed, with a flutter of concern—she saw Frances's face suddenly jolt alive with recognition. She appeared to be speaking to somebody standing on the other side of the doorway; by craning her neck inelegantly, Georgiana could just make out the sleeve of a man gesticulating toward her. He moved, taking a step toward her, and in that moment Georgiana realized who it was.

She got up very suddenly, and Mrs. Burton looked at her quizzically.

"I just . . . I need some air, Aunt. I'll only be a moment."

She patted Georgiana on the arm consolingly but did not attempt to prevent her from leaving.

Georgiana made her way out of their pew and to the doorway, grateful that the room was still loud enough that she went largely unnoticed.

Jeremiah Russell was now standing a little way down the path with Frances, gesturing rather insistently for her to follow him. She was not prepared for the rush of anger and hatred that welled up in her at the sight of him. She wanted to run away—no, she wanted to hit him; she wanted to hit him and *then* run away, very fast, never to cross paths with him again. Frances seemed to be resisting, was shaking her head as he tried to get her to leave with him—and then suddenly he took her quite forcefully by the arm and pulled her away, marching her toward the other end of the churchyard where they were unlikely to be disturbed.

Georgiana hesitated for a moment but then followed them. They were talking in low voices, Frances hissing her responses. Georgiana could sense the thick tension between them in Jeremiah's frown and Frances's hunched shoulders but could not decipher exactly what was happening. Perhaps, Georgiana thought wildly, they had reconciled—perhaps Frances would corroborate *his* side of the story, if it meant being back in his favor? She knew that most of the well-off families had closed ranks to protect him, but surely Frances would not take up such an enormous lie for a man who had treated her so abominably?

As she drew nearer, attempting to remain out of sight among the trees, Georgiana could hear the alcohol in Jeremiah's voice. It was thick and slurred, as if he had been drinking for hours already. Perhaps he had not gone to bed; he certainly didn't look particularly well-rested. He was getting louder and louder, and Frances was shrinking away from him as he did.

"This is getting out of hand. It's starting to affect . . . There are men canceling their meetings with me. My own parents are looking at me like I'm some sort of—some sort of *criminal*, Frances, and it must stop. I even had a letter from *Annabelle,* of all people, from inside that bloody convent, and her parents, too, leveling all sorts of accusations. I know I was unkind to you, I . . . I recognize that things did not go as we had hoped—"

"*Not as we had hoped,* Jeremiah?" Frances's voice was racked with disbelief. "I think they went *exactly* as you had hoped."

"Please, Frances. I am in a . . . a very difficult position." His voice had taken on a wheedling tone, and Georgiana wrinkled her nose in disgust. "Can't we just . . . treasure what we had, for what it was, and leave it in the past?"

"Somehow, Jeremiah, it's hard to treasure a handful of good memories, knowing what came after them," she spat.

"Oh yes, *poor* Miss Campbell. Everyone always says you're the picture of innocence, of course. If you were to talk unfavorably about me, I hope you know that I have plenty to say about *your* particular character, and nobody would have any trouble believing it of you—"

"Be quiet, Jeremiah," Frances said coldly. "You are embarrassing yourself. You have no cause for concern. I am not going to implicate myself in any of your messes."

Georgiana saw some of the tension go out of Jeremiah's shoulders. He was so drunk that he was swaying a little where he stood. When she looked at him now she did not see a rich, handsome young man; she saw a drunken reprobate. A selfish, spoiled boy who had never faced consequences for his actions and reacted like a squalling infant when they came to call. Frances was looking at him as if she was finally seeing the same thing.

"I know you did it," she said quietly, fixing him with a defiant look. "I might not be shouting about it, but I want *you* to know that I understand exactly what kind of man you are. I know—I know that George was telling the truth."

Georgiana's fingers closed tightly around the branch of the tree that concealed her; she hadn't known until that moment how much it would still mean to her to hear Frances say those words.

"That . . . That odious *bitch*," Jeremiah snarled. He had grabbed Frances's arm again; she tried to shake him off, but he would not let her go, drawing her closer. "She's a liar, Frances, she's a liar and a whore who came begging to me for—"

"Let go, Jeremiah. God—you're hurting me!"

Frances struggled, trying to prise his fingers off her—but he was smiling at her triumphantly, clearly enjoying watching her fight against him and lose. Georgiana could stand it no longer.

"Let her go!" she cried.

She stepped out from her cover, and Jeremiah looked around, startled. Frances used the opportunity to break free and backed away; Jeremiah's eyes fixed on Georgiana, and as soon as he realized who he was looking at, they narrowed.

"You! You're trying to *ruin me*!" he shouted.

Georgiana tried and failed to move out of his reach as he ran clumsily toward her. He grabbed her by her shoulders, and up close she saw how bloodshot and unfocused his eyes were. His breath was pungent with drink and smoke, overwhelming her as she tried to twist away from him, and she was suddenly back in the orangery, a scream stuck in her throat; he seemed terrifyingly far gone, a hundred miles past the point of reason. There was no point in trying to refute what he'd said—it was true, and he wouldn't listen to her anyway. Instead she tried in vain to break his grip on her.

"Frances! Get help!" she cried.

Jeremiah knocked her off balance and she fell to the ground, hitting her head hard against a gravestone and struggling to get back up as splitting pain erupted in her temple. Through half-closed eyes she could see Frances scrambling to get away, but Jeremiah had started after her; she reached around for something to throw at him and her hand closed around a large pebble, which she launched at him with as much strength as she could muster. It bounced off his leg, doing him absolutely no harm—but she had his full attention again, leaving Frances free to run.

Georgiana managed to drag herself upright using the crumbling gravestone for support, but by that point he had reached her. In one quick movement he twisted her arm behind her back, pushing so hard she felt it must surely snap. He was so strong, even like this—she *hated* that.

"Take it back," he hissed at her. "Admit that you're a liar. Tell everybody what really happened. That you were asking for it."

"No," said Georgiana, her voice shaking, wondering internally at her stupidity even as she did so.

Jeremiah took a furious breath, his eyes widening, and then suddenly wrenched her arm so violently that it felt as if he had torn it off; now Georgiana *did* hear it break, as clearly and distinctly as she heard herself scream. She had never made a sound like it before and was quite impressed to find herself capable of it. She fell back to the ground, cradling one useless, excruciating arm with the other, her vision narrowing as she wondered if she was going to vomit. Jeremiah seemed genuinely taken aback by what he had done, even on the verge of an apology, taking a few staggering steps toward her with his arms outstretched—and then, as if from nowhere, Thomas was upon him.

He had leaped at Jeremiah with such force that it brought them both tumbling to the ground. They struggled there, Jeremiah trying to push him off and failing, and for a moment it seemed as if it all must be over. Thomas had one arm pressed against Jeremiah's throat, pinning him to the ground—but then Georgiana saw what Thomas had not.

"Look out!" she cried.

Thomas noticed the dagger Jeremiah had pulled from inside his coat a second after she did and threw himself out of the way just in time. Jeremiah pointed it at his former friend with a shaking hand.

"Have you lost your *mind*?" Thomas shouted, scrambling to his feet, blood trickling from a cut on his cheek.

Jeremiah laughed hollowly. "Me? What about *you*? You throw away years of our friendship, for *this*? After all I did for you . . . They are trying to take everything from me, Hawksley. I—I challenge you!" he roared, spittle flying from his mouth as he did.

Georgiana stared at him in horror, focusing on breathing evenly in and out so she would not faint from the pain.

"Don't be ridiculous," Thomas said, raising his hands slowly.

The two men stared at each other for a moment, chests heaving. Jeremiah raised the hand holding the dagger once more—and then suddenly there was a loud *crack,* and Jeremiah was stumbling, listing to one side, then falling limply to the ground.

Betty Walters was standing where Jeremiah had just been, holding a thick section of tree branch aloft like a sword, her expression going from one of deep concentration to one of abject horror in an instant.

"Oh *God*," she whispered. "Oh God, oh God. Have I killed him?"

"I think not," said a breathless Frances, who had just arrived from the direction of the church with the entire congregation in tow; they were all making painfully loud noises of consternation. She stopped for a moment to catch her breath, doubled over from the effort, and then walked over to where Jeremiah lay facedown in the dirt and nudged him with the toe of her boot. "He's still breathing, more's the pity. Just knocked out."

Now that the danger had passed, Georgiana, whose deep breathing had gone more the way of hyperventilating, gave herself permission to faint. As black spots danced and fractured across her vision, she heard Mrs. Burton scream; and then, just as she felt Thomas's arms close around her, the world vanished into darkness.

Chapter Thirty

When Georgiana came to, she found herself lying on a hard wooden pew with a bundle of fabric beneath her head. It seemed to be Mr. Burton's summer coat, judging from his appearance as he stood over her with a worried expression on his face. A stranger was wrangling her arm into a splint with a wooden stick and some strips of fabric, and it was the pain of this that had dragged her back into consciousness.

"Ow," she said, quite unnecessarily.

Thomas, who, it transpired, was sitting behind her where she had not seen him, took her good hand.

"Squeeze it until it breaks," he said as she tilted her face to peer up at him. He was smiling at her weakly, unable to conceal his concern.

"Surely that would defeat the purpose," Georgiana said, wincing and breathing hard while her arm was wrapped tightly against its support. "If I broke your fingers, we would have to make five tiny splints, and you would need to squeeze *my* hand, and we'd begin a never-ending . . . a never-ending cycle of splinting."

She gasped as the last strip was tied off, then thanked the man who had done it through gritted teeth.

"You need a surgeon," he said. "I haven't set this properly, but it'll hold for now. It's a clean break, but it's a bad one, miss."

"Oh," Georgiana said, her head still swimming.

Mrs. Burton was peering down at her, eyes pink from crying.

"Have they arrested him?" Georgiana asked her aunt while her uncle shook hands with her makeshift doctor.

Mrs. Burton shook her head, her worry turning to anger.

"They sent for the constable, but all concern was for you. One man was watching him, but he awoke and slipped out of his grasp. He was long gone by the time help arrived."

"I imagine he'll return to his family's house in Manchester," Thomas said grimly, "where they shall close the doors for a while until they hope all has been forgotten."

Georgiana sighed and gingerly sat up, ignoring Mrs. Burton's protests. Her head was throbbing painfully. When she put her hand to it, she found that her hair was matted with dried blood, but that she did not seem to be currently bleeding. She searched the crowd still assembled in the church—nobody was likely to leave any time soon and render themselves unable to retell even a small part of this story later—until she spotted Frances sitting in a pew, Jane's arm firmly around her shoulders.

"I would like to speak to Miss Campbell, if she'll come," she told Thomas.

He nodded and went to fetch her, politely drawing the Burtons away upon his return so that they could be alone together.

Frances looked shaken but fiercely angry; now that she had summoned her, Georgiana wasn't quite sure what to say.

Luckily, Frances spoke first.

"Betty Walters, hero of the day," she said incredulously, and Georgiana laughed, stopping abruptly when it hurt too much. "She had noticed you were gone, you know. She was coming to look for you when I bumped into her. I went to fetch the others, but she barreled on ahead. Who knew she was so adept with a blunt object?"

"She's wonderful," Georgiana said emphatically.

Frances shrugged. "I wish she had killed him," she said simply.

"If only Ces had brought her bow. You looked like you *had* died, passing out like that with your head all covered in blood."

"I gave it a good go."

"Incidentally," Frances continued, "it was *excessively* stupid of you to follow us." She was fiddling with the fingers of her gloves as if she might actually be nervous. "Frankly, it was none of your business."

"Well, I think we've all made some questionable choices of late," Georgiana said with a wry smile.

Frances stiffened, as if she might be about to take offense, but then just rolled her eyes instead and got to her feet.

"Speak for yourself."

Georgiana tried to sit up straighter and found that it hurt far too much to be feasible.

"Look—I know we're not friends anymore. I won't come to the house again. But if you do want to talk—about any of it—I am still here."

"You look dreadful," said Frances stiffly, ignoring this. "You should burn that dress."

"All right, Frances," Georgiana said, sighing and closing her eyes. "I give up."

She was far too tired for any more of this—it had probably been foolish of her to attempt it in the first place.

When she opened her eyes again she expected Frances to be gone, but she was still hovering, her jaw tensed.

"I'm . . . I suppose, overall," she said with some effort, "I do regret that things have turned out the way they have. He certainly wasn't the man I thought he was, and there are some things I could have . . . Well, anyway. I'm glad. That you're not dead, I mean."

She gave a final nod, blinking rapidly to disguise what Georgiana highly suspected were actual tears, and then walked away.

Georgiana saw her reach the pew that held her former friends, saw Jane reach for Frances—and then to her surprise, saw Frances reach back. She sat down and leaned into Jane, allowing her to put a protective arm around her once more and press a quick, chaste kiss into her hair.

Perhaps, Georgiana thought, there was hope of some sort of happiness for Frances Campbell after all. It was certainly out of the ordinary—but then, so was almost everything else about her.

Thomas sat down beside her.

"Are you all right?"

"Yes," said Georgiana, shifting in her seat and grimacing again as sharp twinges of pain shot up her arm in response. "She told me that she was glad that I wasn't dead. I think that's about as close to an apology as I'm ever likely to get from her."

"I think you're very discerning for somebody with a head injury," Thomas said, and she gave him a squinting smile.

"I haven't thanked you for running headfirst into a fight with an armed man yet, have I?"

"Well, in the retelling of it, I won't mind if you forget to mention that I had no notion he was armed," Thomas said, taking her good hand.

"He's going to get away with it, isn't he?"

There was a tremor in her voice as she spoke; she hated to think that he held any sort of power over her still, but it frightened her to think that one day she might encounter him again, see him from across the room at some party or wedding, or in this very church, and be unable to do a thing about it.

"I don't think he'll be arrested," Thomas said gently, "but we all know who he truly is now. He's not going to return in a hurry. And Mrs. Burton isn't the only one equipped to write angry letters. My father, for one, is very enthusiastic about the prospect of taking up her campaign."

Georgiana sighed and then looked at him properly, taking in their joined hands, and the earnest affection in his expression, and the gash on his temple from where he had quite literally thrown himself to her defense.

"You look quite lovely with blood all over your face," she said, and he laughed, leaning forward and very gently kissing her on the forehead.

"You have very queer and disturbing tastes, for such a nice young lady. Come on—let's get you home."

Chapter Thirty-one

MR. AND MRS. GADFORTH WERE HOSTING PERHAPS THEIR most garish dinner party to date. They had acquired a truly horrific piece for their collection—a real polar bear, captured abroad and stuffed by an acquaintance of Mr. Gadforth's who seemed only to have a vague idea of what a bear—or indeed any beast—should look like. It leered across the hall and upset all who looked upon it—all except the Gadforths, who were treating it as if it were their long-lost son, home from the war. A few drinks in, Mrs. Gadforth was observed giving it sips from her wineglass, until Mr. Gadforth roared at her that she was going to "destroy the integrity of the preservative," and she slapped him with her fan and continued as if she had not heard a word of it.

Due to the presence of the bear, they had announced that the evening would be on the theme of "the Arctic." In the true spirit of the English imagination, they had simply invented what the Arctic might look like based on their own whims, rather than asking a person who might have traveled farther north and been able to give them a true account. To that end, they were serving a strangely blue "polar punch" that mostly seemed to be made of cider, the quartet were playing only jaunty Irish-sounding jigs, and the servants had been costumed with rather moth-eaten fur hats.

Mrs. Burton found all of this perfectly delightful and kept saying so to her husband and to Georgiana, who only clutched her drink and smiled encouragingly when necessary. Her arm was not quite fully healed, and she was very conscious of it, feeling that even though it was no longer in a sling, it needed some sort of support at all times. It still hurt occasionally, but she wasn't sure if that was residual pain from the break or simply the memory of how she had obtained it repeating on her. Whenever she thought of it, she felt an unpleasant dropping sensation in her stomach, and the strange notion that if she did not hold on very tightly, the arm might fall off altogether.

She had not been perilously drunk for almost two months, since the day of the party at Haverton House; she had dabbled a little in the realm of opioids when the surgeon had needed to set her arm properly, but she felt very strongly that this should not count against her. She was perfectly happy to sip Mrs. Gadforth's disgusting punch, knowing that she did not really need another—although this would not seem like such a great feat of restraint to anybody who had tasted the vile concoction.

"Are you well enough to dance, Georgiana?" Mrs. Burton asked eagerly as the band launched into another spirited number and dancers lined up down the hall to begin.

"I think I'll . . . er . . . sit this one out," Georgiana said, gesturing vaguely toward the other side of the room.

Mrs. Burton shrugged, took Mr. Burton's hand, and dragged him toward the fray.

Georgiana had not been to a social gathering this large for quite a while, and she was finding it frankly exhausting. She could no longer hide in anonymity, stand at the back of the room and nurse her drink while the others reveled; since the incidents with Jeremiah, she had been the subject of endless gossip and intrigue, and simply entering the room had been enough to set off a wave of whispers and muttering that had all the subtlety of Mrs. Gadforth's bear. Even now, as the dancers began, she could easily identify the conversations about her that were taking place—people leaning in to each other to discuss her in loud stage whispers, glancing away when they caught her eye. It seemed impossible to her that she had once stood in this very room and been bored out of her wits; now she was so on edge that she ached for quiet.

She put her glass down on an end table and swiftly exited the room. The house was just as darkly lit as it had been on her previous visit—"Well, the Arctic's quite dark, isn't it?" Mrs. Burton had said in the Gadforths' defense—but Georgiana could just about make out the geography of the hallway. She made a beeline for a familiar Grecian pillar that loomed palely out of the darkness.

After all that had happened, it seemed ridiculous to Georgiana that she was once again hiding in an alcove in this dreadful house, listening to the murmur of voices and faint strains of music as she hoped ardently to remain undiscovered. Instead of the intolerable restlessness she had experienced when here last, she felt soothed by the solid feeling of the wall against her back and the promise that absolutely nothing untoward was going to happen at this party. Nobody was going to expect anything more of her than that she be polite and perhaps try one of Mrs. Gadforth's "penguin pies" (Mr. Burton had tried one and assured her that it was chicken, somehow painted blue).

She heard footsteps in the hallway and risked peering out from her refuge—and then smiled widely when she saw who was approaching.

"Betty!" she hissed. "*Betty!* Come over here!"

"What? Why are you *there*?" Betty replied loudly, and Georgiana laughed.

"For the love of God, Betty, be quiet! We're *hiding*," she whispered as loudly as she could manage.

Betty dutifully followed the sound of her voice and joined her in the alcove, hitching up her skirts in a most ungainly fashion as she struggled up onto the ledge next to her friend.

"Why are you hiding? Oh gosh—are they still *talking*? People keep asking me, but I've told it so many times now, I always get a bit lost around the middle of it—and honestly I don't enjoy reliving the part where his head made that dreadful cracking sound," Betty said, shuddering.

She offered Georgiana a fresh glass of Arctic punch, which she quickly declined.

"Yes. They are still talking. To be fair to them, I think it's probably the most interesting thing that's happened around here for centuries."

"That's not very fair of you at all," reprimanded Betty, and Georgiana sighed.

"You're right, of course. I am crotchety and ill-tempered, and I should leave these poor people to enjoy their dead bear party."

Betty nodded, obviously pleased with her friend's moral progress.

"Does it still hurt?" She touched Georgiana's arm gently. "Only I broke my ankle when I was a child and apparently I dragged the leg around after me for months, perhaps even a year—Grandmama says it was all part of a ploy, you see, to get more biscuits, as every time I cried it was the only thing that would stop me—she said that once I realized that pain resulted in sweets, I schemed to get as many as possible—my parents had physicians coming to look at me; there was talk of needing a full-body brace. I think at one point they even considered calling a priest in case it was a malady of a spiritual nature! The funniest thing is, the same thing happened with her dog—not the priest part, I don't think they were afraid for Fifi's soul—but she pretended to have a limp for, you know, personal gain. Biscuits."

"You really are the most fascinating creature," said Georgiana.

"Oh! Is that a bad thing or a good thing? 'Fascinating' doesn't sound half as good as 'charming,' or 'eloquent,' or . . . or . . ."

"It is a marvelous thing," Georgiana reassured her. "Betty Walters, you are a delight to be around. An endless source of fun.

I can honestly say that I never have any idea what you might say next."

"Me neither, to be honest," said Betty, and she sounded so genuinely in horror of it that Georgiana laughed and gave her a spontaneous hug.

"Oh! Be careful of your arm," Betty said, flushing pink as Georgiana released her. "Is Thomas here yet?"

"Not yet."

Georgiana couldn't help but smile, pressing her lips together to try to keep herself in check.

"Do you think he'll . . . he'll *ask*? Would he do it here? Oh, I do hope he asks, Georgiana—it is beyond time for it, and it's clear to all who look upon the two of you together that you are made for each other—I can just picture you as the most radiant bride, although perhaps it would be best to choose another church, go farther afield—I think your head left bloodstains on the pews at St. Anne's, and you would not want to look upon your own blood on your wedding day. Oh! And when you're settled at Highbourne House you must have me to stay—I'd especially like a south-facing room as Grandmama has been and says those are the best, the most charming rooms of all the rooms they have—"

"Betty, he has not asked, and if he asks here, among Mr. and Mrs. Gadforth's odd friends and servants dressed up like wayward explorers, I shall turn him down most vehemently," Georgiana said, laughing.

Thomas had not yet made her a formal offer of marriage, but she was not the least bit concerned—he simply gave her no reason to doubt him. They had been almost inseparable since the day she broke her arm; she had enjoyed many dinners with the Hawksleys, and he had endured just as many at Mrs. Burton's table. They had joined Mr. Burton for his morning walk on a few occasions and gone for gentle hacks on Thomas's horses, returning home wind-chapped and happy. He had played for her at his beloved piano, and she had watched, entranced, as he lost himself entirely in the music and came back to her smiling.

Many parts of his house had been long shut away, but every time she visited they seemed to open another, the rooms coming alive again as Thomas told her their stories.

He had led her through the gardens and to the tree house he had built for his brother, to all the secret places they had shared before they had forgotten how to be children. He had shown her a portrait of his mother, stoic and serious in shades of brown and blue, above the fireplace in the room that had been her parlor, but then pulled out a different painting—one that his father had commissioned when they were married in India, of the two of them wrapped in bright silks and gold jewelry and flowers.

In that one, she had been smiling.

Just last week, Thomas had bade his servants open a room she had somehow not yet entered in the expanse of Highbourne: the library. She had been lost to him immediately, exploring every shelf with her eyes and her hands, pulling out old favorites, reverently tracing the spines of beautiful editions that she was frightened she might ruin with her touch. Half the books had been his mother's, and they expelled little clouds of dust when retrieved, as if they had not been opened for a very long time. She had just been telling him the details of a particular favorite—a Gothic novel so gripping that she had once stayed up all night reading it at her father's desk, only realizing what she had done when dawn began to encroach through the window—when he had gently closed the book, taken it from her hands, and kissed her—not with the passion of the clandestine kisses of their past, but tenderly, with the promise of what was to come.

"We shall have a daybed moved here," he had said, laughing. "Reading all night over a desk tends to give one a terrible crick in the neck."

Betty could not be dissuaded from the topic of marriage, and

Georgiana let her talk about gowns for bridesmaids, and floral arrangements, and the most romantic symphonies to dance to, until she heard more footsteps in the hallway—and suddenly Thomas himself was standing right in front of them.

"Oh! We weren't talking about you," Betty said unconvincingly, and Georgiana raised her eyebrows at him.

"Glad to hear it," said Thomas. "Mrs. Burton said you had vanished and that I would most likely find you hiding somewhere inappropriate."

"It's not inappropriate, Mr. Hawksley, it's an alcove," said Betty helpfully. "I'll leave you two to talk."

She winked exaggeratedly at Georgiana as she slipped off the ledge and then hurried away toward the party.

"Do I want to know what that was about?" Thomas asked, offering his arm so that Georgiana could get down one-handed with some semblance of grace.

She smoothed her dress as she got to her feet.

"*I* didn't want to know what it was about, and I had to hear it all, but I'll spare you out of the goodness of my heart."

"Much obliged, I'm sure. Are you having a pleasant evening?"

"Not particularly," Georgiana said. "It's recently become markedly better, though."

"Excellent news," Thomas said. Georgiana didn't need to turn her head to know exactly how he was looking at her. "Listen, I do have to ask a favor of you—I hope it won't put you out too much."

"What is it?" Georgiana said warily as they approached the drawing room. "I won't drink your punch for you, if that's what you're after—but if you give it to Mrs. Gadforth, she'll feed it to her bear."

"Thank God," Thomas said. "I've already left a glass behind a sculpture, and they immediately tried to give me another."

"Stop stalling—what's the favor?"

"Oh. Well. I know it will inconvenience you terribly, as you are still a little injured, and I'm aware that you are finding public life extremely tiresome of late—but I have a selfish inclination toward dancing with you tonight. What do you say?"

He kissed Georgiana on the hand, and she rolled her eyes, then sighed benevolently.

"Come on, then. You are insufferable for asking—but I suppose I can permit just one, very short dance."

Dear Miss Ellers,

I have received your many letters; please rest assured that there is absolutely no need to send any more. Your penmanship is so poor that it must be a very arduous task, and I do not wish you to risk causing yourself an injury. As I am sure you're aware by now, I have also written to Miss Betty Walters, so you may desist on that account, too. I certainly do not intend to make a habit of it.

In response to your latest note—yes, Miss Woodley and I will be attending your wedding in March. My mother and father will not, as my father is abroad and my mother is in Bath staying with friends, and both intend to be away indefinitely.

Frances Campbell

P.S. Incidentally, I would like to point out that it was very presumptuous and impertinent of you to address the invitation to Jane at my residence. No matter what rumors you may have heard, Jane certainly does not live here.

P.P.S. Jane has asked me to include a recommendation that you do not wear green ribbon, as you look very ill in it. We shall see you on the eighth.

Not in green, Georgiana.

I'm serious.

Acknowledgments

I'VE GOT A LOT OF PEOPLE TO THANK, BUT FIRST A NOTE about the historical context of this book.

At the time of publishing, the UK government and large sections of the media are attempting to whitewash Britain's history. They are actively impeding the progress we have made—and must continue to make—toward understanding the United Kingdom's past, including its imperialism and prominent role in the transatlantic slave trade. This history has shaped and continues to shape the power structures of present-day Britain.

This story portrays a multicultural Regency Britain in a bid to reverse the trend of whitewashing the historical stories we tell. While *Reputation* is fiction, there were many Black and Indian people in various positions in society living in Britain during the Regency period and throughout the history of the isles, and it was important to me that these communities had a place in this narrative.

Now it's time to roll up my sleeves and acknowledge the hell out of some people.

Endless thanks to my brilliant agent, Chloe Seager, for understanding Georgiana straightaway, for always fighting my corner, and for just generally being a good and hilarious egg. This has been a lifelong dream come true, and it wouldn't have happened without all your help. Thanks also to the entire team at Madeleine Milburn for your support and for throwing a truly excellent Christmas party.

Thank you to my editors Sarah Bauer and Katie Lumsden for

making this experience so wonderful, and to Blake, Grace, Jenna, Eleanor, Louise, and everybody else at Bonnier Books who had a hand in birthing this book. Thanks to my cover designer Sophie McDonnell and illustrator Louisa Cannell, for bringing Georgiana and her pals to life. Thanks, too, to Sarah Cantin at St. Martin's, for taking Georgiana on her grand voyage across the big drink to the United States.

This book wouldn't exist without my partner, Nick, who listened to me talk about it endlessly and put meals in front of me when I was more Word doc than human, or my sister, Hannah, who was the first person to convince me, via some light sisterly bullying, that it might actually be worth reading. Thanks every day to my most beloved and particular companion Rosianna, who talked me off ledges many times during the publishing process and wrote to me—in pen and ink—to tell me her favorite parts.

Thanks also to my parents, for all the love and all the books; Kez, who skipped ahead to see if Thomas would be at the ball; Anna and Photine, for reassurance and enthusiasm when I was running out of steam; and Venessa, Jeska, Rose, and Bhavna for their beautiful art.

The early readers I worked with did so much to shape this book, and I am eternally grateful to Helen, Caolinn (who went above and beyond), Sapan, Chloe, Iori, Lynn, and Georgina for their guidance. Hannah and Liberty, thank you for letting me borrow your eyes. Jazza, thanks for letting me steal one of your last names (although frankly you do have a spare, so it was the least you could do).

Thank you especially to the communities I found while writing, including my online writing group (I'll see you all in hell) and the friends I made through the books I love. If you're looking to find people working tirelessly to create things just for the joy of it, supporting each other, and raising each other up in tiny ways every single day, you'll always find them in fandom.

Hannah Croucher

Lex Croucher grew up in Surrey, reading a lot of books and making friends with strangers on the internet, and now lives in London with an elderly cat. *Reputation* is Lex's first novel.